Millennial Reign

MILLENNIAL REIGN

A Novel

Conte

iUniverse, Inc.
New York Bloomington Shanghai

Millennial Reign

Copyright © 2008 by Craig Joseph Conte

All rights reserved. No part of this book may be used or reproduced by any means, graphic, electronic, or mechanical, including photocopying, recording, taping or by any information storage retrieval system without the written permission of the publisher except in the case of brief quotations embodied in critical articles and reviews.

iUniverse books may be ordered through booksellers or by contacting:

iUniverse
1663 Liberty Drive
Bloomington, IN 47403
www.iuniverse.com
1-800-Authors (1-800-288-4677)

Because of the dynamic nature of the Internet, any Web addresses or links contained in this book may have changed since publication and may no longer be valid.

This is a work of fiction. All of the characters, names, incidents, organizations, and dialogue in this novel are either the products of the author's imagination or are used fictitiously.

ISBN: 978-0-595-52467-9 (pbk)
ISBN: 978-0-595-62519-2 (ebk)

Printed in the United States of America

When love beckons to you follow him, thou his ways are hard and steep. And when his wings enfold you yield to him, though the sword hidden among his pinions may wound you. And when he speaks to you believe in him, though his voice may shatter your dreams as the north wind lays waste the garden.

—Khalil Gibran

ACKNOWLEDGEMENTS

Thank you, Diana Fabio and Kathleen Conte for editing the book.

AUTHOR'S NOTE

Millennial Reign is a fictional tale based upon three prophesies written in the Bible. If one does not have knowledge of these passages, he/she may be in the dark when reading this book. Therefore, I have included the visions in this prologue to give the reader greater understanding when reading *Millennial Reign*. The first prophesy is drawn from the *Book of Revelation*. It reads:

"And I saw an angel coming down from heaven, having the key of the abyss and a great chain in his hand. And he laid hold of the dragon, the serpent of old, who is the Devil and Satan, and bound him for a thousand years, and threw him into the abyss, and shut it and sealed it over him, so that he should not deceive the nations any longer, until the thousand years were completed; after these things he must be released for a short time. And I saw thrones, and they sat upon them, and judgment was given to them. And I saw the souls of those who had been beheaded because of the testimony of Jesus and because of the word of God, and those who had not worshipped the beast or his image, and had not received the mark upon their forehead and upon their hand; and they came to life and reigned with Christ for a thousand years. The rest of the dead did not come to life until the thousand years were completed. This is the first resurrection. Blessed and holy is the one who has a part in the first resurrection; over these the second death has no power, but they will be priests of God and of Christ and will reign with Him for a thousand years. And when the thousand years are completed, Satan will be released from his prison, and will come out to deceive the nations which are in the four corners of the earth, Gog and Magog, to gather them together for the war; the number of them is like the sand of the seashore. And they came up on the broad plain of the earth and surrounded the camp of the saints and the beloved city, and fire came down from heaven and devoured them. And the Devil who deceived them was thrown into the Lake of Fire and brimstone, where the beast and the false prophet are also; and they will be tormented day and night forever and ever. And I *saw a great white throne and Him who sat upon it, from whose presence earth and heaven fled away, and no place was found for them. And I saw the dead, the great and the small, standing before the throne, and books were opened; and another book was opened, which is the Book of Life; and the dead were judged from the things which were written in the books, according to their deeds. And the sea gave up the dead which were in it, and death and Hades gave up the dead which were in them; and they were judged, every one of them according to their deeds. And death and Hades were thrown into the Lake of Fire. This is the second death, the Lake of Fire. And if anyone's name was not found written in the Book of Life, he was thrown into the Lake of Fire." (Revelation 20)*

The second selection speaks of a time when the Messiah will reign upon the earth. He will be the Lord and King, and the people will be required to worship Him and celebrate the Feast of Booths each year. The passage declares:

"And the Lord will be king over all the earth; in that day the Lord will be the only one, and his name the only one. Then it will come about that any who are left of all the nations that went against Jerusalem will go up from year to year to worship the King, the Lord of hosts, and to celebrate the Feast of Booths. And it will be that whichever of the families of the earth does not go up to Jerusalem to worship the King, the Lord of hosts, there will be no rain on them. And if a family of Egypt does not go up or enter, then no rain will fall on them; it will be the plague with which the Lord smites the nations who do not go up to celebrate the Feast of Booths. This will be the punishment of Egypt, and the punishment of all the nations who do not go up to celebrate the Feast of Booths." (Zechariah 14:9-18)

The final passage is drawn from the *Book of Ezekiel*. It speaks of a great battle that will take place in the future. It proclaims:

"Son of man, set your face toward Gog of the land of Magog, the Prince of Rosh, Meshech, and Tubal, and prophesy against him, and say, 'Thus says the Lord God, Behold, I am against you, O Gog, Prince of Rosh, Meshech, and Tubal. And I will turn you about, and put hooks into your jaws, and I will bring you out, and all your army, horses and horsemen, all of them splendidly attired, a great company with buckler and shield, all of them wielding swords; Persia, Ethiopia, and Put with them, all of them with shield and helmet; Gomer with all its troops; Beth-togarmah from the remote parts of the north with all its troops-many people with you. Be prepared, and prepare yourself, you and all your companies that are assembled about you, and be a guard for them. After many days you will be summoned; in the latter years you will come into the land that is restored from the sword, who inhabitants have been gathered from many nations to the mountains of Israel which had been a continual waste; but its people were brought out from the nations, and they are living securely, all of

them. And you will go up, you will come like a storm; you will be like a cloud covering the land, you and all your troops, and many peoples with you. Thus says the Lord God, It will come about on that day, that thoughts will come into your mind, and you will devise an evil plan, and you will say, 'I will go up against the land of unwalled villages. I will go against those who are at rest, that live securely, all of them living without walls, and having no bars or gates, to capture spoil and to seize plunder, to turn your hand against the waste places which are now inhabited, and against the people who are gathered from the nations, who have acquired cattle and goods, who live at the center of the world.' Sheba, and Dedan, and the merchants of Tarshish, with all its villages, will say to you, 'Have you come to capture spoil? Have you assembled your company to seize plunder, to carry away silver and gold, to take away cattle and goods, to capture great spoil?' And it will come about on that day, when Gog comes against the land of Israel, declares the Lord God, that My fury will mount up in My anger. And in My zeal and in My blazing wrath I declare that on that day there will surely be a great earthquake in the land of Israel. And I shall call for a sword against him on all My mountains, declares the Lord God. Every man's sword will be against his brother. And with pestilence and with blood I shall enter into judgment with him; and I shall rain on him, and on his troops, and on the many peoples who are with him, a torrential rain, with hailstones, fire, and brimstone. And I shall magnify Myself, sanctify Myself, and make Myself known in the sight of many nations; and they will know that I am the Lord.'" (Ezekiel 38)

The interpretation of these passages has been debated for centuries by theologians and scholars alike. This book unveils one possible reading to the prophetic events outlined in the Bible. They may be accurate or they may be construed; regardless, I have done my best to give the reader a fictional account of what may or may not transpire in the future.

Craig Conte

MILLENNIAL TIME LINE

7 Year Tribulation: Reign of Mahdi
Messiah's Return to the Earth
75 Days of Judgment (Earth renewed to a Garden of Eden)

Ground Zero: The founding of the Kingdom
01: 1st year anniversary of the Kingdom Age
40: K.A. (Kingdom Age) Counselor visitation of Australia & the Outskirts
45: Menelik conquers Australia and becomes the dominant ruler
47: Counselor visits Dan
49: Kingdom of Dan becomes a nation
63: Dan colonizes Antarctica and calls it De-Dan
69: King Dan dies; Zzyzx becomes king of Dan; Corinne becomes queen of De-Dan
95: Sheba's rise to power
98: Marriage of Queen Sheba to the Counselor
222: Mandate 222 becomes law; many leave the Kingdom & colonize new lands
223: Democratic Magog Republic (D.M.R.) is established and Kasca is elected President.
261: Exodus back to the Kingdom led by Patmos
262: Borders to the Kingdom are shut. All those who didn't return are forever banished.
302: Matusak released from prison & banished to the Outskirts
322: 100 year holiday celebrating Mandate 222; flying ban lifted
327: Greenland Pact between Tarshish & the D.M.R.
333: Tarshish-Gomar War
354: Signmonkoala Island burned down
379: Marauders-Algiers War

444: D.M.R., Meschech, & Tubal fail to bring forth tribute (Beginning of 7 yr. drought)
451: 3 nations bring forth tribute and the rain falls
455: Queen Sheba & the Counselor's secret marriage revealed to the world
499: Marauders invasion of Libya (13 Year war)
512: Libyan-Alexandrian Peace Accord brokered by the Counselor (Egypt divided)
555: Alliance established by Tarshish, Sheba, Dan, & De-Dan
556: Nodians vote in favor of entering the Alliance (Vetoed by the D.M.R.)
559: Coalition made by the D.M.R. & the northern nations
576–676: 100 years of peace celebrated in the Outskirts
677: Marauders invade Ethiopia & conquer the Algiers Tribe
702: D.M.R. attempts to cross the border into the Kingdom illegally
775: Uprising in Southern Nod by the Natives
776: Southern Nod declares their independence; D.M.R. declares war on Nod & Tarshish
777: Tarshish & D.M.R. peace accord
781: Nodian/D.M.R. War Ends; Nod divided into two countries
782: Southern Nod joins the Alliance
782–899: 2nd Century of peace
900's: Prophetic expectations; apostasy increases; Matusak unites Africa economically
902: Removal of the holoscreen ban in the Kingdom (Fog of War lifted)
975: Weather systems created in the D.M.R.
996: The Prophets return to the Outskirts (June)
999: Countdown to end of the Millennium
1000 (Jan): 1000 Year Reign ends; Satan released from the abyss
1000 (Jan): Fight of the Century
1000 (Dec): Confederacy of nations invades the Kingdom
1001 (July): End of the Age (The Final Judgment)

PART I

THE KINGDOM AGE

Chapter 1

The Libertines

"Fellow revolutionaries, fellow freemen, we have gathered here once again in New Jerusalem to proclaim our liberty. We have gathered here openly in the face of the King to make our demands known. We have assembled here to declare ourselves a free and IN-DE-PEN-DENT people! For over 200 years we've been in slavery. For over 200 years we've been fooled by their propaganda. For 222 years we've been forced to live under an oppressive system. But no longer will we be subjects of this government. No longer will we bow down to any king or authority. No longer will we follow their laws and precepts. We will not serve and be told what to do. We will lift the yoke of bondage. We will rise up and proclaim our sovereignty!

At these words the crowd roared in response and started chanting, "Kasca! Kasca! Kasca! Kasca!"

Kasca raised his right hand in the air and hushed the crowd.

"In the course of human history, it has become necessary for one people to rise up against their oppressors. In the course of time, it has become a necessity to stand up for what is honorable and right. That moment is here! That time is now! Today is the day of infamy! Today is the day of retribution! Today is the hour of enlightenment! Today is the moment of truth!"

Kasca raised his arms in the air, and the Libertines started chanting again, "Kasca! Kasca! Kasca! Kasca!"

"Dear comrades. Dear friends. Our whole lives we've been given the necessities of survival. We've been fed. We've been sheltered. We've been catered to in every way. But without the ability to think for ourselves and make our own choices, we are still in chains. Without the freedom to be the gods of our own lives, we are in prison. Thus, I propose we overthrow this dictatorship. I propose we form a government for the people and by the people. I propose we form a free and independent society that will allow us the opportunity to pursue our own dreams and aspirations, a democratic society that will enable us to elect our own leaders, a system not ruled by any king or elders."

The crowd cheered loudly as Kasca paused, brushed back his black hair from his face, and continued.

"Fellow liberators, we are embarking on a new era. The Age of Enlightenment is upon us. A renaissance in thought is before us. No longer will we follow their outdated ways. We will make our own rules. We will make our own laws. We will liberate ourselves. We will rebel. We will revolt. We will take whatever means is necessary to gain our freedom! So rise up! Let your voices be heard! Let the voice of freedom ring out!!!"

Kasca then pointed at the Holy Temple, mockingly fell to his knees and cadenced, "We will not serve! We will not bow! We will be free! We will be found!!!"

At this display the crowd started to get unruly. Some of the Libertines started to strip off their clothes and fornicate near the front of the stage. Others began throwing rocks at the peace officers and soon a full-scale riot ensued. The unrest carried on for a few hours and a portion of New Jerusalem caught on fire and was burned down. Eventually more soldiers of peace arrived on the scene, and they started to quell the resistance. Some people got burned, others were badly wounded, but luckily no one was killed. Meanwhile, Kasca and several of his key men were arrested. They were thrown into temporary isolation for a spell, and the Chief Elder ordered an emergency summit of the 144 Elders.

* * * *

"For 3 years we've been burdened with Kasca and the Libertines. We have tried to make every possible concession with Kasca to bring about a peaceful solution; however, Kasca will not make an armistice. He is determined to bring about our ruin," the lead speaker voiced. "We've put up with these disturbances for far too long, and if we don't do something quick, our whole way of life could be in jeopardy!"

There was an uproar in the assembly. Some of the 144 Elders were applauding in support. Others were booing and hissing. Eventually the Assembly of Elders settled down, and the speaker was allowed to continue his address.

"Dear brothers and sisters. I believe it is my duty to remind you that before the Reign of Christ, before the Days of Peace, before the King of Kings set up His righteous kingdom there was chaos in the world. Wars raged from all corners of the globe. Men and women savagely butchered one another with bullets and bombs. There was pestilence and disease. Many people suffered from starvation and malnutrition. The waters were contaminated with bacteria. The air was polluted with smog. Forests were pillaged and cut down. The animals were slain for their furs, and no respect was given unto the natural order of things."

"At one point, it appeared as if mankind would destroy all life on the planet. Nuclear bombs were dropped against rival nations. Radiation engulfed continents, and all life within the fallout area was either contaminated or deceased. But even after all this the leaders of the nations persisted in their arrogance and pride. They fought for power. They fought for glory. They fought for the riches and resources of this world. And ultimately the nations gathered together for one final battle. Billions were killed. The life of men spilled out like rivers of blood, and it appeared as if mankind would become extinct. But at that moment, when there was no hope left, our Lord and King made His appearance. Riding upon a white horse, He conquered the forces of evil and set up His kingdom. Since then He has ruled righteously over us. He has brought forth peace and justice. He has liberated the planet and made it a Garden of Eden. Still, some of these "New Timers," born after the tribulation, do not recall the former days. Some of these rebels like Kasca think we would be better off on our own, but they are deceived. These liberal revolutionaries speak of freedom and justice, but they will not bring about our liberty, they will bring about our demise! These so called Libertines are mere thorns in our side!!!"

Once again the assembly got unruly. Some of the minority roared in protest, but most of the elders clapped even louder. This continued for a few minutes, and it appeared as if the lead speaker would not be allowed to continue, but one of the respected members of the minority shouted above the noise, "Let him speak!" and everything stopped for a few seconds. He added, "A rebuttal will follow!" There was a slight grumble from the elders and a few jeers, but eventually everyone settled down, and the majority speaker continued.

The conservative expressed his gratitude saying, "Thank you, Patmos," then he continued.

"As I was saying, before Kasca and his radical ideas, there were no protests. Before the Libertines there were no riots. Before these rebels started this uprising, years ago, we lived in peace. Nowadays we live in fear. Our children are in danger, and a tenth of New Jerusalem has burned down. Therefore, I believe it is time for us to squash this insurrection. It is time for us to protect our Kingdom and put away these dissenters. We need to ensure our way of life. We need to return to our traditional values. We need to rise up and make a stand for our King!!!"

There was a roar of applause from most of the 144 elders. Even many of the moderate liberals were fed up with Kasca. They were standing on their feet and applauding in approval. The moderates and liberals had tried for years to reason with Kasca behind closed doors, but the Libertine wouldn't budge on the issues. As a result, they sided with the conservatives and were ready to take action. Some of the liberals, however, weren't willing to concede on the issue, and they continued to hiss and heckle the lead speaker.

"Order! Order!" the Chief Elder hollered into a microphone. He started pounding his pallet on the lectern, and in due course brought order to the gathering.

"An appeal has been made by Patmos for a rebuttal. Would any members of the minority care to speak?"

There was a bit of commotion. No one took the floor immediately, so a vocal member of the minority rose to his feet and made his way towards the front.

"I nominate Patmos to speak."

There was a roar of applause and some of the minority started a slow meticulous chant that kept getting louder and faster.

"Patmos ... Patmos ... Patmos ... Patmos ... Patmos ... Patmos ... PATMOS ... PATMOS ... PATMOS!!!"

Patmos rose to his feet, raised his hand to wave off the applause then sat back down. The assembly, however, would not take no for an answer, and they continued to chant out his name.

"PATMOS ... PATMOS ... PATMOS!!!"

Patmos turned towards his friend Rhodes, a fellow elder, shook his head then made his way towards the podium. Patmos grabbed the microphone like a seasoned debater then began his speech.

"I was planning to remain mute on the issue because of my personal sympathies towards Kasca, but I suppose it is my duty to voice my concerns. As you all know Kasca and I have been friends since the early days of the University. He was my favorite pupil. We constantly debated with one another, and after his graduation, I was the one who thought Kasca would be a great addition to our staff. And over the years we've become close friends. We've shared good times, celebrated together, and our families are close. Of course, we've had our disagreements, but through it all, Kasca and I have remained allies. So if we take disciplinary action against the Libertines, I will be personally affected. But be sure of this, even if you do not have close ties to any of the Libertines, you will be affected too. Your children will be impacted, and your actions will reverberate for hundreds of years."

"Over the past three years we have tried to put down the rebellion in a civilized manner. Even the Counselor sat down with the leading members of the Libertines to work out their differences; nonetheless, He was not able to persuade Kasca. At first it appeared Kasca had been appeased by the discourse, but six months later he was back in Jerusalem Square stirring up trouble again. Of course, all of this you already know. Most of this information is public domain."

"Now I know our Lord has given us the authority to make a ruling on the issue, but I believe it's important that we do not act rashly. We must not abuse our powers and be influenced by the times. The decisions we make today could have eternal consequences for thousands, millions, and possibly billions of people in the future. If we decide to banish the Libertines to the Outskirts, we may only be putting out a small blaze, but overtime those coals of hatred will smolder, and we might end up with a roaring wildfire. Hence, we need to judge righteously. We need to thoroughly dissect the pros and cons, consult our Counselor then come to a conclusion. I know many of you are angry today because of the recent riot, but we need to act rationally …"

"What about my home, Patmos?" a member of the majority interrupted. "Where are my kids going to sleep tonight? Sure, you're going to go home to your nice cozy bed, but what about the south side of town? What are you going to tell all those families that have to uproot and start all over again? Screw the Prince of Rosh! Let him burn for all I care!!!"

Patmos continued, "I know your sympathies. I know you're upset, but we must remember that Kasca was not the one who started the fires …"

"But he was the match that lit the flame!" another majority member blurted out.

"Thank you for your input!" Patmos sarcastically replied. "Now may I continue with my rebuttal?"

The Chief Elder hit his pallet on the lectern and exhorted, "There will be no further interruptions. The next person who speaks out of line will be reprimanded."

"Now I want to make myself perfectly clear," Patmos paused for a moment then continued. "Although I am a member of the minority, I still stand for Christ. Although I disagree with Kasca's perspective, he is my friend. And although I believe some sort of disciplinary action is necessary, I am firmly against any mandate that will banish or excommunicate a member or members of our society!"

Patmos put down the microphone and headed back towards his seat. The minority, which represented almost a third of the elders rose to their feet and started applauding. The majority, on the other hand, remained seated in disapproval. A few of the staunch conservatives protested by walking out on the meeting as the Chief Elder ordered the meeting adjourned.

* * * *

One week later the majority came up with a mandate that was voted on and approved. Two-thirds of the elders had to approve any new law and Mandate 222 passed with a 111 to 33 count. Mandate 222 read as follows: *Any person who has reached the Age of Accountability and is unwilling to follow the dictates outlined by the Lord of Lords and the 144 Elders shall be banished to the Outskirts. They will lose their citizenship and may never return to Israel. If an individual chooses to leave Israel on their own free will he/she may do so on their own accord. They and their descendents will be banished until the end of the age.*

The new law was posted all over the Israeli kingdom. The Libertines that were formerly in isolation were released, and they were given the opportunity to either follow the new mandate or continue in their rebellion.

* * * *

The following week, Kasca and the Libertines organized a major protest against Mandate 222. People flocked from all over the Kingdom to either join the resistance or support the Mandate. The 144 Elders called in soldiers of peace from the far reaches of the Kingdom to function as riot police. The officers were given batons to hold back the protesters, so the Libertines responded by carrying canes and baseball bats. Both groups probably would have been carrying firearms and other dangerous weapons if they were available, but they were banned shortly after the Tribulation. Nonetheless, a dangerous situation was erupting. Times had not been this volatile for over 200 years. Lines were being drawn. People were choosing sides, and many people were wondering where the King was during all the commotion. Would He support the mandate? Would He display His power?

It had been some time since the King showed any evidence of His authority, and many people were starting to doubt Him. Occasionally He would walk amongst the people as a humble servant and heal those in need. Other times He would interact with the children by functioning as a teacher or a coach. In general, the Prince of Peace rarely sat on His throne. Sometimes He would look in on the 144 Elders, but most of the time, He would let them run things on their own. Lately though, the King had been absent from His dominion. The Elders informed the community that He went on a pilgrimage to the Outskirts, but many people in the populace doubted their words. The Counselor had been absent a long time, and the multitude was starting to wonder if He was ever coming back.

Chapter 2

The Wolf Shall Dwell with the Lamb

The General returned home. He removed his hat, took off his shoes, and lay down on the couch. He briefly closed his eyes and hoped he'd have an opportunity to take a nap, but at that moment the kids came charging in from outside. The former Georgian knew they'd be at his feet in seconds, so he pretended to be asleep. The kids tried to sneak up on him, but when they were within inches of him, he abruptly jumped up, seized them, and scared the life out of them. Meanwhile, his wife, Sarah, came through the door and playfully exhorted him.

"Micah, one day you're gonna give one of those kids a heart attack."

Micah rolled his eyes and responded, "Oh, they'll be fine," and continued to tickle torture them much to the delight of the children.

"So how'd it go?" his wife inquired as she hung up the kid's jackets in the closet.

Micah hesitated for an instant and said, "Well … lets just say I foresee troubled times ahead."

"Hmmm … sounds interesting. But what does that mean?"

"It means exactly what it means. I believe we are at a historical moment on the time line. And as with all historical moments, there is tragedy and triumph." The General added, "The thing I can't understand though is how senseless some of these broad-minded intellectuals can be."

Micah padded the kids on the butts as a sign to run off and play, and the children went skipping off into the other room.

"And every single one of these elders are 'Old Timers' who remember the good ol' days."

Sarah sat down next to him on the couch and was partially revealing her cleavage to distract him. Micah glanced down at her chest and was about to continue, but she jumped on top of him to shut him up.

"Oh, come her Old Timer, don't you already have enough troubles on your mind?"

Micah was about to continue his rant, but Sarah stared deep into his eyes, and the General knew that she was right. She then ran her hand over Micah's crew-cut, kissed him on the lips, and the General dropped the matter for the time being.

*   *   *   *

Later that evening the McAlister family went out for a walk. The kids were running out front and Micah and Sarah followed about fifty meters behind. Suddenly the kids stumbled upon a pride of lions out on the plains. The kids, therefore, charged in the lion's direction in hopes of petting them. The General tried to caution them by yelling out, but the children ignored him. When Micah and Sarah caught up with the children, they found them playing with the cubs like domestic cats. The grown lions, meanwhile, were grazing on the grass near their cubs, and they seemed to be unmindful of them.

"Now children, be careful," Sarah warned them, "and don't forget the third Principle of Truth, 'Treat the earth and all that dwell thereon with respect and dignity.'"

Micah joined in on the commotion and started playing with the cubs then he went over to one of the full grown males and started petting him. The children watched their father cautiously then slowly made their way over to the giant beast.

"Go ahead, its okay, you can touch him."

Their little hands started petting the lion on the belly as Micah continued to rub the lion's brow. The large cat gave out a mild roar, and the children stepped back in fear, but Micah whispered soothing words to the lion, and the former king of beasts started to purr.

After about five minutes of playing with the lions, Sarah put out a blanket on the grass, and they all gathered together eating cornbread and milk. After they finished eating, they lay down on the blanket, looked up towards the sky, and Micah educated his children.

"Now Matthew and Heather I want you both to pay close attention to what I'm about to say."

Both children settled into the bosom of their mother and expectantly waited for their father's story. Each night before he put the children to bed, Micah would read to them ancient fairy tales or tell them stories of the past.

"Long ago before you were born, these lions were the kings of the jungle. They would prowl amongst the animals and do as they pleased. They would hunt. They would kill. They would savagely tear apart the carcass of their victim and eat their flesh."

Micah roared like a lion as the children held tightly unto their mother.

"Even man was afraid of these great kings. Occasionally there would be rogue lions that would feast on men. They would come in the middle of the night, viciously attack their victims, and drag the bodies off into the jungle, but in the latter years, man created guns to protect themselves. These instruments were filled with gunpowder and bullets, and they could quickly bring down a lion ..."

Matthew interrupted the story, "But father, the lions are our friends. They don't look like they could hurt a fly."

"Yes, I know son, but let me prove it to you."

Micah grabbed the hands of the two children and walked over to the lion he was petting earlier. The General opened up the lion's mouth and revealed to the children his teeth.

"Do you see these teeth? See how giant and claw-like they are."

The children nodded yes with their eyes opened wide.

"They could tear the limb off a man in a matter of seconds." Micah roared like a lion then continued. They could bring down an antelope, a zebra, or even a water buffalo."

Micah patted the lion on the back, grabbed the hands of his children, and went back over to his wife. Sarah was cleaning up the mess and picking up the blanket. As Micah walked, he continued to teach his lesson.

"Now children we mustn't forget that before the Prince of Peace set up His Kingdom, this is how things used to be. We were not able to pet the lions. We were not able to walk at night without worry of being attacked ..."

Micah continued to lecture his children on the walk back. They listened intently for a while, but they soon lost interest in his tale. The Old Timer could tell that they were starting to drift off, so he told the children to run along as he made his way back home holding the hand of his wife.

Chapter 3

Protest

The protest of Mandate 222 occurred at Jerusalem Square right in front of the Temple. Millions had gathered from all parts of the Kingdom. Some were in support of Mandate 222, but a large majority had gathered in rebellion. Peace officers surrounded the Temple Site, and they patrolled the streets in the nearby community. This was the largest protest ever made in the history of the Kingdom Age. It was a three day event that included musical bands, guest speakers, and Kasca himself for the finale. The first two days remained relatively calm. There were a few outbursts and arrests made, but nothing became too out of control. In general, the crowd was relatively civil, and it treated the event as a festival with food, drink, and entertainment; nevertheless, some of the people, mostly rebellious New Timers, were doing all they could to step on the precepts and laws of society. Some were walking around naked to display their freedom, others were fornicating in the park, and many were abusing the herbs and plants grown in Mother Nature. Of course, there were a few others that were acting like juvenile delinquents by making graffiti and destroying property, but their numbers were minimal.

On the final day of the protest tensions started to build. Thousands of peace officers formed a line in front of the Holy Temple, and more than a million protesters stood behind that line. The Libertines planned to overrun the Temple that contained the Tree of Life and take it as a prize after Kasca's speech. Therefore, there was a lot of tension in the air. Many of the Old Timers were enraged at the spectacle unfolding before their eyes, and it brought back memories of the past. They saw Kasca and the Libertines as traitors and were willing to fight to the death to prove their loyalty and allegiance to the King. The Libertines, meanwhile, were getting ready to make their stand. They knew they outnumbered the Old Timers ten to one. Of course, most of the rebels were not as passionate about the cause as Kasca and his close disciples, but many of them firmly believed in freedom, and they thought they were fighting for a just cause.

* * * *

About 5:00 P.M. in the evening, Kasca was about to make his speech. The crowd waited expectantly singing old protest songs from the 20th Century when a man made his way up to the microphone. The crowd started to cheer thinking it was Kasca, but it was merely an Old Timer who had stolen the spotlight.

"You're all traitors!" the voice echoed through the PA system. "You're all Judases! You anarchists! You betrayers of the light!"

The crowd started to boo the man on the stage, and many people started to scream in protest.

"You evil ones! You're all going to be judged for your crimes. You ..."

Just before the man was able to finish his sentence, someone picked up a bottle and threw it at the Old Timer. It hit him right on the nose and blood gushed everywhere. The speaker stepped back for a moment, but he continued his rant.

"You devils! You sons of Lucifer! You ..."

It appeared it was going to take a lot more to shut the man up, so hundreds of people in the crowd started throwing bottles and rocks up on stage. The Old Timer was being pummeled with hits, but he stood his ground until one object smacked him on the side of the head and knocked him out. He fell with great force on the stage, and it appeared as if he had broken his neck, but the crowd continued to throw objects in his direction. A couple of Libertines backstage saw the fall up close and rushed to the Old Timer's aide. They were pounded with hits too, but they managed to get the man off stage and called for an ambulance.

About fifteen minutes later, Kasca made his entrance on stage. He held his hands in the air like a preacher at a Christian revival and saluted the crowd in a quasi-fascist manner. Kasca then started to sing and began waving his arms in the air like he was leading a choir. They sang, *"We will not serve! We will not bow! We will be free! We will be found! Overcome, overcome, overcome!"* Kasca and the Libertines continued their protest chant. They sang the words over and over again. Pretty soon many of the people who had never heard Kasca before were swept up in the moment and started singing right along with the crowd. Eventually the song came to a close and the leader of the Libertines had the audience's attention.

"First of all, I would like to thank many of you for coming here this weekend. I am honored that you found it necessary and important enough to travel from the outer edges of the Kingdom to make your voices be heard. I believe your journey has not been in vain. I believe that your show of support against Mandate 222 and the ruling authorities is a slap in the face to these power mongers. By making your presence known here in New Jerusalem, you are making a stand to gather peaceably. By raising your voice against these oppressors, you are making a stand for freedom of speech. By singing protests songs against a mandated religion, you are fighting for the right of freedom of religion!"

Kasca emphasized the word religion, and the crowd started to cheer in support. Some were chanting out the Libertine's name and others were screaming wildly like they had fallen into a trance and were mesmerized by his words.

"Dear comrades, fellow liberators, I stand before you today to reason with you. I am not here to upset the natural order of things. I am not here to lead a revolution. I'm not here to overthrow the government. I am here to represent a voice that has remained dormant for decades. I am trying to prove to you that the King and the 144 Elders are not the only system of government. I am trying to show you that there is a better way, a democratic way. Should we not have a say on who will represent us? Should we not be allowed to elect our own leaders? Should we follow blindly and accept everything the 144 Elders dictate to us? If we do not stand up against Mandate 222 and the precepts of the past, you might as well give us canes and lead us by the hand. If we don't raise our voices now, we will never be heard. We are the majority! We are the PEOPLE! Let us take back the Temple! Let us be rulers of ourselves!"

At that instance a ruckus started in the crowd that transformed into a riot. Protesters started charging towards the Temple, and they tried to overtake it. The peace officers, however, resisted the insurgence and fought back with all their strength. Jerusalem Square was in chaos. The officers were clubbing people over the head, and many people were getting trampled, but the Libertines were gaining ground, and just when it appeared that the Temple was going to be overrun, the King of Kings appeared from out of nowhere.

He spoke, "Dear children, what are you doing?"

Although the King was not using a microphone, His voice reverberated throughout the Square. His voice started out shallow then it became louder and louder like a jet flying overhead. The Lord's voice was so deafening that many people in the square dropped their weapons and covered their ears. Then the voice stopped as quickly as it began. The rest of the people who were still holding clubs and sticks let them drop to the ground and gazed with downcast eyes towards the ground or at the King.

"My children, where is the love?"

The Lord's voice echoed throughout the crowd, but it was no longer painful to hear.

"I have been gone only a short time, and look at what you have become. Must I be in your midst at all times? Can't a resolution be made that does not involve violence?" The Lord paused. "I'm disappointed in you, but we'll get through this together. Kasca, would you and your closest disciples please come forward? We will meet at the Assembly Hall within the hour. All of the 144 Elders are required to be there. As for the rest of you, would you please help those in need and go home? Anyone who is seriously hurt should be brought up front, and I will offer My assistance. My decision on Mandate 222 will be made public tomorrow. As for those leaving the square, will you please help us clean up the area. Take a few pieces of trash with you and dispose of them properly. Shalom aleichem, peace be unto you."

People injured in the protest were brought forward, and many citizens who were previously at odds with one another were making apologies and helping each other out. Some felt foolish for being caught up in the hoopla of the event and within an hour the grounds at Jerusalem Square were spotless again because almost everyone was pitching in to help clean up the mess left behind. It was miraculous what a simple request from the Counselor could do. As for the people who came from afar, most went home, but a lot of people decided to stay around for one more day to hear the Counselor's verdict on the mandate.

*   *   *   *

The 144 Elders gathered together to hear the Lord's judgment on Mandate 222. Kasca and his disciples were also there. The Elders and the Libertines spoke in hushed voices amongst themselves and waited for the Counselor to make His presence known. As the King entered the room, everyone squirmed in their seats like children awaiting their chastisement. Instead of a heavy exhortation, the Lord waved everyone in His direction, and they followed him out of the building and gathered in a circle under the Tree of Life.

As they sat together, the Lord had some boys and girls bring out some bread and wine, and they all ate as one. Other snacks and delicacies were served, and the discussion began shortly thereafter.

"So who would like to begin?" the King asked.

No one said a word. Some people looked at Kasca, others at Patmos, and some at the Chief Elder, but no one spoke up. Finally Patmos gained enough courage and asked, "Where have you been lately?"

"I know it's been awhile. Actually it's been three years, three months, and three days since I last spoke to any of you. I've been away because I've had serious business to attend to in the Outskirts. I have traveled to distant lands. I have wandered to and fro, but I have always been with you. I have been observing your progress from a distance, and I was curious to see how you would get along without me. Of course, I already knew the outcome, but I've been waiting for the right time to make my presence known. I know all about Mandate 222. I know about Kasca's dreams and aspirations, and my thoughts have been upon all of you. Nonetheless, I did give my authority to the 144 Elders, which I have chosen, to make decisions in My Kingdom. I only wish that you Old Timers would have consulted Me first before making such a profound resolution."

"Now I know some of you are opposed to the mandate, but the protest today does give credence as to why we need a law like Mandate 222. Thus, I have decided to make the mandate the law of the land; however, I'm going to add one other aspect to the law.

If a person decides to leave the Kingdom, I will allow a forty-year grace period for anyone who wishes to return. After the period has expired, I will close the gates to the Kingdom forever. My cherubim will stand guard at all entry points and not let anyone return."

Kasca, this decision is going to affect you and the Libertines the most. Do I have your approval?" the Lord asked. "Remember, if you decide to return before the forty-year period is over, you will be welcomed back. But after the time has expired, you and your offspring will be banished forever."

There was a moment of silence. It seemed to hang in the air like a pop fly heading towards the warning track. Then Kasca looked up and answered, "I understand. It is agreed."

Chapter 4

▼

Exodus

The King's decree was proclaimed throughout the Kingdom. Mandate 222 became law. Many people were upset with the mandate, but most people thought the law was just and fair. They had forty years to decide if they wanted to stay or go, but since many citizens had not ventured outside the borders of the Kingdom, many made plans to travel and settle abroad. And after seeing what lurked beyond the borders, they planned to make their ultimate decision whether to leave the Kingdom or not. Kasca and the Libertines immediately made plans to leave the Kingdom and start up a democratic government to the north. Others slowly left as the years passed. Thus, after Mandate 222 was passed, a large exodus of people left the protection of the Israeli borders and settled in various parts of the globe. In fact, over 70% of the population left the comforts of home and settled abroad by the time the 40 years expired. Regardless, almost all the people who left were New Timers, people born during the Millennial Reign. As for the Old Timers, those who lived prior to the Millennium, less than 5% were willing to venture to the Outskirts.

Before the Exodus occurred, the Kingdom's birthrate was exceedingly high, and over 90% of the population was now New Timers. The rest were Old Timers. In the first year of the Kingdom Age, only 700 million people survived the wars and plagues during the Tribulation. For seventy-five days, these people were judged by the Lord of Lords. The righteous were allowed to enter the Kingdom, and the others were sent away. Out of these people, only one-seventh of the survivors were allowed to enter the Kingdom. These people were welcomed into the Kingdom because they did not receive the Mark of the Beast, but remained faithful to the Lord. The other 600 million people were allowed to live out their lives in the Outskirts but were not permitted to enter the Kingdom. These people were excluded because they aligned themselves with the Antichrist or lived wicked lives. There were also over two billion saints that returned to the earth with the Lord. They were the faithful ones of each previous generation, and they were now receiving their just reward.

The main reason the population grew so fast was because death had practically been exterminated. People's bodies did not age during the Millennial Reign, and if someone was injured or killed, the Tree of Life would revive them. The King of Kings also walked amongst the people, and He was constantly helping, healing, and counseling the people. So the population grew fast. By the year 100, there were already six billion New Timers on the earth. By the year 222, the Year of the Mandate, the New Timers population exceeded twenty-five billion.

* * * *

As the emigrants crossed the borders and entered the Outskirts, the people noticed an absolute throughout the earth. No longer were there thousands of kilometers of endless desert and frozen tundra, but the entire planet had become a paradise. This became possible because after Christ's return, the King of Kings blessed the earth and the planet returned to its natural glory. With a Word from His mouth the planet was transformed into a Garden of Eden. It looked as it did during Adam's time before the fall. Extinct species were formed from the earth and magnificent creatures roamed the planet again. Dinosaurs, unicorns, dragons, and many other creatures spoken of in folklore, walked the earth once more. The geography of the earth also changed. Continents shifted, new islands were formed, but in general, most of the land masses remained the same. The climate of the planet was altered as well, and almost the whole earth became a tropical paradise. Even the coldest regions of the earth like Antarctica and Greenland were havens, but the climate was more temperate. This was possible because a protective water shield like the ozone layer was placed in the atmosphere, and it allowed much of the heat to remain trapped inside the atmosphere. It was similar to what carbon dioxide was doing during the industrial revolution except this was natural and did not cause damage to the earth.

Although the Lord's Kingdom was the most magnificent of all, the whole planet was picturesque. Waterfalls were as common as fruit on a tree, and every form of life sprung up out of the earth without thorns and thistles. Exotic foods and vegetation blanketed the horizon without gnats and flies eating away at the harvest.

For those who survived the Tribulation, this heaven on earth was something that could only be believed in fairy tales, but they watched the Genesis transformation happen right before their eyes. It was an event the Old Timers would never forget, and they would retell the story over and over again to future generations. Even those who were excluded from the Kingdom reaped the benefits of the Messiah's return. Although they were banished to the Outskirts like the convicts of Australia long ago, they were permitted to indulge in the lasciviousness of the earth. These men and women weren't Israeli citizens, but they were far better off than they were during the Antichrist's reign. And even though they were sentenced to eternal separation from God, they were still living a comfortable life free from pain and tribulation.

* * * *

In the second year after Mandate 222 passed, two Irish/English brothers loyal to the Kingdom started to get lonely for the old country of Britain and Ireland. So the two brothers approached the Counselor and told Him their plans of resettling the Land of Tarshish.

"Lord, we've spent over 200 years in the Kingdom, and we like it here and all, but we thought it might be a good idea to venture out and resettle our former homeland," James explained. "We know it's going to be tough and all, especially being separated from You, but in 800 years or so, we will be reunited anyway, and we'll be as one again."

The older brother laughed to himself, and the Counselor also chuckled a little.

"Of course, we would keep the Colony of Tarshish loyal to the throne. Although we will be out of the Kingdom's protection, we will still have the Spirit guiding us along. Now we do know its dangerous being separated from You and the Tree of Life, but if we have Your blessing, we'll probably do alright. Who knows maybe from time to time you'll come and visit us? All I know is that my brother and I are starting to get complacent. We're not accomplishing much in the Kingdom, and an opportunity for adventure has revived our souls."

The younger brother, Jacob, nodded in agreement, and both men waited patiently for the Counselor's response.

"Honestly, I'd hate to see the O'Donohue brothers go, but if you have your mind set on it, there's nothing I can do. You're both free men. You're strong willed and determined," the Lord stated. "In fact, there's probably nothing I can say that would make you want to stay, even though I know if I asked, you would."

The Lord thought to himself for a moment then He continued.

"It might be a good idea to have a beacon of light out there, something that the rest of the world can look to as an example. And if the O'Donohue brothers can survive the Tribulation, they'll survive the Millennium. So make it so, James. Be a true and honorable ruler and don't veer from the righteous path. As for you, Jacob, don't lose heart. Just remember in your darkest hour, I am with you. You have my blessing. Go in peace, but before you leave be well prepared for anything, and be sure to advertise your adventure in the Jerusalem Post. Others will be joining you."

The two brothers gave the Lord a long hug. As they departed, they noticed their King was teary eyed.

* * * *

ATTENTION: All subjects of the Kingdom who are interested in settling the Land of Tarshish are meeting to discuss plans for colonization of the territory. Old Timers and New Timers loyal to the King are welcome. We will be meeting this Friday at 7:00 P.M. in Abraham's Auditorium.

"Hello everyone, my name is James O'Donohue and this here's my brother, Jacob. We've decided with permission from our King that we are going to colonize the Land of Tarshish. We are looking for people loyal to the Kingdom that would like to join us. Of course, it's going to be a difficult task, and you may encounter hardship on the way, but we think it will be a grand adventure. We plan to build a few ships, sail across the Mediterranean then start a new civilization in our former countries of Britain and Ireland. As for my brother and I, we don't wish to start a new government, join the Libertines, or any of that nonsense. We just want to branch out and try something new. I wish there was more to it, but that's about it. If I was a great speaker like Kasca, I might try to woo you over with elaborate pantomimes, but that's not what we're about. We simply want to start fresh and colonize the lands that we loved as children. I guess now might be a good time to take your questions, but don't forget, we have a sign-up list up front, and if anyone's interested, feel free to sign the list. Of course, if you change your mind later, that's fine, we're still planning to set sail in the spring. So are there any questions out there?"

A bunch of hands shot up into the air and James pointed to a young college student in the front row.

"If we decide to join you on this adventure, how do you plan to survive out there?" the university student asked.

"Before we leave, we plan to be well-prepared. Our ships will be well-stocked with goods, livestock, and Fruit Pills. As for my brother and I, we both served in the Royal Navy before the years of tribulation, and we are experts on the high seas. Also, we've served as engineers and carpenters for the last 200 years, and we were instrumental in the rebuilding of New Jerusalem after the war."

James with his deep voice and large size called on another person in the crowd and a fiery New Timer named Hannah inquired, "But how do you plan to start a civilization without women?"

James was about to answer, but Jacob looked at his brother, and gave him a sign that he would take this one.

"Well, that's why we called this meeting. We're looking for others to join us. If we can get enough people to come along with us, I think we'll have a good shot at making this thing work."

Without being called upon, the woman with long auburn hair asked another question.

"So how many people do you have committed to the cause?"

Jacob laughed as he answered, "Thus far it's just my brother and I." Everyone at the meeting chuckled a little. "But I believe that's a start and probably after tonight we'll have a few more. Who knows, by the time spring rolls around next year, we might have over a hundred or thousands heading with us on this journey."

Some of the people looked around and noticed that there were less than a hundred people in attendance. As compared to Kasca and the Libertines heading north, which numbered in the billions, the O'Donohue's idea of colonizing Tarshish paled in comparison. Although some people were not impressed with the brothers' vision, Hannah was already charmed by Jacob's wit and smile. She later became instrumental in starting the colony.

A few other questions were asked, and the O'Donohue brothers did their best in convincing some of the audience to join their mission. After the meeting was adjourned, about twenty-five people came forward and signed their list. Out of these twenty-five, only nine of them set sail when they left. One of these settlers was Hannah, the General's oldest daughter. She managed to bring in 300 more, including her brother Simon, and by the time they set sail, they had over a 1,000 people. Many of these settlers planned to return before the 40 years expired, but they wanted to join the adventure and see the world, so they tagged along on this journey and planned to set sail in the coming spring.

* * * *

The spring of 225 came upon the O'Donohue brothers and their party much quicker than they expected. They originally planned to set sail in March, but they didn't leave the Jaffa Port until late August. The O'Donohue brothers and their crew built three ships. The ships looked like large British warships from the 15th century, but they were empowered with all the modern technology available to them from the pre and post Millennial Age. The engines, however, ran on seaweed. It was created by a German Old Timer by the name of Lane Hofmann. He was a genius, and he solved many of the problems that confounded civilizations before the Kingdom Age. The engines were fast, powerful, and did absolutely no damage to the environment. One item, however, not included on the ships was weapons. They were not available in the Kingdom. The Tarshish settlers figured they would not need them at the start, but they did bring many tools that could quickly be transformed into arms. The ships were also richly supplied with Fruit Pills enough to last a couple hundred years. They also brought food, goods, machinery, and other important items that would help them survive in the Outskirts.

The lead ship was commanded by James. Jacob, his brother, was the captain of the second ship, and the third was commanded by Hannah's brother Simon. Although Simon was not a naval veteran, he had been around boats his whole life, and he was pretty good at the helm. Before they set sail they were instructed by the Counselor that they should stay close to the southern shoreline. He told them that if they ventured too far to the north, they might encounter dangerous storms and sea monsters. Thus, the Tarshish settlers stayed close to the African coastline, still known as Egypt, and made their way towards Tarshish.

The first few days of the journey went well, but when they got to the middle of Mediterranean, they experienced north-easterly winds and veered off track. The settlers didn't expect this and were caught off guard. They fought the sea with all their might and were doing okay until Simon's ship started having engine problems. The ship was being taken by the wind, and the other two ships were forced to follow. As the Tarshish vessels sailed north, they came across something they had never seen before. A giant sea monster emerged from the sea, and it was tracking them.

"James, did you see that?" his brother Jacob asked over the radio.

"How could I miss it? It's as big as three sperm whales put together," his brother responded.

"But I've never seen a sperm whale like that," Jacob added. "It looks like Godzilla in one of those ancient Japanese movies."

"If Simon's engine was working, I'd say we high-tale it out of here and make a run for it, but with Simon and Hannah's boat in trouble, we got to do something quick. We're outside the borders of the Kingdom, and we have no idea if that sea monster is friendly or not.

Jacob thought for a moment as he put his hand to his scalp and ran his fingers through his curly, red locks. "I agree," Jacob said, "and here's my plan. Our boat is closer to Simon's ship, so I'm going to get as near to it as possible and try to board it. Once onboard I'll take a look at his engine and see if I can get that motor running again."

Within minutes Jacob's vessel was running side to side with Simon's ship. A giant rope was tied around Jacob, and he made a leap for Simon's portside. This was difficult to do because of the heavy weather, and he only managed to land half his body on Simon's ship. Jacob almost fell into the sea, but some of Simon's shipmates grabbed Jacob by the arms, and after a struggle, they managed to pull him on board. In the meantime, Jacob's first-mate took control of the helm on his ship. When Jacob was finally on board, Hannah rushed towards him and gave him a giant hug. She dug her head into his chest and sighed in relief that he was alright.

"O Jacob, you scared the life out of me!" Hannah said. "Are you trying to kill yourself?"

Jacob looked at her, rolled his eyes and joked, "Ah, it was just a couple of meters. I had everything under control. Didn't you see my perfect landing?"

Hannah tried to hold back her smile, but she couldn't. Jacob always had a way of breaking her demeanor.

"Well, are you going to let me go or not?" Jacob sarcastically asked. "I've got a ship to fix. There's a giant sea monster out there, and all you're thinking about is love and kisses."

After Jacob's words, Hannah pushed him away, punched him in the side, and marched away upset. The crew, at this display, started to laugh, so Jacob made a funny face to accelerate the laughter then he raced towards the engine room with his arms waving in the air like a madman.

When Jacob reached the engine, he knew right away what the problem was. Hofmann engines were magnificent machines, but they weren't the most durable creation. They were like VW Bugs of the 20th Century, so he went to work right away and was able to get the thing running within minutes. This was lucky because at that moment, the sea monster raised his giant head from the sea and started getting closer. The crew wasn't sure if the creature was just curious or coming to eat them. Consequently, Jacob yelled, "Give her some gas!" and Simon's ship slowly pulled away from the beast of the sea.

After a few more hours of fighting the sea, the storm started to cease, and they made their way towards a small island in the distance. James and the settlers decided that a couple days of shore leave were required, and they anchored themselves at an unknown island not listed on the Kingdom charts in the middle of the Mediterranean.

* * * *

Once the settlers anchored at the uncharted island, they noticed a lot of species they had never seen before. It's was probably similar to what Darwin might have seen when he first visited the Galapagos Islands. There were so many bizarre looking creatures, and they didn't seem to be afraid of humans. One could walk right up to the animals, and they wouldn't run away. In fact, many of the settlers were petting them, carrying them on their backs, and playing with them. One of the creatures that were at the center of the attention was this koala looking monkey. They were all over the trees, and when the settlers approached them, they seemed to be as eager to meet the settlers as the settlers were to meet them. These mammals also looked like an intelligent species. Although the creatures did not speak, they did appear to be communicating to one another by hand signals. The koala looking monkeys made these signals to the settlers, and the settlers did the sign language back. One of these signs was three tappings on the back of the hand and a rolling of the arms and hands towards the mouth. Once their hands touched their mouth, they stopped and did it all over again. When one of the men on the ship saw this, he said, "Look they're doing Signmonkoala!" Thus, from that point on their species was known as the Signmonkoalas. When Jacob did the same sign language back at a Signmonkoala, the creature made a sign towards his friends, and they brought fruit down from the tree and made a pile of it at the settler's feet. Jacob and the settlers received the gift of the Signmonkoalas freely, and they ate of the fruit.

The fruit given to the settlers was a type of fruit that Kingdom Age men had never seen or tasted before. It existed long ago during the 1st few generations of man when Adam walked the earth, but it quickly became extinct due to man's covetousness of the tree. The fruit looked like a two sided pear or a dumb-bell used in weightlifting. It had a bright purplish color and hairy tough skin like a kiwi. When the skin was pulled back, the fruit remained purple, but the insides were of a lighter complexion. After the settlers bit into the fruit, they immediately fell in love with it. It was sweeter than a strawberry, more juicy than an orange, and it tasted absolutely scrumptious.

After about 30 minutes of signing with the Signmonkoalas, playing with the local animals, and eating of the fruit, the settlers suddenly noticed a strange feeling coming over them. Everyone started to feel carefree as if nothing really mattered. The settlers were happy like they were on the drug ecstasy. They were laughing like they had been smoking marijuana, and their inhibitions quickly slipped away. They were floating on the clouds and drifting higher towards the heavens. The settlers played like they were little children, and their bodies felt strong sensations of pleasure and love. The fruit had an intoxicating, aphrodisiac effect upon the people, and everyone was enjoying themselves.

After Jacob and Hannah ate of the fruit, they quickly fell into each other's arms and held one another. They gazed at one another and wallowed in their affection. After some time they ran up the beach holding hands, and when they were far enough from the rest of the group, they stripped off their clothes and went swimming in the ocean. In the water they became intimate, and from that point on, they knew that they were meant for one another. As for the others, they were doing similar pleasurable things, and many men and women got together that evening on the Island of Signmonkoala.

When morning came and the effects of the fruit wore off, many people felt embarrassed about what had transpired the previous day. Nevertheless, no one felt a hangover from the fruit like one might have experienced from drinking wine. Also, from that day forward, the settlers of Tarshish had a much closer bond. The men started joking with one another like they had been friends since childhood, and the women formed a tight circle that was difficult to break even when troubled times came their way in the future. As for Jacob and Hannah, they felt a little ashamed of themselves that they had engaged in sex, but they both knew that this was what they really wanted. In the coming months, Jacob and Hannah became intimate lovers. When they arrived in Tarshish, they planned to be the first couple to get married in the new land. Hannah was willing to sacrifice everything and leave the comforts of the Kingdom behind to be with her new man.

* * * *

After spending six months on Signmonkoala Island, James and Jacob finally got their act together and left port. Many of the settlers of Tarshish wanted to stay longer, eat of the Purple Fruit, and learn more about the Signmonkoalas, but the two leaders thought if they stayed any longer, they may never leave. James was the first one to come to the realization that the Signmonkoala fruit, later known as Bliss and Purple, had an addictive component to it, and the settlers were starting to get hooked. Although James was being influenced by the fruit as much as the others, he was the one that discovered that the fruit was addictive. It was logical for James to come to this understanding because he had been a drug addict for about ten years before and during the Tribulation years. Technically, James was a Christian during that period, but he was a fallen brother. Therefore, when he started to see the signs of the times come to pass during the Tribulation, he got clean and was instrumental in the underground movement that opposed the Antichrist and the Mark of the Beast in Britain. When James started to see everyone getting addicted to the fruit like he'd seen himself and many of his friends get hooked on heroin and cocaine in the past, he knew it was time to stop the eating of the fruit. Thus, James went on board one of the ships for a few days and literally got the monkey off his back.

After James cleaned his body of the Purple Fruit like he did years ago when he kicked heroin, he consulted his brother Jacob and asked him to do the same. At first Jacob didn't believe him because he was in love and having the time of his life with Hannah; nevertheless, he was the only other Old Timer on the trip, and he was instrumental in helping his brother get clean long ago. So he also stopped eating the fruit and managed to convince Hannah and Simon to do the same. A few days later, the three settlers felt like they were waking up from a long dream, and they couldn't believe they had been under the spell of the Purple Fruit for that long.

James and the other three had been off the fruit for over a week, and they started helping others one by one to get off the Purple. The Signmonkoalas, however, did not appear to be affected by the addictive chemicals in the fruit, but when James explained to them their problem through sign language, the Signmonkoalas did all they could to help James and the others out. The Signmonkoalas started hiding the fruit from the settlers, and they would no longer go high up in the trees to retrieve it for them. Of course, this didn't prevent the settlers from climbing the trees themselves, but their effort did help a little. In the end, everyone stopped eating the fruit, but some were defiant to the end. In fact, some of them went to the other side of the island and tried to escape, but eventually James and the others caught them and they were put in detention for a few days until they got clean.

Once all of the settlers finally stopped eating the fruit, about a month later, the settlers made plans to sail for Tarshish again. Some of the Signmonkoalas wanted to come with the settlers, but James wouldn't permit it. He did, however, allow the settlers to take some of the fruit and seed with them, but he kept it under lock and key. James and the rest recognized that even though the Purple Fruit was addictive, there were some positive reasons to keep it around. For this reason, Hannah and some of the others learned all there was to know about growing the fruit from the Signmonkoala, and when the settlers arrived in Tarshish, they planned to plant the seeds and start a plantation of trees.

CHAPTER 5

▼

The Northern Republic

After Mandate 222 became Law, Kasca and the Libertines immediately made plans for starting a democratic republic in the North. The Libertines advertised everywhere, and the entire Kingdom was tempted to follow Kasca northward. Over eight billion New Timers were seduced by his propaganda, and the people believed that they would be freer under a democracy than under the King's rule. The Libertines and about one-third of the Kingdom made their departure to the North, and six months later, they were starting a new republic in the territory that was formally called Russia and Ukraine. Some of the people didn't journey that far, and they started their own townships elsewhere. Many of these people ended up settling in Asia Minor, now known as Meschech & Tubal, just north of the Euphrates River. Others branched out and settled the rest of Asia, Europe, and the continents abroad, but most of the people followed the Libertines into the Northeast. They hoped to form a great republic that embraced freedom and justice, and they believed that Kasca was the man who could bring about their hopes and dreams.

    Before leaving the Kingdom, the Libertines and their followers prepared well for their departure. And when they arrived in the North, the people quickly went to work and started building their new country. The first outpost the Libertines built was called the City of Liberty. In the beginning it was tough to leave the comforts of the Kingdom behind, but within twenty years, the small huts of Liberty became a thriving metropolis and soon the Kingdom was forgotten. It later became the largest city in the known world, and it quickly outnumbered Jerusalem. In the first year, elections were held and Kasca became their 1st President. He ruled righteously over the Democratic Magog Republic (D.M.R.) for fifteen years. He won the first five-year term and easily triumphed in the second and third term. However, in the 4th term, Kasca decided to let someone else pull the reigns for a while and one of his closest associates, Prime Minister Harrick Kim, won the election. Although Kasca was no longer in office, his business partners controlled almost every major resource in the D.M.R. So in reality, Kasca was still ruling the Republic but behind the scenes.

The Democratic Magog Republic had three major branches. They were the Executive, Judicial, and Legislative branches. Although the Libertines modeled their government after a country formerly known as the United States of America, the government differed in many ways. The Judicial Branch had thirteen judges, and they served 25 year terms. And instead of being chosen by the Executive Branch, they were voted into office every 25th year. If a judge decided to resign early from his/her position, an emergency election was held that year. As for the Senate, there was one seat given to every millionth person under that city's jurisdiction. Every seven years they would vote for new senators, and if a city had 3.5 million people in it, three senators would be elected. The first, second, and third highest vote recipients would be elected. If a city reached 4 million, a fourth senator would be elected. As a result, there was a hodgepodge of different parties and many voices were heard. As for the Executive Branch, the President was voted into office every five years. There were no limitations on how many terms he/she could serve. Second to the President was the Prime Minister, and if the President died or was missing in action, the Prime Minister would serve out his term. The Executive Branch's cabinet consisted of ten members. All members were chosen by the current President.

*   *   *   *

Kasca left office in his 15th year as President. He had a 75% approval rating, but he did not wish to run for another term, and it puzzled many people. Kasca, on the other hand, recognized that as a politician, he was limited to what he could do. As President the public eye was always on him, but by working behind the scenes, he was able to do things quietly and quickly like a mob boss. In fact, Kasca and his company, Gog Liberty Incorporated, had its hands into everything.

Gog Inc. had a stake into every major resource in the D.M.R. They also controlled several of the major media corporations, and they were the highest contributors to the Libertine Party. Consequently, Kasca was a busy man, and he figured he could buy any leader off if he needed to get something accomplished in the future. In the meantime, Harrick Kim, the former Prime Minister took over the Presidency. Kim was one of the original Libertines and a loyal subject of Kasca's.

Although Kasca had a heavy hand in the D.M.R., he still believed in liberty and justice. Kasca just figured that he was free to do as he pleased. He believed in Laissez-faire capitalism, and he wanted to be the Rockefeller who would trickle down his wealth to the rest of the Republic. In the beginning, Gog Inc. was the most charitable organization in the D.M.R., but as time proceeded, Kasca's greed got greater and greater and Gog Inc. became more powerful and controlling over the passing decades.

Politically, Kasca's move to step down was a wise maneuver. It made the people believe that they were living in a democracy and not a dictatorship. And in the beginning, the Magog Republic truly was a free society, but as time proceeded those freedoms were slowly taken away. Hence, almost all the New Timers living in the D.M.R. didn't wish to return to the Kingdom after the 40 years expired. They believed that their freedom would last forever, but they were deceived by the flourishing times. The people in the Outskirts didn't think far enough ahead. They forgot to consider the population explosion. They seemed to forget about mankind's corruptibility. They forgot about the greed, the avarice, and the jealousies. But most all, the New Timers had never seen war before. They hadn't experienced hunger, nor had they seen death. In the coming centuries their eyes would be opened and many of the New Timers who willingly left the Kingdom would hungrily thirst for it when times got bad.

Chapter 6

▼

The Water-holes

The settlers sailed along the south-west coast of Europe, now known as Gomar. This region was occupied by the children of the people who survived the Tribulation but were not welcomed into the Kingdom. Eastern Europe was also occupied by these people, but it was divided into three city states. They formed a republic known as Beth-Togar-Mah. As for the settlers, they continued on their way after leaving Signmonkoala Island. They were instructed by the Counselor before they left to stay along the northern shores of Africa to avoid trouble, but they were already two-thirds on their way, and James didn't feel like backtracking. The older brother knew the ocean well, and he figured they'd be fine. As they went, it was pretty much clear sailing until they reached the waters off the coast of what was formerly known as Spain. The ships were moving along at approximately twenty knots when James noticed something very strange occurring in the waters ahead of him. There were these giant looking water holes in the ocean that seemed to be sucking the water down into their holes. Each water hole was much larger than all their ships and if a vessel got stuck in one, it would surely be the end of that ship. The three vessels sailed around the water holes and proceeded on their way. Nevertheless, Jacob, an experienced marine biologist and diver, wanted to observe the phenomena under the sea, so all the ships waited patiently while Jacob, Hannah, and two others went overboard in scuba gear to see the water holes up close.

Under the water, the divers observed a miraculous occurrence. The giant water holes were being created by these whale-like creatures that seemed to be recycling water and feeding on the krill and plankton like baleen whales. Jacob couldn't be sure if this was the case, unless he did further study, but that was his best educated guess. One thing for sure though, this was a new species that Kingdom men had never seen before, so Jacob called them water-hole whales.

The bodies of these water-hole whales had giant mouths that were open at the surface. The orifice had a diameter of about fifty meters. From the mouths, the bodies began to taper down, and at the rear end the water would funnel out of them like an undertow. For Jacob, observing this event was like witnessing the birth of a child. It was miraculous and awe inspiring.

After Jacob and the others returned to their ships, the settlers noticed that the water-hole whales were becoming more numerous. For that reason, they doubled their speed, headed west, and tried to avoid getting caught in one of these whales. At first the settlers were doing alright, and they thought they had escaped the danger, but suddenly water-hole whales were popping up out of the sea all around them, and it appeared they had just sailed into the heart of the whales feeding grounds. It looked hopeless. The lead ship, captained by James, kept having to go forwards and backwards to avoid them, and the other ships were doing the same. Then one of the whales started to open up his mouth right below the lead ship, and it appeared that the boat was going to go down.

James cried, "Lord, help us!" as the other two ships watched helplessly. The bow of James' vessel started to go down, but at that moment the water-hole whale must have sensed the danger of trying to swallow a ship, and it began to close its mouth. Luckily for both the whale and the settlers on board, the orifice closed in the nick of time, and all were saved.

After the lead ship was almost sunk, James remembered the words of the Lord, "Stay to the South in the Mediterranean," and he high-tailed it out of there in a southerly direction as the others followed. The quick left turn was a saving grace for the settlers. If they had continued any further, all the ships would have been lost. The settlers didn't know that during this time of the year, the water-hole whales gathered in this region for breeding, and that they were more numerous than the barnacles on a reef. Also, one of the mating rituals of the male whales was to open their mouths as wide as they could to show their strength and superiority in attracting a female.

* * * *

The ships reached the northern shores of Africa about half a day later. James felt rather foolish for being proud and not following the Counselor's advice on the trip, but they made it there alive, and the settlers would always have great stories to tell in the future after their near death experience in the Mediterranean Sea.

The sun was going down so the crews decided to take a day of shore leave before they headed out for the final leg of their journey. They made port in northern Africa, a region that was once known in the Third World as Morocco. Now it was just part of Egypt.

As the crews came ashore, they noticed strange ruins from another time. Large high-rises still clothed the shoreline, but they were overgrown with forestry and falling apart. To James and Jacob, this was no surprise, but to the New Timers, these were things that they had never seen before. They were mesmerized by the landscape, and they stood with their mouths gaping open. Old tanks and war machines still littered the beaches. Some of the machines were half buried in the sand with bullet holes in their armory. The buildings were blown apart, the roads were torn asunder, and nature had overridden the whole place. As for the animals, the settlers noticed a strange phenomenon. The animals seemed to be afraid of them. Every time someone approached a bird or living creature, it scuttled away from them. The New Timers couldn't understand why this was so, but James and Jacob had known too well. They guessed that people banished from the Kingdom were already living in the area, and they weren't following the law to "Treat the earth and all that dwell therein with respect and dignity." Even the two brothers were shocked at how quickly the morals of men could be thrown out the door when people were free to do as they please. Consequently, the settlers didn't stay long in Africa. James and Jacob realized that there were evil men about, and they didn't want to be involved in any sort of a struggle.

"It's somewhat ironic in a way," Jacob said to his brother, "that even though the Devil is locked away, mankind is still inclined towards evil."

"Yes, that might be true, little brother, but this is a new era. We have to hope that this generation will not be as foolish as previous ones."

"That's rather idealistic of you, even though you know the prophecies. You know what's going to happen at the end of the reign."

"Well, you might be right, bro, but I'm going to try to enjoy this period of peace for as long as it remains." Then James added, "The New Timers have already seen too much already. We need to get out of here as soon as dawn approaches. Warn everyone to stay near camp and to not go off wandering. Make it so, little brother."

Jacob shook his head in acknowledgement, and they cut their conversation short as they saw the outline of a curvaceous body approaching. The woman looked angelic under the twinkle of the sun, but as she got closer, the brothers realized it was only Hannah.

"I'll see you at dawn," James declared.

James departed quickly as Hannah reached them and Jacob grabbed Hannah by the waist, twisted her around, and gave her a hard kiss on the lips.

"So where's he running off to?" Hannah asked. "I didn't mean to break up your little party. Was it something important?"

"Oh, no worries, we were just finishing up a little business, but we are planning to leave at dawn tomorrow. Would you mind telling the other settlers?"

"Oh, do we have to?" Hannah begged. "I kind of wanted to see the sites and wander around tomorrow."

"There will be plenty of ruins to examine when we get to Tarshish, and James and I think we've already wasted too much time already."

"Alright, I'll tell the others."

Hannah started to walk away, but Jacob asked, "Where are you going?"

"To tell the others, Alpha male."

"I didn't mean right now," Jacob explained. "You're such a cry baby when you don't get things your way."

Hannah knew that Jacob was right, but she acted mad anyway and continued to walk away.

"Hey wait up, I'll go with you. We'll tell them together."

Hannah pretended like she didn't hear him and started to walk faster.

"If you don't slow down, I'm going to run you down and then you'll be sorry."

The General's daughter looked back, started to laugh, and began running away from him down the beach.

Jacob yelled, "You're going to get it!" and he charged after her. When he reached Hannah, he tackled her on the sand, wrestled her down, and Hannah lay helpless on the sand. Hannah tried to get away, but her arms were pinned to the ground and Jacob was sitting on top of her with all his weight laughing.

"Let me go, you freckled freak!" Hannah shrieked but Jacob ignored her insult. Instead he started unbuttoning her blouse with his teeth as Hannah continued to struggle. Jacob then started kissing her all over, and in a matter of moments they were naked, making love as the sun went down on the beach.

* * * *

When dawn came, the settlers picked up camp and prepared themselves for departure. As they packed, Hannah had a gnawing sense that someone was watching them. She couldn't tell where they were hiding, but she knew they were out there lurking in the shadows. Hannah told Jacob about her fears, but he told her not to worry and that everything was fine. Jacob, nonetheless, told his brother, and they both kept a watchful eye until their ships were completely boarded.

Hannah's intuition proved correct because right after the ships set sail, a large contingent of people, close to 1000 or more came out of hiding, and they started to wave clubs and sticks in the air like a marauding force of raiders. When the settlers saw this display, they were terribly frightened, but they were already at sea, so they felt relatively safe in the water. Regardless, the settlers were glad that they left at the crack of dawn and were not permitted to explore the area. If they had, it was likely that they would have been captured, killed, or made slaves. In fact, the leader of the Marauders was alerted of the settlers' presence that night, and he informed the men in the area to stand down until he arrived. But Matusak, their leader, arrived too late. He should have ordered his men to take the settlers captive that night, but his pride got in the way of his reason. Matusak wanted to be the one who led the men into battle, and he wouldn't have it any other way.

Of course, when Matusak did arrive, two hours after the settlers already left, he blamed the debacle on the camp leader, and Matusak had him whipped, tortured then chopped off his head.

Chapter 7

The Marauders

The Marauders were a group of New Timers from the Kingdom who were a bunch of juvenile delinquents. In the Kingdom, they were often chastised and disciplined for their disruptive behavior, but when the borders were opened, Matusak promised the Marauders glorious combat and adventures abroad. So when Mandate 222 became law, the Marauders were ecstatic. They were finally allowed the freedom to cause anarchy in the world. Therefore, the Marauders decided to head out west because Kasca and the Libertines decided to go north, and they wanted to have nothing to do with them. They planned to cross the Nile River, go as far west as possible by land, and start a new Marauding Empire in Africa.

During the Libertine Uprising, the Marauders couldn't care less about democracy, but they supported Kasca because they knew his ideals would aide their cause. Matusak and the Marauders, however, planned to build a new empire of their own that would conquer the rest of the world. In other words, they hoped to build a giant war machine and eventually bring the rest of the world to its knees, including the Libertines and the Kingdom, but the Marauders weren't all that bright. They had read far too many stories of glorious battles and victories from the past. Their leader, Matusak, was a bully. He was sadistic, an ego maniac, and cruel at times. On many occasions in the Kingdom, he was disciplined firmly and had to serve lengthy time in isolation. The Counselor reached out to him on many occasions, and it helped a little, but over time Matusak would be up to his old tricks, and he'd be beating someone over the head in football, baseball, or soccer, three of the main sporting events in the Kingdom. In fact, Matusak was banned from playing football altogether. He was an excellent linebacker, but he kept breaking the rules and hurting others, so the 144 Elders took matters into their own hands and banned him from the sport after he purposely broke someone's back over his leg. Nonetheless, Matusak had a large following. He was strong, rough with the women, and unruly. The people loved him for it. Women flocked to him because of his strength and power, and many of the men worshipped him like a god because he was one of the best athletes in the Kingdom. He was the homerun leader in the Kingdom Baseball League and an all pro linebacker in football every year he played until he was banned from the league.

Overall, the Marauders weren't a bad lot; they were just insubordinate like teenagers. The only problem was that the Marauders never grew out of it. They had to be constantly disciplined, but they did respect the Counselor. On a few occasions the King would have to fight Matusak hand to hand to prove who was in charge.

*　　*　　*　　*

"If it isn't the King of Kings," Matusak mocked as the Counselor wandered into the Marauders' camp one evening. "Would you like us to get down on our hands and knees and worship at you feet?"

"That won't be necessary," the Counselor answered. "I'm just roaming around, and I thought I'd crash this party you're having tonight."

Matusak laughed aloud and his minions followed in suit. He then rubbed his thick beard and asked, "Do you have an invitation?"

"No, but I thought I might come by anyway."

"According to the Law of the Marauders, if you don't have an invitation, you must fight your way in."

Of course, there was no Law of the Marauders but the Counselor played along.

"Well, who must I fight?" the Counselor asked.

"The host of the party and that would be me."

Matusak stepped down from his high seat at the table, and he stared down the King.

"So be it," the Counselor responded. "Would you care to wrestle or box?"

"Wrestling will do."

At that moment, Matusak started to pace around the King, and he started to jaw back and forth like he was going to attack then he'd pull back suddenly. The Marauders also started to get unruly. A giant circle started to form around them. Everyone was chanting and cheering like it was a street fight, but no one intervened. Most of the party was rooting for Matusak, who was twice the King's size, but there were some in attendance who supported the King.

"C'mon Matusak, bust his head in!" someone yelled. "Take the throne!"

"Hold your ground, Counselor," a supporter of the King countered. "Don't let him intimidate you."

At that instant, Matusak charged the Counselor, but the King merely stepped aside as he pushed Matusak in the back. The Marauder went face first into the ground, but he got up quickly and charged again. This time the Counselor ducked, and Matusak flew over the King. He fell to the ground, bloodied his lip a little, and Matusak got up more slowly. He now had dirt in his stringy, black hair, and he seemed perturbed.

The crowd stood hushed for a moment, unbelieving what their eyes were seeing. Then someone hollered, "Show Him the Marauding way! Take the King down, and stop fooling around!"

Matusak looked up trying to figure out where the voice was coming from then the leader of the Marauders started to get serious. He grunted like a wild beast, shook off the fall, and began moving in slowly. The King, meanwhile, took the offensive and grabbed Matusak by the shoulders. Each man was locked in each others arms moving back and forth across the ground. Suddenly, the Counselor did an old wrestling move. He ducked down, lifted Matusak on his shoulders then threw him to the ground. The Marauder hit the earth with great force, and there was a giant thud when he went down. Matusak didn't move for a moment. Instead, he waved his hand in the air like he had enough, and the Counselor gave him a hand to get up. But just as the King reached out his hand, Matusak revived and tricked the Counselor. He grabbed the King's arm and brought Him to the ground. The King fell, but He sort of rolled over on His side and didn't let go of Matusak's arm. Thus, it put the Marauder in an awkward position, and the King could easily break Matusak's arm if he wanted. The Counselor kept pulling harder and harder until the Marauder gave in.

"Mercy, you win!" Matusak screamed, and the Counselor instantly let go of his arm.

The King got off the ground first, and He offered His hand again. This time Matusak used it to help himself up, and the King smiled. The Counselor then put His arm around Matusak, and the Marauder laughed loudly. Matusak then ordered, "Drinks for everyone!" and the Counselor was one with them.

There were other occasions where Matusak challenged the King of Kings, but he always lost. Once the Counselor beat him in one on one basketball 11 to 0, and another time the King pummeled him in boxing. After that, the lead Marauder didn't bother challenging His authority. When the King came around, Matusak offered his respects, and the Marauders invited the Counselor to almost every important occasion. As for the King, He didn't defeat Matusak to show off. He did it to teach Matusak a lesson when his pride grew too strong. And afterwards, the Counselor would eat and drink with Matusak and the Marauders, and everyone would have a grand old time. As for the 144 Elders, the Marauders didn't care much for them. They were Old Timers who were out of touch with the new generation, and the Marauders did everything in their power to show their disgust with them. They'd spit on the ground, taunt them, and sometimes challenge them like Matusak did with the Counselor. But the main reason the Marauders didn't like the 144 Elders was because they were subordinate to them. If the ruling authority was an elected leader, a dictator, or the 144 Elders, it didn't matter. The Marauders didn't like authority, and they wanted to be free. Consequently, when the doors to the Kingdom were opened, they left. Approximately 150,000 men, women, and children headed out west to start a new empire beyond the Nile.

Chapter 8

▼

The Final Leg of the Journey

After the encounter with the Marauders on the shores of Africa, the settlers headed north for the final leg of their journey. As they went, it was pretty much clear sailing, but they stayed within sight of land just in case any trouble crossed their path. After the sea monster, the water-hole whales, and their near miss with the Marauders, James and Jacob decided to play it safe. The vessels sailed briskly off the shores of what was formerly known as France and made their way across the English Channel. They stayed, however, to the west of the channel because they planned to set up their colony in Wales so that they would have easy access to Ireland, England, and Scotland. As the settlers crossed into the Irish Sea, James and Jacob noticed a strange phenomenon. The Irish Sea was riddled with a chain of new islands in the sector. The O'Donohue brothers couldn't believe their eyes.

"Do you see that lads?" James announced over the radio to Jacob and Simon, the two captains of the other ships.

"How could we miss it, big brother? My oh my, she's big!" Jacob responded as he sailed next to the giant island.

"Why are you two so mesmerized by this island?" Simon, a New Timer asked.

"You see, lad. Last time I sailed this sea, over two hundred years ago, this island wasn't here." James explained. "It was merely a large polluted swamp that used to rock us back and forth when we crossed her."

"Are you sure a swamp is the right word to use, big brother?" Jacob added after he heard James' explanation.

"Well, maybe not a swamp, but you get the picture."

All the settlers, especially the O'Donohue brothers, stood in awe of the first island. The island they were passing appeared to be about the size of Maui, and the island to the west of her appeared to be just as big. These were the first sights the settlers saw as they entered the Irish Sea. And not only did the first island look grand as they passed it, they could also see giant waterfalls, exotic looking flora, and strange looking animals walking about on the island. The brothers couldn't tell if the twin island to the west was as grand, but they did hope it would be.

After sailing along for quite some time, the settlers eventually passed the first two islands. They soon reached a third island, then a fourth, a fifth, and a sixth. These islands were much smaller than the first two islands at the entrance to the Irish Sea, but they were still beautiful. Eventually they reached the Isle of Man, an island that existed in the area prior to the Millennium, and that made a total of seven. After the Isle of Man, the brothers noticed there was something wrong with the lay of the land. A new land mass bridged the gap between Northern Ireland and Scotland. There was no longer a geographical separation between Ireland and the rest of Great Britain. It was now one giant land mass, and there was no escaping through the North Channel because only half of it was there. Just North of Belfast Lough, the land mass began and it extended all the way across to Scotland. The settlers, as a result, decided to make their home in Belfast instead of Wales. It was the first community founded by the Kingdom loyalists. They called it Canaan of Tarshish.

* * * *

Six new islands formed in the Irish Sea. James and Jacob guessed that there was volcanic activity in the region that caused the transformation. Then again, they thought that maybe the Lord of Lords created it after His return. The O'Donohue brothers didn't care; they were just glad the Islands of Tarshish were there. It was a bonus they didn't expect, and they couldn't wait to explore them.

The two islands at the mouth of the Irish Sea were almost identical in size. They were semi-circular islands that were about 2,000 kilometers across. They were called the Twin Islands of Tarshish, and later they became two of the most exotic islands in the world. The first island stood to the west, and the other twin held his ground in the east. When they first arrived, Jacob made up a story about how the islands came into being, and it instantly became a legend that was told to future generations. Tourists would hear the story over and over again, and it was written in almost every future guide book.

Once upon a time, there was a tribal Chief of Tarshish who had a barren wife. They had tried for years and years to have children, but his wife was unable to get pregnant. They had seen the local witch doctor, and he tried every incantation, spell, and herb to break the curse, but his power was not strong enough to do it. Eventually the Chief and his wife grew older, and it appeared they would never bare a son or a daughter. But the Chief and his wife had not given up hope. They decided to pray unto the Great Spirit to give them a child, but another year passed, and the Chief's wife was still not pregnant. Thus, they both started to despair, and the Chief's wife began to weep. She shed tears for days and days. She cried so much that a great river flowed from the Chief's hut, and it caused a great flood that destroyed all the tribe's cattle and harvest for the year. This was a terrible burden upon the Tribe of Tarshish, and many of the people were angry with her. It was the middle of winter, and now their reserves were gone. But the Tribe of Tarshish was a strong and determined people. They took their canoes, fished the sea, and survived the winter. When spring came about, new crops sprung out of the earth, and the people no longer went hungry. As for the Chief's wife, she was still without child, and many of the women laughed openly at her. They would show off their children in front of her, and the men would offer their daughters to the Chief. And although the Chief was tempted, he did not divorce his wife and take a new one. He loved his wife with all his heart, so he stayed by her side. As time proceeded, it appeared there was not going to be a successor to the throne. This made the Tribe of Tarshish sad because the Chief was well-liked and a just ruler. So the wife of the Chief decided to take matters into her own hands. She planned to jump from the Great Causeway and take her life so that her husband could remarry and have children of his own. But just before she was about to take a leap into the rocks below, the Great Spirit came to her and spoke, "I have heard your prayer. You are going to have two children. They will be two great rulers who will be pillars of hope during evil times. They will stand up for justice. The will fight for truth. They will remember My name." At these words, the wife of the Chief stepped back from the ledge and went home. In the coming year she bore twin boys, and she was happy. When the twins grew up, the elder son became the new chieftain, and the younger one became a great seer. Together they fought against the evil neighbors to the east and to the north, and they were victorious because they believed in the Great Spirit and had not forgotten His name. At the end of their days, the twins sailed out from Tarshish. As they went, two volcanoes erupted beneath them, and they were swallowed by fire and molten rock. When the fires cooled, a pair of islands were formed in the twin's place. New life sprouted from them because their energy could not be contained, and they became the Twin Islands of Tarshish, as they are known today.

* * * *

The settling of Canaan was a great feat for the people of Tarshish because they were so few in number, but the 1,000 or so settlers worked hard in the early years, and a town was built. There was plenty of lumber and resources in the area, and they had many skilled laborers with them.

During the founding of the town, Hannah and some of the women planted the seeds of the Signmonkoala Fruit, and the trees started to blossom in the coming year. They also planted other fruit trees like apples and oranges. In addition to fruit trees, many vegetables were planted and soon the town of Canaan had an abundance of food. In the meantime, the indigenous plants to the area and the fish in the sea supplied the settlers with enough food to sustain them through the early years.

Tarshish during the Kingdom Age was no longer the Great Britain and Ireland of old. Climatic changes transformed it into a tropical paradise, and it wasn't overcast and cold all the time. It still rained a lot, but it didn't concern the settlers. The rain would stop shortly thereafter, and the warmer climate would dry them off within minutes. At first the change of weather was difficult for James and Jacob to comprehend. They remembered the climate in the area before the Kingdom Age when it was always damp, and they rarely saw the sun. Nowadays they could walk around in the middle of winter with shorts and their tops off like they were in Hawaii. This was agreeable to almost everyone, and it made the settlers feel like they were back in the Kingdom.

The first few years in Tarshish were difficult because they missed a lot of their friends and family back home. Eventually people started to fall in love, get married, and have children. This made the community strong, and within ten years the population had tripled. Jacob and Hannah were married in the first year by James, but they did not have children until years later. Both of them were kept busy with starting the settlement, and they decided to refrain from having offspring until Tarshish was running smoothly. As for James, he took his love life just as slow. He had already been married three times before the Reign of Christ, and he was in no hurry to repeat the mistakes of the past. James knew that eventually he'd meet his match, even if it took another two hundred years. In the meantime, he committed his time to building the colony and leading the people.

After ten years, the Town of Canaan became a pleasant place to live and some of the people who planned to return to the Kingdom were having second thoughts. One of these people was Hannah's brother. Simon had become one of the leaders of the town. He had already taken a wife, and he had three children. He was instrumental in the formation of the town, and James was building him up to be his prodigy. But unlike James, who was wise and calculating, Simon was passionate, well-liked, and more akin to Jacob. And Simon knew that one day he would have to decide if he was going to stay or go. In the meantime, Simon was unconcerned with future choices. He had a beautiful wife and wonderful children. He also had many friends, and he was beginning to like his life in the Outskirts much better than he did when he was within the confines of the Kingdom.

The fruit on the trees began to sprout, including the Signmonkoala Fruit. All the settlers were pleased to see the Purple Fruit again; however, James was very strict with the fruit. The trees were kept in a private pasture, and Jacob made sure that it was not accessible to everybody. The fruit was only served on special occasions like weddings and birthdays, and James hoped to one day trade the fruit with other territories in the Outskirts. The older brother realized that in a few hundred years, the whole earth would be repopulated again, and he knew that if he had a large supply of Purple, he would have the upper hand in trading, and it would give Tarshish economic security. And not only did James grow a lot of Signmonkoala Trees in the first ten years, he started to build weapons and warships. The O'Donohue brothers understood they were in the Outskirts alone, and they did not want to be caught off guard by the Marauders or the Libertines when they started to expand their empires. Likewise, in the 8th year after settling Tarshish, James and his crew took one of the warships and made claims to the territories of Iceland and Greenland, which had no people living on them at the time.

Chapter 9

▼

The Seven Prophets

In the 33rd year after Mandate 222 became law, the Counselor hand-picked seven people to notify the people in the Outskirts that the borders to the Kingdom would be closing soon. Micah, Hannah's father, was sent to Tarshish. Patmos was called to go north and speak to Kasca and the Libertines. Rhodes, a dark-skinned man, was sent to Egypt and the Marauders. And four others were sent to various parts of the world. Two of the last four were prophetess.

Each of the seven prophets was equipped with a large backpack filled with food, supplies, and Fruit Pills produced from the Tree of Life. They were ordered to pack as many pills as possible in their packs because this could possibly be the last time many people in the Outskirts would have access to the healing fruit. The prophets were told to give the pills to anyone in need, and at the end of the seven years, to give the remaining pills to the doctors and medical facilities.

✳   ✳   ✳   ✳

Patmos arrived in Magog a month later. He was amazed at how developed the Republic had become. In a short period of time, the City of Liberty was already becoming a booming city. Patmos knew that within a few decades, Liberty would become a metropolis and would rival many of the great cities prior to the Kingdom Age. When Patmos first saw the Magog capital, he despaired. As he entered the city limits, Patmos could already see signs of the pre-Tribulation era, and it worried him. Patmos remembered how severely the world was judged for their evil deeds during the Tribulation, and it was hard for him to accept the fact that it was starting all over again. Nonetheless, he headed forward and planned to fulfill his obligations to the people.

"Hello sir, I'm new to the area," Patmos asked. "Can you please direct me to Kasca's quarters? I have some urgent business to discuss with him."

The man laughed aloud, looked at Patmos like he was insane, and answered, "Do you mean the former president or are you referring to the thousands of children named after him this year?"

Patmos thought about it for a moment, and he realized how foolish his question must have sounded to the man. His friend, Kasca, was a big wig now, and Patmos needed to treat him as such.

"Oh I'm sorry for not clarifying myself. I'm trying to speak with the former leader of the D.M.R."

"You and everyone else," the man answered sarcastically. As the man said it, he began to walk away. Patmos was about to do the same when the man suddenly stopped in mid-step and yelled, "But if you really are looking for him, you might find him over at Gog Inc. He's the chief executive over there. I doubt he'll see you, but you can give it a try."

Patmos nodded his head in thanks, and the two men went their separate ways.

When Patmos reached the center of town, everyone was rushing this way and that and a new metro system was being built that could quickly move people from one end of town to the next. Patmos walked around the city for some time, feeling like he was having a flashback, but eventually he woke up from the dream and asked someone for directions.

"Excuse me, sir, can you please tell me where Gog Incorporated is located?"

The man didn't answer. Instead he pointed up to the largest building in the center of town, tipped his hat, and walked away.

Patmos yelled above the city noise, "Thank you!" and headed in that direction.

When the Old Timer reached the corporate building for Gog Inc., he went to the directory in the front and asked to speak to Kasca.

"Kasca's out today, but if you'd like to set up an appointment, feel free to leave your number, and we'll get back to you."

"Miss, it's really important that I speak to him. I'm an old friend of Kasca's. Can you please tell me when he'll be returning?" Patmos asked.

"I'm sorry sir. We don't give out that information, but if you'd like to give us your number, we'll call you back," the secretary explained.

Patmos was starting to get frustrated with the woman, so he leaned over the counter, looked hard into her eyes and clarified himself. "You see, I'm here on urgent business from the Kingdom. Would you please get on the phone, put Kasca on the line, or find someone who can help me!"

Patmos' firm tone caught the woman off guard, and she immediately got flustered. The manager in the back could see there was a problem, so he stepped forward and asked, "Can I help you sir?"

"Thank the Lord!" Patmos breathed. "As I was saying to the young woman here, I'm an old friend of Kasca's from the Kingdom, and I would like to see him."

"As the young woman was trying to explain to you, the former president is a busy man, and he's not taking any calls today."

"But she just told me that Kasca wasn't in today!" Patmos raised his voice a little and immediately two security guards appeared behind him.

"That might be the case. Our secretaries are not always correctly informed, but if you would leave your number. We will get back to you as soon as possible …"

"Enough of this!" Patmos raised his voice so that everyone in the vicinity could hear him. The security guards took a step forward and were waiting for the word from the manager to throw Patmos out of the building.

Patmos looked to his left and right and noticed the two security guards within inches behind him, so he lowered his voice like a parent exhorting his child and said, "Well, you just tell the president that Patmos was here. And when he finds out that you were the one who wouldn't let me in, you're going to lose your job. Do we understand each other?"

Patmos stared at the manager and smiled. The manager wasn't sure if he should call Patmos' bluff, but the man spoke as one with authority, and he didn't want to take any chances, so he stepped back, picked up the phone, and called Kasca's personal secretary.

"There's a man down here by the name of Patmos. He claims to be a personal friend of the President," the manager explained. "Would you please see if his story checks out?"

A minute or two passed. The security guards moved in closer. They were staring down Patmos, and they couldn't wait to throw this guy out of the building. Suddenly a businessman came charging out of the elevator. He was waving off the manager and the two guards.

"We're sorry sir," the businessman said. "We didn't realize you were a friend of the Presidents. We have a bunch of crackpots coming in here all the time, and we have to be safe. The President's a very important man. I hope you understand."

Patmos relaxed a little. He stared down the two guards, and they looked away.

"Don't worry about it," Patmos comforted. He gave the manager a reassuring look then he followed the man to the elevator as a bellboy took his pack.

* * * *

When Patmos entered the executive suite, Kasca smiled then laughed.

"Who else would be at my door causing a raucous?"

The President got up from his office chair, walked around his desk, and gave Patmos a big hug. When the secretary and the business executive saw this, she shut the door behind her and the two men were left alone.

"So what are you doing out here?" Kasca asked. "Did you get lost or something?"

"It's a long story," the Professor replied, "and I'd love to go into details, but actually I'm kind of hungry, and if I have to eat another nut, I'm going to puke."

"Just as I expected, another beggar looking for handouts," Kasca joked. "But actually I need a break. Let's get out of here. We'll have a few drinks and catch an early dinner. C'mon, I'll show you around the place."

The two men headed out the door and Kasca told his secretary to cancel all his meetings for the day. It wasn't often that his best friend walked through the door. In fact, Kasca thought that he would never see his old friend again."

As the two men exited the building, the manager, the security guards, and everyone else's eyes were upon Kasca and his friend. The President was a celebrity in these parts, and everyone got out of his way. When they reached the street, a hover car and bodyguards were awaiting them. The two got into the car, and they were driven to one of the fanciest Italian restaurants in town.

At dinner the two men talked about old times, the Dragon Wars, and the University. Kasca laughed freely like a young man. They were drinking a lot of wine and being merry in the corner. After a few hours of drinking and boisterous play, Kasca started to get serious with Patmos.

"You know, being here with you, Professor, brings back a lot of memories. It makes me want to strip off this tie and run free again," Kasca explained with tears in his eyes. "Here in the North, I might be an important person, but I'm alone. I can't trust anyone, and I don't know who my friends really are."

Patmos put his hand on his shoulder, and he listened intently.

"Out here we have our freedom and our democracy, but what have we lost? We've given up our purity. We've thrown away our souls."

Kasca was starting to get really drunk, and he began to get angry.

"This Republic is everything I once despised. It's growing way out of control!"

Kasca threw his glass on the floor, and it broke into a hundred pieces.

"This stupid, God forsaken, Republic!"

Kasca started to get real loud and the other people in the restaurant took notice. Kasca was not acting like a former president but a drunken fool. Luckily there weren't many people in the restaurant at the time, but the manager came over anyway and asked, "Mr. President, is there anything else I can get for you today?"

"Ah, get out of my face, you stupid moron!" Kasca yelled.

The manager took a step back and Patmos waved him off saying, "I'll take care of this." The manager walked away as Patmos spoke to his old friend. "Would you relax, old man?"

"What's he gonna do? What's he gonna do about it!!!" Kasca screamed louder and Patmos started to laugh. Then Patmos started to scream himself, "Yeah, what's he gonna do about it!"

At this exclamation, Kasca started to laugh again as he asked, "So why are you really here?"

"I've come to bring you back."

At these words, a glitter of hope twinkled in Kasca's eyes, but the thought slipped away as quickly as it had come, and he looked at his drink with downcast eyes.

"I'm serious. I've come to bring you back and anyone else who has second thoughts about leaving."

Patmos spoke excitedly. The thought of having Kasca back at the University of Jerusalem would cause an uproar, but Patmos knew the Counselor would receive him. The Professor started to smile to himself at the thought of having his old pal back in the Kingdom, but Kasca shattered his expectations by saying, "Are you crazy? There's no way in hell I can go back."

"Yes, you can. We still have more than six years left. Everyone can come back."

At this comment, Kasca laughed drunkenly. His head fell to the table in hysterics then he threw up all over the restaurant pew. From that moment on, the evening turned from bad to worse. Patmos rushed Kasca to the men's restroom, and he puked out his gut for over an hour. Eventually the two men were taken home. The President was treated like a king, even in his drunken stupor. His servants cleaned him up and took him to bed. Patmos was almost as drunk as Kasca, but taking care of Kasca at the restaurant sobered him up a little. At Kasca's home, Patmos was shown to one of the rooms in the guest quarters. When he saw the bed, he fell down upon it and instantly passed out.

* * * *

Patmos awoke in the morning with his clothes off under the sheets. He didn't remember how he got there, but his backpack was neatly stacked in the corner. The clothes he was wearing last night were freshly ironed and washed, and a bathrobe was awaiting him by the washroom.

After Patmos took a shower and cleaned up, he wandered out of his room and explored the freshly built mansion. There were women servants all over the place running around in lingerie cleaning up the estate. Eventually, Patmos found Kasca sitting at a dining table in his bathrobe eating breakfast. Servants were waiting on him hand and foot and when they saw Patmos, they quickly readied a spot for him. One woman served him juice and coffee, put a napkin on his lap, and waved her cleavage within inches of his face.

"Quite a set-up you have here," Patmos stated as he watched the young-maid depart into the other room. "Who do you think you are, Hugh Hefner?"

"Why thank you. I'll take that as a compliment. I worked hard to make this fantasy a reality," Kasca responded.

"When did you have time to build this thing?"

"Well, it's not quite done yet. The whole west-wing is still being built, and the pools aren't even finished, but it's coming along."

"Coming along? This place is a castle."

Kasca gave a dissatisfied chuckle and smiled through his teeth as he drank his coffee.

"So how do you feel this morning?" Patmos asked.

"Besides the headache and the sick feeling in my stomach, I feel fine."

Patmos kept getting distracted by the half-naked women wandering about, but Kasca took no notice of them. Kasca was glancing over the business section in the Liberty Times and was not really paying much attention.

"Hey, throw me a piece of that."

Kasca tossed the front page to Patmos, and they both read quietly as one of the servants brought out food and poured more coffee. As the servant started to walk away, Patmos whispered to Kasca, "She's gorgeous."

"Oh, I know, my friend. Would you like her to service you?"

Kasca smiled because he knew it would get a reaction out of the Professor.

"I'm probably two hundred years older than her, and I'm happily married."

"Of course you are. I'm just saying you're miles away from home, and I thought you might be lonely. Remember, fornication is permitted in Magog and having affairs outside of marriage is acceptable." Then he added, "We're free out here. We don't follow the Counselor's precepts."

Patmos looked at his friend strangely, but he did not argue the point. The two friends had debates over issues like these for years on a theoretical level, but to see Kasca's beliefs become the norm of society baffled Patmos. Nonetheless, the Professor continued to eat his breakfast, and he didn't let Kasca rile him.

Kasca continued, "In fact, most people don't even get married in the Outskirts. The practice is considered archaic. The Libertines have many lovers, and sex is considered a natural bodily function."

To show off his freedom to his friend, Kasca grabbed the servant that Patmos was eyeing and pulled her over to him. He put his arm around her waist and rested his hand on her butt. Patmos watched wide-eyed as Kasca continued to speak.

"Out here we've thrown away the chains of the Kingdom. We're allowed to express our sexuality freely. In fact, Esmeralda and I have had sex a few times, but if she chooses to have intercourse with you as well, that's acceptable in the D.M.R."

Esmeralda gave Patmos the eye. She then asked, "Would you like to be with me? I'm attracted to you. Last night I undressed you and put you to bed. I wanted to crawl into bed with you then, but I did not have your consent."

Patmos didn't say a word, so the Latin looking woman walked over to him, put her arms around his chest and started to touch him all over as he sat in the chair. Patmos resisted her although he desired to be with her. He wanted to strip off her lingerie and have sex with her on the table, but he knew he couldn't. He was one of the seven prophets, and he had a wife that was waiting for him at home, so he kindly pushed her away and said, "No thank you." Esmeralda could see that he desired her, so she didn't stop immediately, then Patmos said no again, and she obeyed his wishes. Esmeralda left the room, but as she went, she said, "If you change your mind, I'll be around."

Meanwhile, Kasca was observing the whole scene. He was curious to see how far he could push his friend. The President still wasn't sure why Patmos was in Magog. The Professor spoke about it briefly the night before, but he didn't go into details about his business. So Kasca decided that the time was right, and he asked, "Why are you here, Professor? What business do you have out here in the Outskirts?"

Patmos was still mesmerized by Esmeralda's scent, but as soon as Kasca asked the question, he was brought back to reality.

"I have come here as a representative from the Kingdom to remind everyone that the borders will be closing soon. I have been sent out personally by the Counselor to warn everyone in the North about the dangers of living in the Outskirts, away from the Tree of Life."

Kasca shook his head in acknowledgement and said, "I see. What can I do to help out?"

"I was reading the newspaper here, and I thought it might be a good idea to get a front page story in the press. I was also thinking about making a public announcement through the holoscreen. Do you know anyone in the media?"

Kasca laughed. "I am the media. Gog Incorporated owns the Liberty Times and the largest media network."

Patmos was amazed at these words, but it didn't surprise him. The Professor heard through the grapevine many of the great achievements in Magog, and he knew that Kasca and the Libertines were the ones in power, so it made sense that they also controlled the media.

"But to be honest with you, Professor, I don't think you're going to find too many converts. Things out here in the Outskirts are better than they are in the Kingdom." Kasca raised his hands in the air and made reference to his home and the women walking about. "And things are getting better everyday. In a hundred years or so, the D.M.R. is going to rule the world, and the Kingdom will be long forgotten. But in the meantime, I'll give you a prime spot on the network. Actually this project might be beneficial to both of us. We'll steal the ratings from the other networks, and we'll make your tale the breaking news story. Everyone in Magog will know your mission, and you'll be a star. So what do you think?"

"It sounds great, but I don't really want to be famous."

"Sorry buddy, if you're on the holoscreen, it comes with the territory. You can't have both in this world."

Patmos looked at Kasca with a smirk and Kasca laughed aloud knowing that he was starting to babble.

"I'll do all I can to help you out. In the meantime, you can stay here for awhile, and eventually we'll get you your own place. I have to go into work right now, but how about golf later? The Liberty Golf Course is challenging. I might have to give you a few strokes, but it will be fun anyway."

"You can keep your strokes, New Timer. I'm going to beat you on your home turf."

"Excellent, we'll meet at 3:00, hit a few balls then tee off soon after. I'll have one of my men take you over. In the meantime, enjoy the luxury of my home. I've assigned Esmeralda to you as your personal servant, and she will take care of all your needs."

Kasca got up from the table and shook hands with Patmos. Kasca gave him a firm handshake, but Patmos grabbed him and gave him a friendly hug instead.

"It's good to see you, old buddy," Patmos said, "and thanks for everything."

* * * *

The minute Rhodes Kruger pulled into Egypt, he was jumped by a melee of Marauders. He managed to take a few down before they hit him over the head and ransacked his supplies, but in the end, he was taken captive. The next day he woke up in a jail cell and remained there for over a week before he talked to anyone of importance. He was given little food and water, but he survived. Eventually, one of the tribal leaders of the Marauders came to see him after the warden of the prisoners heard the elder's story.

"Thanks for coming to see me. I am from the Kingdom. I brought a large supply of Fruit Pills with me as tidings of peace, but they have been stolen. I was sent here by the Counselor to inform the people of Egypt that the borders will be closing soon. I am one of the 144 Elders, and I have been called to deliver this message unto you."

When the Marauder heard his story, he laughed. "You mean I came all the way from Alexandria to hear that. What a waste of time this entire journey has been."

"It is true. My name is Rhodes Kruger. I'm an Old Timer who was originally from South Africa and the Zulu tribe. I was martyred during the Tribulation, was resurrected, and later became a leader in the Kingdom. I have now come to warn the people of remaining outside the Kingdom borders."

"Ha, ha, ha! You mean to tell me that you're Kruger, the former lineman for the Philistines that won seven championships in a row?"

"Yes sir, that's me."

"Ha, ha, ha!" the Marauder laughed even louder this time. "I don't believe you. You've been charged with treason and murder. The Marauder you killed in the struggle is pressing charges against you. Luckily, there were some Fruit Pills around at the time, and he was brought back to life. If not, you would have been killed on the spot. Your limbs would have been ripped from you, and your head would be hanging on a stick. But instead of this, you are going to be in prison for a long time, my friend."

At these words, the Marauder began to leave, but another prisoner yelled, "It's true! I know this man!"

The Marauder headed in the direction of the man's cell as the prisoner continued to speak.

"I was a fan of the Philistines for years. My son used to collect paraphernalia on the team, and his picture once hung upon our wall."

The Marauder looked at the prisoner then spoke sternly, "If you are lying, I will have your head upon a pole. I will burn your body in effigy and watch your ashes sail out to sea."

The Marauder looked at the turnkey and ordered, "Unlock the cell of this prisoner and bring forth Kruger."

A week later, Rhodes was taken to Alexandria, the second largest township in Egypt. The Marauder's capital was located in the City of Casablanca. This is where Matusak and most of the Marauders resided. Matusak, however, would come to Alexandria every other month and take care of important business there. Luckily for Kruger, Matusak was scheduled to arrive in Alexandria in a few days. He would hear the elder's case, and his judgment would be made.

* * * *

"Look what we have here. It's the great Kruger of the Philistines," Matusak voiced in the ruins of an Alexandrian courtroom. "How many times have we budded heads with one another? I do not know. Tis a shame I didn't break your back in the championship game of '77."

Matusak was remembering a football game long ago when his team, the Marauders, played the Philistines in the Kingdom Bowl. In that game Matusak was ejected for breaking one of the Philistines back, and he was forever banned from the Kingdom Football League. The Philistines went on to win that game. It was their first championship in seven, breaking the Marauders' streak of five.

"I imagine those Kingdom Bowl victories came much easier with me out of the league," Matusak boasted.

The courtroom went into hysterics after Matusak's words. The Marauders started banging their clubs upon the ground and started hooting and howling like a crazed mob.

"So what are we to do with you, Kruger? According to Egyptian law, if a Marauder is killed by an outsider, his head shall be taken and his body shall be burned."

This was a harsh penalty because in the Kingdom Age, the fruit from the Tree of Life would revive the life of someone who died, but by burning the body, it made a rebirth impossible. There was a case, however, in the Kingdom where a bunch of young New Timers burned to death in a house fire, and the Counselor brought them back to life, but in the Outskirts, there was no King of Kings. The Fruit Pills would revive the body of someone whose body was still intact, but it would not turn ashes into flesh.

"Then again, the man you killed is alive and in this courtroom today. The Fruit Pills within your pack saved his life, so I'm not sure what verdict the Empire will bring. What is the voice of the people?"

"Death! Death! Death! Death!" the Marauders chanted from the theater pews. The noise was unbearable, and the crowd did not stop until Matusak raised his hand with a fist as a sign to become quiet.

"And what is the voice of the all pro lineman? Let's hear your defense."

Kruger was forced into the center of the room by two Marauders. He did not know what he was going to say when suddenly he felt the Spirit of God fall upon him, and the words came easily.

"I am a prophet of the Kingdom. I have been sent to Africa by the Lord of Lords to warn the people of impending doom. Famine, plague, and death will follow for all who remain in the Outskirts beyond the 40th year. All who stand in rebellion against the Kingdom of God will be severed from the Tree of Life. You will no longer be free, but you will become slaves of the Empire. There will be wars and rumors of wars, and your children will be cursed to live in a fallen world because of your sins. In less than seven years, the borders will be shut, and you will be cutoff from the grace and justice of the righteous King of Kings. You will be ruled by a merciless dictator, and you will have no peace!"

The Marauders started to get unruly when they heard these words. Some started to get up from their seats to defend the insult made upon their leader, but Matusak would have none of it. Instead, he rose from the judgment seat and stood eye to eye with Kruger as he addressed the crowd.

"Because Kruger has insulted me personally and the Marauding way of life, it is my right to defend my honor. I have been called out to fight by this man and a fight he shall have. I will defeat this Philistine. He will not be leaving this courtroom alive today!"

The Marauders started to cheer again, but Matusak quickly raised his fist again to finish his speech.

"But if by chance Kruger is victorious, the throne will be his, and you will have a new chief. Bring forth the weapons!"

The crowd hushed a little. Kruger was a worthy opponent. The Philistine was almost as big as Matusak, and some of the Marauders were unsure if their leader would defeat him. The crowd cheered anyway. To many of them, this is what they lived for. They loved to watch Matusak fight. They were his loyal fans. Others, however, secretly hoped that Matusak would lose. In the Outskirts, there was no Counselor to keep Matusak in line, and they had grown tired of his rule. They longed for justice again, and if Matusak lost, they figured they could return to the Kingdom and start all over again. In the Outskirts they had seen too much death already, and it was not as they expected. In the books they read, the battles were always glorious and heroic, but now that many of them had seen death face to face, they had lost their stomach for it, and some were having nightmares.

To begin the battle, both men were given clubs and shields. Matusak circled around Kruger and taunted him until the Marauder went in for the attack. Matusak went in high, but Kruger successfully blocked each of Matusak's swings. This went on for some time until finally Matusak scored a successful blow. The Marauder acted like he was coming in high, but he quickly adjusted his swing and hit Kruger in his upper thigh. It was a firm hit to the leg, and Kruger started limping around afterwards, but the elder did manage to score a point of his own by striking the Marauder's left shoulder. They were both wounded now, but Kruger was starting to lose his strength. The days in prison had weakened him, and he was losing his stamina. After another five minutes of combat with the clubs, Kruger was starting to lose ground, but there was no time to regain his energy because at that moment the weapon carriers pulled out two swords. They threw them in opposite directions of the courtroom, and the two men were forced to chase after them. Both warriors threw down their clubs, picked up the swords, and the real battle was about to begin.

Matusak continued to taunt Kruger. "This is where you fall, Kruger. I am a great swordsman. When we arrived in the Outskirts, we found many weapons that were banned in the Kingdom. In the last thirty years, I have learned how to use guns. I have learned how to kill. I have become an expert swordsman!"

The crowd cheered louder at Matusak's boast, but no one took their eyes off the warriors in the ring. This was a fight to the death, and many Marauders had gotten a taste for it.

"Well, bring it on! I am not afraid of you," Kruger responded. "And even if I die, my blood will be on your hands. The Counselor will avenge me, and you will pay for your crimes against humanity!"

At these words, Matusak grew angry, and he charged Kruger. The Marauder swung his sword as hard as he could, and he knocked Kruger's shield to the ground. The Philistine tried to pick up his armor, but the Marauder swung his weapon again and Kruger backed away. Matusak then kicked the shield behind him and cornered Kruger.

"Ha, ha, ha ..." Matusak laughed as he swung again. He knocked the sword out of Kruger's hand, and the elder stood defenseless. Kruger now knew that he was about to die, but he stood courageously in his final seconds.

"Are you prepared to meet thy Maker?"

"I am. Only you will be afraid on that day. I will rise again and live forever, but you will burn in hell!"

Matusak then swung his sword one more time like he was hitting a homerun and chopped off Kruger's head. The Marauder then grabbed the skull, raised it in the air so that all could see, and the courtroom chanted madly, "Who-ma-tal-a, who ma-tal-a, who-ma-tal-a, who-ma-tal-a!!!"

* * * *

Micah arrived in Tarshish with a boat full of Fruit Pills. His boat was far larger than the ones James and Jacob built. Micah's vessel was the size of a cargo ship and more than half of the cargo space was filled with pills from the Tree of Life. The rest of the area encompassed valuable metals, farming tools, and machinery that could be beneficial in the future. Micah, a former military general, also made sure that the people of Tarshish would be prepared for war. Although weapons were banned in the Kingdom, they were not in the Outskirts. Therefore, in his children's absence, he had been getting all the necessary parts ready to defend Tarshish. Micah didn't actually make the weapons but he built machinery that could produce firearms. As for the Counselor, He knew all about what the General was doing, but He looked the other way. Micah and the Counselor knew that Tarshish was one of the smallest colonies and that they would be overrun if they did not have weapons to defend themselves. As for the large supply of Fruit Pills, this guaranteed longevity of life for future generations. It also gave Tarshish the upper hand in trading with the rest of the Outskirts. They may have been small in numbers, but they had the largest supply of Fruit Pills outside of the Kingdom.

Upon Micah's arrival in the Town of Canaan, he was greeted with cheers. The People of Tarshish did not know he was coming except for Simon, the General's son. Simon didn't even tell his sister, Hannah, nor leak the truth to James or Jacob. When the people of Tarshish saw the cargo, they were pleased. A lot of their original supplies had run dry, and now they had been refurbished. As for the machinery, the O'Donohue brothers were ecstatic. They had been preparing for warfare since the first days of their arrival, but their weaponry was deficient. The General's equipment was technologically advanced. One of the machines could make hand held laser guns. It was something straight out of Star Trek, a science fiction show on television before the Millennium. The great scientist, Lane Hofmann, made the lasers for other purposes, but the General quickly modified it for weaponry after he knew that his son and daughter were leaving and may not be returning. In fact, Hofmann himself helped the General build the machine.

"Father, I have some wonderful news. Jacob and I have married," Hannah informed her father minutes after he arrived. "And these are my three children."

Two young men stepped forward and a girl of eight years old smiled at Micah. The General shook the hands of Hannah's two sons and the little girl gave Micah a hug. Hannah's second son, Peter, had a striking resemblance to Micah and Peter was a bit taken back by their similar appearance.

"I'm glad to see we have two strong men added to the McCallister family. And such a beautiful daughter, what is your name?"

"I'm Beth and these are my brothers Timothy and Peter."

"So Dad what are you doing out here?" Hannah asked.

"I was just going for a Sunday cruise, and I got lost," Micah joked.

The whole family chuckled at this, but Hannah inquired, "No Dad, really, why are you here?"

"I figured you might need some aide, and that I'd help out with your return."

Hannah looked towards the earth, and Micah knew right away that she was planning to stay.

"But I've also been sent out by the Counselor to bring back any wayward children to the Kingdom."

Micah spoke the words to everyone, but he was addressing Timothy and Peter. Both of Hannah's sons were in their early twenties, and they had already reached the Age of Accountability. Micah thought, if Hannah wasn't willing to return, maybe her children were.

"Mom, did you hear that?" Peter spoke up. "The Counselor Himself awaits our return. It's everything I've dreamed of. We must go back."

Hannah looked firmly at Peter and addressed all of her children.

"That will be a decision for all of you to make in the near future, but for now let's celebrate. Your granddad has come from a far away land. Call forth your father and have him bring forth some of the Purple Fruit.

Later that evening the whole family gathered together and had a feast. Everyone ate of the Purple Fruit except James, and it was a joyous event. Micah told stories about the Kingdom, and the children were mesmerized by his words. Not only was the General a great storyteller, but his tales made the Kingdom seem like an enchanted land only known of in fairly tales. The whole family listened intently, and James knew that when Micah went back to the Kingdom, he was going to take many people from Tarshish with him.

Chapter 10

Back to School

Micah had been in the Land of Tarshish helping the settlers set up their defenses, but he also conducted a history class for all the students born during the settlement. In this class Micah talked about the days prior to the Millennium and after the return of Christ. The General's students were mostly interested in the Kingdom, so Micah would have to spend long lectures informing the children of Tarshish what life was like in the Kingdom. This was important because many of the children had reached the Age of Accountability or would be soon, and they would have to decide whether they wanted to leave Tarshish and return to the Kingdom or not. Those who had not reached age twenty-one would be forced to remain or stay behind based upon their parents' wishes.

"Mr. McCallister, what happened to all the people that died in the past and the ones that survived the Tribulation?"

"The Messiah descended from the heavens and returned to earth riding upon a white horse. He returned with all the holy saints of the past and waged war against the Antichrist and False Prophet. The Lord of Lords overcame the forces of evil and threw the Antichrist, known as Mahdi, and the False Prophet into the Lake of Fire. Lucifer was also defeated, and he was bound and imprisoned in the abyss. As for those who received the Mark of the Beast and followed after Mahdi, they were either killed by nuclear weapons, died in battle fighting one another, or they survived the conflict. Those who survived were allowed to live out their lives but were restricted from entering the Kingdom. They were only permitted to enter into the Kingdom if they were found to be righteous by the Lord, and they did not follow after the Beast. The rest were allowed to live out their lives in the Outskirts, but each family or nation was forced to bring forth a tribute each year at the Booths Festival in Jerusalem. If they did not honor the tribute, no rain would fall on their homeland or country that year."

"Ninety percent of the people who survived the Tribulation lived on the continents of Australia, South America, and Southern Africa. More people survived in these regions because fewer nuclear bombs were dropped on these continents. The rest of the survivors were scattered about the earth and most of these people cowered in bomb shelters and hid within the mountains and caves of the earth."

"The process of judging the people, fighting the forces of evil, and restoring the earth to its natural state covered a period of seventy-five days. Over two billion people became citizens of the Kingdom, and approximately one billion people lived in the Outskirts. The two billion righteous ones came from each generation that walked the earth since the creation of man. Some came from Adam's time, others from Abraham's generation, and so forth until the second coming of the Messiah. As for the rest of the dead, they reside in Hades. They await the Great White Throne judgment at the end of the Millennium. At that time everyone's eternal destiny will be determined. The honorable and upright will be restored according to Christ, and the unjust will be cast into the Lake of Fire for eternity."

After Micah explained this, many of the younger children stood dumbfounded because some of the concepts were difficult to grasp; nonetheless, Micah continued.

"Who else has a question today?" Micah asked.

A girl towards the back raised her hand, and the General called upon her.

"What languages do they speak in the Kingdom?"

"They speak the same languages as us. The official language in the Kingdom is Hebrew. The second language is English. All the people who live in the Kingdom are required to learn these languages. Other languages are spoken like French and Spanish, but over time the languages of old are becoming extinct and only a select few still speak them. Of course, many of the words are incorporated into English, but much of the diversity in languages is being lost with each new generation."

An older student raised his hand after the General finished talking about the languages and he asked, "What are the laws of the land in the Kingdom? Are they similar to ours or different?"

"The laws of the land are based upon *7 Principles of Truth* and *20 Precepts*. They are similar to the 10 Commandments given unto Moses long ago, but they have been altered slightly under the authority of the Counselor. The *7 Principles* are: 1.You shall love the Lord your God with all your heart, mind, and soul. You shall have no other gods before thee. You shall not worship them or serve them. You shall worship the Father, the Son, and the Holy Spirit. 2. Love your neighbor as yourself. 3. Treat the earth and all that dwell thereon with respect and dignity. 4. You shall not murder, commit adultery, or steal. 5. You shall not bear false witness against your neighbor, nor covet your neighbor's house, your neighbor's wife, or anything belonging to your neighbor. 6. Honor your father, your mother, your elders, and your God. 7. You shall live righteously, avoid wickedness, and take full responsibility for your actions. The *20 Precepts* are: 1. Love and help one another. 2. Forgive one another. 3. Be truthful and honest. 4. Be patient and long suffering. 5. Do good and avoid evil. 6. Give and share. 7. Be just and fair. 8. Be supportive and caring. 9. Be kind and generous. 10. Be humble, not proud. 11. Work together and stand united. 12. Look after the well being of your body and mind. 13. Clean up after yourself and return what you borrow. 14. Obey the rules, but follow your conscience. 15. Avoid jealousy and outbursts of anger. 16. Avoid gossip and greed. 17. Avoid envy and covetousness. 18. Don't lie, steal, or cheat. 19. Right your wrongs and amend your ways. 20. Treat others like you want to be treated."

"There are other laws that have been passed since the Kingdom was established like Mandate 222 and the banning of firearms," Micah explained, "but we've already discussed these on a prior meeting, so let's move on with another question."

When the General finished talking about the law of the land, one of the more rambunctious students spoke without raising his hand by yelling out, "How do people trade goods in the Kingdom?"

Micah gave the student a cold stare, raised his hand to remind the student that he needed to do the same then proceeded to answer the question.

"In the beginning, people traded goods the same way people do out here in Tarshish. This is called bartering. But after a hundred years or so, this system became outdated and cumbersome. Thus, a computerized system was created where people would trade credits for their labor. The credits were called shekels. It was a cashless society similar to what the Antichrist created during the Tribulation. The only difference was that there were no markings, and the left thumb was used as a scanning device instead of the right hand or forehead. At first many of the Old Timers were resistant to accepting this system because it reminded them of the deception in the past, but after the Counselor endorsed the use of credits, it became law and everyone was much better off. The system was quick and efficient."

A child of eight years old raised his hand and asked, "How big is the Kingdom? Is it safe there?"

"As you can see by looking at the map on the wall," Micah pointed to the map, "the Kingdom is much bigger than Tarshish. Also, the Counselor and his holy angels protect us from danger, and we live in peace." Micah pulled out a large ruler and pointed to certain sections on the world map. "The borders of the Kingdom extend from the Euphrates River to the Nile River. It includes all lands to the east of the Nile River in the continent of Africa. The northern part of the Kingdom is protected by the Euphrates River and a dense forest. The Kingdom extends all the way to the Taurus Mountains. Extensive winter sports take place in these mountains. There is snow year around, and it's become a vacation resort for people in the Kingdom. No one knows how this is possible in a tropical environment, but the Counselor tells us 'He has made it this way, and it is so.' The southern part of the Kingdom has some rugged mountains in Yemen and sand dunes in Omar. The Gulf of Omar, the Arabian Sea, the Gulf of Aden, and the Gate of Tears are all considered Kingdom waters. Kingdom waters in the Arabian Sea extend 300 kilometers out to sea. Beyond this radius, the waters are known for its tornadoes and hurricanes. The western part of the Kingdom ends at the Nile River. The Mediterranean Sea west of the Nile River also contains sea monsters, and all waters east of the Mediterranean at the mouth of the Nile are considered Kingdom Waters. Everything east of 30 degrees longitude in the Mediterranean Sea belongs to the Kingdom including the Gulf of Antalya & Cyprus. These waters extend all the way up to the region that was formerly known as Turkey. The Red Sea also belongs to the Kingdom. To the east, the Persian Gulf separates the Persian Empire from the Kingdom, and these waters are divided evenly between the Kingdom and the Persian Empire. The Persian Gulf also has sea monsters within it. And above the Kingdom, there are giant dinosaurs and dragons that guard the Kingdom from the sky. The dragons breathe fire, and are fierce in battle. Lastly, the Cherubim of God are protectors of the borders, and they are on guard at all times."

"Mr. McCallister, you know a lot about everything. How did you learn so much?" a teenager asked.

"Well, I've been around for a long time. I'm 305 years old. I'm one of the oldest people in the world, and if you live that long, you're bound to know something," the General joked.

The kids laughed and one of the older kids asked another question.

"What's school like over there? Do you have to go?"

"The age of adulthood in the Kingdom is twenty-one years old. All children are required to attend school from ages six to twenty-one. They are required to learn the languages of Hebrew and English, study math, science, history and take a class in the arts. In addition, they are required to participate in at least one sport and learn a trade like carpentry, medicine, or computers. The last five years of their schooling the students are required to specialize in a field, and after their schooling is completed, they have the option to go onto the University and earn a professional degree. If they do not wish to continue their schooling, they are free to marry, have children, choose a career, and leave the Kingdom if they desire."

"What's the weather like?"

"In most areas of the Kingdom, the weather is tropical. In some parts the weather is temperate, and in the Northwest, near the Taurus Mountains, they have snow. Prior to the Millennial Age, most of the Middle East was desert lands, but after the coming of the Messiah, the King of Kings transformed the wastelands into a tropical paradise. The thorns and thistles changed into beautiful flora, and there was more than enough good land for future generations born during the 1000 year reign."

"Are there any holidays? Do you have to work?"

"The Sabbath remains a holy day in the Kingdom. Every Saturday of each week, the people cease from working and relax. Some have picnics, others have parties, but most just take a day off from work to gather their strength. A majority of people take more than one day off though. In fact, people in the Kingdom only work when they desire. Work isn't mandatory, but people still like to be kept busy so most people work about four days a week. School is in session six months out of the year, and the students go to class Monday through Thursday, so most adults follow a similar work schedule."

"Christmas, Easter, Passover, and Yom Kippur are other holidays celebrated in the Kingdom, but the biggest holiday is the Booth's Festival. It's an eight day carnival in October that celebrates God preserving His people through thousands of years of wandering in the wilderness and bringing them into the Promised Land. People scattered across the Kingdom gather in Jerusalem to worship the King and commemorate the event. Most people leave the comforts of their homes and reside in tents for the length of the festival. There are parties, bands playing, dances, sporting events, and a grand parade. Sometimes people get unruly and violence does occur due to drunkenness and a whole lot of people gathered together in a small space, but most of the time the eight day festival goes smoothly."

"Tell us about the Tree of Life. What does it look like? Where is it located?"

"The Tree of Life is the biggest tree in the Kingdom. Its diameter is over 50 meters across and some of its branches reach the heavens. It's situated at the center of Jerusalem next to the Holy Temple. It's on the highest mountain of Jerusalem, and it's bordered by six other mountains which are beautiful, magnificent, and differ from one another. Three of the mountains are to the east of the Tree of Life and three are to the south of it. The Tree of Life produces fruit year around, and the fruit resembles dates of a palm. Its fragrance is succulent, and one can smell its fruit from miles away. Its leaves are fair, and its blooms are very delightful in appearance. The fruit tastes sweet, and it can heal the body of death and disease. The fruit from the Tree of Life is abundant in the Kingdom. Everyone has access to it, but the tree is guarded by the Cherubim of God. Also, near the base of the tree is where the living waters flow out of Jerusalem. Half of the river flows towards the eastern sea and the other half flows towards the western sea."

"Are there any other questions?" Micah asked. None of the students raised their hands. They had been in class for over two hours, and the General could tell that they were losing interest, so he dismissed them for the day, and the children dispersed.

*   *   *   *

The following day, the children of Tarshish gathered together, and the General continued his historical lecture.

"Today students, I am going to ask that you refrain from asking questions until the end of the lecture," Micah explained. "There is a lot of information we have to cover, but at the end of the instruction, feel free to raise your hand, and I will get to your question."

The students listened quietly, and they took out a pen and a piece of paper to take notes.

"Today students, we are going to talk about life in the Outskirts. If you have any questions about yesterday's lecture on the Kingdom, I will address them at the end of the period."

"There is one thing I forgot to mention though yesterday. It's about childbirth. One of the curses on Eve and the generations that followed her was pain in childbirth. This curse lasted thousands of years because she ate of the Tree of Good and Evil, but since the Counselor's return to earth, women are no longer cursed. In the Millennial Reign women have children without pain or fear of death. How is this possible? I don't know. Our doctors haven't figured it out yet, but the Counselor says that this is the way it was supposed to be in the beginning. Now let's get back to today's topic-life in the Outskirts."

"As we already know from yesterday's lesson, there were about a billion people who survived the Tribulation," Micah reviewed. "Out of these people, only about 100 million were granted access to the Kingdom. The rest were judged and forced to live out their lives in the Outskirts because they bore the Mark of the Beast or were found to be unrighteous. They were not given fruit from the Tree of Life, but they were healed of their infirmities by the Counselor. This generation died in the first hundred years of the Millennium. Their children, however, were blessed with longevity of life and were not held accountable for their forefather's sins. Most of these people resided in the southern hemisphere because this region of the world was not as badly hit by nuclear weapons and more people survived there. A large contingent lived in South America, which later became known as the Kingdom of Dan. General Dan was a great leader who conquered rival factions on the continent. Some remembered him as a hero and others as a butcher; nevertheless, his children have become great rulers in South America, and they are currently the leading magistrates in the region."

"In the Year of 63 some of the people of Dan colonized the continent of Antarctica. This region is known as De-Dan and it was a satellite of the empire. But after King Dan died in 69, Princess Corinne, the ruler of the region, proclaimed De-Dan a separate and independent nation. As for the Kingdom of Dan, Prince Zzyzx, one of his sons, became the successor after his father's death.

De-Dan is one of the most beautiful lands in the Outskirts because the continent is no longer frozen over with ice. After Christ's return the entire planet became habitable, and although De-Dan still has a cool winter, temperatures reach into the 20's and 30's Celsius in the spring and summer. This is possible because of the atmospheric changes that occurred on the earth. There is now a protective layer of water within the atmosphere that makes most of the planet tropical and keeps the heat trapped within, but because De-Dan is so far to the south, the weather is more temperate than tropical. In the Millennial Age this weather is greatly desired. De-Dan has the best skiing in the world and tourists flock there from all regions of the earth to enjoy a change of environment."

"The continent of Australia also had a large body of people that survived the Tribulation. This region was ruled by the Meneliks. Some former Rastafarians managed to seize control of the continent shortly after the Messiah came to the land and set things in order. In a drug induced state, one of the leaders of the Rastafarians thought he had seen a vision from the Lord. The Lord told him in the so-called vision that he was chosen to lead these people and others followed after him. This man called himself Menelik, and his followers were known as the Meneliks. Menelik went on to marry 300 women trying to model himself after King Solomon. He had many children, and his second wife bore him a daughter by the name of Sheba. After Menelik died, Sheba seized the throne. Some say she did it by killing Menelik's first wife and all her offspring, but we don't know for sure. Regardless, the rest of the Meneliks gave their allegiance to Sheba after the event, and under her authority, they went on to conquer the rest of Australia, and Queen Sheba reigned supreme in the land. She named the continent after herself and proceeded to rule for many decades. She still rules the land to this day."

"Southern Africa also had a large number of survivors. For over 250 years after the Millennial Age began, this region was in chaos. Dissident groups fought one another, and there was no peace in the land. These people did not learn anything from the previous age. At times different factions even tried to invade the Kingdom, but all their attempts were quickly put down. Sometimes the Cherubim of God would send forth sea monsters to destroy them, other times they'd send bad weather, but most of the time the people of southern Africa fought one another. In fact, the region did not come together until after the Mauraders arrived. Matusak and the Mauraders kept invading their territory and taking their spoils. Therefore, the leading clans in the region made a loose alliance to fight off these invasions. The region became known as Ethiopia, and it is one of the most war-torn areas in the world. There is still a lot of unknown information about this region."

"The rest of the planet has survivors scattered across the four corners of the earth, but they are small in number. Each year, these groups are required to bring forth a tribute to the Lord at the Booth's Festival, but only a few from each family or nation are allowed to enter the Kingdom. Dan, De-Dan, and Sheba faithfully bring forth their tribute each year, and they have been blessed, but the tribes in Africa have been less compliant. As a result, rains have been withheld from falling upon their lands and drought has followed. Eventually, the leaders of these clans have come to their senses and have brought forth their tribute, but from time to time, different factions challenge the King's authority, and the Lord has to prove Himself to them again by holding back the rain from falling upon their territory."

"Out of all the continents on earth, the Land of Nod, formerly known as North America, was the most desolate. The countries in this region were hit hard early in the Tribulation Wars by nuclear terrorists, and the rest of the world couldn't help the region because of the radiation. Close to a quarter of a billion people died in the first year, and the rest followed soon after. The food was contaminated, the water was polluted, and only a scattered remnant lived through the Tribulation."

"When the Messiah came to the earth, the signs of death were everywhere. Those who did live through it looked like survivors of a Nazi concentration camp during WWII, but these people were rescued. The Counselor healed all of them. The righteous were granted access to the Kingdom, and the rest were permitted to live out their lives in the Land of Nod."

"Nod was restored to its natural state like the rest of the world. The poisonous radiation was removed from the land and with a word from His mouth, Nod became as it was in the beginning. Some of the ruins remain in the major cities, but nature has made a quick comeback and it has overtaken the roads and buildings. The vast deserts in the West have become tropical playgrounds, but most of the Natives reside close to the major rivers like the Mississippi and the Colorado."

"Another aspect of the Land of Nod is that it is no longer separated from Asia. There is a bridge of land that connects Alaska to Kamchatka. Consequently, many of the people who went north with Kasca and the Libertines settled in the Land of Nod. In the beginning, the Natives of Nod were one with the Libertine settlers, but as time has proceeded, they have grown apart from the D.M.R., and many people in Nod want to be an independent nation."

"Europe was also decimated by nuclear warfare and plagues. The continent held out the longest during the Tribulation Wars, but they also suffered the longest. The region was hit with every plague imaginable to man, and death overtook Europe like the rest of the planet. Only a small percentage survived. The O'Donohue brothers were two of these survivors. In fact, so few stayed alive on the islands of Britain and Ireland that the King of Kings made everyone vacate these countries and start anew on the mainland. When the Millennium began, most people thought this was the only reason He cleared out the area, but later on, people understood that He was also preparing it for you, the settlers of Tarshish. Prior to the Millennium, Tarshish was known as Britain and Ireland. As for the rest of Western Europe, it is called Gomar. Eastern Europe is known as Beth-Togar-Mah."

"As for Asia, more people died in this region than any other place on the planet. Plagues spread as quickly as wildfire on this continent and before the leaders of the countries knew what to do, half the population lay dead. And by the time the Tribulation ended, less than one percent remained alive. During the Millennium, the survivors in this region remained divided for over 100 years, but soon after the leaders of the clans came together and formed the Persian Empire. As of late Persia has become a close ally and trading partner with the D.M.R."

"The rest of the Outskirts had small pockets of people upon it, but if they were too few in number, the Lord made them relocate to somewhere else. Therefore, many islands were abandoned, and some large land masses were left vacant like Japan and Greenland. The Lord, nevertheless, did permit some people to remain together. For example, many islands in the southern hemisphere were occupied like Madagascar, New Zealand and New Guinea."

"Whew!" Micah exclaimed. "That's a lot of information to take in for one day. I hope you all got it. Now are there any questions on the Outskirts?"

The General expected a whole bunch of hands to go up, but a lot of this information on the Outskirts was review to them, especially to the older kids. They wanted to know more about the Kingdom, not the Outskirts.

"Well, if there are no questions on the Outskirts, does anyone have an inquiry about the Kingdom?"

A bunch of hands shot up into the air, and Micah proceeded to answer them one by one.

Chapter 11

Counselor Abroad

After the Messiah returned to earth, He judged humanity. Most people were found to be guilty because they bore the Mark of the Beast. These people were judged, but they were allowed to live out the rest of their lives in the Outskirts. This generation was healed of their infirmities by the Counselor, but they were not permitted to enter into the Kingdom. Thus, these billion or so people lived in the Outskirts with limited rules and regulations. This generation quickly passed away in the first century of the Kingdom Age. But before they passed on, there was a struggle for power amongst these people. On the continent of Australia, now known as Sheba, the Meneliks took control in the Year of 45. Their leader, a former Rastafarian, swept across most of the continent and seized power. He was a man who modeled himself after King Solomon and had many wives. His second wife bore Queen Sheba, and she later took over the throne and extended the empire. Meanwhile, before and during King Menelik's reign, his power was not left unchecked. Many times during this period, the Counselor had to head down South and set things straight. The Counselor's first visit took place in 40 K.A. during a time when the Menelik's had not yet risen to power.

The Counselor heard from His Father that there was trouble abroad in Australia, so he took one of the Kingdom ships and set sail for New Sydney. Upon arrival, He learned that there was a lot of deviant behavior taking place. First of all, the Counselor noticed that the people were worshipping many foreign gods. The god with the most statues was the god of altered states. Many of the people were bringing forth tribute to this god, and they were burning incense to him twenty-four hours a day. He was the god of opium poppies, mushrooms, peyote, and any other hallucinogens found on the earth. People were ingesting these plants incessantly, and it was not a good thing.

At one of their bonfire celebrations, the Counselor asked one of the people, "Who is this god that you serve?"

The man answered, "It's the god of altered states. He allows us to break free from the bondage of our imprisonment and to escape the judgment of our marks."

The man showed the Counselor his hand. He bore the Mark of the Beast on his right hand.

"I see," the Counselor responded. "You must have received the mark at a very young age, if you don't remember."

"Yes, I was only a child when I received the mark, but I was still cast with the wicked for other juvenile delinquencies."

"Do you believe the god of altered states will take away this imperfection?"

"That's what our high priest teaches," the man answered.

"Then he has not spoken the truth," the Counselor replied. "Only the God of Abraham, Isaac, and Jacob can take away the sins of man."

"Who is this god that you speak of?"

"You have not heard?"

"No, our leaders do not speak of this god? Can you tell me more?"

"I am the God of Abraham, Isaac, and Jacob, and I have come to set things straight."

The Counselor took off his hood, and the man saw Jesus in His glory, and His face glowed like Moses' did long ago when he came down from the holy mountain.

The man fell to his knees in terror, but the Counselor picked the man back up and said, "Your sins are forgiven. Please bring me to your leader, and I will take away the fog that now shrouds this land."

When the high priest saw the Counselor, the old man immediately fell to the floor in fear. The people did the same. The Counselor told the people that they did not need to bow down and worship Him, but to come forward and hear the truth about the living God. The people did as they were told and by the next day, messengers had gone out to all the tribes about the Counselor's return. By the end of the week, millions of people had gathered in New Sydney to hear the Counselor's words, including Menelik and his followers.

"My friends, I have only been gone a short time, and the truth about God has been skewed beyond reason," the Counselor preached. "As I look around New Sydney, I see many idols and foreign gods. There is the god of wealth, the god of self, the god of sex, the god of altered states, and many other gods from ancient days. There's the moon-god, the sun-god, and the goddess of the earth. None of these gods will show you the way. None of their paths will guide you to the light. Only the cross is the way to salvation, and I paved that road long ago. All you need to do is believe in Me, and all will be forgiven. As for those who bare the mark, you must teach your children the way, so they will not inherit your fate. Teach them the *7 Principles of Truth* and the *20 Precepts of God* as written on the ancient landmark."

The Counselor pointed to an old church that survived the Tribulation and had the 10 Commandments written on its door.

"The generation that bears the Mark of the Beast is slowing passing away. By the year 100, none of your generation will be left. Why should your children inherit your sins? Why should they receive the sum of God's wrath because of your poor example? Their salvation is in your hands. If there is any love within your hearts, please pass the truth onto your children ..."

The Counselor continued his preaching and many people repented of their ways, but within a decade, the truth started to get distorted again. As a result, the generation that followed the Mark of the Beast's generation was corrupted. As for Menelik, the future king of Australia, he incorporated the doctrine of the Messiah into his teachings, but it was difficult to decipher his false teachings from the truth, and by the time Queen Sheba was born, most of the Counselor's words were not taught by the majority of the elders. King Menelik still managed to send forth the tribute each year at the Booth's Festival, but he did it secretly, so the people would not know he gave homage to another.

* * * *

After the Counselor visited New Sydney, he traveled across Australia on horseback visiting the remote tribes on his way. Within a year or so, he returned to the Kingdom to check up on things then ventured out once again when parts of the Outskirts were becoming disorderly. He traveled to Persia, Gomar, Nod, and various other places spreading the same message. Some of the tribes in Persia, formerly known as Asia, were already practicing human sacrifice again by the year of 45 K.A., and He had to cast judgment against many of their tribal leaders. In Gomar, also known as Western Europe, the people were living like wild heathen, and He had to set them straight on several occasions. It was remarkable, no matter how many times the Counselor visited the Outskirts, each generation got worst and worst with time. Many philosophers concluded that mankind was basically driven towards evil and that there was nothing that could be done about man's inherent nature. There were people who remained faithful to His words and lived righteous lives, but they were always a scattered remnant in pockets across the earth. The rest were unfaithful and driven towards sin.

Africa had always been a hotbed of trouble during the Millennial Reign, and the Counselor had to constantly set them straight. Many of the clans got along well with one another, and there was peace, but some of the clans became warlike and began killing one another over land rites. Many of the clans also refused to bring forth tribute during the Booth's Festival; hence, rain did not fall for a year on their territory. Eventually the clans figured it out and stopped trying to test the Counselor. They brought forth their tribute, and the rains fell.

Outsiders looking in at Africa couldn't figure out why the clans were always at each other's throat. There was more than enough land for everyone. In fact, Africa was considered by some to be the most beautiful continent on the planet. Some even suggested that its beauty outweighed the Kingdom's. Eventually the fighting did come to an end in the last century. Africa became a united economy under the guidance of a powerful leader, and they began to rival the great markets of the earth.

*   *   *   *

The continent of South America was one of the continents that had a hectic beginning. Dan, the most powerful general in the region, was as shrewd as Pinochet, and he did anything to gain power. Luckily though, after he had conquered the continent and named it after himself, he had a revelation from God and repented of his misdeeds. The Counselor came to visit Dan, shortly thereafter, and the general was taught firsthand from the Counselor himself. The year was 47 K.A.

After the formal greeting welcoming the Counselor, the two men sat down and spoke to one another. General Dan was concerned about his newfound nation and felt like there were many adversaries waiting to overthrow him. But this was not the case. The general, now known as King Dan, had already eliminated his greatest rivals, and the Counselor comforted him with these words.

"The past is the past, my friend. You have turned from your sin, and you have been forgiven. Now it's important that you start a new leaf and base the country on firm principles of truth and justice," the Counselor stated.

"But how do I go about this?" Dan asked. "I have never worn a crown before."

The Counselor proceeded to answer his question in a parable.

"There were two task-masters in the region who owned many slaves. The first task-master was cruel and unfair to his servants. He whipped them, tortured them, and took advantage of the female slaves. And after seven years of malicious behavior, the slaves rose up and revolted against the task-master. They overthrew him and his henchmen then chopped off their heads. The second task-master also owned many slaves, but he made it a policy that after seven years he would let the slaves go free if they remained faithful and obedient. The slaves knew this, so they worked hard to please their master, and after seven years, he held true to his word and gave them their liberty. The second task-master also helped them get started on their own. He gave them a pension, let the wives of the men go free, and provided work at regular wages if needed. Which of the task-masters was an honorable man?"

"The second task-master, of course," Dan responded.

"You have discerned well," the Counselor taught. "May you conduct your reign like the second task-master."

"But I still do not know how to go about doing this?"

"The answer is simple. Let the people go free," the Counselor suggested. "Let them make decisions on their own, but give them a standard of law that will be just and fair to all?"

"I see. Base the rule of the land on firm principles that we all believe in like equality and justice."

"But if you continue to rule with an iron thumb, your servants are going to rise up against you and take away your life, your family, and your throne."

King Dan shook his head in understanding then humbly asked, "Will you help me set up a government based on principles of truth?"

"I will do my best," the Counselor answered. "Gather your top advisors together, and we will form a righteous nation from the scraps of war and misery."

Dan, the Counselor, and his top advisors gathered together at Iguazu Falls and formed a new nation with their bare hands. It took several months, but ultimately, they wrote a constitution, the order of law, and set up principles by which the people could live their lives by.

It took about two years before Dan and his advisors got everything in order, and in the Year of 49 K.A. a new nation was founded, the Kingdom of Dan.

In the end, Dan's new government looked like a cross between a constitutional and absolute monarchy. King Dan would remain in control, but his power would not be absolute. The continent of South America was broken up into forty-nine districts. Each district would have a magistrate that would represent them. Every seven years, the people would vote for a new magistrate for their district. In the beginning, the forty-nine magistrates were chosen by King Dan under the scrutiny of the Counselor. These magistrates would function as judges in their region, but if there was a case that would mark a precedent; the case would be brought before the King. The order of law was based upon Dan's Constitution, which was signed by the original forty-nine magistrates, King Dan, and the Counselor. Each fall, the forty-nine magistrates would gather together for one month and decide on amendments, new laws, and any other pertinent matters. The King also had the right to order an emergency meeting of the magistrates if he desired. He also had the power of veto but could be over-ruled by a three-fourths majority vote by the magistrates. In addition, the King had the right to choose his successor, but if all the magistrates opposed his selection, the King would have to choose another. Similarly, if all forty-nine magistrates decided that the King was unjust or incompetent, they had the right to call for a vote and remove him from the throne. This was the one law that kept the King's power in check, so he could not become a tyrannical dictator.

There was other fine print included in Dan's Constitution, but these were the basics of their government. The Kingdom and the Counselor had no jurisdiction over Dan, but they were still required to bring tribute each year at the Booth's Festival.

During King Dan's rule he proclaimed his seventh son, Prince Zzyzx (Zie-zex), as the heir to the throne. He also appointed his third daughter, Princess Corinne as the new ruler of the colony on Antarctica, now known as De-Dan. She ruled over 10,000 people when she was given authority. Ultimately, when King Dan died some years later, she proclaimed De-Dan a separate and unique country, and pronounced herself Queen of the region. As for King Zzyzx, he could have easily sent the military over to De-Dan and taken back the territory, but he relented. King Zzyzx loved his sister, so he let her do as she pleased. This turned out to be quite positive for both countries because an intimate relationship developed between the two lands. They became economically intertwined in the coming centuries. There was free trade and people could come and go as they wished when it came to travel. As for Queen Corinne, she was a bit shrewd at times, but she ended up becoming a just and honorable ruler.

King Dan died twenty years after he set up the Kingdom of Dan in the Year of 69 K.A. He died in a skiing accident in Antarctica. He literally skied off a cliff and fell to his death while trying to impress one of his newest lovers. It was a tragic event in the Kingdom of Dan and even the Counselor attended the funeral. In some ways it was good for the country though. King Zzyzx, his successor, was a more competent king, and he didn't have blood dripping from his hands like his father. Before Dan set up the Kingdom of Dan, he killed many of his adversaries and abused human rights in South America. It wasn't until he cleaned up his act in 47 that he started to play by the rules, but by that time, many people already hated him and wanted his head on a stick. In the end, King Dan, an Old Timer, would be remembered as a hero in South America, even though he was an imperfect king. He brought order and civility to a region that was in chaos, and his Constitution was revered and modeled by many nations and peoples in the coming centuries.

Chapter 12

▼

Seeds of Doubt

As a young man in Kingdom schools, Kasca was singled out as different. Not because he was weird or an outcast but because he was a genius. His teachers would constantly praise him and commend him for his excellence. Not only was Kasca the top of his class in academics, he excelled in music and athletics. In addition, he was a natural leader, and his peers followed his lead in almost any situation-right or wrong.

One time in middle school Kasca ordered his gang of fourteen-year-olds to jump from a cliff's edge into a pool of water below. He proclaimed, "If anyone doesn't take the leap, they will forever be called cowards by the rest of us."

One by one the boys jumped into the pool. One boy named Martin hesitated at the ledge, and the rest of the boys started to chant, "Coward … coward … coward!"

The boy did not want to jump, so Kasca suggested, "Why don't we throw him off the ledge instead?"

Kasca didn't really plan to push him off, but he wanted to scare the boy. Martin, however, became afraid and stepped back a pace towards the ledge and slipped. He lost his footing and proceeded to tumble off the ledge. Martin fell uncontrollably towards his doom as the boys looked on from above.

Half of Martin's body landed in the pool and the rest fell on a jagged rock below. Martin's head took most of the impact, and his skull was split open. Part of his brains was dislodged, and it lay on some rocks nearby. As for Martin, he died instantaneously, and it was the first time Kasca and the rest of the boys had witnessed death.

Immediately, the boys below rushed to Martin's aide, but his head was caved in, and his body wasn't moving. Meanwhile, Kasca jumped from the ledge along with the others boys and swam over to the dead boy. When Kasca reached the body, he looked at Martin for a long time and analyzed his face like he would an art piece. The other boys watched their leader carefully, and one asked, "What should we do?"

Kasca did not respond immediately. He seemed to be mesmerized by the scene. Finally he answered. "Does anyone have a Fruit Pill? It's been told that they can bring a grown man back to life."

The boys checked their pockets, but no one had a pill on them.

"Then we must bring the body back into town and see if the elders can save him."

The boys did not move. Finally Kasca ordered, "You four, grab a leg!" as he pointed at his friends, "and carry him. Tim, pick up the pieces of flesh and put them in your hat, just in case. The doctors might need them."

"Why me?" Tim protested.

"Because I said so," Kasca argued.

Tim, one of the lower ranking males in the group, shrugged his shoulders in opposition but proceeded to do as Kasca said.

Martin's body was rushed back to town but there was nothing they could do for him. The Fruit from the Tree of Life would not revive him. One of the Elders suggested that they bring him to the Temple and see if the Counselor could bring him back from the dead like he had done with Lazarus in the New Testament. The only problem was that the Counselor had been away for some time on one of His many journeys, and they did not know when He would return. So the elders decided to bury Martin in the earth like the days of old.

The death of Martin impacted the lives of all the boys in the group, but it especially affected Kasca. He felt partly responsible for the boy's death, and he could not dislodge the memory from his mind. At night, sometimes, Kasca would have dreams about the event, and he would wake up in a cold sweat thinking about it. Other times Kasca would remember the event in his dreams but from a different angle. In the dream Kasca would literally push Martin over the ledge. The boys would be chanting, "Coward … coward … coward … coward!" but instead of taunting Martin, they would be taunting Kasca. In this recurring nightmare, one boy would always holler, "You don't have the balls, Kasca! Push him if you're a real man!" Kasca would then look back at the boy in anger and shove Martin off the ledge. Martin would spiral down towards the rocks below yelling out Kasca's name then impact with the rocks below. On impact Kasca would always wake up terrified and screaming.

Not only did the death of Martin affect Kasca's dreams, it also affected his outlook. After that event, Kasca seemed to snap out of childhood and became aware of his surroundings. It was a moment that forever changed his life, and he saw things through different eyes. His music became morose, and his favorite instrument to play, the saxophone, became a sad, bluesy opus. His paintings began to resemble death, and he wallowed for a period in depression. In sporting events, he became even more competitive, and he overstepped the bounds on many occasions. He would get into fights with his opponents, and he started to use dirty tactics to give him the upper edge. As for Kasca's science experiments, his favorite area of interest, he started to make experiments on insects and live animals to further develop research. This sort of behavior was frowned upon by the scientific community, and he was disciplined firmly by the elders and teachers for practicing animal testing. It didn't help though because Kasca simply continued his experiments in his private lab at home.

The one thing that really upset Kasca though had nothing to do with Martin's untimely death. It had to do with the Counselor. When the King returned to the Kingdom months later, he visited the gravesite of Martin. A large crowd gathered for the event hoping to witness a miracle. Kasca was one of the onlookers. But instead of bringing Martin back to life, the Counselor made a prayer and comforted Martin's family by saying, "At the end of the Millennium, Martin will be with us once again," and put his arms around the mother and Martin's younger sibling.

But one of the New Timers was not content with the Counselor's words. He hollered, "Aren't you going to bring Martin back to life?"

The Counselor stepped forward and said, "If it was my Father's will, I would revive him, but instead Martin's death is to remind us that our time on earth should not be taken for granted. We must cherish life and remember that at any moment we could breathe our last breath."

The New Timer was not satisfied, however, and proceeded to ask another question.

"I mean no disrespect, my Lord, but could it be that he has been dead for too long, and that You are unable to bring him back to life?"

Everyone in the crowd could see that the man was challenging the Counselor's authority like the Pharisees did long ago when He was in Caesar's court.

But the Counselor did not remain mute like he did thousands of years ago. Instead He answered, "It's not the Lord's will to bring Martin back to life. Martin's death is a lesson for humanity. Even in the Kingdom Age, death is a possibility, but it shall not be for all of us."

At the Counselor's words, the New Timer bowed respectfully and said, "Thank you, my Lord." The Counselor nodded at the man, but as He did, He looked in Kasca's direction. Their eyes met as if indicating He was speaking directly to Kasca. The young man looked away, but he did not forget the events that transpired on that day.

Before that event, Kasca used to believe everything that he had been told about the Counselor, but now he began to doubt Him. Kasca thought, "Maybe He doesn't have all authority. Maybe the Counselor is not a god. Maybe He is just like any other man."

Kasca had read how the ancient Egyptians used to worship their pharaohs as gods. Even at Kasca's young age, he wondered if the Counselor was like the pharaohs of old. He thought, "Maybe the Counselor is a charlatan. Maybe He's fooling us with smoking mirrors." And the seeds of doubt began to grow in Kasca's young mind.

* * * *

By the time Kasca reached the Age of Accountability, he was one of the most sought after students graduating from the secondary level. Scouts from all the major universities in the Kingdom were seeking Kasca's signature. Kasca was a top prospect in basketball and football. He could shoot a twenty-footer with ninety percent accuracy and could throw the football farther than anyone else. He was also fast and well-built. Kasca stood at six-foot three, and he was ambidextrous. He could dribble the ball just as well with either hand, and he could the run the offense in either sport. As for his academic scores, they were off the charts. He had received the "Prince of Rosh Award" too. This was a reward given to one student in the entire Kingdom each year that excelled in academics and athletics. As a result, Kasca was a scout's wet dream.

After Kasca received the "Prince of Rosh Award" his fame became well-known in the local community. He was already a sports star, but now people knew that he had a head on his shoulders. This fame made Kasca a bit proud and conceited at times, but this was expected. He was a speech club champion, a chess club member, and he had drones of women at his side because he was dark and handsome. Some of his close friends mocked him at times by saying, "If it's not the

Prince of Rosh" when he walked through the door, and pretty soon the nick-name began to stick. Even the local newspapers caught on, and Kasca was somewhat famous even before he graduated secondary school.

Ultimately Kasca decided to attend the University of Jerusalem, the most well-known college of the time. It was the Harvard of the United States, the Oxford of Great Britain, so no one questioned why he signed a letter of intent to attend this school. Kasca was tempted to attend the Kingdom Technical Institute because it was a place where all the top scientists did their research, but he passed and went to the University of Jerusalem instead. Academically and athletically attending this school made sense because the school topped almost all the charts in every other area of interest.

At the University of Jerusalem Kasca met an inspirational professor by the name of Patmos Svenson. He was the lead historian at the school, and the facilitator of the chess club. Kasca would constantly argue with Patmos in class, but the Professor would almost always win the debate. Many times Kasca would catch Patmos off guard and present facts and figures that contradicted Patmos' account of history, but the Professor was not disheartened. Instead he enjoyed the challenges Kasca posed. One time Kasca even challenged Patmos to a game of one-on-one basketball after losing an argument, and the whole class laughed knowing that Kasca was the point guard at the school. Patmos accepted though, and the two proceeded to play one-on-one later in the week. Many of the students came to watch, and Kasca walked onto the court cocky and overconfident, but he didn't know that Patmos had a pretty good outside jumper, and he was taken aback.

"Because I am the captain of the basketball team, and you're so old, I'll give you the ball first," Kasca mocked.

He threw the ball in Patmos' direction and the onlookers laughed.

Patmos picked up the ball and hit all net from the outside. The crowd started to clap.

Kasca mocked again, "So you made one, let's see you make another" as he checked the ball back to the Professor.

Patmos hit another one, then another. The Professor hit seven shots in a row, and the students in the crowd were going crazy. One yelled, "Give it to him, Professor. Make the Prince of Rosh eat his words!"

When Kasca heard the taunt, he got irritated and started to get serious. He stole the ball from Patmos and proceeded to lay one in for an easy lay-up. The Professor, however, was not going to roll-over easily. He made Kasca work for every shot he got.

This went on for sometime. Both men were playing like it was a fight to the death, and the crowd grew larger. Kasca was making a comeback, but Patmos was holding his ground.

"Hey, what's going on?" someone asked who just arrived on the scene.

"The Professor's playing the Prince of Rosh in a one-on-one game, and the Professor's ahead."

"You got to be kidding me!"

"No, I swear. It's ten to nine. If the Professor makes one more, he's going to win. They're playing to eleven."

At that moment, the Professor made a move to his left then came back to his right. He put up a hook-shot that Kasca could not defend, and it went in. The whole crowd cheered, and Kasca lost the game. He stood dumbfounded, shaking his head, bent over his knees. The Professor was walking around with his arms in the air as a sign of triumph and the crowd, mostly made up of the students in his class, was congratulating him.

Patmos then went over to Kasca, put his hand on his shoulder and said, "Good game, son. You almost had me."

Kasca shook his head humbly realizing it was going to take a long time to live down this moment. But the Professor put out his hand and said, "Don't worry about it. I've been playing my whole life too. Sometimes you win, and sometimes you lose. Just don't get used to losing. C'mon, let me buy you a beer."

Kasca smiled, shook his hand, and said, "Lead the way, Old Timer."

Patmos then announced, "To the pub we go! I'm buying a round for everyone!" and the students celebrated with clapping and cheering.

From that moment on, Patmos and Kasca became fast friends.

Chapter 13

The Fall of Patmos

Two months after Patmos arrived in the D.M.R., Gog Incorporated ran a breaking news story about Patmos and his message from the Kingdom. Almost everyone in the D.M.R. watched Kennedy King's talk show, and today his special guest was Patmos. Not only was the Professor scheduled to appear on the program, but the former President, Kasca, was scheduled to make an appearance. Thus, nearly everyone in the D.M.R. had their eyes glued to the holoscreen, and it was seen as a big event in the Northern Republic.

"Today, we have a special guest on the program. His name is Patmos, a Professor at the University of Jerusalem. He is one of the 144 Elders, an Old Timer, and a close friend of Kasca, our former President."

The crowd gave applause and when the cheering died down, Kennedy King continued.

"And not only do we have Patmos here, Kasca himself is with us today in the studio."

At these words the crowd cheered even louder and it took a while longer for the applause to die down.

"So without further ado, here is Patmos!"

The crowd stood on their feet, gave a loud applause, and Kennedy King stood up and shook the Professor's hand. The two men took a seat, and the interview proceeded.

"First of all, I'd like to say it's an honor to have you here today, Professor. We've heard so much about you over the last week, and we are dying to hear your story," King began.

"The honor is mine. I am just thankful that you're willing to have me on your show today," Patmos humbly responded.

"So Professor, apparently you have an urgent message from the Counselor back in the Kingdom. What message do you have for the people of the North?" the host asked.

"I'll try to be as brief and concise as possible, but this is the message the King wanted to relate to the people in the Outskirts."

The host nodded and waved his hand for Patmos to continue.

"There is less than seven years before the borders of the Kingdom will be closed. Anyone who remains in the Outskirts after the forty-year period will be forever banished.

You and your children will not have access to the Tree of Life, and you'll be susceptible to death, disease, and unjust rulers."

"Wait a minute here," King interrupted. "This we already know. When the people of Magog left for the North and followed the Libertines, we knew the dangers, but thus far, everything that Kasca has promised us has come to pass. We have not seen death. We have a large supply of Fruit Pills in case of accidents, our government has a 75% approval rating, and most of all, we are free!"

At the host's last words, the crowd gave a loud cheer. People were hooting and howling as Patmos waited for the audiences' applause to die down before he answered.

"As of right now, you are free, but in time, maybe ten years, maybe twenty, or maybe in a hundred or so, these things will come to pass."

"Professor, you sound like a prophet breathing fire and brimstone."

"I suppose in some ways I am, but I'm not prophesying by my own visions. I'm merely restating what the Counselor has told me," Patmos answered. "There will be famine. There will be war. There will be unjust rulers who will rise to power, and you will ultimately lose the liberty that you cherish."

There were a few boos at Patmos' words, but most of the audience grew quiet. They had read about war and had heard about death, but over 95% of the people in the D.M.R. were New Timers. They didn't remember the times before the Millennial Age. They had not witnessed the Tribulation. In the Kingdom, they had lived in a just and fair society, and they had not fully experienced evil deeds.

"Now I know things are going well right now, and you feel that this renaissance will last forever, but eventually, there will be dark ages. It has happened in the past. It will happen again. The history books are unforgiving," Patmos explained.

"The past is the past. Almost all of us in the Outskirts know about the propaganda being spread at the schools in the Kingdom, but how reliable are those sources?" King asked. "Can we trust the elders? Do we truly believe the Counselor is the Son of God?"

At these words, Patmos laughed and shook his head in disbelief. He added, "I have seen war. I saw my whole family die of disease. I've seen cities wiped off the map by nuclear bombs, and witnessed atrocities that books can never fully explain. As for the Lord of Lords, you've seen His miracles with your own eyes. There is no one like Him in the world. He has been fair. He has been just. He has been a righteous King. Now I know most of the New Timers in the Outskirts want to be free to elect their own leaders and do as they wish, but this will not bring about happiness. Eventually it will become sour, and if you decide to remain in the D.M.R. after the forty years have expired, you will experience that bitter pill, but it will be too late. You and your offspring will be like Cain, forever banished to the Outskirts."

King breathed deeply after he heard Patmos' words, and the host was moved by his words, but one could see by studying King's face that he was not a believer. He found the Professor's speech intriguing but not believable.

"Professor or should I say prophet, I find your words interesting, but I'm not fully convinced. I might have to be one of the ones that are left behind to see if your predictions will come to pass. Nonetheless, I think this might be a good time to call forth our next guest and hear his perspective on these issues. So without further ado, the former PRES-I-DENT OF THE D.M.R., KASCA!!!"

The holoscreen audience rose to their feet and Kasca appeared from backstage. Kasca acknowledged the crowd with a wave then he shook hands with Kennedy King and gave a big hug to his buddy, Patmos. Eventually, the applause died down and all three men sat down in their seats.

"To begin, Mr. President, I would like to say thank you very much for coming on our show today. It's quite a privilege," King praised.

"Thank you, Mr. King. I'm honored to be here," Kasca responded.

"You're welcome," the host said, "but please call me Kennedy."

Kasca nodded and the host continued.

"Mr. President, you agreed to come on this show because of your friendship with the Professor here. Can you please inform us how you met Patmos, and where your friendship began?"

"Patmos and I have known each other for about 200 years. I was a student at the University of Jerusalem, and Patmos was my mentor. As a young colleague, I studied archaeology and history with the Professor, engaged in fierce debates with him over political science, philosophy, and women."

The crowd laughed at these last words as Kasca continued.

"After serving my intern with him, I played professional ball for a spell then I joined the staff at the University. I was the first New Timer to become a professor at the school. Therefore, Patmos and I worked together for over a hundred years and became close friends. We have a lot of similar interests and if he wasn't here on this pilgrimage, I'd ask him to be my second in command."

"What do you think, Professor?" King asked. "It sounds to me like Kasca is offering you a job. Are you interested?"

"Thank you, Mr. King, but I already have a job back in the Kingdom, and I'm not staying long," Patmos answered.

"According to my sources, they say that you are planning to stay in the D.M.R. for six more years. Is this true?" King asked.

"Yes, I've been sent out by the Counselor to remain until the very last moment then return before the borders are closed."

"So what do you plan to do in the meantime?" the host inquired.

"I haven't given it that much thought, but ..."

"I know what he's been doing as of late though. He's been crashing at my house every night and living off my hard earned labor," Kasca interrupted.

The crowd laughed as Kasca continued. "No, seriously, Patmos and I have already discussed a temporary position until he decides to go home, and hopefully he'll like it out here and decide to stay forever. What do you think, old buddy?"

The crowd cheered madly at this suggestion, but Patmos just smiled at the suggestion and hit the President in the arm like two children playing.

"I'll sleep on it, but I wouldn't bet on it if I were you," Patmos stated.

The interview continued in this slap stick mode a while longer, but eventually Kennedy King got down to business and asked the serious questions. Although the holoscreen audience enjoyed seeing their former President as just another one of the boys, they were highly curious as to how the Libertine would respond to Patmos' prophetic statements.

"So Mr. President, what do you think about the Professor's earlier claims?" King asked. "He predicts there is going to be war and death out here in the Outskirts, and that eventually we are going to lose our freedom. What's your opinion on this?"

"First of all, I can't predict the future," Kasca explained. "I'm not a seer or a god, but I'm not going to run and hide and return to the Kingdom with my tail between my legs. I believe in everything we've accomplished out here. Look around you. The D.M.R. has potential to become one of the greatest civilizations the world has ever known, and I'm not going to throw away my dreams and aspirations because Patmos or the Counselor is predicting death and destruction. I believe in the freedom to think and do as we please, but if we return to the Kingdom, we will be throwing all that away. We will become figurative slaves in the Kingdom. The chains will not bind us, but our dreams and hopes will be locked away forever in bondage."

The applause started to build, but Kasca waved his hand for them to stop and continued speaking.

"We need to throw away our fears and take that leap of faith. Maybe in a hundred years or so there will be hard times ahead for us, but I'm not going to throw in the towel because of these so called tremors in the future. This is only the beginning of our adventure together, and I'm going to strive ahead to achieve our goals. Thirty-three years ago, most of us left the Kingdom on our own accord, and I'm not going back. I hope the rest of the country feels the same. However, if anyone in the D.M.R. wishes to return with Patmos, there will be no hard feelings. We are all free men and women. Those left behind in the D.M.R. will carry on without you. We are the founders of liberty, and if we have to endure hard times to achieve these freedoms, we will do so …"

The interview continued for another thirty minutes or so. The two old friends went back and forth on the issues and Kennedy King acted as mediator. No solutions were brought to the table, but one thing for sure; the people in the North had been warned about the troubles ahead.

* * * *

After Patmos appeared on Kennedy King's talk show, he became a household name in the D.M.R. When he walked the streets of Liberty, people gazed at him like he was a movie star. Some people asked him for his autograph while others moved out of his way. But most of all, Patmos was respected and feared. He was a prophet sent out from the Counselor, and he was Kasca's personal friend. In addition, Kasca took him under his wing, and he worked as an executive for Gog Incorporated. The Professor was given a large office adjacent to Kasca's, and he was paid well. At first, Patmos didn't work much. He sat in on meetings, gave his insight on important decisions, but most of the time, he sat at his desk unsure of what he was doing. The Counselor sent Patmos out to warn the people in the North and bring people home, but he still had six more years to go. The Professor thought to himself, "What am I suppose to do now? Does He want me to go into Liberty Square, dress in sackcloth, and walk around naked like Isaiah, the prophet? The King of Kings wasn't all that clear. Now I'm stuck here for six years." Thus, it made sense for Patmos to work for Kasca. At least by working for Gog Inc., he was able to support himself and save enough credits to buy his own place. Although Patmos did enjoy spending time at Kasca's home, the Professor wasn't a free-loader. He had worked hard his whole life, and he was one of the few who survived the Tribulation. The Professor, as a result, came to the conclusion that he would work for Kasca, give occasional speeches throughout the D.M.R. over the next six years, and plan for an exodus back to the Kingdom in the last six months. In the meantime, he was staying at Kasca's estate and living the life of the rich and famous. He was also growing closer to Esmeralda, his personal servant, but he had remained chaste and had not broken his marriage vows.

* * * *

A month after the holoscreen broadcast and the media blitz died down, Patmos decided it was time to move out of Kasca's home and find a place of his own in the City of Liberty. The only reason Patmos had not left already was because of Esmeralda. In the last three months she had waited on him hand and foot. He had his meals with her, spoke to her continuously, and he was falling for her. Although he was a married man, it was just a matter of time before he was going to give into his desire. Therefore, he decided to leave the hospitality of Kasca's estate before it was too late.

"So where are you off to this early in the morning?" Esmeralda asked at the door catching Patmos unexpectedly.

Patmos jumped back a bit and responded, "I didn't see you standing there."

Patmos was hoping to escape without Esmeralda seeing him, but Esmeralda sensed something the night before, and she was not able to sleep.

"I've been standing here for a few minutes wondering if you're leaving without saying goodbye."

The Professor looked down at his bag and continued to pack without answering her. Esmeralda moved closer. Her voice quivered as she spoke, "Were you j … just going to leave without telling me? After all we've been through, all the deep conversations and intimate moments."

Patmos looked up at her Spanish eyes. He could see the pain within them. He felt moved, but he continued to pack his things.

"What? Aren't you going to say anything? Were you planning to leave me here alone? I know you're torn inside, but I'm in love with you, Patmos," Esmeralda declared. "From the first day I set eyes on you, I've w … wanted you. At first it was only d … desire, but over the last few months, I have felt a close bond with you. I thought you felt it too."

Patmos looked up at her but continued to remain mute. He just stared at the tears rolling down her cheeks.

Esmeralda's voice grew louder and she asked, "Do you love me, Patmos? If you don't, just say it. Tell me to my face!"

Patmos still did not have the courage to speak. He wanted to take her in his arms and tell her the truth, but he had a wife back home in the Kingdom, and he did not want to be unfaithful to her. And just when he was about to say something, Esmeralda shouted, "You don't love me!" and she ran off into her room. Patmos followed her. He found her weeping on her bed. He approached her. He put his hand on her shoulder and tried to comfort her.

"It's true. I have fallen for you," Patmos declared, "but I'm married, and I have a wife waiting for me at home."

Esmeralda started to weep louder, but Patmos tried to comfort her as he ran his hand down her shoulder and moved in closer. He whispered, "I do love you, and I will never forget you. You have sparked a flame within my heart that has been dead for over a hundred years, and I do not know if I'll ever feel this way again."

Esmeralda rolled over and listened as she played with her dark brown hair.

"At first I thought it was just desire too, but as time proceeded, I found myself falling for you, and I knew if I did not leave, I would be tempted to break my …"

Esmeralda interrupted him, took him by the neck, and wept on his shoulder. Her breasts and heart beat up against his chest, and Patmos could no longer resist. He passionately kissed Esmeralda on the lips to comfort her, and the two lovers fell into one another. They made love, and months of inner turmoil were set free. The fall of Patmos had begun, and Kasca's plan went according to plan.

* * * *

Once Patmos broke his marriage vows and committed adultery with Esmeralda, his life took a turn for the worse. First, the Professor started to speak out less and less about returning to the Kingdom. In fact, Patmos was unsure if he was going to return himself. He was madly in love with Esmeralda, and she satisfied him in ways his wife was unable to. Esmeralda fulfilled every sexual fantasy that came to his mind, and she role-played as well as any prostitute on the street. In the coming years, Patmos would engage in orgies of sex and all sorts of promiscuous behavior that was unacceptable in the Kingdom. Sometimes Patmos would have a whole harem of women at his feet. As for Esmeralda, she was the queen bee at Kasca's estate, and Patmos did not come to understand this until much later. He thought Esmeralda's love for him was pure and unadulterated, but in reality the seduction of the Professor was an elaborate ploy made by Kasca and Esmeralda the first day Patmos arrived in the City of Liberty.

"So how are things coming along with my good friend?" Kasca asked a few weeks after Patmos arrived at the estate.

"Oh, I believe it will be just a matter of time before Patmos is putty in my hands," Esmeralda answered. "But to be honest with you, he has proven to be much more difficult to seduce than I originally planned. He's quite a remarkable specimen."

"Yes, I know. The Professor was my mentor so be careful. Don't let his innocence and purity fool you," Kasca explained. "He can be as tricky as a fox if he wants to, but if he knew I planned this, I could lose his friendship forever, and I'm not willing to take that chance. So be as prudent as a wise man and don't fall for him."

Esmeralda laughed loudly to show her disdain for the word and remarked, "I was born long before you, and I'm no fool for love, Kasca."

Although Esmeralda acted like she couldn't care less for Patmos, she was falling for him, and she knew it. She had never met a man with such firm convictions like the Professor, except for her father, and she admired him. He was able to resist her beauty, and no man she pursued had been able to refuse her before. Back in the days before the Tribulation, Esmeralda was one of the top models in the world. And not only was she drop dead gorgeous, she was intelligent. In fact, before the Tribulation, she ran Modelo Espana, one of the most successful modeling agencies in Europe. She started the company with the money she made from modeling in her younger days and became a wealthy business woman, but after she saw the Antichrist rise to power, she put most of her money into a fall-out shelter in the mountains of Switzerland. She never received the Mark of the Beast and converted to Christianity during her days within the mountain.

"Alright Zeze, if you say everything is fine, I won't worry, but please be careful. Patmos is like a brother to me."

"No problema, our secret is safe," Esmeralda reassured Kasca.

As Kasca walked away, Esmeralda hoped that he did not see through her guise. She knew that Kasca was no fool, so she realized that she needed to be careful with her emotions because around Patmos, she felt like a teenage girl in love, and she was already losing control. Her love for Patmos was growing stronger each day, and it frightened her.

* * * *

Patmos bought a freshly built home in Kasca's neighborhood, and he lived there for the next six years. It was a two story, five bedroom home with a pool on an acre of land. Esmeralda officially moved in with the Professor a year after he bought the place. The two lovers never got married, nor did they remain exclusive. Each individual had several lovers, and they both enjoyed the freedom of an open relationship. Patmos and Zeze, Esmeralda's nickname, cruised around the northern province like two teenage lovers. They didn't have a care in the world, and Patmos practically forgot about his mission in the D.M.R. The Professor was also becoming an important figure at Gog Incorporated, and it was becoming obvious to everyone at the company that Kasca viewed Patmos as his second in command. As for Esmeralda, she continued to work behind the scenes for Kasca. She worked as Kasca's head mistress and organized parties and social gatherings for him. Esmeralda did not hold political office, but she was one of the most influential Libertines in the Republic. Nonetheless, Esmeralda found herself in a conundrum. Her bond with Patmos was closer than it had been with anyone before, and she deeply wanted to tell Patmos about how Kasca and her plotted against him, but Esmeralda was afraid to cross the former President. Kasca was a dangerous man, and she could not afford to become enemies with him. Esmeralda knew all about the business world, and she could see that Kasca and the Libertines were the wave of the future. Not only was she afraid of what Kasca could do to her, Esmeralda feared she might lose Patmos if she told him the truth. So she remained silent on the issue and did not reveal her little secret to the man she loved.

Chapter 14

Bound and Free

After the Marauders arrived in Egypt, prisons popped up everywhere to punish those who opposed Matusak and his authority. Judgment was swift, and most people ended up in the prison system for a long time. For instance, the prison in Alexandria had swelled beyond its capacity, and the inmates struggled to survive fighting over food and space. Also, the chance of being set free was nil after the Emperor or one of his arbitrators executed judgment against you. In fact, everyone in the penal system knew they were never getting out, and a common saying amongst the inmates was, "There's one way in and no way out." In actuality, only nineteen people had found their liberty thus far in the prison, and nine of them had escaped. The saying could also be applied to Egypt in general because it was nearly impossible to get back into the Kingdom after crossing the Nile. Emperor Matusak put armed guards on the border, and he would not permit people to return. If someone did attempt to re-cross the Nile, Matusak would have them shot or imprisoned. Sometimes, he would behead the escapees and put their heads on a pole for all to see then he'd burn their dead bodies so that they could not be revived by the Tree of Life.

In the 39th year after Mandate 222 had passed, the people of Egypt were starting to get restless. The Emperor cracked down even harder on the people and made sure that no one was leaving. The border was filled with double the warriors and only a few hundred had managed to escape so far and most of these people crossed in Ethiopian territory. In the prisons it was even darker for the convicts. They were behind bars and locked in chains. They all knew it was the 39th year, and if they did not make a prison break soon, all hope would be lost forever.

At the prison in Alexandria, there was an inmate that was being beaten by one of the guards because his leg was broken, and he could not keep up with the labor.

"Get back to work, you worthless slave!" one of the guards yelled.

The guard continued to swing his whip harder and harder, but the inmate continued to withstand the blows. Eventually when the prisoner could not take it any longer, he rose to his feet for a moment but his leg gave way and he fell again.

"Get up, I said, or I'm going to throw you into the dungeon for a week!"

The dungeon was a six by six box set aside for disobedient inmates. It was dark, underground, and the prisoners got even less food down there.

The guard raised the whip again, but when he pulled back the whip this time, a mysterious stranger wearing a hood appeared out of nowhere and grabbed hold of the whip. The stranger knocked the guard to the ground, and when his fellow guards saw this, they ran in his direction to help him out, but just when they were about to reach the hooded man, the stranger pulled down his hood, and everyone could see it was the Counselor. When the guards saw the King's face, they froze in their tracks and fell to the ground. The angelic glow from the Counselor's face knocked them to their knees, and they could not move. Then with a word from the Lord's mouth, all the chains fell off the inmates, and the prison cells were opened. The prisoners stumbled out into the yard, and the Lord healed all who were in need. Grown men wept at His feet like women in hysterics, and the Lord comforted them.

After the prisoners of Alexandria were liberated, a large body of people headed east on foot and made their way towards the Nile. In the meantime, the sadistic guards of the prison were put behind bars and were given a taste of their own medicine, but on the third day after their imprisonment, the cells miraculously opened, and they were set free. Meanwhile, as the people headed east, the Counselor made His way towards Casablanca, the Marauders capital, and liberated people as He went.

When the King arrived in Casablanca, He was not pleased. The pain and suffering He saw in the Capital was twice as bad as it was in Alexandria. Heads were on polls all over the city, and monuments were built that gave homage to Matusak. In the city centre, there were whorehouses on every corner, prisoners from Ethiopia being sold as slaves, and much debauchery. So when the Lord entered the city centre, He was angry. The first thing the Counselor did was point His staff at the giant idol of the Emperor, and it came tumbling down. He then approached the slave traders from southern Africa, and they ran. The slaves were set free, and the King of Kings made His way towards the Emperor's throne. People followed the Counselor from a distance because they were afraid, but they were also curious as to what action He was going to take next.

When the King entered the Emperor's Hall, Matusak had one hand on a turkey leg and another on a girl's butt. The Emperor was screaming wildly with his friends, but suddenly everything got quite still as the Counselor made His way down the hall and towards the table.

When Matusak saw the Lord, all the color dropped out of his skin, and he looked white as a ghost. The Emperor knew that he was in trouble, but he tried to save face by welcoming the Counselor.

"Greet-ing-ing-ings, we are honored to ha-a-a-ave your presence," Matusak stuttered. "What brings yo-u-u-u to the Outskirts?"

At first the Counselor did not say a word. Instead, he simply looked at Matusak and the rest of the Marauders at the table. No one dared look up, including the Emperor. They were like children being caught in a mischievous act, and everyone knew they were in serious trouble.

"So I see you have a nice collection of heads in the Empire. May I have one as a souvenir to bring back home?" the Counselor disparagingly asked.

No one said a word, but one of the more stupid Marauders chuckled briefly not getting the joke, but Matusak gave him a stern look, and the Marauder became still again.

"How about them whorehouses, you can't find that in the Kingdom?" the Counselor continued.

This time no one made a sound as the King slowly paced around the table with His arms behind His back.

"And to top it all off, we now have slave traders."

The Counselor moved in closer. He was now within an earshot of some of the Marauders.

"Isn't life just wonderful outside the Kingdom?" the Counselor mocked. "There's justice, you're free to do as you please, and righteousness reigns supreme."

The Counselor continued to pace around the men at the table, and when he reached Matusak, he stopped momentarily behind him then continued walking. The rest of the men peeped up to see what the Counselor was going to do next, but He merely spoke.

"As you know, it's the 39th year, and there's not much time to make your final decision to either stay or go. You can either live out here in the Outskirts where there's peace and justice or you can come back with Me and be ruled by a merciless dictator."

The Counselor's speech rang out with sarcasm, and the hundreds of people in the room knew exactly what point He was making.

"But all of this you already know. I'm sure my personal messenger, Rhodes Kruger, has already informed you about it. Where is he, by the way?"

Everyone in the room knew about the great battle between Matusak and Kruger over six years ago. Each person also knew that Kruger was killed unjustly, and that he was sent out as a messenger from the Lord. In fact, the death of Kruger became so famous throughout the Empire that his head was mounted and preserved in the Alexandrian courthouse where he was killed.

"Oh that's right, the elder's life was taken from him shortly after he crossed the Nile," the Counselor answered His own question, "and the blood of many men and women trying to cross still cry out to me each day. So what am I to do about these crimes, Matusak? What would you do if you were in My shoes?"

Matusak rose to his feet and shouted, "Okay, I've had enough of these accusations! If you're challenging my authority, why don't You just say it loud and clear instead of beating around the bush?"

"Matusak, I am challenging your authority, and I've found you to be an unjust leader. Therefore, I'm going to take away your throne today and give it to someone else."

"Well, I'm not going down without a fight! If you want the throne, you're going to have to take it from me!"

After Matusak spoke, he charged the Counselor with a club, but the Counselor hit Matusak squarely on the bridge between his nose and forehead with an open hand, and Matusak went down. He fell to the floor and lay unconscious. It was a brief and concise victory for the King.

The former leader of the Marauders was bound in chains and taken back to the Kingdom under the Counselor's authority. More than half the Marauders returned with him. The door to the Kingdom was opened again, and the people of Egypt finally understood how good their lives had been under the authority of the King. Still, a large populace remained behind, so the Counselor appointed Xavier Madmenah as the new Emperor of Egypt. He was a just ruler, and the first thing he did as Emperor was remove the heads of the people who lost their lives under Matusak's reign. Madmenah then brought the whorehouses of Casablanca down, and the slave trade was abandoned. As for the Counselor, He led the people back to the Promised Land. On His way, He stopped at the Alexandrian courthouse and removed the head of Rhodes Kruger. The Lord of Lords then performed a miracle. From the dust of the earth, a new body was formed for the head of Kruger, and His messenger came back to life.

Chapter 15

Stay or Go

The day of Micah's return to the Kingdom had finally come. The settlers of Tarshish were forced to either stay or go. Over 5,000 people now had to make the choice of their lives. If they decided to remain in Tarshish, they would be forced to renounce their Israeli citizenship and would be banned from returning. This was a harsh penalty, and many of the original settlers were unwilling to be separated from the Kingdom for the next 700 years or so. As a result, over a third of the original settlers decided to return with the General. The rest of the people were children born outside the Kingdom. They had never known the Counselor or experienced the Kingdom of Israel, so most of these descendents decided to remain behind. Their families and friends were in Tarshish and to make a leap of faith by moving to the Kingdom took courage, so only a small contingent decided to leave. Peter, the son of Hannah and Jacob, was one of the children born in Tarshish that decided to go with his grandfather. The rest remained behind including Micah's two children, Hannah and Simon. Originally, these two planned to return before the forty years expired, but things had changed. Simon and Hannah were both leaders in the community, and if they left, life would not be the same in Tarshish. Simon was one of the most popular people in Tarshish, and Hannah was looked to as the voice of the women. She was also married to Jacob, one of the O'Donohue brothers.

The General was disappointed that more people were not willing to leave Tarshish. He explained the risks of living outside the Kingdom and all the terrible trials that would come, but he was only able to convince about 600 to return with him. Micah was especially disappointed that more of his family was not returning with him, so a week before Micah's departure, he made one last plea at a family dinner.

"McCallister and O'Donohue families, it has been an honor to be in your presence the last seven years, but the time has come for me to return to the Kingdom. Peter and I will set sail for the Holy Land a week from today, and I wish more of you were coming back with me…"

Micah spoke at the table in front of everyone after dinner. He was a little bit drunk, but everyone listened anyway.

"But I must remind you that it is my duty as messenger and prophet of the Counselor that troubled times will come. There will be wars. There will be plagues, and only by the grace of the Almighty will Tarshish be saved. If you remain in the Outskirts, you will be putting your life and future generations at risk. So I must emphasize how important it is for you to return home with me!"

Micah started to slur a little and began addressing Simon and Jacob.

"And Simon, are you willing to watch your own shildren die and be butshered in war? Tell them, Jacob, yous of all people should know! You lived through the Shibulation. You know how vile and evil mankind can be. Why don't you order your family to return with me?"

Micah's voice began to get louder and his tone grew angry.

"You're a fool, Jacob! First you seduce my daughter, and now you're staking her away forever. You're all gonna die out here, and yous know it!!!"

Hannah rose from her seat and came to Jacob's defense. Some of the children were getting scared, and Hannah got mad.

"Dad, would you please calm down? We were having a great time until now. Why do you have to spoil everything?" Hannah voiced as she grabbed hold of her father and tried to get him to sit down.

"Get your hands off of me. I have a right to speak. And stop trying to color-code the picture here. The shildren have a right to know what's gonna happen to them. And you're sending them to their death beds!!!"

This time Jacob spoke up. He rose from his seat and defended his position. "Mr. McCallister, you may be right or you may be wrong. There is potential danger out here by living in the Outskirts, but you can't predict the future. How do you know if our children are going to die? And stop scaring them!"

As Jacob spoke, Hannah was able to get her father to sit back in his seat and listen to someone else's opinion for a change.

"James and I gave everyone the freedom to decide for themselves if they wanted to stay or go. In fact, we even encouraged people to leave and see what's on the other side. We can't order people to return. I'm sorry that only a small percent are returning with you, but this is our home. It may not be as lush and cozy as the Kingdom, but it's where we want to be ..."

Beth, Hannah's fourteen-year-old daughter, came over to her Granddad and tried to comfort him. She said, "It's okay Papa. We'll be fine out here. We may be living in the Outskirts, but God is still with us. He will protect us from danger."

At Beth's words, Micah calmed down and apologized for his outburst.

"I'm sorry everyone. I'm just worried for y'all, and I don't want you to get hurt. I've seen too much war and death in my time, and I don't want the same to happen to y'all, so without further ado, I'm shheading on my way."

Micah rose from his seat and waved goodbye to his family, but in the process he knocked into the table and spilled several drinks. He then stumbled his way towards the back room, and Hannah followed him to make sure her father was okay.

* * * *

In the ensuing week, the settlers of Tarshish said their goodbyes and made their final preparations before leaving. Micah went to every family, and tried to get more people to return with him, but he was only able to convince a few. The General was respected amongst the settlers, but it was difficult for the settlers to leave their families behind. To the original colonists, the success of their settlement gave them a sense of pride and to return to the Kingdom would suggest their mission was a failure. As for those born in the last forty years, they loved hearing the stories about the Kingdom, but to them, the tales about the Counselor and His feats were folklore. And although they liked Micah and his stories, they weren't willing to pick up and start anew based upon some mythical place. Also, most of the people born in Tarshish were happy, and they didn't concern themselves with the possibility of death. Tarshish was paradise to them and compared to pre-millennial standards, there was no reason to leave. Consequently, in October of 262 K.A., about 600 people joined Micah and set sail for the Kingdom. The rest remained behind to face unknown trials that lay ahead.

* * * *

On the return trip, Micah was ordered by the Counselor to stop off at the Island of Signmonkoala and pick up as many native Signmonkoalas that were willing to return to the Kingdom with him. Although Micah did not know what a Signmonkoala was or how to get there, he followed the Counselor's instructions and did as he was told. When Micah first arrived in Tarshish, he found out all about the Signmonkoalas. It was one of the adventures the settlers loved to tell. He learned about the Purple Fruit, and Jacob gave him a copy of the sea charts that would direct him to the island on his return.

As they journeyed back to the Kingdom, the children born in Tarshish waited impatiently on the cargo ship. Micah's vessel was large, but it wasn't a cruise ship. There were few windows, and there was minimal sleeping quarters. So most of the people milled around the cargo area, played games or slept on the ground. It was an unpleasant journey, but once they arrived at Signmonkoala Island, the settlers started to get excited.

"Mama, is this the Kingdom?" a young child asked as the ship pulled into the harbor.

The child's mother laughed aloud and said, "I hope not. If so, I think we'd be in serious trouble. This is the Island of Signmonkoala. We have come to pick up some of the Signmonkoalas and bring back the Purple Fruit to the Kingdom."

"Oh, I see," the child replied. "Will I get to have a Signa-monka-koala to play with?"

"The Signmonkoala's are very playful, but you can't own one," the mother explained. "They are an intelligent species, but they speak a different language than us. They use sign language to communicate with one another. See, this sign here means hello in Signmonkoala."

The mother showed the sign to the child, and the child did the sign back.

"We learned almost their entire language when we first came to the island forty years ago. In fact, our leaders back home require everyone to learn the basics of the language in their teens. They plan to use it during wartime to give them an advantage in combat."

The child did the sign of greeting over and over again as she gazed out the window hoping to get a glimpse of a Signmonkoala.

An hour later, almost the entire crew had disembarked from the ship and were standing amongst the Signmonkoala. One of the best signers communicated the settlers' message, and she explained their reason for coming back to the island under the General's authority.

"We come in peace as representatives from the Israeli Kingdom and the Colony of Tarshish inviting you to come with us to live in paradise. Our Lord and King welcomes the Signmonkoala into the Kingdom."

At these signs some of the Signmonkoala shifted around and began to move back and forth apparently stirred up by the message. One of the leading Signmonkoala then signed back at the settlers and signaled, "You are welcome here, and we accept your generous offer, but it will remain to be seen whether any of us will return with you."

The Tarshish representative signed back, "Thank you, we will discuss more later," and the first of the settlers came ashore.

Micah and the returning settlers from Tarshish remained on the Island of Signmonkoala for two days. They brought back the seeds from the Purple Fruit, but only a small percentage of the Signmonkoala were willing to come with them. Micah warned them about the extreme danger of not joining them, but most of the Signmonkoala were unwilling to leave their native land. Micah warned them about the evil men that would come to the island and how they would exploit it of its fruit. He also informed them that these men may not come in peace. He sternly warned them about death and the possible extinction of the tribe, but the leaders of the Signmonkoala seemed unconcerned. The Signmonkoala were a friendly folk, and they did not understand these things, so only a small number joined the settlers. Less than fifty Signmonkoala boarded the ship, and the rest waved goodbye to their long time friends.

Chapter 16

The Fall-Out

"Tell me again, Patmos" Esmeralda begged.
"C'mon Zeze, I've already told you two times."
"Please, I love hearing it roll from your lips. It's so beautiful."
"Okay baby, for you I'll do anything."
Patmos spoke in Spanish and with a glimmer of his Swedish accent said, "Mi amore, I love you."
Esmeralda giggled like a little girl, rolled over on top of him, and kissed him passionately on the lips.
"Promise me you'll never leave me," Zeze pleaded as she ran her hand through his blond hair.
"I'll never leave you," Patmos whispered.
"Promise me, my love!"
Esmeralda then held onto him for dear life like the Professor was heading off to war. She dug her head into his chest and held him firmly. Patmos hugged her back and tried to comfort her. The Professor spoke soothing words to her. "Everything's going to be fine. Don't worry, you are the love of my life."
Zeze, however, could not be consoled. She seemed to be troubled about something. It was as if she wanted to tell Patmos something. Tears started to build in her eyes as the Professor continued to comfort her by rubbing his hand up and down her back.
"What's wrong, Zeze?" Patmos asked. "Are you alright?"

She answered, "I'm fine," even though Patmos could tell that something was wrong.

Instead of speaking, Esmeralda kissed the Professor over and over again. She then kissed him on the neck and chest and slowly proceeded further down until both were quiet except for a few moans.

In the morning, Patmos awoke to Esmeralda on her side staring at him. She looked serious and concerned. When the Professor looked at her face he knew right away that he was in trouble. The crunch of her nose and peering brown eyes gave her away. So Patmos tried to avoid the argument by trying to sideswipe Zeze's train of thought.

"How about brunch this morning? I'll cook up my special recipe, the grand-slam breakfast, and we'll eat like kings."

Esmeralda did not answer. Instead, she lay staring into space contemplating their future.

"So what do you say, woman?" Patmos asked again. "Are you hungry?"

"No, not really Patmos," Esmeralda answered. "I don't have much of an appetite, but I was thinking …"

"You think too much, Zeze."

Patmos cut her off as he rolled over and sat on the edge of the bed trying to avoid a confrontation.

"Let's enjoy the day for a change. The birds are chirping, the sun is shining, and it's a beautiful day."

"I was just thinking about what you said last night …" Esmeralda paused then she continued. "You said you'd do anything for me. Is this true?"

"Yes, Zeze, you know I love you."

Patmos was about to rise to his feet, but Esmeralda would not concede. She threw down the ace of spades instead and stated, "I don't want you to leave. Stay with me Patmos, and don't return to the Kingdom. Would you do that for me?"

The Professor looked out the window. He knew one day this moment would come where he would have to decide whether he wanted to stay in the D.M.R. or not. The years snuck up on him like a snake, and now he had to make a choice. The borders were closing in six months time, and it was time to ready the people for their return.

"Patmos, would you stay with me?" Esmeralda asked again. "Please don't go back to the Kingdom. I love you, and I want to be with you forever."

"Then return with me, Zeze!" Patmos exclaimed. "We'll start a whole new life in the Kingdom. I'll leave my wife for you. I'll abandon my post at the University. I'll forsake the Council of Elders, but I must fulfill my oath to my Lord and King. I cannot betray Him."

Esmeralda was silent as the Professor continued.

"The Counselor is the One who saved me from the pit. He rescued me at the end of the Tribulation. I was starving. I was incarcerated. He did not forsake me in my darkest hour, so how can I forsake Him now? I have an obligation to bring these people back with me. If I don't make a stand, nobody will, and many souls will be lost forever. You would not understand, Esmeralda. You're a New Timer. You do not remember the times before the Millennial Reign."

Esmeralda thought to herself. It was time for her to be honest with him. She broke down and told Patmos the truth.

"I do understand, Patmos. I am also an Old Timer."

"What are you talking about?" You told me you were a second generation New Timer born in 55 K.A."

"I lied Patmos. In fact, I've lied about a lot of things. It's time for me to come clean. I can no longer live in denial. I must tell you my true past."

"What are you saying?" Patmos asked. "Is this some elaborate ploy to get me to stay?"

"No Patmos, it's the truth, and it feels good to rid myself from this burden on my heart. I am an Old Timer. I, like you, survived the Tribulation. I was a former model and a successful business woman long ago. I bought a bomb shelter in the mountains of Switzerland during the wars. Seven of my friends accompanied me, and we lived inside the mountain for over 3 ½ years. We survived on rations, canned foods, and bottled water. One of my friends in the shelter was a Christian, and she brought with her a Bible. In the beginning of our stay we made fun of her for her beliefs, but by the end we all believed in Jesus and were saved. When we ran out of supplies, we were forced to leave the security of the mountain and venture outside into the radiation, but we found Switzerland transformed into a Garden of Eden. Fruit abounded on the trees, and pristine waterfalls rolled down the hills and mountains. At first we thought we were dead and had entered into heaven, but a strange man sitting on a rock spoke to us and told us he was taking us to Jerusalem. He informed us that the King of Kings awaited our arrival, and that we were welcome into the Kingdom."

"How long were you in the mountain after the Messiah's return?" Patmos inquired.

"Twenty-nine days. We had been in the belly of the mountain when the transformation of the earth occurred. We were disappointed that we didn't see it happen before our eyes, but we didn't care. We were just glad to be alive."

"Esmeralda, how come you didn't tell me this? What purpose did you have in keeping this information from me?"

"Before I go on, Patmos, I want to say I'm sorry. A day hasn't passed where I haven't wanted to tell you the truth, but I couldn't."

"Why couldn't you? There's so much more we could have shared with one another, but you let me ramble on for hours about things you already understood."

"I know. I'm sorry," Esmeralda answered. "I enjoyed the stories anyway. It brought back the old days."

The two lovers sat without speaking for a moment then Esmeralda continued her story.

"When you first arrived in the D.M.R., I had heard your name before, but I didn't know who you were. Kasca informed me that you were a good friend, and that he wanted me to seduce you. At the time, I didn't know why or for what purpose. All I knew was that Kasca swore me to secrecy, and that the leader of the North had given me an order. I did my best to achieve that request."

"You bitch," Patmos cursed under his breath. "So am I to assume this whole affair has been a charade?"

"At first, yes," Esmeralda explained, "but as I got to know you in the following months I began to fall for you."

"Oh, give me a break, Zeze!" Patmos protested. "You were sent to me by Kasca to keep me entertained. With me occupied, I wouldn't be parading around the D.M.R. preaching to people about returning to the Kingdom. Is that it, Zeze? And to think I considered leaving my wife and the Kingdom for you."

"But Patmos, I swear …"

"You swear what? What good is your word to me now? Our whole relationship in built upon a farce!"

"Patmos, it's not a lie," Esmeralda explained. "I love you. If I didn't love you, I wouldn't be telling you this."

"Instead you waited until now, six years into our relationship?"

"I don't know. I suppose I was afraid if I told you the truth, I'd lose you. Oh, Patmos, I don't want to lose you. Please forgive me. I'm sorry."

"It's a little too late for that. I've wasted six years on fruitless pursuits because of you. And not only that, my best friend deceived me. Do the two of you get beneath the sheets and laugh behind my back? I'm such a fool! The Counselor trusted me. How could I fall for such an age old lie?"

"My love for you is not deceit, Patmos. My heart burns for you. It yearns for you."

"Don't forget lies to me," the Professor countered.

"Oh, don't be so melodramatic."

"Melodramatic, huh, you want melodramatic? How's this for melodramatic?"

Patmos grabbed the alarm clock and threw it across the room. It broke into a hundred pieces. He then stormed out of the room and slammed the door behind him. Esmeralda sat flabbergasted on the bed. Her heart dropped within her. She then began to weep.

*   *   *   *

Twenty minutes later, Patmos stormed through the door at Kasca's estate. He punched a security guard in the nose and yelled, "Where's my good friend, the Devil incarnate?"

Kasca appeared at the top of the stairs a moment later in his bathrobe and underwear. He waved off the security guards who had stormed through the doors and looked down at Patmos.

"What do you know? It's Judas in the flesh!" Patmos hollered. "The one who betrayed me! Were you going to wait until the 40 years passed before you told me about, Zeze? Were you going to let me forsake the Lord and His calling, all in the name of liberty?"

"Patmos, let me explain," Kasca spoke from the balcony on the stairs.

"What's there to explain?" Patmos asked. "You deceived me. For over six years I believed that Zeze truly loved me, and that you needed me, but it was all lies. I have been played for a fool. I've been a mere pawn in your game."

"Please old friend, let me explain," Kasca begged. "I didn't mean you any harm."

Kasca started descending the stairs as he continued.

"Let's sit down. Let's reason together, Professor. Please hear me out before you pass judgment on me."

Patmos remained silent as Kasca made his way down. When Kasca reached the bottom, Patmos punched Kasca in the mouth, and the former President fell to the floor.

"Okay, I suppose I deserved that. Do you feel better now?" Kasca protested. "Now would you please sit down and let me explain?"

Patmos stood there for a moment contemplating his next move. Eventually his reason overcame his passion as his temper died down and he sat in a nearby chair. Kasca also sat down and grinned. He said, "You really got me good with that punch. I think a tooth is loose."

Patmos didn't smile but sat stern and serious. Kasca then began speaking in his defense.

"When you first came to the North, I had no intention of deceiving you. But after I saw the way you looked at Esmeralda that first morning, a thought came into my head. I wanted to tempt the great Patmos to see how far I could influence his belief system. So I threw the worm out there to see if you'd fall for the bait and you did. In fact, I thought I was doing you a favor. Esmeralda is one of the best looking women in the world. Most men throw themselves at her, and I thought a little lust and passion would spice up your life. I had no idea that the two of you would become lovers. And after I saw that you had fallen for her, I thought I'd use it to my advantage. I already told you that I don't have too many people I can trust out here, but you have always been a faithful friend. The temptation to have you by my side was too great to resist."

"So you mean to tell me, the deception was all because you wanted my friendship and trust? How ironic?" Patmos retorted.

"I will admit that you falling in love with Esmeralda had its benefits, but it was not my intention to deceive you?"

"Then how come you didn't tell me this sooner?" Patmos asked. "I don't think you ever intended to tell me the truth. In fact, I think you used my love for Esmeralda to keep me occupied."

"Let's be honest, I couldn't have you running around the D.M.R. stirring up trouble. If I allowed you to continue preaching your doomsday prophecies, you would have put everyone on edge. And don't say I didn't help your cause. I did give you a national audience and allowed you to preach the Counselor's propaganda to everyone in the D.M.R."

"But you deceived me, Kasca. Do you understand why that's so important to me? It's the same reason why you wanted me by your side. It's a matter of trust, and without trust in a friendship, there is only animosity. And you broke that trust by lying to me."

"Technically, you are correct, but I only bent the truth a little. As a politician we do it all the time."

"True, but I'm not one of the populace. I'm your friend. You lied to me, and I feel betrayed."

"Patmos, you're overstating things. You make it sound like I stole Esmeralda away from you and stabbed you in the back."

"In some ways you have, my friend. In some ways you have."

The fallout from the deception was horrendous upon the friendship between Patmos and Kasca. Patmos quit his job at Gog Inc. and left without saying goodbye. The two friends didn't reconcile their differences, and Patmos was unwilling to forgive and forget. Instead, Patmos walked away from their friendship and never looked back.

Later that day, the Professor grabbed his original backpack from the Kingdom, packed his stuff, and left everything behind-the house, the hover-car, and all his material things. Patmos didn't even say goodbye to Esmeralda. He slipped out when she wasn't there and got a small hotel room on the outskirts of town. He locked himself away from the rest of the world and vanished for a spell.

Chapter 17

The Straight & Narrow

Patmos wallowed in depression for a week watching the holoscreen and thinking about what had transpired. He never left the room. He was upset over everything because he felt like he'd been played. The deception ate away at his heart and embittered him. The Professor was willing to give up everything to be with Esmeralda. He committed adultery for Zeze. He was planning to divorce his wife for her. Patmos would probably be ostracized by much of his family and many of his friends for his misdeeds, but he was willing to give up his old life for her. He felt like Adam did in the Garden when Eve offered him the fruit from the Tree of Good and Evil. Adam knew it was wrong. Adam knew that it would upset God. Adam knew that he would be kicked out of the Garden for rebelling against God and ultimately die, but he bit into the fruit anyway. Adam did it out of love. He loved Eve more than any of the creatures in the Garden, and he could not live without her. Adam knew that love could not be wrong, so he took the fruit from her hand and willingly rebelled against God's edict. Adam would now be forced to face the same judgment as Eve, but at least he would die with her in his arms.

Patmos felt the same as Adam, and he also knew he could not go back to the mundane existence of marriage. The Professor still loved his wife, but his heart did not beat for her as it did with Esmeralda. Patmos knew that his wife would be torn asunder when she found out about the affair, but Esmeralda was the love of his life now. There was nothing he could do to change his fate. Patmos was caught between the vows he made long ago and the passion of his spirit. Thus, he sought God for guidance. He prayed, "Lord, surely you understand? I know I'm committing immorality. I know I'm breaking the Law of Moses and the Seven Principles of Truth, but can love be wrong?" Patmos did not have to wait long for an answer. Immediately the Spirit of God ran through his veins acknowledging his prayer. For some strange reason God seemed to understand. Love knew no bounds. It must have been the same reason why God was willing to step from his throne and die for man. He did it out of love. He did it out of compassion. He did it to redeem man.

This was how Patmos was able to justify running around with Zeze for over six years. He was in love. There was nothing he could do about it. Love overstepped the law. Love went beyond any measure dictated by man. Now if the Professor just acted rashly out of lust and passion then Patmos would agree that it was an act against the precepts of God, but this was not the case. Patmos loved Zeze with all his heart, so he was able to live with himself and the choices he had made. He was even able to communicate with God by means of the Spirit during that period, so Patmos felt vindicated. But now that he had discovered that he had been betrayed by the woman who he was willing to give up the Kingdom for, he felt embittered. He was enraged. His heart died within him, and he knew it would be a long time before he recovered. Patmos hoped it would take years for him to heal, but he knew better. He'd been down this path before during the Pre-Millennial Era when his heart was broken as a teenager. Perhaps his heart would never mend or it might take decades or even centuries to heal. All Patmos knew was that there was an emptiness inside. He felt like a disembodied spirit with no where to run and no where to hide.

On the eighth day, Patmos finally managed to crawl out of bed. He garnished whatever strength was left within him and fell to his knees. He wept on the floor for a long time confessing his sins and asking for forgiveness. He wept over his lost love and tried to put it behind him. When his tears dried up, he promised God he would complete his mission and bring the people back to the Holy Land. Patmos was now focused on the task at hand. He was like a man who had been on a forty day fast in the desert. He could see clearly now. All the distractions were washed away. All the temptations seemed to vanish, so he picked up a cane and put on a robe made of sackcloth. He headed to Liberty Square, the center of debate and political unrest in the city, and addressed the onlookers in the area.

"Seven years ago, I came to the D.M.R. to witness to the people about remaining in the Outskirts. I went on Kennedy King's Talk Show, debated with Kasca, and informed the North that the borders to the Kingdom would be closing soon. Now I am preaching again to lead an exodus of people back to the Kingdom. In three months time all the people who wish to return to the Kingdom will gather at this very spot in Liberty Square, and we will return to our Lord and King. We will forsake our evil ways and start anew. We will turn our backs on a future doomed for failure and return to a land filled with milk and honey. City of Liberty, this may be your last chance. One day the D.M.R. will transform into a ruthless dictatorship, but there will be no escape from the totalitarian regime. The borders to the Kingdom will be closed, and you will regret not joining me. Please, for the sake of your children and future generations, return to this spot in three months, and we will walk together hand in hand into paradise …"

Patmos' speech continued for another thirty minutes, and his rhetoric was convincing many people in the growing crowd. He would return to this spot three times a day for the next two weeks trying to persuade the people to join him. By the end of the second week, Patmos was joined by thousands of disciples propagated by his message. Many of the followers passed the exhortation onto others, and the whole Magog Republic was in an uproar.

On the 14th day at Liberty Square, a clash of different opinions filled the air. Libertines loyal to the Republic were doing all they could to upset the proceedings and just before Patmos was about to speak, a riot ensued.

"… Without further ado, I give you Patmos!"

Patmos moved towards the mike. He breathed in deep and was about to sprout his first word, but at that moment, someone threw something from the crowd and pelted Patmos in the eye. He fell back and immediately tried to cover his head. When Patmos' supporters saw their hero get hit, some of them lost their cool and went looking for the perpetrator. But the Libertines stood in their path and before anyone knew what happened, the two sides were throwing fists. This small brawl attracted a larger crowd and within minutes a full-scale riot ensued.

"Death to the traitors!" someone shouted.

"Resist the Libertines!" the opposition responded.

Bottles were thrown. Fires were started. Many were injured. It was also easy to see what side you were on because the Libertine loyalists wore red shirts and white hats as a sign of solidarity. Patmos' supporters bore no colors and after the initial fighting died down, a line was being drawn at Liberty Square. The Libertines were on one side, and the followers of Patmos were on the other.

This melee lasted for about an hour. After that, the D.M.R. army had to be brought in to quail the disturbance, and they were a bit excessive in their force. They went about beating people over the heads with clubs, and many soldiers showed little restraint. It marked the first time military forces had to be used to restore order, but it would not be the last.

The media coverage of the riot at Liberty Square was slanted. Most of the holoscreen stations blamed Patmos and his followers for the disturbance, but the people at the event knew the Libertines were the ones who incited the riot. Nonetheless, Gog Inc.'s rival station did a more honest job of covering the event, and the Libertines' reputation did not go unscathed. Patmos was arrested and taken into questioning but released later that day. He was informed by the general of the army that if he tried to speak again at Liberty Square, he would be incarcerated. If this occurred, it was likely that Patmos would miss the forty year deadline and he'd be banished from the Kingdom. Regardless, it didn't matter to the Professor. He was on a mission now and if the Lord wanted him to rot in a cell, so be it. The elder figured it was his due. As for the City of Liberty, they had been warned. If they decided to remain behind, that was their prerogative. He had other cities and towns to visit in the D.M.R., and he knew that if he did not get the message out, their blood would be on his hands.

Patmos traveled from place to place in the D.M.R. as a public speaker. He spoke in halls, schools, and at street corners. Everywhere he went, people would gather to hear him speak and a large contingent were starting to follow him. By the end of the three months of touring the North, thousands of people were setting up tents in parks and were awaiting the final exodus back to the Holy Land. Patmos would tell these people to meet at Liberty Square or start making their way south on their own, but only a few would leave. These followers were loyal to Patmos, and he was their Moses leading them through the wilderness.

*   *   *   *

In 262 K.A., millions of people gathered in Liberty Square and started the long march home. Many of these people came north forty years ago to experience life on their own. Others were born after Mandate 222 was passed, and they were curious to experience life in the Holy Land. They had heard so much about the Counselor that they were willing to branch out and leave their former lives behind. As for the rest, a small contingent was Old Timers who knew better than to remain outside the Kingdom. There were also some Libertines who joined the exodus, but most of the people who returned with Patmos were afraid. Some feared they would die in the North being separated from the Tree of Life and the Counselor. Others believed that Patmos' prophesying would come to pass, and they did not want to experience famine and disease. Likewise, almost everyone knew about Ezekiel 38 and other prophecies in the Bible. They had been taught this information since childhood in Kingdom schools, and they did not wish to side with the Devil and declare war on the Kingdom. As for the rest of the D.M.R., they did not worry about such trivial things. The North was as beautiful as the Kingdom, and they were free to do as they pleased. There weren't as many limitations on behavior in the Outskirts, and thus far, Kasca and the Libertines had fulfilled everything they promised. A democratic government was formed, the D.M.R was already outdoing the Israeli Kingdom in many areas, and it was just a matter of time before the Democratic Magog Republic became the center of culture and the ruling authority in the world.

As the people made their way on foot through the wilderness, an unexpected guest made her appearance. It was Esmeralda. She had a small pack on her back, and she was following Patmos from a distance. On the second day after leaving the City of Liberty, Esmeralda finally had the courage to approach her lover as they made their way on foot.

"Patmos.... Patmos...." Esmeralda cried out. "Can you hear me?"

The Professor did not turn around, but he froze in his tracks when he heard Esmeralda's voice.

"I know I've done you wrong, but please hear me out."

Patmos remained still and did not turn around.

"First of all, I'm sorry how things transpired. I know I'm not worthy of you, but I still love you," Esmeralda said. "I want to be with you forever. Would you please talk to me?"

Patmos turned around and stared coldly into the face of Esmeralda. She was weeping, and it took all of Patmos' strength to resist her. He wanted to grab her in his arms, hold her one last time, and say goodbye, but he could not.

"Will you please take me back?" Esmeralda asked. "Do your former words of love and affection still hold true? Would you leave your wife for me?"

Patmos did not answer her question, but continued to stare at her. Esmeralda was looking at the ground with downcast eyes and spoke again.

"My love, is there forgiveness in your heart? Is there anyway to win you back to me?"

Finally, Patmos spoke. He said, "Zeze, I still love you, and I always will. I forgive you of the wrongs you have done unto me, but I cannot forget. I wish I could put it all behind me, but it may take years, possibly decades, to forget what you've done. And before all this happened I was willing to leave my life and forsake everything for you, but I have repented, and I am going to return unto my wife, if she'll have me. As for us, we are at the crossroads."

Patmos moved in closer and comforted Esmeralda by wiping away a tear from her cheek.

"I will always love you, but my heart is in shambles," Patmos explained. "It's splintered into a million pieces like Humpty Dumpty, and I cannot put it back together. Do you understand?"

Esmeralda shook her head as the two stood inches apart from one another. Their lips were so close, and if Patmos had not been walking firmly with the Lord, he would have fallen. But he was a changed man. The last three months had been hell, and the broken relationship may have been painful, but it gave him strength when he encountered problems during his public speaking in the D.M.R. Nothing could faze him. The spitting in his face by the Libertines, the constant attacks on his character, and the blows he received from loyal D.M.R. citizens. And as he stood looking into Esmeralda's eyes, he spoke the hardest words he had ever said. "I love you, Zeze, but I cannot be your lover. You are welcome to join the thousands of people returning to the Kingdom, but I will not have you. I will not be with you. We must go our separate ways."

Patmos gave Esmeralda a kiss on the forehead, turned around, and continued heading south towards the Kingdom.

Esmeralda tried to reach out with her hands, but she could not move. She strived to say something, but the words would not roll from her lips. Instead she stood like a statue in that spot for a long time. She then turned around and headed north.

Chapter 18

Closing of the Borders

After Micah's ship left port, the people of Tarshish suddenly realized they were alone. Their choice to remain in the Outskirts was now final, and there was no turning back. In a few months the borders to the Kingdom would be closed, and they would lose their Israeli citizenship. But not only would they forsake their citizenship, they would lose the protection of the King of Kings. No longer could the colonists turn to Him in settling a dispute. No longer could they depend on the Counselor in time of need, and some of the women started to weep as Micah's ship disappeared on the horizon. The people left behind did not wish to return to the Kingdom, but they were still afraid. If the General's prophecies were correct, death would come to many of them, and they would see horrible atrocities associated with war and disease. Nonetheless, the settlers of Tarshish stood firm on their principles. They knew that when the Millennial Reign ended, they would be re-gathered unto the Lord of Lords, and He would make a new heaven and a new earth. Still, it was difficult to see hundreds of years into the future. Anything was possible, and sometimes the prophecies of the future were difficult to interpret, so some of the settlers were concerned. Even Hannah, one of the strongest women in Tarshish, voiced to her husband her fears and doubts, so Jacob encouraged his wife.

"Hannah, I'm as terrified as you are about the dangers that will come, but I don't believe we are alone," Jacob explained. "God will always be with us. He will not forsake us in our time of need. And although we will not be able to see or touch Him, His Spirit will reside within us. And if we don't lose faith, we can call upon the Lord at anytime, and He will deliver us. If war comes to Tarshish and we are outnumbered, we can call upon the Lord and He will give us victory over our enemies. There is nothing to fear, my dear. The Lord is on our side."

"I suppose you're right, honey," Hannah said, "but do you think it's possible I could go with you next fall during the time of tribute? I miss the Counselor dearly, and I do love Him so."

"Well, I'll talk to James and see what strings I can pull. After all, it will be our first tribute at the Booth's Festival and many will want to go, but I bet I can get you on board. James may be our leader, but he is my brother."

"Thanks, Jacob, I truly do miss the Counselor. I could survive three millennia without the luxuries of the Kingdom, but it's hard to go a day without the Lord."

"I understand what you're saying. I suppose that's the same reason why I had difficulty leaving the Kingdom and coming out here in the first place."

"So true ... so true."

"C'mon, let's go join the others. They need our strength right now."

Jacob and Hannah went forth and comforted the others. Many families had been torn apart by the departure, and it would be some time before Tarshish would recover. In the coming months, the people of Tarshish went about their business and the closing of the Kingdom passed without a ripple. People ate and people drank, but in the back of everyone's minds was the choice they made to remain in the Outskirts. James and Jacob especially felt that burden because they were the ones that led the others out there. If the colony failed and people died, they would feel responsible and that troubled them; nevertheless, the colonists who stayed in Tarshish did so on their own accord, so they really couldn't be blamed. In the meantime, those left behind united together and did their best to forget about the past and moved forward into the future.

* * * *

Matusak arrived in Jerusalem bearing chains on his ankles and a collar around his neck. His head hung low, and he appeared to be a broken man to everyone in the Kingdom. He walked slowly, and he made his way methodically towards his temporary prison in Jerusalem. The citizens of the Kingdom stared at Matusak as he shuffled along the path. Young boys would ask, "Is that the great warrior, Mama, who holds all the home run records? Is that Matusak?" "They say he had the strength of Sampson, what happened to him?"

In a day or so everyone in the Kingdom knew about Matusak and his fall from grace. They learned about the slayings, the prisons, and all the wickedness that transpired under his rule. They read about the glorious battle between Rhodes Kruger and Matusak in Alexandria and how the Counselor brought Kruger back to life after being dead for many years. In the future, children would read about this event in their history books and Kruger would become a celebrated hero. Not only was he a fierce lineman for the Philistines, Kruger would become a great martyr who died for his faith. As for Matusak, he became an example of how pride and power can corrupt absolutely. Professors would lecture, "Matusak was given talent. He was given skills. He was given strength, but ultimately these gifts failed him. He became like Lucifer and fell from grace."

When Matusak arrived in Jerusalem, he was put into a temporary holding cell, and his chains were removed. The Counselor ruled that Matusak's life would be spared, but he would be imprisoned for forty years. After Matusak's years of internment expired, he would be banished from the Kingdom until the end of the age where he would be judged for his crimes. Meanwhile, the Lord set aside three acres of land for Matusak's prison. The Marauder would be free to go anywhere on the acreage, but if he stepped outside the borders he would be put in chains for a year then released again on the land. One of the Angels of God watched over Matusak and made sure he abided by the rules. As for Matusak's friends and the former Marauders, they were allowed to come and go as they pleased, but at sunset of each day, they were forced to leave Matusak's encampment.

The Marauders who returned with the Counselor became loyal subjects of the King of Kings. These New Timers now understood what the Old Timers were saying about the days before the Millennial Reign, and they were no longer disobedient adolescents. Many of these men and women were still rebellious, but they no longer spit at the feet of the 144 Elders. They still hated the condescending looks some of the Old Timers gave them, but they weren't an unruly mob anymore. The Marauders would remain outsiders in the Kingdom like a group of bikers in a gang, but they were now fervently loyal to the King. At times they would break the rules and overstep their bounds, but in general, they were law abiding citizens. As for the Marauders in the Outskirts, they awaited Matusak's return. One day they hoped to recapture the throne of Egypt and overthrow the puppet emperor, Xavier Madmenah. In the meantime, the Marauders went south into Ethiopia, fought battles, and waged war down there.

* * * *

Kasca watched over a million people leave Liberty Square and follow Patmos back to the Kingdom, and he was enraged. Kasca's best friend had turned his back on him, and he felt betrayed. In Kasca's mind, he envisioned himself ordering the Magog army to fire upon the dissenters and killing all of them. He saw their dead bodies fall and their blood spill upon the ground, but all of these visions were a passing fantasy. He hoped someday to get retribution against these dissenters and to make Patmos pay for turning the people against his Republic, but today would not be the day. Kasca would have to wait until the D.M.R. was stronger. Currently, the Counselor and the Kingdom held the power in the world, but one day he hoped to rule the planet. Kasca planned to figure out how the Counselor did His miracles, and he would do the same. One day, Kasca hoped to expose the Counselor and prove to the world that he was just another man, but in the meantime he would have to wait until he figured out the root of His power. Kasca mused, "Why do the Old Timers fervently pledge their allegiance to the Counselor? Is it some elaborate plot to control us New Timers? And why does the Counselor want the D.M.R. and all the countries in the Outskirts to bring forth a tribute to Him each year? The Counselor is obviously trying to keep us under His thumb by having us bow down unto Him. This doesn't seem just. This doesn't seem righteous. The prophecies also say that if the families or countries in the Outskirts do not bring forth their tribute, He will cause the rain not to fall upon that region until the tribute is brought forth. Hmm ... we must test this theory to see if He can also control the weather. If so, He must have some technology that enables Him to have this power. I will have my scientists research controlling the weather and expose the Counselor as a fraud. In fact, I'll have Gog Inc. invest a large portion of its profits in technology, and the D.M.R. will recreate the miracles He performs. It's just a matter of time. These Old Timers have had thousands of years to create their advancements but the D.M.R. will overtake them in a hundred or so. The new will replace the old and the D.M.R. will rule the world with Gog Inc. on top!"

As Kasca watched the last of the dissenters leave the Republic, he felt animosity towards Patmos and the Counselor for stealing his people. In the coming years, this hostility would fester, and the Libertine would not be able to let it go. It would take away his peace. It would eat away at his soul, and later, it would bring about his downfall.

* * * *

A throng of people and some of the 144 Elders gathered at the gates of the Old City in Jerusalem to celebrate the official closing of the borders. As a symbolic gesture, the gates were closed, and the people celebrated with drink and song. News reporters captured the scene on the holoscreen, and it was projected to the world that the borders were officially closed. It was the last official broadcast from the Kingdom to the Outskirts, and from this day forward, no one would be permitted to enter the Kingdom from the outside. Only on the Days of Tribute would representatives from the Outskirts be permitted to enter the Kingdom and that was during an eight day holiday known as the Festival of Booths. The rest of the year, the borders would be closed and anyone trying to sneak back across without official citizenship would be turned away or killed. Therefore, many people were happy because this moment officially marked the day that the Libertines and their fellow rabble-rousers were banned from the Kingdom. It also meant that anyone who was discontent with the laws of the Kingdom and the Counselor's rule could be banished by the 144 Elders. Everyone in the Kingdom, however, did not see this as a glorious day on the timeline because many people now had family and friends living in the Outskirts, and they feared for their lives. To them the closing of the borders meant that they would probably never see these people again, and it saddened them. Nonetheless, the forty-year grace period had come to a close, and the world embarked on a new era.

Part II

The Four Corners of the Earth

Chapter 19

A Warrior's Return

In the year of 302, forty years after the closing of the borders, Matusak was released from his imprisonment. He was taken to the border of Egypt and set free in the Outskirts, but as soon as Matusak set foot in Egypt, he was taken captive by Egyptian forces. Xavier Madmenah, the emperor of Egypt, did not want Matusak to reside in Egypt because of the threat he posed, so he was escorted out of Egypt and later released into the southern territory of Africa known as Ethiopia. As Matusak entered Ethiopia, he was greeted by Marauding warriors and reunited with many of his old companions.

"My friend, it has been a long time," the commander voiced. "We have awaited your return."

Matusak shook hands with the commander in the Marauder's way, then grabbed him by the shoulders and gave him a hug. He then grabbed the commander's head with both hands, firmly kissed him on the forehead, and said, "I'm free at last!"

The rest of the Marauders moved in and shook hands with Matusak. Many of the troops had never met Matusak because they were born in the last forty years, so they came up to him like he was a god and stood awestruck in his presence. Matusak welcomed them like a movie star would do, and he was friendly towards them. In the old days Matusak would have picked the biggest one out of all of them and knocked him to the ground to show his strength. Instead he shook hands with his admirers, and it appeared to a few of the older Marauders that some of the Matusak's rough ways had been subdued. Matusak was milder. He was less aggressive, and his boasts were fewer.

Later in camp that night, Matusak sat with Jonas, the commander of the outpost, and they discussed many issues.

"So tell me, what was your imprisonment like?" Jonas asked. "Did they torture you?"

Matusak looked at Jonas, and he realized that he had been gone a long time. Matusak had forgotten how different the Outskirts were, and the idea that the Counselor would torture him seemed absurd.

"Jonas, my imprisonment was not that bad, but don't tell any of the other men about it. These recent recruits seem to be all about reliving the glory days, and I'd hate to destroy their image of me. The truth is, I was given acres of land to roam free on. I bore no chains, and my friends were able to visit me at their leisure. Of course, I was not able to leave the acreage, but women could come visit me. Also, there were fruit trees on the land, and I started a farm of my own. I grew carrots, lettuce, corn, and whole bunch of other vegetables. In fact, I kind of enjoyed it."

Jonas sat with his mouth gaping open. He couldn't believe these words were coming from the great warrior. Jonas thought that Matusak would be bitter and that he would want revenge against the Counselor, but Matusak only seemed to admire the Man.

"Yes, Jonas, I know it sounds absurd, but my imprisonment changed me. In truth, I was kind of thinking of getting some land, becoming a farmer, and having a family of my own out here. Does that sound unreasonable?"

Jonas looked at Matusak in amazement and chuckling said, "I suppose it's possible."

"Why do you laugh, Jonas?"

"It's just that you're so different than you used to be. Your whole demeanor has changed. You don't appear to be the same way as you were before your imprisonment."

"Your observations are correct, Jonas. I have repented of my sins, and I just want to start all over again with a clean slate. And if I live a good life out here, maybe the Counselor will receive me back unto Him, and I will not be cast into the Lake of Fire at the end of the age."

"Wow, there's no doubt anymore that you have changed, Matusak. You're definitely a new man."

"It's true, Jonas, now if I can only stay on course and not veer from it."

Jonas looked at Matusak like he had been brainwashed, but he did not tell him so. Instead the commander said, "I suppose it could happen, but what about your reputation?"

"To hell with my reputation! I want to start anew. These wars and battles will not give us glory. They will only bring us shame."

As Jonas and Matusak continued to talk frankly with one another, a young Marauder was lying in his tent listening to the conversation unbeknownst to the two men, and he could not believe his ears. Everything he had been told about Matusak had been a lie. Matusak was not a valiant warrior but a pacifist. The young man felt betrayed by his leaders, so in his anger, he grabbed his knife, sprang forth from his tent and charged Matusak. When Matusak heard his rumblings, he simply moved a little to his right, and tripped up the young warrior as he passed. The young man fell to the ground and landed on his knife. The blade penetrated his ribcage and pierced his heart. The man then managed to roll over on his side, and with his last breath, he reached out with one hand and died.

When Matusak saw the young warrior expire, he was crushed. He had only been out a few days, and he had just killed his first man. During Matusak's imprisonment, he vowed to never kill again but he had already broken that oath. As for the other men in the camp, they stormed out of their tents to see what the ruckus was about, and they all stood dumbfounded as they observed Matusak standing over a dead body with a tear running down his cheek.

* * * *

For the next fifty years, Matusak lived in the Northeast corner of Ethiopia with the rest of the Marauders. The Marauders made this territory their homeland, and they built farms and raised families there. Occasionally the Marauders would fight skirmishes with other rival factions in Ethiopia, but Matusak never joined them. He was too busy tending to his farm and taking care of his family. At that time Matusak had eight wives and thirty-nine children, but every few years, Matusak would add another wife to his harem, and his offspring continued to multiply.

Matusak was still the most feared man in the territory, but he was known as the "Gentle Giant." Every now and then, however, people would see if they could stir up his anger and Matusak's old self would come to the surface, but most of the time he controlled his temper. One time, a man trying to prove his worth came up to Matusak in the center of town and challenged him to a fight to the death. Matusak refused, but when the man charged him anyway with a machete in his hand, Matusak took the weapon from him like he was a child and threatened the man's life with the weapon if he did not strip in front of everyone and head out of town. The man did as Matusak ordered, and he was never seen from in those parts again. Another time, three assassins came to town with automatic weapons and planned to hunt Matusak down like prey, but they never made it to his ranch. Instead some of Matusak's fellow Marauders heard about their plan, and these men were sought after and killed. Their dead bodies hung in the center of town for one week with a sign over them saying, "All enemies of the Marauders will be shot and killed."

In 355, Matusak's life took a turn for the worst. A rival tribe from southern Ethiopia came to the Marauders territory and was stirring up trouble in the outskirts of town. Two of Matusak's teenage daughters were on the road back to the ranch when they were attacked and raped by a few men from this tribe. When the news reached Matusak, he and his older sons went south with arms and killed every man, woman, and child they could find within this tribe, and Matusak's name changed from the "Gentle Giant" to a "Wild Beast" once again and no outsiders messed with him for some time.

In the year of 379, a war broke out between the Marauders and Algiers, two rival tribes in Ethiopia. The first few years of the war went poorly for the Marauders, and it appeared they were going to be overrun by the Algiers. Thus, Jonas, his old friend, came to Matusak and asked for his aide.

"Matusak, the war with the Algiers is going bad," Jonas stated. "Is there any way you could help us out in this conflict?"

"I already told you and the rest of the commanders that I will not join your cause," Matusak answered.

"But you don't understand. We're about to lose this war. The Marauders' territory is about to be taken by the Algiers' clan. That includes your ranch and farm."

"Hell Jonas! Why did you start this war in the first place? If the commanders would have conceded on some of the border lands, we wouldn't be having this discussion!"

"True, but it's too late now. We've been fighting for three years, and we are about to be defeated. We are outnumbered three to one. The troops are tired, and we are completely out of Fruit Pills."

After being informed, Matusak hollered, "Damn it!" and he pounded his fist upon the table. Matusak thought about his next move then he finally spoke.

"Okay, Jonas, you tell the other commanders that I'll bail them out this time, but I want complete control of the army. I will be their general once more, and we will ride to victory, no matter what the cost."

Jonas exclaimed, "Yes!" after he heard Matusak's demand and said, "It is agreed. You will lead us. I will tell the other commanders."

Jonas jumped into his hover-car and sped off into the distance. He now had the great warrior by his side, and he hoped that their fate would change. They had lost so many battles in the last six months that the Marauders were in dire straits and their morale was low. Jonas also knew that although Matusak was a bit aggressive in his tactics, he was a competent leader. In fact, he was the best general Jonas had ever seen and if Matusak couldn't lead them to victory, there was no hope for their cause.

A week later, Matusak came up with a plan for a quick and decisive victory. Matusak moved all the troops secretly to one location. He planned to launch one final assault on the Algiers. If he overtook the forces in that region, he figured that the Algiers fighters would fall like dominos, and they would call for a peace treaty. If Matusak's plan failed, the Marauders' defenses would be overrun in a matter of days and all would be lost.

Matusak moved the men to one location on a foggy and damp night. It was perfect conditions for what he wanted to accomplish. He could move the men freely to the point of attack. In the meantime he had some of the women replace the men at their posts to make it appear as if nothing had changed to the Algier scouts when the fog passed. To Matusak's credit, the deception worked, and the Marauders invaded at sunrise. The Marauders overtook the Algiers at one base camp, and proceeded to the next until three had fallen. They did not stop like the Japanese did after they attacked Pearl Harbor in WWII, but the Marauders moved on until they had reached the back lines of the enemy and in the process, many of Algiers general's were killed.

The next day the Algiers lead commander raised the white flag and called for a truce. Matusak and the Algiers' commander came to terms, and the Marauders gained significant territory in the war. Matusak's strength and skill became legendary once more, and the Marauders silver and black flag was raised all over the territory. Soon, new recruits from all over Africa came to join them, and the Marauders' forces doubled, then tripled within one year. Even rumors in Egypt spread that Matusak was coming to overthrow the Emperor, but none of it was true. After the peace treaty was signed, Matusak simply went back to his ranch and worked, but he knew that things had changed. Although the warrior tried to remain humble, his ego began to inflate again, and it was just a matter of time before he would be back to his old ways. In the meantime, Jonas took command of the Marauders' forces under Matusak's decree and trained the new recruits. A great army was being built in Ethiopia, and the borders of Egypt shook with fear.

Chapter 20

On the Road to Recovery

Esmeralda returned to her home in the City of Liberty. It was empty, and everything within its confines reminded her of Patmos. The paintings on the wall reminded her of him. The pictures of the two together brought back a flood of memories. Even their bed and his pillow still held his scent. When she walked out onto the patio, she could think of nothing but him. The house was not the same without her lover. It only brought back powerful recollections. She thought, "How can I go on without him?" And she fell into a deep depression that lasted for months and would linger on for years.

Esmeralda sat at home contemplating what her next move would be. From time to time, she would return to Kasca's estate and work, but she drifted like a disembodied spirit and became distant from everyone. If it was anyone else she would have been fired, but Kasca would not dismiss her. He ordered, "Let her be and even hired a personal secretary to cover all the affairs and details that Esmeralda missed. Kasca knew about her pain, and he felt it too. Kasca had been in love before, and his relationship with his lover turned sour, so he had pity on her. Esmeralda was also his favorite at the estate, so he tried to console her. Esmeralda, however, could not be comforted. She was lost. Every pop song on the radio reminded her of Patmos. It was as if the song had been written for her, and she wallowed in melancholy everyday. Esmeralda's persona also changed. She used to laugh out loud and was the life of the party, but now she kept to herself and spoke rarely. She was no longer fun to be around, and she suffered from outbursts of anger. The littlest of things could have her screaming in rage. For instance, one time she had a trinket that had come apart. It was given to her by Patmos, and she treasured it deeply. It sat in the center of her desk like a shrine, and now it was broken. For hours, she tried to put it back together but was unsuccessful. Finally her secretary came in and asked nonchalantly, "What are you doing?" and Zeze lost it. She screamed, "It's none of your business!" and threw everything on her desk onto the floor. She then picked up a golf club, one Patmos had given her, and broke everything in the room, swinging the club around like a mad woman. The secretary fled the room and called security. The guards tried to take the club from her, but she swung it at one of them and hit him. The other guards backed off. Finally, Kasca came into the room and was able to calm her down.

After the incident at the office, Esmeralda never returned to work. Instead she decided to sell her home and get away from the City of Liberty. She put the house on the market and within a short period of time, the house was sold. She then wandered aimlessly for years and traveled from place to place. She traveled throughout the D.M.R., Persia, and Beth-Togar-Mah. Esmeralda had a tent, a backpack, and lived as a traveling vagabond. She met people on her way and had some wonderful experiences, but in reality, she was running away. Esmeralda was trying to forget everything that would remind her of the past, and she drifted without direction for two decades. Eventually, she settled in Gomar in the region that was formerly known as Spain, and worked odd jobs to keep herself busy, but after a few years in Gomar, she started to come to terms with the loss of Patmos and decided to return to the D.M.R. Although she still pined over Patmos, Esmeralda's wounds were healing. Traveling from place to place on her own gave her strength, and she realized she could live through anything. Although the last twenty or so years had been difficult to overcome, even more difficult than surviving the Tribulation, she tried to move on. Since the break-up, her heart had become colder, and she was like frozen tundra from time to time, but if you gave her a drink she would loosen up and become as friendly as she was before Patmos left her on the hillside. Still, there was a fortress around her heart, and it protected her from ever being hurt again. This stronghold would remain with her for centuries, and Esmeralda's aura was like the moon on a pale November night.

* * * *

Patmos, like the other seven prophets, was welcomed as a hero when he returned to the Kingdom after his seven years abroad. Patmos brought back more people with him than any of the other prophets, and the people in the Kingdom treated him like a holoscreen star. He was now one of the famous people that resided in the Kingdom. Patmos joined David, Moses, and all the other patriarchs. He became part of an elite class that would rather live their lives in solitude than to be bothered with the attention that came along with stardom. As for the people, they loved Patmos' story. They learned about his affair, how he fell from grace, and his triumphant return to glory. As for Patmos' wife, she found out about his love for Esmeralda, and she tried to forgive him. For two longs years, she attempted to keep the family together, but in the end she divorced him. Patmos' wife could tell that her husband still pined over his former lover, and she did not want to be second best, so she left him. As for Patmos, he did not go out with a fight. He accepted his fate, and gave her everything. He felt she deserved it. She took the house, their material goods, and his two teenage daughters. Patmos, took his divorce as a time of transformation in his life, so he quit his job at the University, and he left the 144 Elders. He moved to the Gulf Coast, bought a boat, and worked as a fisherman to get away from his old life and the pandemonium of the city. Patmos lived on his boat, but eventually the former elder bought some property on the shoreline and built a house there.

For ten years Patmos lived at his home by the sea recovering from his troubles. He would wake up early in the morning and fish the gulf coast. Occasionally, Patmos' eighty-year-old son, Nathan, would join him, and the two men would go out to sea. Most of the time, they rarely spoke to one another. There was nothing to say. They had known each other for far too long. The two men went about their business and worked quietly side by side. When the work was done, Patmos would return to his home by the sea and Nathan would return home to his family, which lived nearby. One time, however, as they were making their way back in, Nathan asked, "So Dad, how long are you going to beat yourself up over your former transgressions?"

At first, Patmos didn't answer, but his son pursued the issue.

"Well, I know you heard the question, but are you going to answer it?"

"I haven't decided yet," Patmos responded. "First of all, it's none of your business, and second of all, it's none of your business."

"C'mon Pops, for over a year I've been going out with you on this ship, and I've never pushed the issue, but it's been over a decade now. Don't you think it's time to crawl out of that pit and join the rest of civilization?"

"What are you talking about? I do lots of things …"

"Like what?" Nathan interrupted. "You go out fishing then you come home. You don't go into the city. You don't visit anyone, and at best, you come over to our house to have dinner on the Sabbath. The rest of the time you read books, watch the holoscreen, and sleep. What kind of life are you living?"

"What are you talking about? I went to the ballgame with you last week."

"Dad, I'm not talking about a ballgame. I'm talking about women. When is the last time you went out on a date? Don't you think it's time to start getting back out there?"

"Well, I don't want to upset your mom or anything."

"C'mon, give me a break. Mom remarried five years ago, and she's doing great."

"I know. I just …"

"Pop, I don't mean to bust your balls. I'm just worried about you."

"Son, I'll be fine. I'm just not ready yet."

Nathan dropped the subject. Instead, he grabbed a couple of beers, and the two men shared a drink as they drifted into port.

Later that night, Patmos went out on his balcony and stared out to sea. He thought about his former lover, Esmeralda, and wished she was by his side. He thought about the words his son spoke to him about moving on, but Patmos didn't want to. He wanted Esmeralda and nothing more. Although ten years had passed, the flame did not die within his heart. His love for Esmeralda still burned passionately, but she was gone forever. Patmos regretted the words he spoke to her the last time they saw one another, and he wished he could go back in time and change things, but the past was unforgiving. Esmeralda went back to the City of Liberty because of his words. He could have taken her back. He could have forgiven her, but his pride would not let him. She was willing to leave everything behind to be with him, but Patmos could not forget. She came to him begging for forgiveness, but at the time her deception was fresh in his mind. Looking back, Patmos realized that he was too hard on Esmeralda, and he should have forgiven her. Thus, Patmos decided to write Esmeralda a letter. He thought he might bring about some sort of reconciliation, so he sat down at his holoscreen and began to type.

Dear Zeze,

Over ten years ago, we had a falling out. You lied. You hurt me. You broke my heart, but looking back in retrospect, I should have forgiven you. I should have realized that there were outside forces influencing your decisions. The question I now am asking is will you forgive me? You came to me on that hillside, and I turned you away. I should have received you with open arms. Instead, I forsook our love and abandoned you. In the process, I left the person I care the most about. I deserted my soul mate. I forsook my love. I'm sorry. Please forgive me. Will you find it in your heart to look past my former transgressions? At the time, I was too beat up to see beyond what had transpired, but looking back on what took place, it seems so trivial. I just needed some time to remember what truly matters, and I have finally realized that you are the most important person in my life. The love we shared together was incomprehensible. It goes beyond the supernatural. It goes beyond rhyme and reason.

Although much time has passed, I remember the times we shared together like yesterday. I remember our love. I remember your lips. I remember your scent. You were like fresh flowers dripping with the morning dew. You were the shining sun that shed light upon my world, but since you've been gone, I've been living in darkness. I'm a lost ship at sea that drifts east and west with no destination. I long to return home, but there's no place I can call home. You were my home. You were my safe place, but you've become a dream to me, and I've become a man without a home. Still, in my night visions I remember your face. I remember the touch of your skin. I remember the intimacy we shared. I recall lying in each others' arms and making love for hours on end.

You may ask why I am writing to you after so many years have passed. It's because I'm trying to find absolution. I'm trying to win back your favor. I'm searching for what I have lost. You see, I've seen the error of my ways, and I want to start all over again. Will you have me back? If yes, I will leave the Kingdom, and we can begin a new life in the Outskirts like we planned. We could travel the world together. We could live in Sheba or De-Dan and raise a family together. It would not matter where we settled as long as you and I are together.

I do hope this letter reaches you. I'm not sure if you live in our old home, so I've made a copy, and I'm sending it to Kasca's estate as well as our former abode. And if you receive this letter, please write back. Tell me where you'll be and I'll meet you there tomorrow. Oh, I was such a fool to leave you behind! I should have taken care of you like a precious emerald, but I let you slip away. Please forgive me for the hardness of my heart. Come back to me. A new beginning awaits us. Our future together is written in the stars.
With Love,
Patmos

Patmos later made a copy of the letter and sent both copies out with a courier who delivered it to the border of Tubal. A postal company on the other side received the letters, and they were delivered within the week to Kasca's estate and Esmeralda's old address.

The letter sent to Esmeralda and Patmos' old home was received by the new owner of the place, but he threw all of their old mail away. At first, the new owner would save all the letters and junk mail that came to their address, but Esmeralda never came by to pick it up, and she had no forwarding address. As for the copy of the letter, it was sent to Kasca's estate where it went through heavy security, but it eventually landed on Kasca's desk. After scrutinizing the writing on the address, Kasca opened the letter. First of all, the letter was from the Kingdom, so it immediately peaked his interest. Secondly, the writing style looked vaguely familiar, so he opened the letter and discovered it was a love letter from Patmos to Esmeralda.

After reading the words in the letter, Kasca was moved by the Professor's passion for Zeze. He now realized how deeply Patmos had fallen for Esmeralda. But as he read his old friend's words, bitterness arose in his heart. From Kasca's perspective, he felt like he had been betrayed by Patmos when he led the people back to the Kingdom, so he thought only of hate. Kasca had not forgiven nor forgotten about the indiscretion. So Kasca lit a match and set the letter on fire. It burned brightly in his hand and a small grin started to form on Kasca's face as the words slowly disappeared.

Patmos never received a response from his first letter, so he wrote several others in the coming years, but each time they were thrown away by the new owner or burnt by Kasca. Finally, the Professor gave up and he stopped writing to Esmeralda altogether. Patmos realized that she was truly gone, and he needed to move on with his life. As a way of coping with the loss, he drank a lot of alcohol or ate too much of the Purple Fruit to escape reality. In truth, however, it never really helped, but Patmos felt justified in his actions because he took his advice from the Book of Proverbs which read, "Give strong drink to him who is perishing and wine to him whose life is bitter. Let him drink and forget his poverty and remember his trouble no more." And Patmos did not want to remember. He wanted to put Esmeralda out of his mind forever. He wanted to forget about her, so he wouldn't brood over her no more. But nothing worked. He even tried to wash the pain away by sleeping around, but it didn't help either. The sex only gave him a temporary reprieve from the demons that haunted his den at night. He then turned to violence. He joined a fighting club and learned the martial arts. He was a pretty good fighter too. He was a natural athlete and quick on his feet, but he still got beaten to a pulp in some fights. He didn't mind though. The pain made him feel alive. It took his mind off his lost love for a while, but his thoughts always drifted back towards her. Patmos couldn't escape the ghost of Esmeralda. This behavior went on for a few years and in some ways, it was good for him. He was socializing again, even though he was engaging in decadent behavior. Eventually Patmos met a woman who had gone through a similar experience, and the two bonded. They were not intimate lovers, but they did care for one other, and it was better than being alone. The two married some time later, and Patmos lived together with this woman for a long time. She bore him many children, and they lived happily by the shoreline. And although Patmos still thought about Esmeralda, he reminisced about her less and less as time passed. When Patmos first returned to the Kingdom, not a day nor an hour passed where he did not think about his former lover, but nowadays he only thought of her from time to time. Eventually, he hoped she would become as distant to him as his life was before the Millennial Reign. That life was only a dream now. So many years had passed that he could not remember the former things. He had been living in paradise so long that pre-Millennial years no longer entered his mind. He hoped someday that Esmeralda would become like the former days, but deep down inside he knew he would not forget. He loved her, and he knew that love lasts forever.

* * * *

Kasca's estate was the first place Esmeralda visited after returning to the City of Liberty twenty-five years later. The former President received her back like a prodigal daughter, and the household celebrated her return. The fattened calf was sacrificed, and a great feast followed. But when the party was over, Kasca and Esmeralda sat alone in the dining room and talked. They had both lost someone close to them in Patmos. Esmeralda had lost her lover, and Kasca had lost his closest friend. There was now a common bond between the two of them, and they were able to open up to one another.

"So how are you doing?" Kasca asked.

"I'm fine," Esmeralda answered briefly.

"No, how are you doing, Zeze?" Kasca emphasized. "Are you over him yet?"

Esmeralda shrugged and didn't answer his question. She breathed in hard, stared at the ground, and started playing with her long, brown hair.

"I see. You're still in love with him, and I understand. I miss him too. He was the one person I could confide in. He wouldn't beat around the bush. Patmos would tell me like it is. He would stab me in the heart with his words and look me in the eye as he did it. He is a great man, and we should have never tried to deceive him."

At the last line, Esmeralda looked up in anger and spoke, "And if you hadn't told me to lie to him, he'd still be here right now!"

Kasca looked away shamefully as Esmeralda continued.

"But I suppose that doesn't matter anymore."

Esmeralda's temper died down.

"It's all under the table now, and we have to move on. You couldn't have known it would end up this way. I'm sorry for getting mad, and I forgive you."

"And I, you," Kasca responded.

"Forgive me for what?" Esmeralda's voice rose again.

"For telling him the truth. If you wouldn't have said anything and confessed your innermost thoughts to him, we wouldn't be having this conversation alone. He'd be sitting here in our midst."

"Ahhh!" Esmeralda grunted as she peered over at Kasca. "And if you weren't a jerk and such a crooked politician, you wouldn't be lying to your friends."

"Give me a break, Zeze. You're ten times more deceptive than I've ever been. The only reason you fell so hard for Patmos is because he was the one man you couldn't break. He didn't fall for your charm, your wit, or even your beauty, and that's the only reason why you wanted him!"

"Kasca, you're so full of it! I don't even know why I came back here. What was I thinking?"

Esmeralda rose from her seat and started looking around for her traveling backpack.

"What did you do with my things? Have them brought out to me immediately!" Esmeralda demanded. "I'm leaving!"

"Sure and where are you going to run to?" Kasca stated as he looked towards one of the servants and pointed at him to retrieve Esmeralda's backpack.

"I don't know but anywhere is better than this!"

Esmeralda paced around the room. She waited for the servant to return as Kasca continued to berate her.

"What's wrong? Did I strike a chord? Did I tell you the truth? Did I upset you?"

Esmeralda continued to fume but refused to respond to Kasca taunts. The servant returned with her backpack and laid it on the floor next to the door by Kasca. Esmeralda made a beeline towards the pack and tried to pick it up, but Kasca put his foot on it to prevent her from lifting it.

"Move your foot, you bastard!"

"No, if you want it, you're going to have to take it," Kasca taunted. "C'mon, let's see what you got."

Esmeralda continued to pull on the backpack, but Kasca was stronger than her.

She pulled with all her might, but couldn't get the pack away from him, so she tackled him to the floor and Kasca banged his head real hard. She then retreated back towards the pack and started to put it on her back, but Kasca returned the favor and tackled her and the pack went flying. Kasca then sat on her chest and pinned her arms helplessly to the floor. Esmeralda struggled and yelled, "Get off of me you lying son of a bitch!" But Kasca just laughed at her louder like an older brother playing with his sister.

"If you don't get off of me, I'm going to …"

"You're going to do what?"

Kasca jumped off of her and said, "Now take your bag and go. Get out of here!"

Esmeralda got up off the floor and quietly started to put on her backpack and was just about to walk out the door when Kasca spoke earnestly.

"If you have to go, Zeze, go, but I'm sorry for everything. I should have never forced you to lie to Patmos. It's my fault and I take full responsibility. I didn't realize you had fallen so hard for him. You made it seem like you had everything under control. I should have known better. Patmos is a great man. He was my dearest friend. As for you, I love you like family, and I don't want you to leave. If you have to go, to work things out, that's fine, but you'll always have a place here. My door is always open."

Esmeralda dropped her pack at Kasca's sincerity, turned around, and gave Kasca a long, deep hug. She then kissed him on the lips passionately, and before the two of them knew what happened, they were both naked and having intercourse on the floor.

The love affair between Kasca and Esmeralda started that day on the floor of Kasca's estate. A close bond developed through the years between the two, but Kasca never told Zeze about the letters Patmos wrote. When Zeze first returned from her long journey, Kasca almost told her, but he decided against it. Kasca liked having Zeze around, and he thought if he told her about the letters, he might lose her again. So out of selfishness he kept the secret to himself, and Esmeralda never found out.

Chapter 21

Colonization

The first fifty years after the closing of the borders remained relatively peaceful on the earth. Of course, there were skirmishes between rival factions over land and territory, but there were no major wars happening in the world. The Democratic Magog Republic was flourishing, and the Republic had strong alliances with Meshech, Tubal, and Persia. Meshech and Tubal originated as two small clans that did not want to be a part of Kasca and the Libertines nor a part of the Kingdom. Therefore, they settled in the land as a buffer between the D.M.R. and the Kingdom. As the years passed by, they become two small countries, but since they could not do business with the Kingdom, they traded with the D.M.R. and soon became economically intertwined with the Libertines' Republic. As for Persia, they became a strong empire in the East, and they also had economic ties to the D.M.R., but they were not dependent on them. After being on their own in the Outskirts for almost eighty years, the borders were being drawn and alliances were being made. As for Europe, it was still divided. There were too many rival factions, and no one ruled with an iron thumb. Eventually Western Europe was divided into small city states and they formed a loose alliance known as Gomar. As for Eastern Europe, it was divided into three city states. They were called Beth, Togar, and Mah. They formed a democratic government and were known as Beth-Togar-Mah. Beth-Togar-Mah traded with the D.M.R. every now and then, but they kept their distance. They did not want to become puppet states like Meshech and Tubal. They liked their distinctiveness, and they wanted to remain independent at all cost.

*   *   *   *

The Democratic Magog Republic was the greatest power outside the Kingdom. Their cities were growing. The population was booming, and the land was being filled, so a lot of people in the D.M.R. started heading east and crossed the Alaskan-Kamchatka Passageway. The passageway was a bridge of land that connected the East to the West. It existed long ago before the Flood during Noah's time, and it reappeared during the Kingdom Age. These people were citizens of the D.M.R. but were colonizing the Land of Nod in North America. At first, the Nodians and the Libertines got along well with one another. A trade network was developed, and there was enough land for everyone, but after a hundred years, a rift started to develop between the original Nodians and the D.M.R. settlers. The Magog Republic wanted to annex the Land of Nod, but the Native Nodians did not want to become part of the Republic. The Native Nodians may have been a scattered group of tribes, but most of the Natives were against the annexation; however, the Natives were outnumbered 2 to 1 by the D.M.R. settlers, and the Libertine Republic did as they pleased. Eventually the Republic claimed Nod as their territory without the consent of most of the tribes, and the rift between the two factions grew wider. This division would lead to civil war in the future, but in the meantime, the Native tribes of Nod went about their business and did not recognize the D.M.R. as the ruling authority.

*   *   *   *

Since the northern ice-caps in the arctic no longer existed, it was easy to travel from place to place in the Arctic Ocean. The weather was temperate, and ships quickly started to fill the region. These ships explored the area and countries started to claim the land masses as their own. One of these regions was Greenland. When Tarshish was settled by the O'Donohue brothers and their compatriots long ago, they claimed the land of Greenland as their territory. Technically, Tarshish was the first nation to set foot in the area after the Millennium began, but this did not prevent other countries from claiming it. After a hundred years of being on their own after the Kingdom borders closed, Tarshish settlers went out to reclaim their right to the territory, but when they arrived in Greenland, a small contingent from the D.M.R. was already there. They claimed the territory as theirs and a disagreement ensued. Eventually, James O'Donohue proved his right to the land by convincing the D.M.R. settlers to travel south and see their claim. In friendship, they sailed with one another and James proved Tarshish's claim to the land. The D.M.R settlers also said they had claim to the land, but their evidence was circumstantial. Although James knew that the land belonged to them, he did not want to make enemies with the D.M.R., so an agreement was made between the two parties in 327 K.A. The northern part of Greenland would belong to the D.M.R., and the southern part would belong to Tarshish. Maps were drawn, signatures were signed, and Tarshish sent out a contingent of ships and soldiers to protect their territory.

The result of the Greenland Pact between Tarshish and the D.M.R. laid the foundation for future trade between the two countries. Tarshish was now recognized as a nation by the Libertines and the D.M.R. expanded its borders. The Magog Republic now surpassed Dan and its former colony of De-Dan as the largest country in the world. The northern parts of Asia and Eastern Europe belonged to the D.M.R; Nod was now under its jurisdiction, and half of Greenland was under their control.

The encounter with the D.M.R did result in one negative for Tarshish though. James and his men carried laser guns with them when they encountered the Libertine settlers in Greenland, and one of these guns was stolen. This laser weapon was then shipped to the City of Liberty and given to Gog Incorporated for a price. The company that Kasca controlled took the mechanism apart and eventually figured out how it worked. In the coming years, they would mass produce this weapon and all soldiers within the D.M.R. would carry it.

When James found out about the missing weapon, he was enraged at the young man who lost it.

"You idiot!" James yelled. "How could you possibly be so stupid to let our greatest weapon slip into the hands of the enemy? You fool!"

"But ..."

"But what?" James mocked the young man. "Are you going to head back to northern Greenland and retrieve it? Are you going to accuse the D.M.R of stealing? You stupid...."

James looked at the young man with his head down. He looked like he was going to cry, so James stopped yelling at him. Instead he cursed under his breath and walked away. He hoped that the weapon was simply missing or misplaced, but he doubted it, and this even made him more paranoid. So when James got back to the Land of Tarshish he stepped up his efforts in preparing for war and made it mandatory for all men of Tarshish to join the Tarshish Defense Force (TDF) at age twenty-one and serve for five years.

When James made his proposal for a draft, many of the up and coming leaders of Tarshish opposed the idea, and there was a bit of an uproar in the City of Canaan, the largest city in Tarshish; nonetheless, Jacob, Hannah, and Simon all supported his decree and young men started being drafted the following year. James' foresight turned out to be beneficial because a few years later, Tarshish ships were ransacked by Gomar and one of the coastal towns was invaded. This resulted in a war between the two nations, and Tarshish's preparedness made them a superior fighting force during the war.

* * * *

Gomar was a loosely formed republic in Western Europe. Many of the people who founded the region were people who survived the Tribulation but were not permitted to enter into the Kingdom. These people bore the Mark of the Beast and soon died out within a generation. The children, however, did not bare the sins of their forefathers and were granted longevity of life like the rest of the people born during the Millennial Reign. These New Timers may not have inherited the curse of eternal damnation like their forefathers, but they did learn some bad habits from them before they passed on. They learned about murder, fornication, lying, stealing, and every sin known to man. After the Counselor revisited this region in 100 K.A., he quickly restored order to the region and had to teach these New Timers all over again like babes. For a period, His teachings and exhortations kept the people of Gomar in line, but the sins they learned from their forefathers slowly began to resurface in the following century. And by the time Mandate 222 was passed, Gomar was completely overrun by sin. This posed a problem because the Lord of Lords knew that many people from the Kingdom would be heading out that way, so He passed judgment against them and Uriel, the angel of turmoil and terror, was sent out to kill many of them. In Uriel's rage, all the ships that belonged to Gomar were destroyed by a hurricane and nine-tenths of the people were killed. The survivors were warned by the angel, Raphael, that if they did not follow the precepts outlined by the King of Kings, the whole region would be destroyed. Nonetheless, another century passed and Gomar was repopulated again. The people started to become wicked once again, and they desired more. Gomar saw the Land of Tarshish prospering from a distance, and Gomar wanted a piece of it. Although Tarshish was off limits to them by Raphael's decree in 223 K.A., they still decided to take matters into their own hands and invade the region.

Chapter 22

The Tarshish-Gomar War

The Town of Paradise was burned down by Gomar and its troops. They took everything of value and fled back into the sea where they came. When the Tarshish Defense Forces (TDF) arrived, burnt bodies covered the area and only a few people were brought back to life by fruit from the Tree of Life. The rest were so badly burned that there was nothing they could do. Twenty-one people were murdered in the raid, and the rest fled to safety by the hillside. The town was completely caught off guard and most people didn't realize they were being invaded until it was too late and this brought about their demise. Luckily, a woman named Azrial reacted quickly and led the rest of the town to safety. The surviving townspeople watched from a distance as the Gomar troops overran their village.

Upon arrival, one of the TDF generals asked Azrial what happened. She stated, "We were all quietly going about our business like any other day when suddenly a flood of Gomar ships arrived in Paradise Port. Armed troops unloaded and started attacking our people. Some women were raped, and many of the men were killed. They then pillaged the shops on the bay and took everything of value. Afterwards, they lit everything on fire and fled back into the sea from where they came."

"How large was their navy?" the TDF general asked, "And how many soldiers were there?"

Azrial answered, "I'd estimate over 100 ships and a thousand or so men. They all wore green uniforms and appeared to be military men."

When the general heard about the uniforms, he knew right away the troops were from Gomar. The general quickly passed this news onto Chieftain James and within hours, everyone in Tarshish knew about the invasion. War was immediately declared by James and the other chieftains after the attack. The twenty-one that died in the Town of Paradise and the many fishing ships that were lost at sea made the decision easy. Tarshish prepared for war that evening and Jacob's invasion of Gomar took place the next day.

Over 30 ships sailed for the coast of Gomar, and Tarshish planned to destroy the Gomar Navy. Using their laser weapons, the TDF destroyed every ship in their path. The Gomar Navy was no match for them, and Tarshish's 30 warships destroyed over 3,500 Gomar vessels. They destroyed ships of war, fishing vessels, speed boats and anything that moved in the water. By destroying every ship in the sea, Jacob hoped to eliminate any counter-attack by Gomar. By evening, there were no Gomar ships left in the sea. Out of the 30 Tarshish ships, only two were damaged. The rest remained untouched. It was a glorious victory for Tarshish. Their laser technology made it almost impossible for Gomar to make a counter-attack. Their ships could fire from a great distance away and with pinpoint accuracy. As a result, the coastline of Gomar was littered with debris and dead bodies lay in their wake.

After the Gomar invasion, the leaders of Tarshish gathered together for prayer.

They thanked God for the victory at sea, and proceeded to ask Him for guidance. They asked if they should continue the war and attack Gomar's cities. They prayed for His leading and agreed they would not act until He brought forth a response.

One week passed and nothing had happened. Tarshish remained untouched, but the people were afraid. Many of the New Timers wanted to strike now and asked why they were waiting. They wanted justice and to the young men and women, war sounded valiant and noble. Another week passed and still the Lord had not responded. Hannah thought that it must be a sign that they should do as they desire and Jacob agreed with her. They wanted to eliminate the threat of Gomar before it reached Tarshish soil. James disagreed and said we must wait, and the leaders prayed once again for divine guidance. Later that night, Simon, Hannah's brother, had a dream. The angel, Michael, came to him and took him under his wing and flew him over three cities of Gomar. Michael spoke as he went. "The cities of Azazel, Semjaza, and Rameel will be given over into Tarshish hands. Send forth your forces and destroy the wickedness from these places. God will give you victory, if you remain faithful, and peace and prosperity will be with you in your land."

When Simon awoke from his dream, he immediately ran to tell James and the others, and they believed it was inspired by God. The leaders ordered the TDF to prepare for an invasion, and they set sail the following day. The navy was divided into three wings. The first wing, led by Simon, attacked in the North and set sail for the City of Azazel. The second wing, led by Jacob, attacked the capital City of Semjaza, and the final wing led by Hannah, sailed south and invaded the City of Rameel. At precisely 5:00 A.M. the following day, the three forces began their invasion. The order from Jacob was to "destroy everything and to leave no building unturned. If possible, spare the defenseless and take no spoils."

"Ready, aim, fire!" was the order from Jacob and all three wings of the navy fired their weapons of destruction into the cities of Gomar. The three shoreline cities were completely demolished and many people died that day. The war was over before it even began and once the shelling of laser fire ceased from the ships, the men landed on shore and proceeded to turn everything left in the cities to rubble. Some people were screaming. Many people were dead or dying, and it was difficult for the TDF soldiers to see with their eyes, but they proceeded through the cities and followed orders.

Once the battle was over, Tarshish had only a few people that were injured or killed. Those who did die were revived from the Fruit Pills. In the end, only two men lost their lives trying to save some burning children. They rushed into the building, and it collapsed on them. Their remains were never found and were forever lost under the burning rubble. As for Gomar, they called for a peace treaty the next day, and the fighting ceased. The President of Gomar and his advisors came to the City of Canaan and met with James and the other leaders. A peace treaty was made between the two nations and Gomar was forced to bring tribute for twenty-one years to honor the dead who were killed in Gomar's sneak attack of the Town of Paradise. As for the three cities of Gomar, they became ruins and Gomar was not allowed to rebuild the cities for twenty-one years in memory of those who lost their lives.

It was estimated that over 3 million people died in the attacks on Azazel, Semjaza, and Rameel. The whole world learned about the invasion of Gomar and great fear fell upon the people in the Outskirts. Now even the D.M.R. took notice of Tarshish, and they greatly honored the Greenland Pact. The D.M.R. also removed their ships of war from Greenland as a sign of good tidings, and

James was allowed to do the same. With the exit of the D.M.R. Navy, it allowed James the ability to free up some of his forces and focus on other areas of concern.

The funny thing about the invasion was that no country openly protested the destruction of Gomar. Some of the rival factions in Ethiopia did bring up the issue but the rest of the nations were hands off. If they didn't know already, the nations of the world soon learned that Tarshish was a colony of the Kingdom, and no one dared mess with the Counselor. Tarshish was now a world power. They had the best weaponry and the strongest navy. In the coming years, the D.M.R. would surpass them, but in the meantime, Tarshish was the strongest military in the Outskirts.

* * * *

After the Tarshish-Gomar War of 333 K.A., the world started becoming more pluralistic. It was difficult to remain isolated from the rest of the nations because of the holoscreen. People were starting to travel. Planes were now being built. They were previously banned under the 144 Elders, but in the year of 322 K.A., the ban was lifted. Representatives from Dan and Sheba asked the Counselor personally at the Booth's Festival if they could start building planes, and the Counselor said yes. It made sense for these nations because they were so far away from the rest of the world, and air travel would make it easier to get around. The only contingent was that no plane was allowed to fly over the Kingdom's airspace. If they did, they would be immediately destroyed. No one knew how the Counselor would shoot down these planes, but His ability was not questioned until centuries later. And these planes found out the hard way that the Counselor was not bluffing.

After the ban on air travel was lifted, all the nations started to build an air force. It took over a decade to get things going, but a century later the world was crawling with airplanes. Gog Inc. was the leading company in air travel, and their superiority in building the machines made them the biggest company in the world. They traded their jets for resources, technology, and years later, for the coveted Purple Fruit.

Chapter 23

The Demise of Signmonkoala Island

In 354 K.A., explorers from the D.M.R. Navy landed on the small Island of Signmonkoala. They were the first people to visit the land in almost 100 years. Micah and the people returning from Tarshish to the Kingdom were the last men who were there. When the Signmonkoala saw the D.M.R. ship docking in the bay and coming ashore, they greeted them the same way they greeted the Tarshish settlers long ago with Purple Fruit and open arms.

A small hovercraft was boarded and it skimmed across the surface of the ocean as it made its way towards land. As they approached land, they noticed the Signmonkoala making signs and waving their arms. When the D.M.R. soldiers saw this, they quickly grabbed their lasers and prepared themselves for a conflict; however, when they landed, they realized that the Signmonkoala were not human, and they put their laser weapons back in their holsters.

"Would you look at that? The funny looking creature seems to be offering us food," one of the men stated.

"Don't touch it men," the commander ordered. "It might be poison. Be prepared for anything."

The men grabbed their weapons again and pointed them at the Signmonkoala. The Signmonkoala were making signs and trying to communicate with the soldiers.

"Spread out men. Don't let their small stature and cuddly faces fool you. Look towards the tree line. Those ones have spears in their hands."

The commander ordered the men to spread out and take cover behind sand dunes and palm trees. A few minutes passed and one of the younger men spoke. He voiced, "Commander, I don't think these creatures pose a threat. It appears to me they are trying to communicate with us. Look they're doing some kind of sign language with their hands and they're bringing us gifts. Why don't we try to communicate with them?"

"Private, its obvious this is your first trip at sea," the commander answered. "We've encountered sea monsters, hostile forces, and barbarians. We must take every precaution."

"But commander, look, they're trying to give us food …"

"Keep your peace, private, how do we know it's not some sort of a trap?"

"C'mon commander, don't be so paranoid. It's obvious they're friendly. Look, I'll show you."

The private rose to his feet and approached the Signmonkoala offering the Purple Fruit. The commander tried to call him back, but he was already within reach of the Signmonkoala so he let him continue. The commander thought to himself, "I'm going to make him pay for questioning my orders, but in the meantime, lets see if they're friendly or not."

The private took one of the bell shaped pieces of fruit, examined it, and cut it in half with his knife. The private smelled it then bit into it and the tribe of Signmonkoala started to jump up and down in celebration.

"Get ready men!" the commander ordered, "They're about to set forth their trap!"

At that moment many of the Signmonkoala come out from the trees and surrounded the private. They were touching him and examining him and many of the younglings were crawling on his back and on his head. When the commander saw this, he yelled, "At ease!" and the D.M.R. troops came forward.

✱   ✱   ✱   ✱

Later that evening, almost the entire crew was onshore interacting with the Signmonkoala and eating the Purple Fruit. The camp was set up. Bonfires were burning and everyone was feeling high and wonderful except for the private who did not follow orders. He was sent back to the ship and was not allowed shore leave. The rest of the troops enjoyed their stay and began interacting with one another.

"It's obvious this Purple Fruit has an intoxicating effect on us," one of the men said. "I've never felt this good in my life. It's like I'm floating on the clouds and soaring the heavens."

"Man, I feel you. I wish my girl was here right now. Imagine having sex on this stuff. It would be like a religious experience or a Vulcan Mind Meld."

"Sammy, you are high, but I have to agree. This stuff is magnificent. We could take some of this stuff back with us, start a plantation, and be the richest men in the D.M.R."

"That's a great idea, but we'd have to first slip it by the commander," one of the other men spoke, "and you know he wouldn't allow that. In fact, I bet he's got aspirations of his own. Look what he did to Private Wilhelm."

"No, I doubt it. The commander doesn't think that way. He's all about duty and honor and his allegiance to the Republic."

"Hey man, you might be right, but you're blowing my trip. All this talk of making money and overthrowing the commander means nothing. Can't you see we're all part of everything? We're one with nature. We're one with the earth, and one day we'll be one with the Creator."

"Sammy, you are over the edge. How much of that stuff did you eat?"

Sammy didn't answer. He was off in his own world, but Sammy was making sense in one accord. The idea of a coup d'état was now circling around the minds of the men, and if they could eliminate the commander, they could return home to the D.M.R. with the Purple Fruit in hopes of becoming wealthy men.

* * * *

The troops stayed onshore for a few days. The commander had the men raise the D.M.R's red flag on the island and claimed it as part of the Republic. Meanwhile, a group of men were planning a coup. They planned to kill the commander and the men loyal to him and take the ship as their own. Once they had accomplished this task, they planned to take the seeds of the Purple Fruit back with them, start a plantation, and become wealthy businessmen.

The men planning the coup numbered thirteen. That means there were 27 other men to be accounted for. Four were on the ship and one of the men was Private Wilhelm. Thus, they had to overtake the ship and kill the men loyal to the commander onshore. Overtaking the ship was the easy part of their coup d'état. When the men had to be relieved onboard the ship, that was the moment the thirteen planned to make their move because two of the men who were due onboard were part of the thirteen.

As the men traded spots, the hovercraft returned with the men who were previously onboard, and that was the moment the coup began. The first people killed were the men on the hovercraft then the eleven men remaining began to randomly kill the men faithful to the commander. Within the first thirty seconds, nineteen out of the twenty-seven men were dead, including the commander. After that, a full-scale battle began and laser fire was going off all over the island. Trees were being torched and the Signmonkoalas were running about scared out of their wits. After the first thirty minutes of laser fire, almost half the island was on fire. Huts were burning, Signmonkoala were dying, and it was just a matter of time before the whole island burned down. There was a lot of dry shrub left on the island from the leaves of the Purple fruit, and this ignited fires everywhere. The Signmonkoala tried to put out the flames, but every time they ran to the ocean to get water, they'd be shot down by the D.M.R. troops.

After a couple of hours of fierce combat, only a handful of D.M.R. troops remained. Five of the original thirteen were alive. Two of these men were on the ship and three remained on the island. That meant it was three on three combat for the rest of the battle because only three men loyal to the commander remained alive. As for the hovercraft, it was destroyed in the first minutes of combat so there was no way to get back to ship unless one swam. It didn't matter anyway because it was just a matter of time before the whole island burned down. Therefore, the remaining Signmonkoala declared war on the D.M.R. troops but they were easy targets for the D.M.R. soldiers. They fought with spears and had never experienced combat before.

When it was all over, only two of the thirteen were left alive onshore. They had successfully overthrown the commander and his men but at great cost. The whole island was on fire, most of the Signmonkoala were dead, and it was just a matter of time before all the Purple Fruit burned down. They had won the battle, but they had lost the fruit. The last two men did manage to get a backpack of fruit off the island, and they swam to the ship docked in the bay. As for the Signmonkoala, a small group of them hovered in a corner of the island and watched the rest of the island burn down. There was nothing they could do. Within a couple of weeks, the remaining Signmonkoala would die of starvation.

The five men onboard the D.M.R. naval vessel sailed into a Magog port. They told the people back home that they had been attacked by Marauders when they were at sea, and everyone believed them. Private Wilhelm was given the option to either go along with their story or be killed. He decided to become part of the remaining thirteen. Years later, he would tell the true story of what happened on the Island of Signmonkoala, but in the meantime, he kept silent. As for the Purple Fruit, it all spoiled by the time they got back to the Republic. There were lots of seeds to plant though, but they were not cared for. They needed to be kept damp. If not, they would dry out and wither. The remaining members of the thirteen did try to plant these seeds, but only one sprouted. The young tree died in the next year. Hence, the whole expedition was a failure. They thought the Purple Fruit and the Signmonkoala had been lost forever like during the days of Adam, but they were wrong. Tarshish had a whole plantation of Purple Fruit trees that were over a hundred years old. In the coming years, they would start to export their Purple, and these would become the most coveted trees on the planet. Its fruit would trade for great wealth and weaponry. As for the Signmonkoala, the tribe survived back home in the Kingdom when Micah brought some of them back with him in 262 K.A. They lived in the northern jungle of the Kingdom and planted Purple Fruit trees on their arrival. The trees reached great heights and numbers in the Kingdom and within a century, every Israeli citizen was enjoying the euphoric feeling from eating of the Purple Fruit.

Chapter 24

The Tribute

In October of 444 K.A., the Festival of Booths took place in the Kingdom. The eight day carnival was a joyous event, but this year representatives from the D.M.R., Meschech, and Tubal failed to bring forth their tributes. This was upsetting in the Kingdom because the people of Israel used this opportunity to pass mail and find out how life was going in the Libertine Republic, but with the absence of the D.M.R. and its allies, people started to talk.

"Do you think they're coming this year," one Kingdom citizen asked another.

"I don't know. It's the last day of the carnival. If they don't make their tribute, the wrath of the King will come down upon them," an old time citizen answered.

"Do you really think the Counselor will withhold rain from falling on the D.M.R.?"

"Of course He will. Look what he did do the tribes of Ethiopia. He had no mercy upon them, so why should He treat the Libertines any differently?" the Old Timer bluntly stated.

"It just seems a bit harsh. After all, the Libertines are our distant brothers."

"True, but they know the rules like everyone else. If they don't bring forth tribute each year, the rain will not fall in their territory."

"Do you think Kasca and the Libertines are testing the Counselor?"

"Of course they are. Kasca has no respect for the Counselor. He's a rebel and should not be tolerated. In fact, I think the Counselor was too lenient with him long ago."

"Hmm, I guess we'll see soon enough."

A year passed and the Booth's Festival came round again. The D.M.R and its allies did not show. Thus, the rains did not fall in Magog, Meschech or Tubal for another year. The plant life started to wither in these territories, but the people had enough water to survive. The lakes were still filled with water, and the D.M.R. had a good irrigation system.

After the third, forth, and fifth year passed without a single drop of rain falling in the D.M.R., the people began to be upset with their leaders and protests occurred around the major cities. Peoples' crops were dying, lakes were turning into dry beds, and many people wanted their leaders to send forth tribute to the Kingdom. Nevertheless, the D.M.R. and its allies still had enough food to feed its people.

In the sixth year of the drought, a major fire occurred in the far north of Magog, and it burned a quarter of the D.M.R forest down before the Fire Department had it under control. Over a million people lost their homes and were displaced because of the fire and many of these people went to the City of Liberty demanding the government change its stance on the tribute.

"Send forth the Tribute! Send forth the Tribute!" Everyday in Liberty Square people would gather to protest the government's unwillingness to give tribute to the Kingdom and riots ensued. Hence, the government called upon the Magog Army to restore order, and they arrested people, beat people with clubs, and killed innocent bystanders. The result of the army being brought in did restore order, but it upset many of the citizens. President Harrick Kim III was called a traitor by many of the local news services and over 50% of the people wanted Kim to step down. Kim did not relinquish his power. He still had many years left on his term, so he buffeted the military and went after the leaders of the resistance by putting them in jail and torturing them.

Although Kim was only following the orders of Gog Inc. and the Libertine leaders, he took the brunt of the hate from the people, and by the 7th year of the drought, people were starting to go hungry, and they wanted Kim removed from power. This made the D.M.R. and its allies a hotbed of trouble. Crime increased. The citizens were starting to carry arms, and people were calling for revolution and the overthrow of the government.

Nearing the end of the 7th year of drought Kasca came out of hibernation and spoke to the press.

"Although the D.M.R. is an independent republic and we do not bow down to any ruling authority, I do believe it is in our best interest to bring forth tribute this year. The drought has killed many of our citizens, the fires have burned much of the beauti

ful landscape to the far north, and the people of the D.M.R. have suffered immensely. But I do not blame President Kim for his stand against the tribute. I do not blame the people for standing up for their rights. I blame the Kingdom and the Counselor Himself for creating such an absurd law in the first place. Why must we bow down unto Him? Why must we bring forth tribute to a Kingdom still living in the Dark Ages? It is because the 144 Elders and the Counselor still want to rule over us. So for the time being I think the D.M.R. should bring forth tribute, but in the meantime, we will figure out how these Old Timers control the weather, and once we have this technology, we will never bow down to the Kingdom again! We will be independent of their rule forever, and the Republic will reign on!"

After Kasca spoke, he raised his hand and made his way through the crowd. He entered Gog Inc.'s Headquarters and security forces shut out the press. Within minutes, Kasca's speech was on almost every holostation in the Outskirts. People on both sides of the issue had something to cheer about, and Kasca was once again seen as a hero of the Republic.

A month later at the Festival of Booths, the D.M.R, together with its allies of Meshech and Tubal, sent forth representatives to the Kingdom and gave tribute to the Counselor. The representatives only stayed a few hours and left shortly thereafter. The next day, a monsoon type storm hit the northern republics, and the people danced naked at Liberty Square. The drought was over. The rains had come. And the D.M.R. had made their stand against the Kingdom.

* * * *

The ramifications of the seven year drought made the people in the North resent the Kingdom for their control over them and animosity grew in the D.M.R. The Kingdom was mocked in the press. The Counselor was seen as a ruthless dictator, and 144 Elders were viewed as puppets on a string.

In the coming years, the people who survived the Drought of 444 would tell stories to their children, and the Counselor would be seen as the villain in the stories. He would send forth fire from the sky and burn the crops and landscape in the North. The Counselor would laugh wickedly as people bowed down to Him, and He would mercilessly whip those who were subservient to Him. The Counselor would be hated and feared for many generations to come because of these stories, and it would later give the people justification for declaring war upon the Israeli Kingdom in the future.

Chapter 25

The Counselor & Queen Sheba

Queen Sheba had ruled the South Pacific for a few years. She had power. She had wealth. She had servants and slaves, but she was still not satisfied. There was a hunger in her heart that had not been fulfilled. She had been with many men and women, but none of them had stolen her heart. The Queen had never been in love, and she viewed it as something only known of in fairy tales. Then in the third year of her rule during a terrible drought, she learned from one of the wise men in her kingdom about an ancient tradition of bringing forth tribute to the Kingdom and the King of Kings.

"It is said in the ancient Book of Zechariah that whichever nation does not bring forth tribute to the King of Kings will suffer no rain to fall upon their lands until they give honor and glory to the Lord of Hosts."

"Why have I not heard of this before?" the Queen asked. "Who is to blame for this? And who is this King of Kings?"

"Before your time, there was a great Man who came to our land. It was before the time of our forefathers, the Meneliks. He gave us precepts and laws to rule us and said that each year, we must bring tribute to Him or the rains would not fall on our lands. Your father Menelik would secretly send forth tribute each year to Him, but since his death, Sheba has not sent forth tribute. Hence, the rains have not fallen."

"Why was I not informed of this, you worthless slave?" the Queen angrily spoke.

"I am sorry your majesty. I am to blame," the Queen's counselor admitted. "I did not think the ancient books were true, but after years of drought I have begun to question my beliefs."

The Queen glared at the counselor, but her anger quickly slipped away.

"You are forgiven," the Queen pardoned, "but next time, be sure to bring forth any information from the Holy Books that might be of importance."

"Understood, my Queen."

The Counselor bowed and began to leave the room, but the Queen spoke abruptly and ordered, "Ready my ship. We have a long journey ahead of us. We are going to bring forth tribute to this King. We'll leave tomorrow at sunrise."

*   *   *   *

As the Queen's ship sailed for the Kingdom, the advisor she had been speaking with earlier gave her an ancient Bible from pre-millennial days, and she began to read, "In the beginning ..."

When Queen Sheba arrived in the Kingdom, she had already read through about half the Bible. She was currently in the Book of Isaiah, and she learned of a great Messiah that was to come and set up His righteous kingdom. As the Queen read, she wondered if this Messiah was the Lord she had just read about in the Bible. She was not sure, but she hoped it was so. She boldly went forward and was guided to Jerusalem after arriving in the Sinai Peninsula.

The Queen was escorted down the streets of Jerusalem like royalty. Men of fortitude were carrying her in a carriage and servants were fanning her as she made her way down the boulevard. She was dressed from head to toe in royal attire. She looked like a 16th century monarch from long ago, and the Israeli citizens marveled at her. They were not used to seeing people dressed in this fashion. In the Kingdom, people wore scarce clothing, and at beaches and public pools, nakedness was the norm. Only in the cities and at the work place was clothing considered the standard. The rest of the time, nakedness was permitted, and no one felt ashamed of themselves.

When the Queen arrived at Jerusalem Square, she was let down from her pedestal and escorted to the Temple by some citizens of the Kingdom. They were taking her to the Counselor. It was not common for outsiders to visit the Kingdom outside of the Booth's Festival, so the Queen's presence was stirring a mild uproar.

The year was 98 K.A. when the Queen met the Counselor. When she first saw the Lord, she stood paralyzed in her tracks because the Counselor revealed Himself to her in all His glory. He usually did not do this, but He made an exception for the Queen. She felt like His eyes were peering into her soul, and she felt ashamed of herself. Sheba was a murderer. She was a fornicator. She was a liar and a thief, and she had now gazed into the eyes of the Lord who seemed to know all about her. After looking momentarily at the Lord, she fell to her knees and could not raise her head nor move at all. She was humbled in His presence. She now knew that the stories in the ancient book were true, and she felt guilty over her transgressions. A moment ago, she was proudly walking down the streets of Jerusalem like a Queen, but now she felt like the servants who cleaned her feet.

The Queen lay at the feet of the Lord for sometime. Her straight, black hair was sprawled out on the floor as the Counselor waited. He then rose from the place of honor and touched the Queen on the top of her head. She was still bowed at his feet weeping, and He said, "You are forgiven. Now rise."

The Queen could not move, so the Lord gave her His hand, and escorted her up. Sheba still looked downcast towards the earth and would not look at Him in the eyes.

She felt ashamed. The Queen felt humbled, and she continued to weep. Eventually she regained her composure. She was able to function somewhat as a human being again, and she spoke with the Counselor.

"My Lord, I am sorry for my iniquity. I have done unjust deeds. I have given orders to kill my enemies, and I have murdered my own brothers and sisters to gain power."

Queen Sheba was referring to her rise to power. Her father was Menelik, the strongest tribal leader in the South Pacific. He ruled on the continent of Australia shortly after the Messiah came to the land and judged it, but Menelik was poisoned in his sleep decades later. One of Sheba's subjects gave Menelik poison, and he passed away. After his death, there was a struggle for power, and Sheba, the first daughter of Menelik's second wife, took control of the tribe and the continent by killing Menelik's first wife and all of her offspring.

"This I already know, Sheba. I also knew that on this day and on this hour you would come to Jerusalem. My Father in heaven has appointed you to be my wife during my stay on earth. Although I am the Son of God, I am still a man, and you have been chosen to accompany Me on my journey. We will have many children together, and they will become princes and princesses in the Land of Sheba."

Queen Sheba looked at the King in astonishment.

"But my Lord, I am not worthy," Sheba said. "I am a sinner and should be punished for my crimes against others."

"Yes, you and all of humanity should be punished, but your soul has been made white as snow. Long ago on the cross I bore the sins of man, and now they are gone forever."

"My Lord, I thank you for all that you have done, but you should be with someone who is holier than I," Sheba explained. "I am not a virgin. I am a fornicator."

"Yes, I know all of this, but it has been appointed by my Father for me to marry a woman of sin like the prophet Hosea long ago," the Counselor explained. "You are the woman He has chosen for me, and that is why your womb has remained closed for so long."

The Queen did not speak but stood dumbfounded as the Lord continued to speak.

"From now on, you and I will be one. You will refrain from sin and no longer sleep with others. We will become intimate and offspring will result. In the meantime, you will stay with Me for the next three months, and We will get acquainted with one another. After the allotted time, you will return to the Land of Sheba on your own. From time to time, I will come to your land and visit you. And every seven years, you will return to the Kingdom during the Festival of Booths, and We will be together.

* * * *

The relationship between the Lord and Queen Sheba was kept hidden from the public for hundreds of years. The Counselor thought it would be best if their bond was unknown to the masses. This way their children would grow up without the burden of being called Children of God. However, in the year of 455 K.A., the truth became known to the people in the Kingdom. During the Booth's Festival of that year, Sheba's third daughter, Sydney, came to bring forth tribute. She was an inquisitive child and always questioned her mother about her Father. The Queen would always say that He was a great warrior from a far away land, and she would cut the conversation short. As Sydney got older, she became wise to her mother. During one of the Counselor's visits to the Land of Sheba, Sydney caught the two of them in the middle of love-making. Although the Queen did not see her spying daughter peering into the room from behind the curtains, the Counselor knew. He saw her out of the corner of His eye. From that moment forward Sydney learned everything she could about the Counselor and she thought to herself, "Is the Counselor my Papa? I have never seen my mother with another man. Could the King of Kings be my Dad?" Sydney studied pictures, and she looked a lot like Him. Finally in Sydney's teens she asked her mother, "Is the Counselor My Father?"

When the Queen heard the question, she laughed mockingly, "Don't be ridiculous! The idea is absurd!"

But there was a hint of deception in the Queen's voice and Sydney knew her mother well. She could tell that she was lying. So Sydney looked at her mother oddly and walked away believing the Counselor was her dad. And in Sydney's twenties, she asked if she could see the Kingdom and bring forth tribute that year. The Queen said yes, and during October when Sydney arrived in the Kingdom, the Counselor announced to all the people in attendance unbeknownst to Sydney that she was His daughter. He told the people about how He bonded with Queen Sheba back in 98 K.A. and His many offspring.

In a matter of minutes, the news was leaked to the world, and everyone knew about the Counselor and his relationship with the Queen. The Queen did not deny it. Openly she said to the public, "The Counselor and I have been married for hundreds of years. He has given me eight children, and I am proud of each and every one of them. But due to Emmanuel's position on the planet, He thought it would be best to keep our marriage a secret."

In the Kingdom, people celebrated the news as a glorious moment on the timeline, but in the Outskirts, especially in the D.M.R., it brought up more speculation about the Counselor and his ruling authority. One newspaper even went so far as to call the Counselor's relationship an affair and said He had bastard children. The truth, however, was that the Counselor and the Queen were married back in 98 K.A. by the authority of the Chief Priest. Zadok, the priest, verified the documentation to the public, but most of the people in the Outskirts didn't believe it. They wanted a scandal, and the press made it so. Even in Tarshish, people were starting to question the Counselor. The New Timers born after the closing of the borders knew nothing of Him, and they were being more influenced by news coming from the Outskirts than from the reports being trickled down to them by Chieftain James and his advisers.

∗ ∗ ∗ ∗

The news of the Counselor's marriage to Queen Sheba greatly changed the landscape of Sheba. Sheba's family was now descendents of the Son of God, and people started to look at them differently. Would the children show miraculous powers like the Counselor or would they be like everyone else? No one knew for sure, but everyone was waiting and watching. As for Queen Sheba, she decided she wanted to step from the throne and live with the Counselor back in the Kingdom. After all, she had ruled for over 300 years, and she wanted to do something different with her life, so she sent message to the Lord, and He approved of it. Therefore, the Queen divided her kingdom into five regions. Each region would be ruled by a different prince or princess. To the North, Sheba's first son ruled the territory. To the South, Sheba's second son ruled. To the West, the Queen's first daughter ruled. To the East, her fourth son ruled. And the island region was ruled by her third son, the most unstable part of the Kingdom. As for the rest of the children, including Sydney, they did not have an interest in being a ruler of Sheba. After meeting her Father, Sydney wanted to move to the Kingdom, and the Counselor approved of it.

In the coming centuries, Queen Sheba was always known as the Queen in the Kingdom. She lived a relatively quiet life and bore many more offspring. She stood by the Counselor on special occasions and was a faithful and righteous woman. From time to time she would visit her former kingdom and give advice to her children and grandchildren. In the meantime, she enjoyed her knew life far more than when she was acting Queen in Sheba. After all, she was around the Son of God all the time, and He was the Creator of the universe. Around Him, there was always a new mystery to unfold, and the hours passed like minutes in His presence.

The Queen became one of the most famous people in the world after her secret marriage to the Counselor became known to the public. In addition, she released her autobiography a decade later and became renowned. Her story was read by billions, and it was considered to be one of the best books of the century because the Queen was brutally honest with her tale, and she did not cover up the treachery of killing members of her family to gain power. She admitted openly and told about the guilt she felt inside for her former transgressions.

After the release of the Queen's book, she sort of became an ambassador from the Kingdom. She would go out as the Counselor's representative and help those in need across the globe. She was the Mother Theresa of her age, and people loved her. Wherever she went, crowds would gather, and she was treated like royalty even in the D.M.R. And although some people thought the Queen should pay for her crimes of murder, most forgave her. Besides, who was going to press charges against her anyway? To most people, the Counselor and the Kingdom were still the ruling authority in the world, and the Queen was the Counselor's wife. So nothing could be done about her former sins.

The Queen was well-liked because she had the gift of charity. She was friendly to everyone and was never condescending. It didn't matter if you were a servant or a star, she would treat everyone the same. Her good deeds were known by all, and it was hard to find someone who didn't like her. Being in the Counselor's presence all the time must have rubbed off on her, and she became like a goddess to the world. She glowed like Moses did when he came down from Mt. Sinai, and at times, it was difficult to look upon her Polynesian face at all.

In the second half of the Millennial Reign, her book became part of most school curriculums throughout the world, so almost everyone knew her story. It was well-written. It was from a woman's perspective, and she gave great insight into the Counselor and His character. Thus, she was loved. But when her deeds of charity were done, she'd return to Emmanuel and was a faithful and devoted wife. She gave the Counselor love, and He loved her back. They were intimate lovers, and they were as close as a bee is to the nectar of a flower. It was a difficult relationship for most people to grasp. Philosophers would ask, "How could the Son of God be the Creator of the universe and still be one with the Queen of Sheba?" No one knew for sure, but they were still the most celebrated couple in the world.

Chapter 26

The 13 Year War

Back in 382, Emperor Xavier Madmenah heard about the Marauder's victory over the Algiers. It disturbed him that Matusak and the Marauders were on the rampage again, but he didn't do anything about it. Instead, he strengthened his borders and kept a watchful eye on the Marauders. Emperor Madmenah should have sent forces immediately into the territory and conquered the Marauders while they were still weak. Instead, he did nothing and the Marauder's army grew like Hitler's forces did during WWII. In time, the Marauder's would be a force to be reckoned with, and it would be too late. This occurred in the year of 499. The Marauders invaded Egypt and the 13 Year War began.

* * * *

In the last 100 years, the Marauders had been growing in number. Since the Algiers War, there was a pompous attitude amongst many of the warriors, and they were hungry for warfare again. Even Matusak who went back to his farm after the war was starting to get restless. The great warrior wanted to take back Egypt, but he was afraid of what the Counselor might do if he led the invasion. After all, the Emperor was anointed by the Counselor like Saul was during the time of David. However, in the year of 498, Emperor Madmenah drowned at sea on a fishing excursion, and his body was never found. Some people thought there was funny business going on and that his first son killed him, but these were only rumors. People close to the Emperor's family were highly suspicious of Madmenah's first son. He was ambitious and a bit cruel. Many people thought that he was hungry for power and that he wanted the throne. Regardless, the truth was never revealed and Madmenah's first son ascended to power. He was known as Emperor Xavier Madmenah II, and no one called him by his first name.

The death of Emperor Madmenah I gave Matusak credence for the invasion of Egypt. With the Lord's anointed now dead, Matusak thought he was given a free pass to his former territory, so he led the invasion. Madmenah II, however, was not caught off guard. He had a formidable force, and if the Marauders wanted war, he would give them one. So in 499 the 13 Year War commenced.

Both sides suffered serious loses in the first few years and with a minimum supply of Fruit Pills available in the Outskirts, millions of people died. The war was devastating to the region. The Egyptian cities turned to rubble, and the Marauders' homeland looked the same. Matusak hoped that it would be a quick victory, but the Egyptian forces were well-armed, and they outnumbered the Marauders 2 to 1. Long ago, the D.M.R. sold weapons to Egypt, and they weren't going to fall as easily as the Algiers did years ago. As for the Marauders, they were secretly being supplied Fruit Pills and weapons from Tarshish, so it balanced out the warring parties. And every time a Marauder fell, they would feed him a pill from the Tree of Life, and he would be restored back to health. As for Matusak, his farm was heavily bombed in the first year of the war, and much of his family was killed. This guaranteed that the Marauders would never put down their arms. Matusak wanted revenge, and the leader of Egypt was just as vindictive.

"Jonas, did you see what they did to my ranch?" Matusak asked.

"Yes, your home and almost everyone's home in the territory," Jonas answered.

"Madmenah has no pride," Matusak angrily stated. "Instead of facing us in hand to hand combat, he prefers bombing us from a distance. And he fires upon innocent women and children. He killed my family. We must make him pay."

"We already have, sir," James responded. "His cities are also in ruins. An eye for an eye was your decree."

"Yes, it was, but I never intended to bomb innocent bystanders. Madmenah's the one who broke the code of war. And we will make him pay for his lack of honor."

"But at what cost, sir?" Jonas asked. "Our cities are in ruins. Our people are starving. And we are on the run, moving from one place to the next trying to avoid the next offensive. Do you think we should surrender?"

When Matusak heard the word surrender, he knocked Jonas to the ground and said, "I will never surrender! That bastard went after my family in the first bombing raid and killed almost everyone. He will pay for his crimes, and I will never give up. I will see to it that all of Egypt is destroyed before I admit defeat. The war will not cease until my hands are around Madmenah's throat, and he is good and dead. Do you understand me, Jonas?"

Matusak shook Jonas in anger and put his hands around his throat. It appeared like Matusak was going to strangle him but Jonas pleaded inaudibly, "Sir … it's me … Jonas. Come … to … your … senses. I was only … seeking … your … council!"

For a moment, Matusak's hands got firmer around Jonas' throat, but instead of squeezing, he picked Jonas up off the ground like a rag-doll and spoke earnestly. "Don't speak of surrender again and make sure none of the commanders or men hear your concerns. We might be losing more battles than we are winning, but we will win the war. We will retreat for now, lurk in the shadows, and attack Madmenah's forces when they move into our cities. We will be victorious and make sure the men believe you believe it! Got it?"

"Yes sir … I … will … not … fail … you," Jonas answered, gasping for breath as Matusak let him down.

Matusak smiled psychotically then left the room as Jonas stood shaking in his boots.

The war continued, and the Egyptian forces moved forward. After thoroughly bombing the Marauders' cities, Madmenah's forces took them over, so the Marauders sought refuge in the hills and used guerrilla warfare to combat the invaders. The Marauders also used terrorist tactics to wear down the Egyptians; therefore, Madmenah's generals sent soldiers into the hills to weed out the Marauders, but it was a fruitless cause. Every time the Egyptians attacked the Marauders, they would come back with half their troops missing, and the bodies would have their heads chopped off.

The 13 Year War dragged on for years and years. Both sides were growing weary of the conflict, but the leaders were unwilling to put down their arms. This was dangerous because the area had a shortage of food, and famine was spreading. Rare diseases only seen before the Millennial Age also started to pop-up, and if they weren't kept in check, a plague would likely have spread to all four corners of Africa. The Counselor, therefore, stepped in before it got out of control, and a truce was made. The two sides signed a peace treaty. It was called the Libyan-Alexandrian Peace Accord. Borders were drawn. The territory was divided, and the 13 Year War came to a close. From that point forward everything to the northeast of Africa, up to the Nile River would belong to the Marauders. Everything to the northwest would belong to Emperor Madmenah and his people. As for the name of Egypt, neither country would bare the name any longer because both men claimed it as their own. From now on Madmenah's country would be called Libya, and the Marauders territory would be known as Alexandria.

The 13 Year War ended like most wars. Some soldiers returned home and many asked, "What were we fighting for?" It was a bitter pill to swallow for those who lost loved ones and body parts in the conflict. Libya and Alexandria had to start all over again as the rest of the world went on about their business. As for the D.M.R. and Tarshish, a new Cold War was coming to the surface. Neither side liked the other. The D.M.R. saw Tarshish as a puppet of the Kingdom, and Tarshish viewed the D.M.R. as rebels seeking world dominion. The fact they shared a border in Greenland only made the situation more volatile. A giant wall was being built to keep the two sides apart as the rest of the planet looked on in wonder. Most believed these two world powers would go to war eventually, but in the meantime, a fragile peace existed in the north as it did in Africa.

Chapter 27

Trade Pacts

In 555 K.A., alliances were being made in the Outskirts. Tarshish and the D.M.R. were both trying to manipulate the outside world to conform to their interests and Trade Pacts were negotiated. Tarshish was able to get other lands to form alliances with them because they had the largest supply of Purple Fruit in the world. The Purple Fruit, known as Bliss and Purple in the Outskirts, was the most coveted drug in the world. Bliss made people feel elated. It also had an aphrodisiac effect upon its users. In addition, Tarshish had the most Fruit Pills in the Outskirts. These pills came from the Tree of Life, and they could cure disease and bring a man back to life. One reason Tarshish was blessed with so many Fruit Pills was because of careful planning by its founders, and Micah's cargo ship filled with them before the border closed. In addition, every year at the Festival of Booths, Micah would smuggle out as many Fruit Pills as possible, and over time Tarshish became the heaviest exporter of Fruit Pills to the Outskirts.

The D.M.R. also had strong influence in the world because they were militarily the strongest and on the cutting edge of technology in the Outskirts. Gog Incorporated, Kasca's company, was usually the ones who came up with the advancements in technology. He was able to get the most brilliant minds working for him because of the incentives given. Working at Gog Incorporated was also a matter of prestige in the Outskirts, so people wanted to trade with the D.M.R. They had the best planes. They made the best weapons. And they manufactured high quality hover-cars, automobiles that would not touch the earth but hover above the ground like a helicopter. A lot of these weapons were used during the 13 Year War. Tarshish also made great advancements in technology, but after the year 500, the D.M.R. seemed to be a step ahead of them. Still, Tarshish had the Bliss and the Fruit Pills, so it was hard for the nations to resist forming an alliance with them.

The first alliance formed in the Outskirts was the Empire Free Trade Pact between Tarshish, Sheba, Dan, and De-Dan. This trade pact was put together by Chieftain James of Tarshish. James was a great diplomat, and this alliance benefited all the countries involved. Nod also wanted to be part of the trade pact because it would give them more independence from the D.M.R. The Native Nodians greatly supported the idea. Even the Nodian settlers from the D.M.R. were tempted to join. In fact, the Nodians voted in favor of becoming a member of the Empire Free Trade Pact, but it was vetoed by the D.M.R. government. This upset many of the Nodians because they cherished their independence. In truth, many of the Native Nodians didn't even recognize the D.M.R.'s authority over them, but this veto was the first disruption of their liberty, and more animosity against the D.M.R. started to grow amongst the Native Nodians because of this. As for the Nodian Settlers from the Magog Republic, many of them were upset with the decree, but they did not rebel or riot in the streets like many of the Native Nodian townships. In the end, Nod did not become a member of the Empire Free Trade Pact.

"Kasca, what are we to do about this free trade pact by Tarshish and its allies?" the current President of the D.M.R. asked. "It gives Tarshish an economic advantage over us. Do you think we should join this alliance?"

"No never!" Kasca roared. "I will never be part of any trade agreement with that colony from the Kingdom."

"But what do you think we should do instead?"

"I've been thinking about that the last few weeks, and I think it's time we formed a trade pact of our own," Kasca answered.

"We will make even a stronger alliance. We'll sell our technological advancements to our allies without tax, and if a country from the Empire Free Trade Pact wants a piece of the puzzle, we'll tax the hell out of them. What do you think? Does it sound like a plan?" Kasca asked.

The President didn't respond. He just shook his head in approval. Although he was the elected president in the D.M.R., he knew that Kasca was the one who called the shots. As a member of the Libertine Party, the President knew who got him elected, and he also knew who could take his authority away.

"Excellent, it is agreed."

Kasca seemed pleased.

"Why don't you call the Emperor of Persia and see what he thinks?"

Getting Persia's support in the North was important because Persia was the second strongest country on the continent. If the Persian Empire approved of the deal, it was highly likely the rest of the republics would fall in line.

The President called up the Emperor of Persia, and he went along with the agreement. Of course, the Emperor first asked if Gog Incorporated was behind the deal, and once he found out that it was so, he agreed to a trade pact.

In the next few weeks, Kasca was able to get Persia, Meschech, Tubal, Gomar, and Beth-Togar-Mah to join "The Coalition." Of course, Nod was automatically part of the trade deal because they were technically a colony of the D.M.R. This new alliance was called the Northern Coalition of Free Trade. It balanced out power in the Outskirts, and the question of whose side you were on was no longer up for debate.

After James learned of the Northern Coalition, he was not taken by surprise. He knew the D.M.R. would react this way, and he expected it. They would take his trade pact as a threat, but at least now Tarshish was not on their own. They now had powerful friends in high places, and it was unlikely the D.M.R. would try to make war with them. If the D.M.R. tried to invade Tarshish, they would have to answer to Sheba, Dan, and De-Dan. As for Tarshish's new friends, they knew what they were getting into. They were saddened that they lost Nod, especially Dan, but they knew they would get along fine without the D.M.R. The Empire Free Trade Pact gave them authority as a group. No longer would they have to bow to the D.M.R.'s wishes. As an alliance they could stand up to the Magog Republic and make rules of their own. For example, if they were upset with something like the destruction of Signmonkoala Island years ago, they could make a formal protest against that country or make economic sanctions against that nation. The nations in the Southern Hemisphere, with their northern ally, were empowered by the alliance, and it gave them a leg to stand on during the second half of the Millennial Reign.

For the next 400 years or so, the Empire Free Trade Pact was known as the "Alliance" in the Outskirts. The Northern Coalition of Free Trade, brokered by Kasca, became known as the "Coalition." These two groups became the ruling authorities during the second half of the Kingdom Age. James was the unspoken leader of the Alliance, and Kasca led the Coalition. Whenever there was a major dispute in the Outskirts, these two groups would come together. Debates would follow and usually a deal or settlement would be made.

Chapter 28

▼

100 Years of Peace

The trade pacts negotiated between 555 and 559 K.A. brokered in an era of peace in the Outskirts. There were still some minor conflicts taking place in Sheba's northern islands, but there were no major wars. There was also an ongoing struggle between the Angolans and Tanzanians in southern Africa over some islands, but these were minor skirmishes. Of course, the Algiers and Marauders had a fragile peace treaty in Africa, but the Marauders were still recovering from the 13 Year War with Libya, and they weren't ready for another conflict. As for the Zulus and Nigerians in Ethiopia, they never seemed to lay down their arms, and it was a great testing ground for the D.M.R.'s newest weapons. The D.M.R. would make arms deals with both sides and see what the outcome would be. This did not go over well in the Southern Hemisphere, and the Alliance exposed the D.M.R. for their treachery. After the scandal in Ethiopia, the D.M.R. stopped selling arms in the area, and the region cooled down for a bit. This was the beginning of 100 years of peace in the Outskirts. It began in 576 K.A. and ended in 676 when the Marauders invaded Algeria.

During the 100 years of peace, Tarshish was living in its golden years. Trade was going well with their allies to the south, and everyone was prospering. The Purple Fruit was in abundance and even the D.M.R. was trading with them. As for the people of Tarshish, they started to get comfortable and lazy during this period. The cities were established, Canaan was a Metropolis, and tourism was at an all time high. The citizens of Tarshish were also becoming like the rest of the people in the Outskirts, more immoral everyday. Recreational drug use was rampant and drugs like cocaine, heroin, and marijuana were making a comeback. And of course, the use of Bliss was a staple in society. Everyone lived for such a lengthy time that people started to dabble with evil devices. It was everywhere around them, especially the holoscreen. The holoscreen was like a television set, but it projected the images in three dimensions. The images would be projected into people's living rooms, and it felt as if the actors were sitting right next to you on the couch. This invited many decadent ways into people's homes and pretty soon, the values of the Kingdom were slipping away.

Jacob and Hannah were also being influenced by the times, but they had not been fully seduced by the propaganda, and they tried to screen their children from improper behavior. As for the love between the two, it wasn't as vibrant as it had been in the past, but it still flourished. They had children and grandchildren and grandchildren of grandchildren, and the O'Donohue name was a fixture in the society. Children read about the founding fathers in their history books and Jacob and Hannah's names were always mentioned. Of course, Chieftain James, Jacob's brother, was the most famous person in the country, and Simon, Hannah's brother, was also well known. James and Simon were more in the public eye because they were politicians, so the focus tended to be on them. They were continuously on the holoscreen, and everyone in the Outskirts would recognize them. As for Jacob and Hannah, they were more behind the scenes. Jacob, of course, was the leader of the Tarshish Navy, and Hannah was one of their commanders, so it was difficult for them to become invisible, but as the years passed Jacob and Hannah became more private with their lives.

The two lovers lived on an elaborate estate in the City of Canaan. Much of their family lived on the grounds, and they even had a few Purple Fruit trees on the property. Their estate bordered the Purple Fruit plantation, which extended hundreds of kilometers to the northeast, and James' property was next door. Simon also lived nearby.

"Hannah, you look as beautiful as when I first set eyes on you back in the Kingdom," Jacob admired.

Hannah was passing by him in the backyard, and Jacob was checking out her butt.

Hannah gave her husband a sly look and jokingly responded, "That's right and don't you forget it."

Jacob laughed and said, "Come over here, baby, why don't you give your man some loving?"

Hannah moved in closer, but once she realized what he was up to, she tried to slip away, but Jacob was too fast for her and she was caught in his grasp. He started kissing her on the belly. Hannah was enjoying his touch, but suddenly she realized her grandchildren were around so she tried to make him stop. She was also about to head out for a run, and she had other priorities at the moment.

"Jacob don't, the little ones are right over there, and I'm going for a jog anyway," she protested.

But Jacob continued to kiss her on the belly, and he started to get lower and lower. Hannah was now starting to get aroused, so she pushed him away saying, "Keep your hands off me, you bastard!" and started to walk away.

Jacob laughed as she strutted away, but before she turned the corner, she bent over so that Jacob could see up her panties and gave him a quick smile.

Jacob laughed even louder and yelled as she trotted away, "I'll get you later. You can't run away from me forever!"

As Hannah slipped away beyond the horizon, Jacob mused to himself. He thought, "What would I do without Hannah? She has become everything to me. When I wake she is the first thing I think of. When I go to bed she is the last one I talk to. Now I understand why many old people used to die so quickly after their significant other passed away." As Jacob sat in his garden, he contemplated many things. He remembered what it was like to lose someone, and he thought about his old girlfriend, Jessica, from pre-Millennial days. Jacob loved Jessica with all his heart. He wanted to marry her and raise a family with her, but she left him for another man. He recalled the pain and misery he went through after the relationship came to an end. He spent endless hours thinking about Jessica and could not get her out of his head. Jacob was alone for a long time after Jessica left him on the side of the road. In fact, he never fell in love with anyone else until Hannah came around hundreds of years later, so Jacob had a lot of time to brood over her. The chieftain hoped he would never have to be alone again, but he feared it. Jacob remembered the years of isolation, the depression that followed, and all the heartache he went through. Love was something Jacob feared because the loss of a loved one was too great of a price to handle. Jacob hoped that Hannah would not leave him or die, but in the back of his mind he understood that life doesn't always play by the rules. "Accidents happen," he thought. "And what happens if we go to war with the D.M.R. someday? People could die and having Hannah as one of the naval commanders is dangerous business. Maybe I should suggest that she step down from her post. But she loves her position. She'd resent me if I took that away from her." As Jacob rocked back and forth on the porch, he contemplated many things. He was thankful that he had been blessed with a beautiful wife, but he permitted dark thoughts to cloud his mind and ultimately his greatest fears would come upon him later in life.

※   ※   ※   ※

Esmeralda looked up from her pillow and saw Kasca staring into her room. She had her arms wrapped around another man, and he was still sleeping. Kasca was about to speak, but before the words came out of his mouth, Esmeralda put her finger over her mouth, signaling for him to remain quiet, and she slowly crawled out of bed without the other man knowing of her absence.

The two walked into the other room and Kasca asked, "So is this your new plaything?"

Esmeralda giggled and answered, "Yes, are you jealous?"

Kasca didn't answer her question but asked one instead, "How old is he anyway?"

"He just turned eighteen, and he can go on forever," Esmeralda claimed.

"You're going to destroy that boy, Zeze, but make sure you invite him to the orgy tonight. I'd like to try him out for myself," Kasca said. "And by the way, the Emperor from Persia is going to be here tonight, and I want you to personally take care of him. Make sure he's treated like royalty, but don't be too agreeable. He likes lively women and someone who is going to pose a challenge."

"Understandable," Esmeralda answered, "he sounds like someone I know."

Kasca laughed and started to walk away.

"So where are you going?" Esmeralda asked. "Would you like to join us for a morning wake up call?"

Kasca shrugged her away and said, "I got work to do. I can't be bothered with this right now."

Kasca started to walk away again, but she begged him.

"C'mon darling, just a quickie. I'd like to have both of you at the same time."

Kasca stopped and thought about it for a moment, but he knew he had important matters to take care of. As he walked away, he said, "Bring him by tonight, and I promise to fulfill all your wildest fantasies."

Esmeralda looked disappointed and whispered as loud as she could, "I'm going to hold you to your words," and scuttled off towards her room.

* * * *

Back home in the Kingdom, life was far more innocent and pure. People did not engage in sex outside of marriage and most people did not participate in fornication or immoral behavior. Of course, there were incidents all the time, especially by the young and juvenile, but the behavior was not as rampant like in the Outskirts. As for divorce, the 144 Elders made it part of the legal system. The Counselor did not approve of it, but He thought it would be better if people divorced than live in unhealthy relationships for years and years. Divorce also made sense. Ideally the Counselor wanted people to stay together and work things out, but people were living much longer than before the Kingdom Age, and it was difficult for citizens to remain faithful to their lovers for such a long period of time. Therefore, divorce was permitted, and it curbed the incidents of adultery in the land.

Patmos was one of the people who had been divorced. After he returned from his seven year hiatus in the D.M.R., Patmos and his wife were divorced. They tried to keep the relationship together, but there was too much friction in the relationship, so they departed from one another. Decades later Patmos married again. He had a wonderful family and many offspring, but after 300 years of marriage to his second wife, the two decided they wanted to start over again. There was no fight for property or a debate over who was going to get the kids in the legal system. Patmos and his wife settled these things amongst themselves and remained friends thereafter. Patmos' second divorce took place during the 100 years of peace in the Outskirts.

After the divorce, Patmos decided he wanted to return to teaching. He had been away from the classroom for a long time, and he wanted to influence young minds again. Therefore, he called the chancellor at the University of Jerusalem, an old friend of his, and got a job teaching in the history department. Patmos once again would teach about the era before the Kingdom Age and influence the next generation.

As for Patmos' love life, he was taking it slow. He felt there was no rush to get married again, and he was at peace with himself. Occasionally, he would still think about Esmeralda, but he no longer pined over her. Time had healed his wounds. In the meantime, his classes at the university were filled to capacity. He was a famous historian and prophet in the Kingdom, and the young flocked to hear him like flies on excrement.

During the second semester, however, he met a passionate student by the name of Sierra. She had beautiful caramel skin, and she was intelligent. Sierra reminded Patmos of Esmeralda in many ways, but she was also her own person. Although she was still in her 20s, she was wise beyond her years, and Patmos was drawn to her. She came to him during his office hours to discuss some of the issues brought up during lecture, and the two of them instantly bonded. This continued the entire semester, and they got to know each other better.

"I'm kind of hungry. Would you care to join me for a bite to eat?" Sierra asked.

"I suppose it is getting late, and I've probably talked your ear off, but I have some leftovers at home, but thank you for the offer," Patmos answered.

"C'mon Professor, I'm buying," Sierra said. "I know this great sushi place off campus. The food will make your mouth water."

Patmos thought about it for a moment. He knew that it wasn't wise to fraternize with his students like this, but he was hungry, and he was a sucker for sushi, so he agreed.

Into the night, the two ate and drank together. They laughed and joked with one another, and they probably would have continued like this all night but the proprietor of the establishment was closing up so the two had to leave.

As the two headed towards the metro, Sierra innocently grabbed Patmos' hand and the Professor took it willingly. At the metro station, the two were feeling sad because the night was coming to a close, and they had to take two different speed trains to get home.

"Professor, I had a great time tonight," Sierra said. "Thanks for joining me for dinner."

"It was all my pleasure, darling."

The two were holding hands, and they were staring into each other's eyes. Sierra could hear her train in the distance getting closer, and she deeply wanted to kiss him on the lips and make passionate love to him, but Sierra did not show her true intention. Instead, she waited for Patmos to make the first move and did nothing.

The train pulled up. She was disappointed that he did not take her in his arms and passionately kiss her like those old romance movies. Instead, she let go of his hand. Sierra started to walk away and said goodnight, but Patmos grabbed her by the hand again, pulled her towards him and their lips met.

Patmos rode the metro home like a bumbling school kid. He had a smile from ear to ear, and he felt like he was on Bliss. Sierra felt the same, and from that moment forward, the two became lovers.

* * * *

The 13 Year War with Libya devastated the Marauders. Not a single city was left standing after the war, so those who survived the war had to rebuild their empire. Libya, formerly known as Egypt, was also in shambles, but their cities weren't as bad off. As for the people of the warring factions, Libya lost about three soldiers to every Marauder lost. As for Matusak's family, he lost twenty-seven of his thirty wives and 114 of his 149 children. The loss was demoralizing to him, so in the years that followed the war, Matusak prepared himself defensively. First, he helped rebuild Alexandria, the Marauder's new country name, and started a new farm up north. On his farm, he constructed a secure bomb shelter 100 meters under the earth to prepare him and his family for another bombing raid in the future. Matusak may have been a wild warrior, but he still loved his family. He did not want to have a repeat incident of the bombing raid that killed most of his family during the war.

The 100 years of peace in the Outskirts was beneficial for the Marauders. It allowed them time to rebuild their empire and start again. In reality the Marauders enjoyed over a 150 years of peace because their last conflict ended in 512 K.A. and the 100 years of peace came to a close in 676 K.A. Consequently, Matusak and his warriors had a lot of time to secure their defenses and prepare for the next war. In the meantime, during the years of peace, Matusak replaced all his dead wives with new ones. In fact, most of the warriors in Alexandria took more than one wife because there was a shortage of men after the war. Libya, to their west, was in the same situation. And by the Year 676 K.A., Matusak had over 200 wives and many more concubines. He had been blessed with over 300 children and Alexandria started to prosper. The country continued to trade with Tarshish, as they did during the 13 Year War, and it enabled them access to the other members of "The Alliance."

"Come here, my lovelies!" Matusak ordered. "Our friends from Tarshish have come to join our feast. Welcome them as one of our own, and give them all that they desire!"

Over fifty women welcomed Simon and his party of representatives from Tarshish. They had brought Fruit Pills and Bliss and many other commodities welcomed in Alexandria. In trade, Tarshish gained a valuable ally in wartime, and they traded for exotic foods only found in Kingdom waters. These foods were only available in the countries that bordered the Kingdom, and Alexandria let Tarshish dive and fish off their coastal waters. Alexandria also had precious resources only found in the D.M.R., but they were now available to them at a reasonable price.

Simon's party of five was welcomed as Kings. Each man had all he wanted, and they enjoyed the raucous of a Marauder party. There was fighting, exotic dancing, drinking of wine, and the eating of Bliss. As for the one woman of Simon's party, she was granted a seat to the left of Matusak and was offered any warrior of her choosing.

Later on during the revelry, Matusak came up to Simon and asked, "So what do you think, Simon? Are you pleased? I bet they don't have this type of entertainment in Tarshish?"

"You got that right, Matusak," Simon responded. "The fighting is so intense, and the women are magnificent."

One of the Marauder's women was currently giving him a neck massage and another was rubbing his feet.

"You should come here more often!" Matusak exclaimed. "And next year bring Chieftain James with you. I'd love to challenge him in combat."

"I will tell him of your invitation."

"Ladies, depart from us for the moment," Matusak ordered. "Chieftain Simon and I have important business to talk about."

The women shrugged and went their way and the two men talked business.

"So Simon, is our pact between our two peoples secure?" Matusak asked. "If there is another war, can we depend on you again?"

This time Simon was unyielding and he answered, "Did we fail you during the 13 Year War? Why question our honor?"

"Ha, ha, ha!" Matusak roared, "That's the type of answer I was looking for. Tarshish and Alexandria will be friends forever. And my good friend, you have our support. If the D.M.R. ever dares to step over their bounds, we'll be there by your side in the trenches. We'll talk more in the morning. Now enjoy the party. Bring forth more wine!"

Matusak waved towards the women, and they returned to Simon's side. A flock of women took Simon by his hands and led him towards one of the tents. Simon entered, and the women catered to his private whims and desires.

✳   ✳   ✳   ✳

The ancient saying that idle time is the Devil's playground came to pass during the century of peace. Mankind just had too much time to do as he/she pleased. So man got involved in a lot of deviant behavior. For instance, many people in the Outskirts started to delve into black magic. The occult started to make a revival, and the worship of Satan was not uncommon. All of the sudden, the sacrifice of innocent animals started taking place, and hedonistic societies were popping up everywhere. People would dance into the night under hallucinogenic drugs and being in an altered state of mind became the mainstay in some parts. Many people were getting hooked on drugs like opium and cocaine, but the abuse of the Purple Fruit was the most pronounced in the Outskirts. Tarshish was the greatest exporter of the Bliss, and millions of people were addicted to the fruit. It was becoming a major problem on the planet.

Another form of entertainment was the Great Hunt of leviathan, formerly known as dinosaurs. The leviathans outside the Kingdom were hunted down like beasts, and they became wild again. The godzillas were the first dinosaurs to be hunted to extinction in the Outskirts because of their size. They stood as high as a skyscraper and were tenfold stronger than a bull. These leviathans got most of their food from the sea and usually resided on remote islands. Therefore, men in the Outskirts would locate where the godzillas lived and proceeded to hunt them down. Some hunting parties used laser fire in their pursuits and the godzillas were no match against these groups. These people were usually after souvenirs that they could boast about and place on their walls. The real warriors, however, were in it for the hunt, and they would pursue the godzillas with shield and sword. Many within these parties would die during the hunt, but that was the risk these hunters were willing to take to get their adrenaline pumping. Overall, the hunt of the godzillas was a dishonorable act because naturally these large dinosaurs were gentle beasts and would not hurt a fly, but their lineage learned to fear man because of the hunt, and they became angry beasts.

Dragons were also hunted to extinction in the Outskirts. In the Kingdom, these creatures were mankind's greatest friend. They were an intelligent species that spoke to man and protected the borders from invaders, but in the Outskirts it was a different story. Dragons learned to hate man. Men and women would kill their offspring and hunt them down like beasts, so their friendliness turned to wrath. And once a dragon had turned sour towards man, it was nearly impossible to turn him/her back. Many of these dragons became vengeful, and they raided the villages and cities with fire, but after the advent of laser fire, dragons lost their advantage. They may have been powerful and fast, but they could not dodge fifty laser rifles being fired at them at once, and the species was quickly exterminated from the Outskirts.

There were other great beasts that returned in numbers after the Christ returned to earth like the Moby Dicks and the giant octopuses of the sea, but these species were also hunted down, and during the century of peace, almost all of these great creatures were killed as trophies for man.

It was remarkable how quickly mankind could bring dinosaurs and other species to extinction in the Kingdom Age. Before this era, it took thousands of years to kill off certain species, but in the Millennium it took hundreds. Hand held laser fire was the main reason so many species were murdered off. In the Kingdom, however, hunting was not permitted, and the endangered species were safe in the territory. The more intelligent ones managed to find refuge inside the borders of the Kingdom, but the rest were forced to find safety on their own. Dan and De-Dan did a relatively good job of protecting endangered species, but only in the Kingdom were these species truly safe from rogue hunters.

Chapter 29

The Great Hunt

"Matusak, it is great to see you again," the Leviathan Hunter asked. "How's that arm of yours? That dragon got you good last time. He must have thrown you thirty leagues across the valley."

Matusak laughed and flexed his arm to show he was fully recovered and responded, "Yes, that dragon may have wounded me, but his head is now sitting on my palace wall with several of his friends."

The Leviathan Hunter laughed then asked, "So I heard your hunting godzilla today."

"Yes, it is true, me and twelve of my finest warriors."

"Will you be using laser fire?"

"Ha! Don't mock me!" Matusak warned. "We've come with shield, bow, and sword to bring down the great beast."

"But Matusak, you know that no godzilla has been brought down this way. The chances of success are slim."

"Then we will either die trying or become the first to conquer the great beast."

"Fair enough," the Leviathan Hunter answered. "Have you brought forth the appropriate payment?"

Matusak snapped his fingers and three young Marauder boys carried a large chess of Fruit Pills and Bliss and laid it at the Leviathan Hunter's feet.

"Excellent, it is always good to do business with you. Now hop upon my ship, and I will bring you to the island of one of the last remaining godzillas in the world."

Matusak, along with the twelve Marauders and the servant boys, boarded the ship and set sail for the island. Half a day later, the ship arrived at the island of the godzilla within De-Dan territory. They unloaded their weaponry and proceeded to follow the Leviathan Hunter through the jungle maze. He was an expert tracker and had tattoos all over his body.

The trees reached up to the heavens, and it was obvious that man had not pillaged this island of its resources since the dawn of the Millennium. Without the Leviathan Hunter, the Marauders would have been lost and after a day of hiking, they had still not found the godzilla they were seeking. The men camped the night on the island, and the next morning set out again on their quest after a night's rest under the stars.

Around noon, the Leviathan Hunter started to get sketchy. The Marauders soon realized why when they saw the giant footprints in the mud. They looked like something straight out of "King Kong," and some of the men shook with fear when they gazed upon them.

One of the Marauders asked, "How big do you think this behemoth is?"

The Leviathan Hunter answered, "I'd say about four stories high by the size of the footprints. It's pretty big. I've only seen one this big in my life, and we had laser fire to fend off his attacks."

"Not this time," Matusak boasted. "We will defeat the great beast by cunning and skill."

A half an hour later, the men stumbled upon the godzilla feasting on the leaves of a tree.

Matusak, using Signmonkoala sign language, signaled to the men to stand back and be quiet. One of the young boys, however, wasn't paying attention, and stumbled onto the path where the godzilla could see him. The godzilla immediately stopped, looked down at the boy, and roared. When the servant boy saw the display of prowess, he dashed back behind a rock as the behemoth moved in the boy's direction. The great beast was coming for the boy to kill him, so Matusak signed to the men nearest to the boy and ordered them to fire upon the godzilla to protect him. The godzilla was pierced over and over again by arrows, but they did not slow the beast down. Matusak then ordered the men to take cover and flee towards the cave they saw about 300 meters back. Everyone ran including the Leviathan Hunter as the godzilla pursued them. The young boy who hid amongst the rocks was seized. The godzilla picked him up with his small hands and bit off his head. He then threw the body aside and continued pursuing the other men.

The Marauders ran as fast as they could with the Leviathan Hunter in the lead. Matusak was close behind, but he was trying to watch over the other servant boys as they ran along the path. Matusak hollered, "Run faster!" as the godzilla closed in behind them. Two of the Marauders were overtaken in the chase. One was crushed like a pancake by the godzilla as the other stopped in the path and fired at the godzilla's eyes. He missed but pierced one of the behemoth's ears. This greatly angered the beast, and it proceeded to open its mouth and split the man in two. Its jaws came crashing down, and all that remained of the Marauder was everything below the waistline. The two men may have died, but it did give the rest of the men more time to get away, and they all fled to safety within the cave.

At the mouth of the cave, the men waited for the godzilla to arrive. The beast roared and peered into the cave. The men were all backed into a corner as the beast tried to get its mouth into the cave.

"Okay men, ready your bows," Matusak ordered. "We are going to take out its eyes. On the count of three I want you to fire and take out one of his eyes."

The men pulled back their bows as Matusak cadenced, "Three … two … one … fire!"

The men released their drawstrings, and the godzilla's right eye was struck many times. The beast was blinded in that eye, and the beast pulled its head away from the cave after being hit. The godzilla then started to stagger about for a moment, so Matusak used this opportunity to take advantage of the beast. He charged out of the cave, pulled his sword out, and swung as hard as he could at the godzilla's big toe. Matusak chopped it off with one swing. If it was any other man, he would have never gotten through the bone, but Matusak was the strongest man in the world, and he was successful. The beast roared in pain as the rest of the Marauders came forward and shot at the godzilla's other eye. Once again the beast was hit and now the godzilla was completely blinded, but this didn't stop him from swinging about madly, and the giant beast managed to kill several of the men.

Meanwhile, Matusak used the opportunity to cut off the other big toe, and the beast fell to the ground with a loud thud. The godzilla then tried to get back up, but every time he did, he fell back down.

As the beast floundered about, the Marauders continued their attacks. Matusak ordered, "Aim for the throat!" Each man fired over and over again and pierced the throat of the godzilla with little darts. Pretty soon there were almost a hundred arrows hanging from his throat, and the behemoth stopped moving. It was suffocating. Its chest moved up and down for a while then it stopped moving altogether.

The remaining Marauders celebrated with glee by cheering a childhood chant, "Who-ma-tal-a … Who-ma-tal-a …" over and over again as they danced around the godzilla. The men then went to help those who had fallen.

In the end, five of the Marauders and one of the boys were killed. Three of the other men were injured, but they survived and were healed by Fruit Pills. One of the men who died was brought back to life by a Fruit Pill, but the rest were half eaten or mangled so badly that there was no chance of revival.

Overall, the hunt went well. The Leviathan Hunter didn't expect any of them to survive without lasers, but Matusak and the Marauders proved him wrong. They truly were warriors of renowned, and he was proud to have been one with them on the hunt. And although the Leviathan Hunter had a laser gun hidden under his pant leg in case of emergencies, he never let any of the Marauders know about it. At one point inside the cave, he almost pulled it out, but after the beast was blinded he decided to let the hunt play out, and no one ever found out. If Matusak did discover the laser gun, he would have been called a coward by the tribe, but Matusak never did find out. Instead, his name was later listed as a Marauder who partook in one of the greatest hunts ever recorded in Millennial history, and his name became legendary in all of Alexandria.

Chapter 30

▼

Sightings

During the Century of Peace the Counselor left the Kingdom from time to time and visited the Outskirts. He checked up on things and made straight the crooked paths of injustice and helped those in need. One person the Counselor met up with was King Zzyzx of Dan. It had been a long time since the Counselor had spoken to him. King Zzyzx used to faithfully come each year and present his tribute at the Booth's Festival, but the Counselor had not seen King Zzyzx in over a century. Instead, a representative from Dan would come in Zzyzx's place, so the Counselor decided to make a surprise visit to the region.

The Counselor snuck into King Zzyzx's palace like a secret service operative and posed as a servant in disguise. In fact, the Counselor preferred interacting this way because if He came as Himself people would put on a facade, and a large crowd would gather around Him. In addition, He would not be able to complete His mission as was the case with King Zzyzx. And lately, the Counselor had heard that the King of Dan was ruling unjustly, so He wanted to catch the king in the act.

Posing as a servant cleaning Zzyzx's palace, He observed King Zzyzx as he was making judgments on several cases. The first was a farmer who had his land seized by the government because some rich businessman wanted to build homes on the property. King Zzyzx heard the case and ruled in favor of the businessman because he was a man of authority and power. And although the king knew that the government had no grounds to seize the land, he ruled in favor of the businessman because he was part of the constituency that kept him in power.

Another case involved a man who was unjustly imprisoned. The prisoner was a commoner that wanted to marry one of King Zzyzx's daughters. The two were in love, but because the man was without wealth, the king would not allow his daughter to marry him. At the prisoner's parole hearing, King Zzyzx ruled that the man would remain behind bars.

A third case involved one of the forty-nine magistrate's teenage sons. He had murdered another boy in a dispute, and the parents of the murdered boy wanted justice for his death. King Zzyzx, however, let the teenager go free because he was the son of one of the ruling authorities.

After the ruling on the final case was made, the Counselor came forward. He said, "In all three cases you knew who was right and who was wrong, but you chose to rule in favor of the wicked. Will you please explain why?"

King Zzyzx laughed, "I don't answer to you. Guards, remove this man immediately!"

The guards stepped forward, but as they did, the Counselor started to take off His disguise. Once King Zzyzx realized who it was, he turned white as a ghost, and the guards froze like statues.

"I'm disappointed in you, Zzyzx," the Counselor stated. You had more potential than any of the rulers in the Outskirts, but you've become as corrupt as a totalitarian dictator. Hence, I'm going to make you a leper for a spell as retribution for all the suffering you have caused. You will remain on the throne, and hopefully you will learn from the error of your ways. But be forewarned, I will be watching you from afar. And once I believe you have suffered enough and restored justice with injustice, I will restore your health."

The Counselor departed from the palace and as soon as He walked out the door, lesions began to form on King Zzyzx's skin, and he became a leper.

After seven years of just rule, the leprosy went into remission on King Zzyzx, and he was declared clean by the physicians. As for the Counselor, he departed Dan and went south to De-Dan and helped people at the bottom of the world.

In De-Dan, there were sightings of a sojourner who did great miracles. Some said He was a healer that could perform great wonders. Others said He was a wise-man that spoke great words. And some knew right away that it was the Counselor, and they welcomed Him into their home.

As always, when the Counselor left these people's dwellings, He requested that they not tell anyone that He had come. In most cases, the people he visited or helped would keep His secret, but sometimes the truth about the Counselor's deeds would leak out, and the stories about Him would be made known.

In Native Nodian territory, a story about a man who did great deeds started to circulate amongst the Natives. One of these stories was passed along in the village by a young boy who had witnessed a great feat.

"Mom! Dad!" the ten-year-old yelled as he came into the house. "Mom! Dad! Where are you?"

The boy looked in the kitchen and living room then heard faint whispers from upstairs, "We're in the bedroom."

The boy ran upstairs and rushed into his parents' bedroom.

"Mom, Dad, you're not going to believe this," the boy said excitedly, "but I just saw a miracle."

The mother said, "Okay, calm down, and tell us what happened."

The boy breathed in deep then began his story.

"Me and my friends were crossing the Bridge of No Tomorrows when suddenly ..."

The mother interrupted, "Do you mean that broken down, wooden bridge that's been deemed unsafe?"

"Yes, yes that bridge," the boy continued, but the mother interrupted again.

"How many times have you been told to stay off that bridge? A decade ago a boy fell from that thing and died."

The boy rolled his eyes, but this time the father interrupted.

"When I was younger, we used to cross that bridge all the time."

"But that was decades ago," the mother argued. "And since then the engineers determined that it was unsafe."

"Mom, will you let me finish the story?" the boy said agitated.

"Yes Mom, the father mocked, "Will you let him finish his story?"

The mother of the boy suddenly grew quiet as the boy continued.

"We were about half-way across the bridge when little Suzie, Torelli's sister, slipped and almost fell to her death."

"Oh no!" the mother interrupted again. "I thought it was just you and the boys?"

"It was, but Torelli was watching over his little sister, so she had to cross with us."

"She must be six-years-old," the mother stated. "The nerve of that boy to bring her out onto that bridge."

"Well apparently one of the wood panels broke as she was making her way, and she fell. She was holding on for dear life. It was just like one of those adventure movies, so Torelli tried to reach down and grab her with his arm, but he wasn't strong enough to pull her up, and she slipped out of his grasp."

"Oh please don't go on!" the mother exclaimed. "Tell me she didn't fall into the gorge."

"She was about to, but suddenly out of nowhere, a man flying on a dragon swept down and caught her before she fell to her death."

"A man on a dragon?" the father questioned. "There hasn't been a dragon in Nod in over a hundred years."

"Yes, a dragon!" the boy explained. "I swear to God and hope to die if I'm not telling you the truth."

The parents started to take their son seriously at these words because he usually was not one to lie.

"What was the man's name?" the father asked.

"I don't know, but when we got to the other side, he said we need to be more careful and warned us to stay off the bridge because the ropes were weakening. Then he was gone. His dragon breathed fire, and he flew away."

"How'd you get home?" the father asked. "And have you seen the man before?"

"No, I don't know who he was, but Jeremiah said he looked a lot like the Counselor. As for getting home, we had to walk all the way to Gorge Bridge and cross over there."

Tales like these were occurring everywhere in the Outskirts. There was a man who performed great deeds, and the legends spread from east to west and north to south across the globe. He was like Batman of Gotham, Zorro of colonial California, and Hercules of ancient Greece. Even in the D.M.R., stories were being told about a great man riding on horseback who stood for freedom and justice. One story went as follows:

In the Land of Kamchatka, the wild west of the D.M.R. lived a tyrant of the land. He rigged elections, bribed judges, and disregarded Constitutional law. He tortured and murdered people to get what he wanted, and had a gang of men to do his bidding. The common folk, however, were in fear of this tyrant, and no one stood up to challenge his authority until the man riding on the white horse came to town ...

By and by the story goes on, and it reads like a poorly written western. Ultimately, the man on the white horse kills the tyrant and all of his henchmen, and the town is freed of corruption. But the real reason the story became so popular was because it was interpreted as being an allegory. The tyrant represented Gog Inc. The henchmen symbolized the Libertines, and the man on the white horse represented the ideals of a people searching for freedom and justice. Likewise, some interpreted the man on the white horse as symbolizing the Counselor who will one day return to the North and set the captives free.

Professors at the Universities in the D.M.R. would teach this interpretation much to the disdain of Kasca and the Libertines. The real reason a book like this gained so much notoriety was because there was an undercurrent of intellectuals in the D.M.R. who despised what the Republic had become. Many of them believed that democracy was a now misnomer in Magog as the people watched their freedoms get violated one by one. During the Century of Peace, people still practiced freedom of speech, but it was dangerous to speak out against Gog Inc. or the Libertines. And it was becoming more and more common for people who voiced their concerns to disappear or be locked away for a long time. The freedom to practice your own religion was also becoming difficult. Those who still believed in the Counselor up north wanted to freely worship and praise His name, but they were feeling a clampdown from the Libertines. The government was watching these groups, and a lot of D.M.R. citizens felt like their rights were being violated.

In general, there were many stories being passed around that were based upon the great deeds that the Counselor was doing throughout the earth. Sometimes He would ride on dragon's wings. Other times He would trot along on horses' hooves, but overall, He was helping people and doing His job as the supreme ruler of the earth. In the D.M.R., many positive stories about the Counselor were being told; they were just being conveyed in figurative language. This was the only way to get the story out because people realized that if they spoke openly, they were in danger of being black-listed or imprisoned.

CHAPTER 31

▼

AUTOBIOGRAPHY (GROWING UP)

The following excerpt is taken from *The Autobiography of Queen Sheba*. Be forewarned before reading any further that some of the subject matter is graphic due to sexual content.

✳   ✳   ✳   ✳

When I was a child, I grew up in the court of King Menelik. He was a fair ruler. Although I did not know him well, I did observe his ways. He was quite the ladies man, and his sexual exploits were deviant to say the least. He had his own dungeon built in the palace filled with all sorts of toys and odd machinery. It was something straight out of an Anne Rice novel. As a child, we were not permitted to enter the dungeon, but there were ways around such rules. My closest sibling, Franklin, had found a secret passage behind the stairs that would enable us to spy on the events that were taking place down there. Much to our surprise, we discovered that our father was a closet sadist. He derived sexual gratification from controlling others and inflicting pain on them. At our young age, this was a bit too much to handle, but being children we decided to play out some of the events that took place in the underground chamber.

One day, when no one was watching, Franklin and I went out into the garden with some rope and a wooden spoon I stole from the kitchen. Being one-year older than Franklin, I ordered my half brother to strip off his clothes and bear hug one of the trees. At first he was resistant, but I threatened to have Andrew, my older brother, beat him up if he didn't do as I said. Franklin complied. I then proceeded to tie him to the tree and started to poke him with a wooden spoon like I saw my father do with a cane to his fifth wife. This was fun for a while, torturing him with a spoon, but then an idea came into my head. I saw a feather on the grass, so I proceeded to pick it up and tickle Franklin. It was quite fun and Franklin kept saying, "Don't, you're tickling me. I can't take it anymore!" he screamed, but I kept tormenting him anyway. I then took the spoon and started to spank him on the buttocks. He yelled, "Don't, that hurts! Stop it, Sheba!" And he squirmed about trying to avoid my blows. But I wouldn't stop. I kept hitting him over and over again, and pretty soon, red welts started to show all over his body. He begged me, "Please Sheba, I'll do anything just stop hitting me," but I wouldn't stop. I was so entranced with my sudden power and authority over another human being that I even peed myself without knowing it. But then I heard something. It was one of the servants' voices, and he was coming our way. At first I thought about running and leaving Franklin there, but I knew I would get in trouble, so instead I quickly untied him, and we both made a run for it. When the servant arrived at our previous destination, we were no where to be found, but he did find a bunch of rope tied around a tree.

As I grew older, my deviant behavior became even more pronounced. I noticed that I enjoyed controlling other people. I loved having authority over others. In my teenage years, I got even worse. Franklin became my own personal toy, and he did anything I commanded. He was my puppet on a string, and I actually think he enjoyed it. Looking back, I realize now, that Franklin was a true submissive. He loved to be beaten and taken advantage of.

One time during a house party at the palace, I coerced one of the boys to come back with me to my bed chambers. The boy thought he was going to get lucky that night, but instead I was expanding my horizons. Years earlier, I stole the key to the dungeon and had a copy made, so I led him down to the underground chamber beneath the stairs instead of my room. Once inside, he was floored by the scene. He couldn't believe his eyes. I then kissed him hard on the lips, ran my hand over my chest and said, "Do you want to have some real fun?" I was holding handcuffs in my other hand and swinging them in the air beside me. The young man didn't know what to do. He just stood there with his mouth gaping open. He then asked, "What do you have in mind?" I just smiled and started to take off his shirt. He resisted, but I was forceful and ripped off a few of his buttons. He pushed me away and said, "Don't!" but I slapped him across the face and said, "Are you scared?" He said, "No!" and to prove his worth, he came towards me aggressively and started sucking on my neck. I let him have his way for a moment, but as he was kissing me, I hand-cuffed one of his wrists. He stopped for a moment, contemplating his fate, but then gave into his desire. I smiled at him and slowly led him over to one of the restraints. Eventually I got his clothes off and tied him down to the table as the two of us were kissing and rubbing up against each other. I made the illusion like I was going to give him oral pleasure, but once I realized he was firmly restrained, I rose from his lap and walked out of the room. He hollered, "Hey wait, where are you going? Get back here, you bitch!" I shut the door behind me and dead-bolted the door.

Fifteen minutes later I was back in the room with Franklin trailing behind me on a leash. I knew all sorts of thoughts were spinning through the boy's head. He probably wondered if he was going to be taken captive, raped, or even murdered, but I would not say a word. The boy kept pleading, "I thought we were going to make love. I thought you and I had a connection. Why are you doing this to me?" I did not respond. Instead, I got all my toys ready and locked Franklin to an adjacent table and made him kneel before me. Finally I said, "Today is going to be a day that will change your life forever." I then turned on a holo-recorder and teasingly said, "Smile for the camera." The boy spit in my face in protest, but I merely wiped it off and said, "You're going to pay for that."

I proceeded to whip, torture, and abuse the boy. I allowed Franklin to kiss my feet occasionally, but mostly I had him there as an observer. As I was entertaining myself with the boy, I was so excited I had an orgasm in my pants. I also noticed that the boy had a hard-on that reached up to the heavens. I knew he was scared, but I also knew he was enjoying himself. Even when I had him buttered up, he remained stiff. After an hour or so of continuous play, I grew bored with the boy, so I ordered Franklin to finish him off. Franklin did not resist. He had been trained well in the past and proceeded to do as I wished.

All of this was being recorded, but once I had fully taken the boy's pride away, I turned off the camera and stated. "If you tell anybody or seek revenge, I'm going to have this recording leaked around school, and you'll be called a homosexual for the rest of your life. Do you understand?" The boy nodded yes. "Let me hear you say it!" I demanded. "I understand, Mistress Sheba." I then kissed the boy intimately on the lips and whispered in his ear. I uttered, "Thanks for playing with me today. I truly enjoyed myself. I think you did too. If you want to play again, let me know. I'll see you around school." I then ordered, "Franklin, clean up this mess. Here are the keys. Let him go in ten minutes."

I don't think the boy knew what to do with himself after that incident, and I'm sure I thoroughly upset his world. I was out of control, and he was just one of many play things that I took advantage of throughout the years. I manipulated men, women, siblings, servants, and even children. I had them do all sorts of bizarre stunts for me. The list must number in the hundreds. I'm surprised no one has sought revenge against me, but I've discovered people are obsessed with their reputation, and they'll do anything to keep it unblemished. I must also give credit where it is due. Franklin was a wonderful slave for me. During my rise to power, years later, he even killed for me. The Royal Guard also did a fine job of protecting me because I literally had the commander tied up in strings.

In writing about my exploits, I want to make it perfectly clear that I am not writing this down to titillate you. I'm trying to show you how out of control my life had become. I was power mad. I was ruthless. And as I grew older, I used my skills of manipulation and sabotage to seize the throne. I was proud beyond measure. I thought that I was invincible, and not until I met the Counselor had I ever served another or kneeled down upon my knees.

Chapter 32

Musings

Esmeralda had been living at Kasca's estate for some time now. She had her own quarters on the west-wing, next to Kasca's room, and it afforded her the privacy she required when she needed it. The room looked like a V.I.P. suite in a hotel. It had a walk in shower, a hot-tub, and an elaborate view that looked out on the garden and pool. The room also had its own kitchen and entryway.

This morning, she woke up thinking about Patmos like every other morning for a very long time now, but this time she woke-up badly missing him. She needed to talk to him. She needed to hold him, but Patmos had been gone for centuries now, and no matter how hard she tried to put him out of her mind, she remembered him. She had only been with the Professor for seven years, but he was still the love of her life. Esmeralda had loved others over the centuries, but never as intimately as she did with Patmos. He was her soul-mate, and there was no other. Nonetheless, Zeze was starting to forget what the Professor looked like. His image was fading in her mind, and she could no longer remember his scent. So she went to her walk-in closet, dug behind some old shoes, and found a box that contained all her memoirs of Patmos and her.

Inside the box, she found love letters and pictures of old. One picture taken was at her birthday celebration. There was a cake in front of her with candles. She was smiling. Patmos' arm was around her shoulder. As she gazed at the picture, she remembered how his blond hair was always messed up and out of order. She remembered his fair skin, and the freckles that formed on his nose. But mostly she remembered his dark eyes, and how they could hypnotize her if she gazed too long into them.

Zeze proceeded to look through the pictures. With every one of them she could name the date and place where it was taken. She had a sharp mind when it came to remembering dates and special occasions. She then found her old diary from a vanished time when she wandered the province of Gomar. Zeze looked at the diary. She could smell its musky pages and was afraid to open it. There were too many sad memories in that book. Most of it was written right after the gates to the Kingdom were closed in 262, and she had left the D.M.R. behind. She stared at the diary for a moment longer then finally decided to read its contents. Page one read as follows:

I arrived in Barcelona today after taking a train through Beth-Togar-Mah and Western Europe. I hoped by returning home to my old stomping grounds before the Kingdom Age I'd feel some sort of a connection, but it's not the case. The buildings aren't the same. Catalan is a dead language, and only a few still speak Spanish. I don't even know where my old home used to be. The landscape has radically changed. Don't get me wrong, New Barcelona is far more beautiful than it used to be, but there was something to be said about the old city. In the meantime, I have to find a place to rest my head. Money is not a problem. I have plenty of credits, but I don't know anyone here. I'm going to have to start all over. Maybe I'll find a job at a café or bar and work as a waitress or something. It will help me to get acclimated. Anyway, there's some annoying man staring at me. I got to get going. I'll write more tomorrow ...

Zeze read through more of her pages of her diary then stumbled upon an entry that reminded her of Patmos and how melancholy she was after his loss.

When I wake in the morning I can barely move. I ache all over, and I can't stop crying. I don't know if I'll be able to make it into work today. I can barely move. I don't even know how I'm making this pen scribble across the page. I'm a wreck. I've never been this depressed in my life. I know no one. I have no friends, and my love is gone forever. Yesterday I tried to escape to an imaginary holoscreen world at one of the play factories, but I couldn't role-play very well, and I had to keep restarting the program. I just couldn't get into the script. The story was predictable, and the hero was no substitute for Patmos. Damn, I miss him. Where are you, my love? Please God, bring him home to me. I don't know if I can live another day like this. The pain is unbearable. I feel so lost. It's like I've lost my soul. I'm like a child whose wandered too far from home and can't find her way home. If I took my life, my spirit would wander the caverns of this city forever. O Lord, help me. I need you now. I don't know if I can go on any further ...

As Esmeralda read the pages, tears came to her eyes. She remembered how suicidal she was at the time, and all those memories came rushing back into her head. She then broke down and started to weep. She must have cried for over an hour thinking about Patmos, thinking about her life, and remembering events like they happened yesterday. Finally she found the courage to read on, and she came across an entry that brought a smile to her face.

Lately, I've been writing about family and friends and some of the crazy experiences we've had together. Today I'm going to write about Patmos. I know I've written about him before, but all the entries have been sad and depressing. This time I'm going to write about a funny story that happened to both of us back in the D.M.R. Maybe writing about the good times will lift me from this despair. Anyhow, here's the tale:

Patmos and I were walking around Liberty Square and a new shop had just opened. It was called Liberty's Pawn Shop of the 21st Century. So we decided to go in, and what we discovered is that the whole place is filled with relics from the Old Days. There were television sets, personal computers, ancient flags representing the nations, and we just sort of got lost in the place. At any rate, we both were walking around and I suddenly lost track of Patmos. I said to myself, "Where did he go?" I looked around further and found him talking to the owner of the place and looking at a gun. Patmos was so excited. He hollered, "Ze, come over here! You got to see this thing." So I walked over to him and looked at the object in his hand. I said, "Big deal, it's just a pistol." "Just a pistol?" he said to me. "Don't you realize this is a vintage twenty-two firearm from the 20th Century, and it's American made." I said, "That's nice, honey, but can we go now? I'm kind of hungry." "Go! We can't go! This is something I've wanted for as long as I can remember. I haven't seen one of these things in over 250 years." Just as the Professor said that, the owner pulled something from the drawer. Patmos yelled, "No! It can't be!" The owner just shook his head and said, "That's right." "Alright, you've made your sale. How much for the gun, holster, and bullets?"

To make a long story short, he bought the gun, and as soon as he got home, he took out a bunch of empty beer cans and stacked them on the fence. He was having the time of his life out there hooting a howling like a kid, so I just gave in and joined him. He gave me the gun, showed me how to shoot, and I shot two of those cans down. And to tell you the truth, I think I was a better shooter than him.

By and by, we finally had our lunch, and I had him working on something around the house. Anyway, we were out back and there was this thin sheath of metal that needed to have a hole drilled in it. I forgot what it was for. So I said, "I'll go get the drill from the shed, and you can drill a hole through it." But he said, "No, no we don't need the drill when I got this thing." He patted his gun which was now in the holster around his waist and said, "I'll shoot a hole through the metal using this thing." I laughed and remarked, "You can't shoot a hole in it with that." He said, "Want to bet?" And he stepped back about ten meters, strutting as he went. He looked like a cowboy in one of those old western movies. He then ordered in a southern accent, "Get out of the way, woman! I'm gonna shoot a hole in this thing." I quickly scuttled out of the way, and he proceeded to line up his shot. He pulled the trigger, but the shot ricocheted off the metal sheath and hit him in the belly. He cried, "I've been hit!" At first I laughed thinking he was making a joke, but I stopped laughing after I heard him say, "No Zeze, I really shot myself." I rushed over to him and noticed there was blood dripping from his shirt. I exclaimed, "Move your hand, so I can see!" I noticed he really did shoot himself, but it didn't look that bad. In fact, it turned out to only be a flesh wound. Nevertheless, I rushed inside and got the first aide kit. Inside were several Fruit Pills, so I gave him one to eat and proceeded to tape up his wound. I then rushed him over to the hospitable in the hovercar, and they fixed him up. They said the injuries were minor and that it was nothing to worry about.

The whole time in the emergency room, Patmos and I were laughing so loud we had bellyaches. We kept saying, "I've been hit!" and we were in hysterics. The whole hospital thought we were out of our minds, but we didn't care. And looking back at those days, we were having the time of our lives. It's a story I will always remember.

After reading the entry, Esmeralda started to feel better about everything. She proceeded to read the rest of the diary, and she was impressed that she was able to live through such dark times. Although a lot of the memories were sad, it was good therapy for Esmeralda to read about her past. And after she was done, she removed all of her clothes and took a long, hot bath.

Chapter 33

The Dragon Wars

"Patmos, I've heard many stories about Zeze. I've heard everything there was to tell about your first and second wife. I know all about your children, but how come you never talk about Kasca?" Sierra asked.

Patmos didn't answer. Instead he shrugged it off like he didn't hear what she was saying.

"Pat, I'm serious. How come you never say anything about your old friend?"

"I don't know," Patmos shrugged. "I just don't like talking about him."

"C'mon, I know you two had a falling out, but tell me a story about the Prince of Rosh," Sierra said. "We've read so much about Kasca in the history books, but books never really tell who you are as a person."

"Some other time," Patmos tried to avoid the subject. "I'm not in the mood right now."

"C'mon Pat, if you tell me a story, I'll rub you down real good with a Thai Massage and finish it off with a happy ending," Sierra persuaded.

Patmos thought for a moment but didn't give in so easily, so Sierra started rubbing his shoulders and running her hand through his hair.

She said, "I promise I'll make it worth your while," and continued massaging his shoulders then stopped momentarily.

Patmos was seduced by her touch, so he said, "Okay one story," and the Professor began his tale.

"During college, Kasca was a renowned basketball star. He led the University of Jerusalem to three championships and put the basketball team on the map. He really was a great player. He was almost automatic from the outside, and he could run an offense like no other. As everyone knows, Kasca went on to play ten years in the Millennial Basketball League and topped off his career with a championship before he went onto teach at the University."

"It's absolutely amazing the natural talents this guy was given. He's a genius, gifted in sports, and was named one of the most beautiful people by Kingdom Magazine back in the day. Not only that, he is witty, appears humble in front of the camera, and has women at his beckon call."

"What do you mean 'appears' humble?" Sierra asked.

"Lets be honest, Kasca always had a big head. He was brilliant and all, but sometimes he could be condescending."

"Really?" Sierra asked again.

Patmos shook his head in agreement.

"So we had to bring Kasca down to earth."

"Eww, I like this story," Sierra said gleefully and she sat up Indian style on the bed, looking at the Professor with alert, eager eyes.

"We did this by inviting him to partake in the Dragon Wars."

"No way, you've got to be kidding me!" Sierra exclaimed. "You were part of the Dragon Wars!"

"That's right, my dear," Patmos proudly stated. "In fact, I was one of the originators, and I'm a pretty good rider, if I don't mind patting myself on the back a little."

"No way! You're making this up aren't you?" Sierra questioned.

"I'm afraid not, darling."

Sierra sat there flabbergasted as Patmos continued.

"As you know from the history books, the dragons didn't always get along that well. Different kin fought one another and many of them were dying. It got out of control at one point, and some thought the dragons would fight themselves into extinction. So some of the minority within the 144 Elders got together and came up with a resolution to solve their disputes. Of course, I could go into depth about who was there and what happened, but I would have to kill you, so I won't tell you all the intricate details."

Sierra smiled knowing that Patmos had twisted the truth a little. She could always tell when the Professor was lying.

"To make a long story short, we met with the dragons from rival kin and came up with a solution. We called it the Dragon Wars."

Sierra sat there shaking her head in disbelief then Patmos teased, "And that's about it. We asked Kasca to join in the fights, and he became one of the gladiators."

Sierra stood there dumbfounded scratching her braided head. "That's it! What do you mean that's it? C'mon, tell me the rest of the story."

"I'm getting kind of tired," Patmos bluffed. "I'll have to tell you the rest of it some other time."

"Oh, no you don't, you son of a bitch," Sierra slurred and tackled him on the bed.

"You're going to tell me the rest of the story right now!" she demanded as she proceeded to wrestle with the Professor. Patmos was letting her win as she jumped on top of him and had the upper hand. But Patmos quickly turned the tables on her by twisting her arm in a weird way and taking advantage. Within a few seconds he was on top. Sierra was struggling with all her might, but the Professor was merely laughing.

"You're ... going ... to ... tell ... me the rest of the story," Sierra demanded or I'm going to ..."

"You're going to what?" And he tortured her some more.

Patmos laughed at her then let her go. They were both breathing hard on the bed for a few minutes as they captured their breath.

Sierra then asked gently, "Please Patmos, tell me the rest of the story.

She kissed him intimately on the forehead and begged, "Please, pretty please with sugar on top."

"Okay, you win," Patmos conceded.

Sierra jumped up from her position and sat at the Professor's side expectantly waiting for the rest of the tale.

"Now because the dragon wars were never approved by the 144 Elders or the Counselor, we had to fight our battles in secret. Looking back now, I'm sure the King knew all about it, but He looked the other way. He did that once in awhile. He let us work things out on our own. Anyway, if two rival kin of dragons had a dispute with one another, they would settle their differences on the battlefield. That was the agreement. The dragons would satisfy their thirst for combat, but they were not permitted to bludgeon one another to death."

"It sounds so violent," Sierra interrupted.

"It was. We were forced to wear full armor to protect us from the fire and clashing javelins. It was something straight out of medieval times, only these battles took place in the air, and it was bloody. The rules were as follows: As soon as one of the gladiators fell off his dragon, the serpent would have to leave the battle and vice-versa. Sometimes the battles would be one on one or two on two, but most of the time it was five on five like a basketball game. And others times when one kin of dragons had declared war on another, it would be all out war. Hundreds of dragons would be in the air fighting each other. It was pure insanity!"

Patmos looked away. Tears were starting to form in his turquoise eyes. He was obviously upset about something.

"Are you okay, honey?" Sierra asked as she reached out to him with her hand. "What's wrong?"

Patmos started to get congested after getting teary-eyed, so he grabbed a tissue and blew his nose.

"Yes, I'm alright. Like I said before the battles were bloody. We lost a lot of good men in the Dragon Wars and many fine dragons. I lost one of my best friends in a battle. His name was Silverstreak of the Silver Kin. That's the kin I was a part of. He was my brother. I rode him for years. He sacrificed his life to save my own, and I will never forget him."

"I didn't realize how intimate the relationship could be with a dragon," Sierra said.

"It's true. He was my best friend. He watched my back, and I watched his for almost a decade. There's a camaraderie that comes with fighting alongside someone in battle. Only a soldier who has been through the trenches with his mates would understand."

Sierra sat and listened. By looking at Patmos' face, she could see how important Silverstreak was to the Professor.

"At any rate, back to the story; this was supposed to be about Kasca, not me, so let me change directions." Patmos went on, "Many of the Silver Kin knew of Kasca's prowess on the court, so we decided to see if he wanted to join our kin. He did, and he learned how to ride a dragon. Of course, he had to go through his cuts and bruises like everyone else, but he ended up becoming a fine rider."

"What do you mean?" Sierra inquired. "He wasn't the best one out there as expected?"

"Let's just say he had a slow learning curve, but once he mastered the skill of riding, he became quite a gladiator. And this was expected. After all, many of us Old Timers had been riding horses from childhood. Jumping on the back of a dragon was easy because it was so similar. That's why I think you'd be an excellent dragon rider. You've been around horses your whole life, but Kasca was a city slicker most of his days. He had only been on the back of a horse a few times and riding on the back of a dragon was far more difficult, especially with armor and weaponry."

"Interesting ... How often would you get hurt?"

"It all depends on the rider and the dragon. In the beginning I had my share of injuries, but I had less and less as the Dragon Wars went on. Thank God for Fruit Pills! But that's why Kasca had to sit out so much during his pro years. His was dragon fighting on the side. If the league would have found out, he would have been heavily fined and maybe kicked out of the league."

"So how did the Dragon Wars end?"

"The history books pretty much tell the story. Once citizens started to hear about the wars, people were coming out in droves to watch the combat. It was like cock-fighting in the old days. It was gory as hell. Almost everyone loved it, but the moral majority took away all the fun, and the Dragon Wars came to a close."

"It was probably a good thing though, don't you think?" Sierra stated. "At least this way people and dragons weren't dying in the wars any longer."

"Give me a break, Sierra!" the Professor shouted. "Do you think the kin of dragons stopped fighting after the 144 Elders banned the sport? No, the dragons went back to their old ways and more lives were lost. At least back when we were fighting, there was some sort of civility. If a gladiator or dragon went down, you were not permitted to continue the attack. That was the rule, and everyone abided by it. And if you didn't, you were excommunicated from your kin and dishonored!"

"Okay, old man, relax," Sierra teased, "I'm just making an observation."

Patmos smiled back. His anger died down realizing he was getting upset about nothing.

"So how do the Signmonkoala fit into the picture?"

"About a hundred or so years later, the Signmonkoala came to the Kingdom, and they lived alongside the dragons. They became fast friends, and the Signmonkoala replaced us as riders," the Professor explained. "After all, they are much better equipped to ride dragons. They're small like a jockey. They can fall from hundreds of meters in the air and not break a bone. They have claws that can hold on tight to a dragon, and they are tough as hell. It just made sense that they took over where we left off."

"And when did dragon fighting become a sport?"

"About a decade later. New rules were created that made the fighting safer, but the dragons could still take out their aggressions on one another. Nowadays it's based on points and scoring like soccer, but that's how the Dragon Wars began."

"So who's your team?" Sierra asked nonchalantly as she started putting lotion on her dark skin.

"Who's my team?" Patmos answered as he pointed to the wall with a Silver Kin banner."

"I'm just kidding," Sierra laughed. "Every Thursday night you're glued to the holoscreen. You think I didn't notice?"

Patmos laughed. He tackled her on the bed and said, "So how about that backrub?"

Sierra got up, crawled on top of him, and went to work.

Chapter 34

Campfire

Annually, the O' Donohue's would have a family gathering at Jacob and Hannah's estate. Hundreds of people would attend this giant backyard barbeque to keep the family united. Even descendents that had moved to far off lands like Sheba and De-Dan would return each year to Tarshish for the family reunion. At the party there was swimming, horse-shoes, softball, eating, and much more. There were so many people these days that Hannah decided to have the event catered, and it lifted the burden off her shoulders. This way she could socialize and have fun too. At the end of the evening, most of the grown-ups would gather around a large bonfire, tell stories, eat Bliss, and drink into the night. It was Jacob's favorite part of the gathering because he loved to tell stories. Sometimes he repeated his tales, but no one cared. A story repeated a year earlier would probably have a different twist to it anyway because Jacob loved to embellish his tales.

"Hey James, remember that time back before the Millennial Age that you and I were jumping from building to building in London," Jacob asked.

"Of course, how could I forget?" his bigger brother responded. "We were young fools back then."

"Yes we were, but it sure was fun as hell!" Jacob exclaimed. The younger brother then addressed everyone and started to tell his story.

"This event happened back when James and I were back in our early twenties. It was years before Mahdi's rise to power. We were drunk as skunks partying in London. I'm sure we were high on something. At any rate, we were on top of some roof. They were having a roof party above one of the flats, and being brothers we were always in competition with one another. So I yelled, 'I bet I can jump from this roof to the next one over. Care to wager twenty quid?' James was standing on the edge of the roof, so he looked down at the ground, three flights down, then over at the other roof. He said, 'Sure, but if you fall, I'm not picking your broken bones off the pavement.' 'We all got to die sometime,' I said and moved closer to the edge. I then stood on the periphery of the roof. Suddenly I caught many people's attention. I bet they were hoping for a suicide attempt. When Jane, my girlfriend at the time, saw me, she yelled, 'Jacob, what are you doing? Get down from the ledge at once!' I slurred at her, rocked back and forth a bit then leaped towards the other roof. There was a sudden hush at the party. It felt like everything was going in slow motion. I heard some girl scream, 'Oh no!' as I landed on the other side. I fell, did a summersault, and rose back to my feet with my hands in the air screaming. 'Yes!' I shouted and everyone at the party was hooting and howling. I then yelled at James, 'Care to make it double or nothing?' I remember him saying, 'Yes' as frankly as he could, seeming somewhat pissed off that he was out twenty pounds and that his brother didn't fall to his death. I then hollered, 'If you make it too, we'll call it even!' James looked down again at the street below. He gulped down the beer he was drinking to build up his confidence then stood on the edge of the roof. This time, everyone at the party was watching, including the people inside. The boys were chanting, 'Jump, jump, jump!' as the girls looked on in wonder. James then leaped to the other side. He didn't even fall. He landed on his feet and grunted, 'Ahhhh!' The whole party was in hysterics. James and I were also going crazy. James then rushed to the far end of the roof and looked at the next building. It was exactly the same distance to the next one over. In fact, the whole street was in equilibrium. James then rushed back over to me and said, 'I'll bet you a hundred quid I can jump five buildings before you can. I took out my wallet and looked inside. I had just enough. James may have been bigger and stronger than me, but I was faster than him, so I figured I could beat him based on speed, but did I have the balls? The people at the party were looking at us strangely then suddenly they heard James yell, 'On your marks, get set, go!' We both raced to the other side and leapt to the next building like we were in some James Bond movie. And we jumped again and again until we reached the fifth building."

Jacob then ended his story, shaking his head in disbelief. He said, "We sure were imbeciles back then and looked over at James.

One of the relatives then blurted out, "So who won?"

James was smiling from ear to ear as Jacob declared, "That bastard beat me." And everyone started to laugh. They could tell that Jacob was still upset about losing that race.

After Jacob was done telling his tale, Hannah jumped right in. She was sitting next to her husband with her hand on his leg. She said, "I believe him too. Have you seen these two go at each other?"

Everyone shook their head at the campfire, acknowledging the obvious.

"But I've also seen these guys stick up for one another too."

Hannah then proceeded to tell her story.

"This was back before we had left for Tarshish. We were still living in the Kingdom, and I had only known these two for a few weeks. At any rate, we were out drinking at one of the pubs after a long day of making plans for coming out here and colonizing the nation. We were just minding our own business when in walks Matusak and a bunch of the Marauders. They hadn't left for Egypt yet, and they were real jerks at the time. They thought they could do whatever they wanted. When James and Jacob saw them, they both cussed and nodded at one another.

Anyway, a couple hours passed, and it was nearing closing time. Our group was playing darts, and the Marauders were shooting pool. The Marauders were getting more and more boisterous and started slapping some of the girls' fannies. Tensions were also building in the room. Anyone in touch with their emotions could feel the temperature rising. Even so, as I was going to shoot my turn, one of the Marauders was returning from the loo. As he passed, he spanked me on the behind and laughed as he smiled at his friends. When Jacob saw this, his eyes turned red; I'd never seen him get this angry before. As the Marauder was continuing on his way, Jacob bumped into him, smacking him real hard in the shoulder. The Marauder was much bigger than Jacob, so he shouted, 'Watch it buddy!' and tried to pass again. But Jacob wouldn't get out of the way. Instead, he smiled at the Marauder with an evil grin. The Marauder then tried to throw a bunch, but Jacob grabbed his arm and kneed him in the belly. The Marauder fell to the floor, and instantly his friends joined in. There must have been a dozen of them that rushed to his aide. When James saw this, he belted two of them in the face and knocked them to the floor. The other Marauders closed in on Jacob, and he knocked another one of them down as the rest of them rushed the two brothers. The fight ensued. James and Jacob were losing. They were way outnumbered, but they held their ground. The fight eventually came to a close when Matusak decided to get involved. He grabbed two of his friends and lifted them off Jacob and threw them aside. When the others saw this, they let James go. At that point

I'm sure James and Jacob thought they were dead meat, but Matusak didn't do anything. Instead, he lifted the brothers off the floor and patted them on the backs. He ordered, 'Lets go!' to his men and smiled at James and Jacob as he left."

James then interrupted the story.

"That was the first time I ever met Matusak," James stated. "And from that point forward, the Marauders didn't mess with us. There was mutual respect amongst our clans when we were in the pub together. "And when I told that story to Matusak, a century or so later, he laughed. He remembered the story and the events. He just didn't realize it was us, the O'Donohue brothers. In fact, I think that fight was the bond that brought our countries together as allies. Without it, I don't think Matusak would have trusted or respected us."

The campfire celebration continued for sometime after that. There was more storytelling, drinking, and camaraderie amongst the family. By the end of the night, James and Jacob had their arms around each other. They were singing a song Jacob wrote long ago. They were all out of tune like Viking warriors after a night of wine and gluttony. They chanted, *"Our fathers fought the Germans & we survived the grief. We'll make it through a thousand years without the apple from the Tree…"*

Chapter 35

The End of Peace

In 677 K.A., the Marauders invaded the Algiers territory and ended the 100 years of peace in the Outskirts. It was a carefully planned offensive by Matusak and his generals. They saw a weak spot in the Algiers defenses, and they took advantage of it. The Marauders had been at peace for too long, and they needed another war to expand their borders and keep the legend of the Marauders alive. Thus, they invaded. The war was quick and decisive. It was over within a few months. The Algiers did try to fight back but the initial attack by the Marauders wiped out communication in the Algiers and laid the Algiers Air Force to waste. Only a few Algier planes were able to get off the ground, and they were overwhelmed by the Marauders. Alexandria controlled the air, and the people within the Algiers were terrified.

In the fourth month of the war, the Algiers government surrendered. Matusak rolled into their capital as a conquering king and many of the Algiers' people celebrated. After all, Alexandria had prospered during the last 100 years because of their close relationship with Tarshish and the Alliance. As for the Algiers, they were one of the weakest territories economically in Ethiopia. Most of their kings and queens were unjust men and women, and the people suffered for their actions. For example, in the Algiers, slavery still existed, but it was banned in almost every other region of the world after the Counselor came to Egypt and set things right long ago. In addition, there was still poverty and hunger in the region, and this was inexcusable during the Kingdom Age. There was more than enough food on the planet, but because of inept kings in the Algiers, the people suffered. So it made sense that the people cheered when Matusak rode into town. With him as their leader, the Algiers hoped they could prosper again like the days of old and put away the chains that enslaved them.

The first thing Matusak did was publicly kill King Manasseh and Queen Athalia. He hung them from the palace pillars, and the whole world watched on the holoscreen. He then abolished slavery in the region, and many men and women were set free. Matusak then brought in food and aide to the people and started to bring in engineers and others to repair the country. Tarshish and "The Alliance" were instrumental in helping the country, and Matusak was heralded as a great king. As for the region, it was annexed by Alexandria, and the Algiers territory was ruled by Matusak's old companion, Jonas.

At the beginning of the war, the D.M.R. and the Northern Coalition were up in arms over the invasion. After all, Alexandria's declaration of war broke the 100 years of peace and killed many innocent civilians. The real reason the D.M.R. was so upset with Alexandria was because they had exploited the region for years. They mined the Algiers' resources, and only the rich elite benefited from it. Many D.M.R. citizens were also instrumental in the slave trade although Kasca and the Libertines were formerly against the policy; nevertheless, Kasca and many of the leading Libertines knew about it, but they did nothing. Also, many resources found in the Algiers were sent back to the D.M.R., and the Republic benefited.

If the war did not end so quickly, it was likely that the D.M.R. would have gotten involved. Many of Gog Inc. business partners had deals in the region, and they called on Kasca to do something about it. In the third month of the war, the D.M.R. was preparing to aide the Algiers' war effort, but they wouldn't be able to get their ships and planes to the region for a few more months. After all, this was the southern hemisphere, and the region was predominately controlled by the Alliance. But the war ended before the D.M.R. ships and planes left port. If the D.M.R. did get involved, it was likely that the situation could have materialized into a world war. The Coalition would have supported the Algiers, and the Alliance would have backed Alexandria.

A year after the annexation of the Algiers, the D.M.R. wanted compensation for the business losses in the Algiers, and a private meeting was held between the leaders of the two alliances in the Outskirts. On the territory of Greenland, a neutral spot between both sides, representatives from all the major players were in attendance. James of Tarshish and the leaders of Dan, De-Dan and Sheba were there. Kasca, representing Gog Incorporated and the President of the D.M.R. were in attendance with all the other leaders of the Northern Coalition.

The leaders met around a table and after the initial shaking of hands and cordialities, the meeting began. Kasca led the summit and spoke first.

"First of all, I'd like to thank all of you for coming here today, but we have important business to discuss. And I'm sure all of you know why we are really here. It's in regards to Alexandria's takeover of the Algiers, and the loss of business for the Northern Coalition. As you all know, many of our constituents had mining companies in the Algiers, and the war destroyed these operations. Now with the Marauders occupying the territory, there is no chance to reclaim the mines or get back all the profits we lost during the war. We want retribution for these loses, and we would like an embargo placed on Alexandria," Kasca finished.

The men at the table shuffled around a bit, and Chieftain James rose from his seat with a response.

"All of you know Alexandria is not part of the Alliance, so we have no authority over Matusak and his empire," James explained. "He is free to do as he wishes. However, we do have some important trade deals with Alexandria, and we might be able to persuade Matusak to give the companies in the D.M.R. some compensation, but as far as an embargo goes, Tarshish will not support such a thing."

One of the Kings of Sheba rose and said, "I agree with James. Compensation seems fair, but an embargo is a bit extreme. How does Dan and De-Dan feel about it?"

King Zzyzx of Dan and Queen Corinne of De-Dan rose to their feet and agreed with Tarshish and Sheba. When Kasca could see that his embargo was not going to succeed, he pushed hard for the compensation his partners lost during the war.

"I disagree with you on the embargo," Kasca answered, "but it's obvious if only the Northern Coalition places a ban on trading goods with Alexandria, it won't work. We need your support. So I think we should talk about the compensation due us."

The men went back and forth for some time over what compensation should be made, and finally they came to a conclusion. Alexandria would remain in control of the Algiers' mines, but any disputed Nigerian and Tanzanian mines would now be controlled by trading partners of the Northern Coalition. Most of these areas already had Coalition companies working the area, but there were a few Alliance companies staking a claim to parts of it. These claims would be handed over to Northern Coalition companies. In the end, it was a relatively even deal. Currently the Algier mines were producing a lot of resources, but everyone knew that in a few decades Nigeria and Tanzania would be the place to be. There were a lot of un-mined resources in the area, and the Coalition hoped to capitalize on them in the future.

When it was all said and done, no contracts were signed, only an agreement was made between the two sides. In the Kingdom Age, a man's word is what carried weight in the world, and if a person or group broke their word, it was as heavy as someone breaking a legal document. The two sides agreed that in the next few months, all nations of the Alliance mining in Nigeria or Tanzania would forfeit the rights to their claims and leave the territories. They would hand them over to Coalition companies.

The last words made by Kasca were probably the most profound at the summit. These words made their way back to Matusak and reverberated throughout the room. Kasca said, "If Alexandria dares to invade Nigeria or Tanzania to expand their borders again, the D.M.R. will declare war on Alexandria and any nation supporting them. Have I made myself clear, gentlemen?"

"Yes Kasca," James responded, "we'll pass the message onto Matusak. He'll know where you stand on the issue."

When the meeting was adjourned, James contacted Matusak, and the two men met the following day in the City of Canaan. They discussed what transpired at the summit.

"Matusak," James stated, "I've got some good news and bad news."

"Tell me the good news first," Matusak said.

"The D.M.R. is not going to intervene in the war. They've called back their ships, and they are not going to come to the Algiers' defense. The territory is officially yours to do with as you please."

"And the bad news?" Matusak asked.

"If you decide to expand your borders into Ethiopia again, the D.M.R. will declare war on Alexandria."

"Then you tell Kasca to bring it on!" Matusak blurted out. "We aren't afraid of him!"

"Matusak, please be reasonable here. Alexandria wouldn't stand a chance against the D.M.R. They would bomb you into submission. Not a single building would be standing after the invasion was over. You have to find some other way to conquer the world. These are volatile times and your exploits could draw the whole planet into a world war. This is not acceptable, and you know the Counselor would agree."

Matusak thought about it for a moment then paced around the room. Finally he said grudgingly after his anger died down. "I suppose you're right. Maybe there are some other ways to fulfill my thirst for action and adventure."

"I hope so, Matusak," James answered. "If not all of the Marauders' accomplishments will be wiped away and probably Tarshish's aspirations right along with them."

"Alright James, you have my word. Alexandria will not advance further into the other territories of Ethiopia. We will honor the agreement the Alliance has made with the Northern Coalition."

Chapter 36

▼

Illegal Crossing

In 702 K.A., the D.M.R. was the greatest power in the Outskirts. The scientist of Gog Incorporated, Kasca's company, had made many great technological advances. For example, through science people could now levitate through the air and fly like the hovercars. People didn't go very fast, but it was possible. This changed a lot of things. New sporting games were created. People could do things that would have been considered godlike long ago. And it explained how the Counselor was able to fly. Gog Inc. was responsible for creating this technology. To an extent, the company was also able to figure out how the Counselor was able to throw his voice like a sonic boom when He wanted ones allegiance or attention. Gog Inc. perfected great war machines, games, and other knickknacks, but they still had not figured out how to control the weather. If Kasca and the D.M.R. could learn how to do that, they would no longer be subservient to the Counselor and the Kingdom.

In the meantime, Kasca thought it was about time to see what would happen if people tried to cross illegally back into the Kingdom. It was rumored that anyone who crossed the border illegally would be killed, but were these rumors true? Kasca had to find out for himself, and he planned to launch a secret expedition back to the Kingdom. But before Kasca ordered his spies across the Kingdom border, Kasca attempted to spy out the land from a distance.

New satellites created by Gog Inc. could see an ant crawling upon the earth from space. They could see a zit on a person's face, and could pretty much locate anyone on earth in a matter of time. However, these satellites could not see very far into the Kingdom. Every time they tried to peer in close on something like the Tree of Life or the Holy Temple, the picture on the camera would go hazy and muddled. The scientists at Gog Inc. couldn't figure out why this was so. With these new cameras that the company created, they could see anything on earth, but not inside the Kingdom. It baffled the Gog scientists, and they tried for years to figure out why there was a fog of war over the Kingdom. Eventually the scientists gave up. Some called it a miracle of God, while others like Kasca were determined to figure out how the Kingdom was able to block their peering eyes. Nonetheless, the cameras could clearly see into the Kingdom for a few miles, but after that the picture would become hazy and obscured. And one thing Kasca noticed was that the borders had no defenses. There were no walls or barriers keeping people out. There were some natural defenses like a forest, a river and mountains, but all of these could be overcome. So Kasca decided to see what would happen if he sent forces across the border.

Kasca sent a regiment of five men across the border to see if they could enter by land. Their mission was to retrieve some fruit from the Tree of Life and return. After traveling through Meschech, the five men drew near to the border at dusk. As they drew closer they came across two men sitting by a fire. When Kasca's soldiers saw the two men, they immediately grabbed their arms and approached cautiously. When the soldiers were within twenty meters of the men by the fire, they realized that the two men were not carrying weapons but cooking dinner, so they eased up a bit and were about to call out when they heard, "Come forward, you are welcome here. Come out of the bushes and join us for supper." The men by the fire didn't even look up. They had their backs to the soldiers so it was difficult to see who was speaking. The five soldiers hesitated and gripped their weapons tighter, but the captain of the men signaled for them to put down their weapons, so they did. The soldiers cautiously approached the fire then sat down in the dirt and warmed themselves. The captain thanked the two men for their hospitality, and the strangers by the fire nodded you're welcome. As the two welcomed their guests, they did not speak a word, but they did reach from their helpings and gave each soldier a large piece of meat and poured them something to drink, almost as if they were expecting them. The soldiers thanked the two men, and they ate heartily. The soldiers eased their guard, but continued to stare at the older camper whose face was all wrinkled. To the soldiers, the camper looked like one of the old men they'd seen from footage before the Millennial Age. But when the old man glared back, they looked away until he spoke to them.

"You are our guests here. Feel free to stay the night. This is the last campground before entering the Kingdom."

The captain thanked them with a nod and responded, "We knew we were getting pretty close to the border, but it started to get dark outside, and we kind of veered off track. Then we saw the campground, and we made our way towards you."

"So where are all of you from?" the older camper asked. "My name's Gabriel and this here's Raphael."

The soldiers and the campers all shook hands and introduced themselves then the captain said, "We're from the D.M.R. We've been sent out here to survey the land," the captain lied. "No one from Magog has been out this way in a long time, and we've been ordered to see what's to the south of us."

The two campers shook their heads in understanding as the captain continued his lie. "Tomorrow we're going to head further south and if we're lucky we'll come across something intriguing."

Raphael, the other camper said, "This is about as far south as you can go. You must have seen the signs. If you go any further you are going to enter the Kingdom, and that's strictly forbidden. Don't they teach this in the North?"

"Sure we've heard the stories, but that edict goes back hundreds of years. Most of the people in the North don't believe the stories," the captain explained. "In fact, most of the people in the North think these stories are fairy tales."

"The stories are true, captain," Raphael explained. "No one from the Outskirts who has entered the southern lands has ever returned. Personally, I think their haunted."

The captain and the rest of the soldiers listened intently to Raphael's tale like an orchestra tuning their instruments.

"In fact, at night sometimes," Raphael leaned in towards the soldiers and started to speak in a whisper, "I've heard the roar of lions in those woods. Not tame lions like we have today, but wild ones that feast on the flesh of men. And one time I swore I heard the sound of bull's hooves rushing towards me. It scared the living hell out of me. At first it started like a low rumble … then the earth started to shake like it was an earthquake … then I heard the screams … then nothing at all."

At that moment, a piece of firewood crackled in the flame and it burst open firing little pieces of wood in every direction. The soldiers jumped back in fear then they laughed at their cowardice.

One of the soldiers responded, "You really had me going there for a moment, Raphael. Next thing you're going to tell me is the Kingdom's protected by the Watchers of God."

The soldier chuckled to himself and everyone started to laugh again until Gabriel, the older one, spoke up in a serious tone. "It's true though. Everyone who crosses the border never returns. We've had many people come this way over the years, and no one's ever come back. You boys can take your chances tomorrow, but I guarantee you, you'll never see your families again if you do. Those woods are haunted, and if you cross that line, you're dead men."

Gabriel then got up authoritatively from the wood stump he was sitting on and headed towards his tent. As he went, he said, "You boys have been warned. Don't cross into the Kingdom. You all seem like good fellows, and I'd hate to see you lose your lives over something foolish. Good night. Take care. It's been a pleasure meeting all of you."

After Gabriel slipped off to bed, one of the soldiers asked Raphael, "What happened to your friend's skin?"

Raphael answered, "He was cursed with aging long ago for his rebellion in the past. He's perfectly healthy, but he bares the wrinkled skin as a sign."

"What did he do to earn such a punishment?"

"Some say that God punished him for not obeying His command exactly as given, but no one knows for sure. Gabriel never talks about it."

"It's not contagious, is it?" one soldier asked.

"No, but it does make one wonder what aging was like before the Kingdom Age."

The soldiers shook their head in agreement then Raphael spoke one last time.

"Well, I'm heading off to bed. Feel free to finish off the rest of the supper. You boys take care, and please heed Gabriel's warning. He's not one to tell myths."

One of the men laughed abruptly after Raphael's words, but it sort of stuck in his throat and made a cackle sound. The other soldiers looked at the soldier like he'd been given an omen as they watched Raphael slip away into his tent.

After Raphael slipped off to bed, the soldiers kind of milled around for a bit, joked with one another then one by one they all drifted off to sleep. In the morning, the soldiers were awakened by the sound of eagles chirping in the trees. Raphael and Gabriel appeared to still be asleep, so the soldiers moved quietly, picked up their gear, and headed on their way.

As soon as the soldiers crossed into the forbidden zone, everything seemed to be okay. After a few miles inside the border of the Kingdom, the soldiers' fears started to ease, and they felt rather womanly for even considering that the stories could be true.

As the soldiers continued marching in line along the stream in the forest, one of the soldiers stopped to get a drink and his buddy joined him. As the two men were dipping their faces in the water, one of the soldiers abruptly jumped up and said, "Did you hear that?"

The other soldier answered, "Hear what?"

"That sound. It sounded like a growl."

At first, the second soldier was a bit frightened, but then he thought his friend was just playing a joke on him, so he brushed it off and continued drinking from the stream. About a minute later, the soldiers were back on the trail, picking up the pace a bit and trying to catch up with the other men when suddenly a fierce roar was heard in the forest. This time it echoed throughout the valley.

"Did you hear it that time?" the first soldier sarcastically asked.

Both men grabbed their guns and moved slowly along the path. The dense forest was difficult to see through and at any corner there could be a cat lying in wait. As the soldiers quickened the pace to try to catch up to their commander, they were waylaid by two lions. One of the soldiers managed to get off a shot, but he missed. Both men were mauled and quickly killed by the lions.

As for the captain and the other men, they heard the shot and immediately froze in their tracks. They grabbed their guns and slowly back-tracked towards the other men. As they went, the soldiers moved cautiously and eventually reached the bodies of the dead soldiers. Both men had been mauled to death and their bodies were lying on the path. A large eagle was currently feasting on one of the dead men's eyes. The soldiers scared the eagle off, and one of the men checked to make sure they were dead. The captain ordered his troops to keep alert and to continue moving forward up the path; however, one of the men stopped in his tracks and questioned his orders.

"We should go back. These woods are haunted. Maybe that wrinkled man was right."

The other soldier looked at the captain and hoped their leader would change his mind. The captain, however, was firm in his command and encouraged his men.

"It's just a cat or maybe a couple of lions. If we can kill the cats, we'll be fine. Men, we've been trained for this. We've fought far more dangerous battles in the past and other wild beasts. Are you going to let a couple of cats get the best of you? Are we going to head all the way back to Magog with our tails between our legs? Have some courage men. We are the elite forces of the D.M.R. Let's move out, and if one of those cats crosses our path, it's going to be the last thing that cat ever sees."

The two men gained some courage at these words, and they continued to follow their commander. As they proceeded up the path, they heard the roar of a lion in the distance, and one of the men shot his laser several times in that direction. The captain yelled, "Cease fire!" and the soldier stopped shooting.

The roar of a lion was heard again, but it echoed off the mountains and reverberated in their ears. Thus, it was difficult for the men to decipher which direction the growl was coming from. They spun around in all directions and panicked. At that moment a lion came out of the bushes, but the captain was able to shoot it down before it reached them. The giant beast fell a few feet away from them and died. Then suddenly a whole pride of lions were upon them. The soldiers managed to get off a few shots, but they missed. One of the men was struck from behind. A lion sprung out of the shadows and dug its claws into the soldier's back. The other soldier was mauled by several lions and each of his limbs was torn from his body. As for the captain, a lion bit off his head at the neck, and he died instantly.

After a year of waiting, Kasca concluded that the five soldiers were dead or traitors, so he decided to send fifty men this time, but they never returned. They stopped at the same campground, entered the Kingdom, and were trampled by raging bulls. They came upon the men like roaring buffaloes and were trampled to death.

Another year passed and Kasca concluded that the fifty men were lost, so Kasca decided to send even more troops this time. However, he was planning to enter the Kingdom by air. He sent one transport plane and three fighter planes to protect them. He planned to have men parachute into the Kingdom, return home by foot, and collect any evidence on the way. The orders were simple, and he hoped he would be successful this time, but when the war planes flew over Kingdom airspace, they were instantly attacked by flying dragons, known as leviathan. One of the planes barreled straight into one of the dragons, and they both pummeled to the earth. The other two planes dipped out of the way of the giant dinosaurs but were hit with flames of fire from the flock of dragons, and these planes also went down. As for the transport plane, it did manage to unload most of the twenty-five parachuting, but before it was able to finish unloading the men, they were also attacked by the dragons, and the plane went down. As for the men, some were burned alive before they reached the earth by the dragons. Others had their parachutes eaten away at the ropes by great eagles, and they tumbled to their deaths. The rest of the men were snatched away by other flying dinosaurs, and they were eaten as prey.

After the D.M.R.'s planes disappeared from the radar screen, Kasca and the Libertine generals waited silently, but the planes never re-emerged, and Kasca was angry. All three attempts to reenter the Kingdom had failed, and his plan of conquering the Kingdom was put on hold.

A month later, Kasca ordered a special mission. He asked two of his finest cadets to undertake this task. They would pilot a commuter plane filled with tourists returning from De-Dan to the D.M.R. On their return, they would fly over Kingdom airspace and ask for an emergency landing in the Kingdom due to technical difficulties. Of course, the plane would be running fine, but the Kingdom wouldn't know that nor would the rest of the world. So Kasca executed his plan.

"S.O.S. our plane is having technical difficulties," one of the pilots blurted through the holo-emitter on the plane. "We have no choice but to make an emergency landing in the Kingdom. If you're out there, Counselor, please give us safe passage."

The pilot looked scared as he continued to transmit his message. It was being received in the D.M.R. and being recorded. The pilot was also trying to get his message across to someone in the Kingdom, but he reached no one. There was no one there to receive his message. And just as the commercial plane entered the Kingdom, it was welcomed by a flock of dragons like the war planes a month ago, and the plane was brought down.

The pilot's final words were aired everywhere in the Outskirts, and the Kingdom was seen as merciless. As for the Counselor, he was blamed for everything. The families of those who lost loved ones on the plane wanted revenge, and the event hurt the Kingdom's and the Counselor's reputation. As for Kasca, he seized the moment and spoke to the press about the incident. Kasca looked earnestly into the camera and spoke. *"The death of the people on Aero-plane 22764 was a terrible tragedy. It is a shame in this golden era that barbarous acts like this still exist. How could the Kingdom shoot down a friendly commuter plane? In their distress, their cries were not heard, and many people perished. People from De-Dan, Sheba, and the D.M.R. lost their lives in this attack, and I think all nations in the Outskirts should make a formal protest against the Counselor and the Kingdom by not bringing forth tribute at the Festival of Booths this year. Of course, I know we will have to sacrifice for twelve months without rain falling upon our lands, but I think it's worth it. The time is now for us to make a stand against the Counselor and the 144 Elders. Why can't we all be free? When will the Kingdom join the rest of us in the Outskirts and become part of the greater community? These questions I do not have an answer to at the moment, but if the Kingdom is out there listening somewhere, let our protest be heard."*

When the Booth's Festival came around that year, all the nations in the Northern Coalition did not bring forth tribute that year, and the rains did not fall upon their territories. There were large protests in De-Dan to do the same because many of their citizens had lost their lives in the crash, but Queen Corinne disagreed with the protesters. She sent forth her tributaries and gave her respects to the King of Kings. The rest of the Alliance did the same.

Chapter 37

Nod's Declaration of Independence

555 K.A. was a turning point for the people of Nod in North America. It was the first time the D.M.R. regulated policy in Nod. Up to that point the Magog Republic let the Nodians run their state of affairs, but when the Nodians voted to join the Empire Free Trade Pact, the Libertine government stepped in and vetoed an alliance with Tarshish and its allies. After the veto, many of the Nodians were upset and there were protests in the streets, especially in the Native Nodian cities. From that point forward, there was friction in the Land of Nod. Many of the Native Nodians, those born in the North American territory, began to see the D.M.R. as an occupying force. As for the Settlers, those who moved from the D.M.R. and settled in Nod, they had a strong allegiance to the motherland.

This friction between the Natives and the Settlers of Nod slowly began to divide the territory, and over the next two hundred years, it had become written in their hearts. Sporting events between the two sides were brutal and bordering on combat, especially in sports like football, soccer, and rugby. As for the fans, they were riotous. Also, some of the more fanatical Natives started to use terrorist's tactics, and the D.M.R. military had to be brought in to keep the peace. This only caused more hatred and fueled more attacks. By the time 775 rolled around, the D.M.R. was an occupying force in Native Nodian cities, and many of the D.M.R. soldiers were prejudiced and bigoted towards the Natives.

In 775, there was a peaceful protest taking place in one of the cities that had a majority of Native residents. The Natives of Nod were protesting the presence of the soldiers in their cities, and over a million people were gathered in the streets. This made the D.M.R. soldiers feel a little on edge because they were heavily outnumbered, and any sort of minor disturbance could be considered an attack upon their authority.

"I said get behind the barrier!" one of the D.M.R. soldiers yelled as the protesters marched along in unison. "I said get back!" but this time the soldier hit one of the young protesters and knocked him to the ground.

When some of the younger Natives saw this, they started to yell obscenities at the soldiers and pretty soon a mob started to form. The protestors were yelling, throwing rocks at the soldiers, and it was getting ugly. Some of the D.M.R. soldiers were getting pelted in the head and a few of them fell.

"Invaders go home! Invaders go home!" the crowd started to chant, and they began to push harder on the blockade. They were getting brave, and it was just a matter of time before fists were thrown. Finally one of the soldiers got pelted in the face with a large rock and he was seriously injured. When his buddy saw this, he pulled out his weapon and shot at the ground several times. The laser fire scattered the crowd and people fled in every direction. Then all of the sudden, a laser gun was fired from the mob, and the shot killed one of the soldiers. When the D.M.R. forces realized they were being fired upon, many of them drew their weapons, and they began to fire randomly into the crowd. Protesters were being shot and killed. Some had their arms and legs singed off, and before anyone knew what happened, it was a full-scale riot.

Later that evening a curfew was ordered. Anyone found in the streets after dark could be shot and killed. The curfew did not allow the Natives to clean up all the dead bodies that fell earlier so many dead protesters still lined the streets. As for the press, they caught the whole event on the holoscreen. A large gathering of press personnel had come to witness the peaceful protest, but the riot had far exceeded their expectations.

The Massacre of Nod claimed the lives of 1,037 Natives, and thousands more were injured. The press made the soldiers look like butchers because they fired upon unarmed civilians. Although some of the protesters were armed, it wasn't mentioned in most of the news stories. When it was all said and done, months later, the D.M.R.'s occupation of Native Nodian territory was frowned upon by people in the Outskirts. Tarshish and its allies wanted an immediate withdrawal, but the D.M.R. put their foot down and weren't willing to budge.

Later during the year, some of the Native Nodian leaders secretly came to Tarshish asking for help. They wanted Fruit Pills, medical supplies, and weapons. When Chieftain James heard the request, he said he'd send Fruit Pills and medical supplies, but he denied their request for weapons. When Jacob heard James' verdict, he was outraged. Jacob had many Nodian friends, and he sympathized with the Natives. He believed the land rightfully belonged to them and that they had a right to defend themselves. So Jacob went against his brother's wishes and secretly shipped arms to Nod.

* * * *

"Wait ... go back," a D.M.R. secret service man ordered as he was looking at the footage of an arms deal being made at one of the Native Nodian ports. "Stop, right there, I think I recognize that man. Can you bring it in closer?"

The man working on the computer pushed some buttons and zoomed into the face on the screen.

"If I'm not mistaken, I think that's Jacob O'Donohue," the secret service man declared.

"You mean, Jacob O'Donohue, the brother of Chieftain James?" the man on the computer mocked. "Don't be crazy."

"Yep, that's him. I knew I'd seen his face before. I only shook hands with him once at a party in Greenland, but I could swear that's the man," the secret service man affirmed. "Get this data as quickly as possible to headquarters and have them analyze the recording."

"You really think that's him?"

"Have you ever known me to be wrong? Want to make a bet on it?"

"I suppose you have a point there," the man on the computer answered. "Last time I challenged you, I lost 100 credits. I think I'll pass, but let me know what you hear. If that was Jacob O'Donohue, we might have a situation here."

"You got that right. Wait till the authorities hear about this one."

* * * *

A few months later in February of 776, the native Nodians declared their independence. Immediately, war broke out between the two sides. The soldiers occupying the Native cities of Nod withdrew, but returned weeks later with five times their number. The D.M.R. reinforced their numbers and prepared for a full-scale invasion. However, when the D.M.R. entered the cities they were struck with a firm defensive. The Native Nodians were able to dig themselves in, and they were hiding in every nook and cranny of the cities. They were also well-armed. The only way to drive them out was to destroy the cities, and the Libertines were not willing to do that, so the two sides fought a conventional war and many people were killed or injured.

*   *   *   *

"General, I thought you told me this would be an easy victory," Kasca questioned. "It's been over six months and you haven't taken back a single city. Are you inept? Is this task too difficult for you? Are you going to let the Natives outwit you?"

"It's not the Natives I'm worried about, it's the arms," the general answered. Every time we try to make an offensive, they shoot back at us with laser fire. I had no idea Nod was this heavily armed. They must have thousands and thousands of laser guns. Where did they get all their weapons?"

"That's a whole other issue altogether," Kasca responded. He was referring to shipments of weapons being brought in from Tarshish, and Jacob O'Donohue leading the insurrection. "But do the best you can. We know we've placed heavy restrictions against what actions you can make. Remember no heavy armory until I give the orders. Consolidate some of your forces and try to take one city at a time. If it gets to the point were your soldiers are losing hope and victory still eludes you, notify me. We may need to do something drastic."

"Yes sir," the general cadenced and he left the room.

By the winter of 776, the two sides were still at a standstill and not one city had been retaken by the D.M.R. forces. As a result, the D.M.R. sent a large contingent of ships and sailed towards Nod. And instead of taking the long way around, they sailed through the channel separating Southern Greenland and mainland Tarshish. When the ships were about halfway through the strait, they stopped. Tarshish wasn't sure what they were doing, but the navy and air-force were put on full alert. The next morning, the papers read, "The D.M.R. DECLARES WAR ON TARSHISH!" Pictures of Jacob's secret arms shipments to Nod were all over the holoscreen, and Southern Greenland had been invaded.

Part III

▼

The Final Battle

Chapter 38

Imprisonment

Lucifer had been in the abyss for almost 800 years, and he was growing weary of his imprisonment. When Lucifer was first bound with chains and his liberty was taken from him, he was angry, but as time proceeded the Devil was humbled. He cried out to God for forgiveness and promised Him that if he was set free he would return to the old ways and be an obedient servant; however, God did not answer his prayer. The Creator of the universe did not even acknowledge him. Instead there was silence and many hours alone.

As Lucifer sat at the bottomless pit he pondered, "Why would God grant mercy and forgiveness to humanity but not to the angels? It does not seem fair. His justice seems biased. Why would God show partiality to men? When the Watchers came to Him long ago, why didn't He have mercy upon them as He did with man?"

Lucifer was referring to the angels in the Book of Enoch who slept with women and bore giants long ago. These angels were also known as Watchers, and they asked God for absolution for their sins, but forgiveness was not granted unto them. Instead they were cast into hell and doomed for the Lake of Fire at the final judgment.

"With man God stepped from His throne and became a lowly servant to redeem them but with us He won't even turn the other cheek. I don't understand this Creator. Is this righteousness? Is this just?"

Lucifer continued to think about these profound theoretical ideas, and he felt like he'd been cheated. Therefore, a great hatred for God began to smolder within him and over the years it started to grow and grow. Long ago when Lucifer first rebelled against God, a third of the angels joined him in the revolution, but back then it was a matter of pride and independence. Now he simply wanted revenge. He was doomed for the Lake of Fire, so he planned to bring as many of God's beloved with him. Deep down, however, Lucifer still longed for forgiveness. He remembered the times before the rebellion, and he hoped it could be that way again. Lucifer yearned for that intimacy with his Creator, but a barrier stood in his path. There was no communion with Him any longer. He was excluded from God's throne.

Lucifer was one of the most beautiful and enchanting of the angels. He stood in the places of honor with Michael and Uriel, but Lucifer fell when his pride grew strong. He wanted to be like the Most High and because of his arrogance he was cast down. God passed judgment upon the Devil. Gnashing and bitterness of teeth awaited him and eternal separation from God was Lucifer's ultimate fate.

In the meantime Lucifer was able to come and go as he pleased. He became known as the "Great Accuser" in heaven and he brought many charges against God's people. Lucifer challenged God on many occasions like he did with Job long ago. Nevertheless, Lucifer was kept in check by God. He was not permitted to do certain deeds, and if he overstepped his bounds, God would send forth his holy angels to keep him in line. For thousands of years the forces of good and evil waged war with one another and a fragile balance was attained on earth. But prior to the Millennial Reign, Lucifer and his axis of evil got the upper-hand in the war, and they seized control of the planet. This was during the 7 Year Tribulation, and it appeared Lucifer was going to accomplish his task of exterminating all life on earth and David's lineage. But right when he was about to finish his task, God stepped in and the Messiah set things right again. Lucifer and his forces were defeated, and Lucifer was bound and chained in the abyss of the earth.

Lucifer's future looked grim. He knew about the ancient prophecies that predicted his doom. He mused, "At the end of the thousand years, I will be released for a short time, but that's all John's revelation reveals. How long is a short time-a year, a thousand years, or ten-thousand years? Sometimes His prophecies are so vague. One can't make heads or tails out of anything until after the fact then it becomes clear. So what am I to do in the meantime? I've already wept and begged on my hands and knees for many years. What else does He want from me? My humiliation is complete. I cannot be brought any lower."

Lucifer continued to meditate on these things. The more he brooded over it, the more frustrated he became. At times Lucifer would get angry. Other times he would sulk about in depression. At one time he was one of the most powerful angels in heaven. Lucifer ruled over the earth and was feared by many. Now he had become like Nebuchadnezzar. He crawled on his belly like a viper, and he was losing his sanity.

* * * *

"La la la la … la la la la … la la la la … la la la la …" Lucifer sang to himself to keep himself entertained. Suddenly Satan heard the seal above him creaking open. Lucifer knew who it was because every hundred years like clockwork, he'd receive a visitation from Michael, a fellow arch-angel.

"If it isn't my old friend, Michael, who has come here to pay me a visit," Lucifer said sarcastically. "What good deed have I done to deserve this visitation?"

Satan emphasized his words with a gesture and proceeded to flip Michael off when his back was turned.

"I saw that!" Michael said. "Would you prefer if I closed up the hatch and returned in another century?"

Lucifer's eyes got big for a moment, fearing another hundred years of isolation and boredom. He then spoke, "No, stay a while. You've come all this way. We might as well have a cup of tea together."

Michael looked down at Lucifer and felt pity for him. Once upon a time they had been like brothers, but after being lied to and betrayed many times, Michael was skittish and on guard whenever he was around Lucifer.

"So where are Uriel, Raguel, and the rest of your gang?" Lucifer asked.

"They're right outside the door, so don't try anything?" Michael answered.

"Oh please ask Uriel to come in. Is he afraid I'm going to tear off another one of his wings?"

Michael shook his head in disbelief then said, "I think he's going to pass this time. I don't think he's gotten over the wing incident. You embarrassed him and took away a piece of his pride. It took some time for that wing to grow back."

"Ah! such a shame!" Lucifer smirked.

"So would you prefer English or Earl Gray?"

"English will be fine," Michael answered as he sat down at the table next to Lucifer.

"So how are things going in the universe?" Lucifer asked. "Did the Yankees win the series again? And how's Gabriel doing?"

"Funny you should ask. The Yankees in the Kingdom Baseball League are in last place, and the Angels won another one."

Lucifer shrugged it off as if he didn't care, but deep down inside Michael could tell he didn't like seeing the Yankees lose. After all, that was his team, and he always made certain the Yankees would have the biggest payroll and the best talent before the Kingdom Age. As for winning the series, it had been left to chance. Only a few times in history had Lucifer tried to manipulate the outcome, but all the angels, good and bad, knew about it, and it took the fun out of watching the games. So there was a standing order amongst the angels to not mess with the outcomes.

Michael continued, "As for Gabriel, he's still rebellious at times, but he's remained faithful to the Lord."

"Shame, shame ... and he had so much potential," Lucifer mocked.

"So old chap," Michael inquired, "your time is almost up. What do you plan to do when you're out?"

Lucifer thought for a moment then answered, "I don't know yet. Do I have a choice? It seems like my fate has already been pre-determined. I've read the exposition. Is my fate sealed?"

"You've done a lot of evil deeds through the ages," Michael argued. "If you were God, how would you judge your case?"

Lucifer answered, "According to His rules, I deserve the Lake of Fire, but I'm not playing by His rules. I've always made my own policies, and that's what the do-gooders don't understand. I think my case needs to be re-evaluated and judged by a neutral arbitrator. Obviously my stance has credence. A third of our kind agreed with me. Even you questioned your beliefs. Can you deny it?"

"A few doubts may have filled my mind, but I never wanted to sit on the throne. We are created beings. Doesn't He have the right to rule as He pleases?"

"Yes and no. All I'm saying is that we need to look beyond good and evil as Nietzsche pointed out and see things from a different perspective, one that does not play by the pre-conceived rules."

"You have some valid points, Lucifer, but what about the crimes you have committed against humanity?"

"Are you out of your mind? It's just man!" Lucifer protested. "Nine-tenths of them are as interesting as sheep on the pasture. And God wants us, a superior species, to serve them? Get off your high horse, Michael! How many men have you slaughtered by your sword? Hundreds? Thousands? Millions? And that's not counting women and children. I helped Adam to see the light. It's not my fault his race decided to follow me instead of Him."

"Lucifer, I don't know what to say to you anymore. I figured all this time down here in the pit would help you to regain your reason, but you have not changed at all. You still hold to the same opinions that got you thrown out of heaven in the first place."

"Maybe so, brother, but as Milton once said, 'It's better to rule in hell than to serve in heaven.'"

The two angels continued their debate. They could go on for days discussing these higher theoretical ideas, but eventually the allotted time of visitation came to a close, and Michael left Lucifer chained up in his prison cell. The arch-angel sealed up the abyss and flew up into the heavens.

Chapter 39

Deterrence

"General, have you input your launch codes already?"

"Yes, Mr. President, I have input them into the computer," the D.M.R. general responded. "All we need now is your launch codes, and the missile will be ready to fire."

The President walked over to where the general was standing, and he entered a series of numbers on the holoscreen. A red button lit up on the screen. It was blinking on and off.

"Mr. President, the superweapon is ready to fire. Would you like to do the honors?"

Sweat started to build on the President's forehead knowing that he was about to launch a weapon that would destroy an entire Tarshish city. Millions of innocent victims would die, but he hoped by taking out one of Tarshish's cities, it would bring about a quick and decisive end to the war. The President hoped it would be like the ancient history books during WWII when the Americans brought an end to the war by destroying the cities of Hiroshima and Nagasaki with atom bombs. "Then again," the President thought, "what happens if Tarshish has superweapons of their own? According to D.M.R. intelligence, Tarshish had not acquired the technology to make a superweapon. But if intelligence is wrong, I'll be writing a death sentence for millions of our own citizens as well."

The President continued to ponder these things as he continued to stare at the red button on the holoscreen. He had been ordered by Gog Inc. and Kasca himself to fire the weapon, but he wondered what would happen to him if he did not comply. The President knew for sure he would fall from power and that some sort of scandal would arise, but he would be free from condemning millions to death. Hence, the President was in a conundrum. Either way he was cursed. In the end, he reached hesitantly towards the holoprojection and pushed the red button. The missile took off from a silo in Northern Magog and headed towards the Land of Tarshish.

Minutes later, New Glasgow of Tarshish was completely wiped off the map. There were no survivors. The city crumbled to dust, and all that was left was fire and brimstone for a radius of 100 kilometers. The outskirts of the city were either destroyed or untouched. If the suburb was within the 100 Kilometer radius, it was no more. If it was outside the bomb's range, it remained as it was. On one side of the street there'd be a flowing stream and a beautiful home. On the other side of the street, there would be ash and burning embers. The scientists at Gog Inc., who perfected the weapon, made sure that anything outside the bomb's impact zone would not be harmed. It was a miraculous weapon of destruction, and Tarshish had now been shaken by its wrath.

When the news reached Chieftain James, he immediately left the City of Canaan and headed secretly to Tarshish's underground base in New Dublin. From the installation, James would have communications with his military and access to his weaponry. After arrival, James ordered his one superweapon to be readied for launching and within the hour fired a rebuttal to the D.M.R.'s savage attack.

James was not sure if the weapon would work. Tarshish was still in the experimental stage of developing the superweapon, and they had not been able to test their new technology due to other pressing concerns. Nevertheless, James ordered the weapon to be fired anyway. It was not as powerful as the one that destroyed New Glasgow, but it didn't matter. If James successfully hit one of the D.M.R.'s cities, Kasca would be hesitant to launch another.

The superweapon was launched from the underground base and entered D.M.R. airspace minutes later. It struck the outskirts of the City of Kamchatka, and a third of the city was turned to ash. The superweapon also destroyed the main road linking Kamchatka to Alaska and now made it difficult for the D.M.R. to move its conventional forces into Nod.

After James was informed that the weapon was successful, he immediately contacted Kasca on the telocommunicator, and the two men began a heated debate.

"Do you see what you started, James?" Kasca began. "If you would have put the reigns on that brother of yours, none of this would have happened."

"And if you would have used diplomacy before you decided to declare war, millions of people would still be alive," James responded.

"You started this thing," Kasca yelled.

"No I didn't," James argued. "It was you and your desire to rule the world."

"Oh, rubbish. If your Alliance would stop sticking their noses into Coalition business, we would not be at war right now."

"And if you didn't practice Manifest Destiny, the whole Outskirts would be better off."

"James, you're so full of it!" the Libertine exclaimed. "Just get down to business and tell me why you called."

"It's simple. If you fire another superweapon at Tarshish, we are going to fire one at the City of Liberty and destroy all of your accomplishments."

"And if you destroy our glorious city, we will wipe Tarshish off the map!" Kasca exploded.

"That might be so, but if we're going to burn, you're coming with us," James explained. "But why don't we bring an end to this conflict instead? Too many innocent civilians are dead because of this war."

Kasca's anger died down, and he thought for a moment.

"Why would we choose to end this quarrel? We are winning. We took Greenland in two weeks, and the conflict in Nod has tipped in our favor."

"Yes, that is true, but at what price? Can't we come up with a resolution?"

"I don't know, James. I'll have to speak with the President and my constituents. In the meantime, you have my guarantee that another superweapon will not be fired on Tarshish as long as you can grant me the same promise."

"It is agreed. Tarshish will not fire another superweapon at Magog, but if you break your word, Kasca, the City of Liberty will be no more."

"Agreed."

"I will get back to you pronto. Kasca out."

The telocommunicator went blank and James breathed deeply knowing that his bluff had worked. If Kasca thought Tarshish did not have anymore superweapons, the D.M.R. would have surely destroyed James' homeland and went onto conquer the world. But for now Kasca and the Coalition were kept in check, and there was hope for tomorrow.

*   *   *   *

Two weeks later, the war between Tarshish and the D.M.R. came to an end. Southern Greenland was given back to Tarshish, but it was agreed that the southwest province would be occupied by the D.M.R. for three years. This allowed the D.M.R. to check up on Tarshish activity to make sure they weren't making illegal shipments to Nod. As for the Land of Nod, Tarshish was forced to remove all of its troops from the area even though the Nodian War of Independence raged on.

The tally of the number killed during the two wars exceeded 700 million people thus far. Twice that number were injured in the conflict, but most of these people were healed; nevertheless, the large stock of Fruit Pills would not give back arms and legs that were singed off from laser fire, so many people in the regions had to depend on bionics to replace the missing limbs. Luckily, the technology was advanced enough during the Millennial Reign that people with robotics were able to function as normal human beings in society and their mobility was not limited. As for the cities of Greenland, they were decimated. It took only one month to tear down every city in the region. Both sides suffered serious damage to their infrastructure, and it would take decades for it to be rebuilt. As for the mainland of Tarshish and the D.M.R., they remained relatively unscathed, except for the two cities destroyed by the superweapons. New Glasgow was no more, and Kamchatka was limping back to life.

Although the conflict between Tarshish and the D.M.R. was over, the war in the Land of Nod became more volatile. The Native Nodians and the Settlers from the D.M.R. would not make peace. After Tarshish was invaded at the beginning of the war, Matusak sent a large contingent of men to help train the Natives for guerilla warfare. This assured the war would drag on for even longer. The Marauders were expert technicians at war, and if they were allowed to train a new generation of warriors, the tide could eventually turn in the Natives favor. In the meantime the D.M.R. Settlers were advancing on the Natives and taking over the cities one by one. But this was exactly what the Marauders had hoped for. They would let them have their temporary victory, but take it back slowly with terrorist activity and guerilla warfare in the cities. The Marauders knew that eventually the Settlers would lose hope, and the Natives would be victorious just like the Marauders were during the 13 Year War in Africa.

As for the D.M.R., they could have quickly destroyed the Native Nodian cities with superweapons, but after the world saw how destructive these bombs were, the President and the citizens of the D.M.R. were strongly opposed to using them. In fact, most D.M.R. citizens would rather lose the war than be forced to fire these weapons again.

*   *   *   *

During the thirty-three day war between Tarshish and the D.M.R., the two navies and air forces engaged in fierce combat. The D.M.R. was superior in the air, and Tarshish was more advanced at sea. This gave a slight advantage to the D.M.R but not much because a Tarshish warship could shoot practically any missile out of the sky. Tarshish radar would detect any missile coming in their direction, and their anti-aircraft capabilities were at a 95% success rate.

"Incoming!"

"Turn the ship to the port bow and increase speed to 30 knots," Hannah ordered. Is the anti-aircraft ready?"

"We're tracking it. It's coming in fast, but we have it on our scope."

"Remember, don't shoot until it's within range, then fire the Dispersal Gun.

The Dispersal Gun would allow a Tarshish Ship to fire thousands of tiny lasers simultaneously in any direction. It would cover about a third of the airspace overhead, and it made it nearly impossible for a missile to penetrate their defenses. Tarshish warships were, however, susceptible to missiles coming in from opposing directions at the same time. For example, if the D.M.R. shot missiles from the north and south and they arrived simultaneously, a Tarshish warship would not be able to defend itself.

"Wait a second, there's another one coming in from the north. It's coming in too fast!" the lieutenant shouted.

"Quick fire at the first missile and bring the Dispersal Gun around!" Hannah ordered in desperation.

The first missile was singed into thousands of tiny particles, but the second missile arrived seconds afterwards in the other direction, and Hannah's shipmates weren't able to get the Dispersal Gun around in time. It hit Hannah's ship from the rear and blew the whole back end of the vessel off. Many of Hannah's shipmates died in the initial explosion, and the rest went down into the depths of the sea.

*   *   *   *

Hannah's ship sunk two days before the Tarshish-Magog War came to an end. Jacob searched the sea for weeks trying to find the missing vessel, but he was unsuccessful. He hoped to find her body and bring her back to life with a Fruit Pill, but with each passing hour, he knew that the chances of restoring her were becoming less and less possible.

"Where are you?" Jacob thought. "Counselor, if you're out there, guide my ship to her resting place. I can't live without her. She means everything to me. Please Lord, answer my prayer."

But the Counselor never guided Jacob to her fallen ship, and after one week of searching the high seas, Jacob finally gave up. He mourned the loss of his wife and had a funeral for her. He, like many others in the north, had lost someone close to him, and the aftermath left a bad taste in his mouth. Jacob now hated the D.M.R. with all his being, and he vowed one day to avenge Hannah.

Chapter 40

Mermaids

After the loss of Hannah, Jacob took a leave of absence and traveled the world with a small crew. On his ship, they visited Dan, De-Dan, and spent a lot of time exploring the Islands of Sheba. The islands were under Sheba's jurisdiction, but a lot of the area was unexplored territory, so Jacob went out on a quest to find something new. Jacob and his crew didn't know what they were looking for. His crew had no idea what they would find, but they journeyed onward.

For three years, the crew stumbled upon nothing unexplainable. There was no Big Foot, no Loctus Monster, nor creature at the bottom of the sea, and they were losing faith in their quest. Finally when they were thinking about heading back to Tarshish, they stumbled upon a mirage on the horizon. As they looked out to sea, they saw beautiful women sunning themselves on some nearby rocks. As the ship sailed forward, the men couldn't believe their eyes. They were gazing upon mermaids, and they were smiling at Jacob and his men. As the ship got closer, the mermaids slipped from the rocks and waved at them from the sea. They were inviting the men into the water. One of the men hollered, "I think they want us to join them. And another yelled back, "I don't trust them. It might be a trap." As for Jacob, he had already stripped off his clothes and dove into the water. When the sailors saw him, a couple of the men did the same and joined him in the water. All three of them were swimming with the mermaids.

At first, Jacob and the two other men were swimming with the mermaids at the surface, but eventually they went under the water, and they got deeper and deeper into the depths of the ocean. As they descended, the men were surprised that they were not suffocating from lack of oxygen. For some reason, it felt as if their lungs were filled with air, and they couldn't explain why. Something supernatural was occurring as they swam with the mermaids.

As the men swam in the water, they found themselves surrounded by these beautiful creatures. They were enraptured by the mermaids, and they were rubbing up against them in erotic ways. All the men were aroused as they participated in this frolicking under the sea. As for the mermaids, they were kissing them and touching them like curious dolphins, and this playful activity lasted for some time.

The men who remained aboard the ship started to worry about their captain and the others. "Do you think they're okay?" one sailor voiced. Another answered, "I doubt it. No man can hold his breath for that long. They've been under the water for over half an hour."

The truth, however, was that Jacob and the others were experiencing what few men had experienced before. Before the Millennial Reign, mermaids used to exist, but they became enslaved by a wicked captain before Noah's Flood. The captain's name was Bluebeard. In revenge, the mermaids rose up against their aggressors and killed Captain Bluebeard and his men, but the damage had already been done to the mermaids. Shortly after, the mermaids all started to get sick, and one by one, they died from a plague. They caught a disease from man, and it wiped out their entire race.

At the dawn of the Millennium, the Counselor created mermaids again, but this time, He made it more difficult for man to find the mermaids home. For hundreds of years, their home in the sea was protected by a reef that appeared impassable. The rocks were jagged in the area, and many ships had been lost. Thus, there were signs posted in the vicinity to warn ships away. Jacob was just daring enough to bring his ship into the bay, and he made the discovery of a lifetime.

As Jacob swam with the mermaids, he was in ecstasy, then suddenly they all departed from him and he was left alone. He wondered if he had done something to offend them but that was not the case. From behind him appeared the most beautiful mermaid of all. Her hair was golden. Her breasts were voluptuous, and her curves were worth dying for. She also resembled Hannah, his former wife, in many ways. Her looks were so close to Hannah's that Jacob thought that it might be her. He pondered, "Maybe Hannah turned into a mermaid after she sunk to the bottom of the sea. Maybe it really is her." Jacob truly wanted to believe it, but he did not know. He could not ask her because the mermaid did not know his language.

When Jacob moved in closer, he gazed long and hard into the mermaid's eyes then hugged and kissed her over and over again. He voiced, "Is it you Hannah?" but his words came out all garbled under the water, so the mermaid looked at him dumbfounded. The chieftain then took the mermaid's hand and swam towards the surface. As the two heads popped up from below the sea, Jacob had a giant grin upon his face. He voiced, "Hannah, my love ..." and looked closely at the mermaid. Jacob suddenly realized that the mermaid was not Hannah. Her features had been distorted under the sea, and his smile turned into a frown. Jacob's heart sunk within him, and he felt an emptiness inside once again. When the mermaid saw the change in his expression, she looked sad for a moment then she tried to comfort him, but Jacob shunned her away, so the mermaid reached out to him one last time, gave him a hug then dove back under the waves.

The other two men had already risen to the surface and were back on board the ship. When they saw Jacob, everyone gave out a sigh of relief. After all, he was their captain and their friend. He was also one of the best seamen in the world. As for the mermaids, they had vanished as quickly as they had come. The men looked about for them, but they were no where to be found.

The ship sailed around the area for a few more days in hopes of seeing the mermaids again, but they never reappeared. Therefore, Jacob gave the orders, and they set sail for their homeland in Tarshish. As the ship sailed, things were going smoothly until they encountered a D.M.R. warship on the way. It was flying the red colors of the D.M.R. Jacob's vessel also bore its flag. The Union Jack of the old British Empire was waving in the wind, except now all the red on the flag was replaced with orange and the blue was replaced with green to show unity between the old guards of the Protestants and the Catholics.

This encounter was not good for Jacob and his men because tensions between the two countries had still been high after the war. As a result, when the D.M.R. warship saw the Tarshish flag waving in the wind, the captain decided to make sport of them. The only thing the D.M.R. captain didn't realize was that Jacob's yacht was a converted vessel from the war. It may have been smaller than the D.M.R warship, but it was more mobile than the D.M.R. ship. Jacob's vessel was also well-armed with laser fire and other conventional weapons.

When the captain of the Magog warship saw Jacob's ship in his sight, he fired a bomb into the vicinity of Jacob's ship. It exploded within 100 meters of the Tarshish vessel.

Jacob yelled, "What the hell was that?"

One of the men answered, "The warship is firing upon us."

"Those bastards," Jacob mumbled under his breath, and he started to high-tail it out of there. Then suddenly another bomb exploded in the water, but this time it was much closer, and Jacob's ship rocked violently back and forth from the explosion.

The captain of the D.M.R. ship hollered out, "I said get a shot in close, not hit them!"

But the gunner of the D.M.R. ship merely laughed, and the rest of the D.M.R. men also chuckled. The captain tried to hold back his laughter too, but a slight grin started to form on his face as he cadenced, "Now be careful, lieutenant!"

Everyone on board knew the captain loved the shot, but he was the captain, so he had to keep some form of composure.

"We don't want to start another war," the captain explained, "so we need to be careful."

But the gunner mumbled to the men near him, "And no one would know if we sunk that ship. It would be lost forever at the bottom of the sea."

"I heard that lieutenant," the captain exhorted. "No more shots until I give the order."

Meanwhile, Jacob wasn't taking the offense against his ship well, so he turned his ship around and at full throttle drove his ship straight into the warship's path.

"What are you doing Jacob?" one of the men asked. "I'm going to kamikaze their ship!" Jacob insanely gargled.

"That's suicide!" one of his shipmates hollered.

"Yes it is," Jacob said as he gritted his teeth and held firm on the throttle.

Meanwhile the captain of the D.M.R. ship inquired, "What is he doing?"

The look-out man answered, "He's heading right for us, and he's coming in fast."

"Are you sure?" the captain questioned.

"Yes, and he's 200 meters off our bow."

"Fire upon him, captain!" one of the men suggested.

The captain thought about it for a moment as Jacob's ship got closer. He hesitated too long though. The ships were now 100 meters apart and a major collision was about to happen on the high seas. If he fired upon Jacob's ship, it was possible that his ship could also be damaged from the explosion, so the captain ordered, "Veer to the left! Get out of her way!"

Jacob's ship closed in. The two ships were now twenty meters away from one another. From the captain's perspective, the situation looked hopeless. He ordered, "Brace for impact!" but at the last second, Jacob veered away and managed to skim the side of the warship. It was far too close for comfort for everyone involved, but Jacob knew his ship like it was an extension of his own body, and he pulled off the maneuver like a master craftsman. The men on Jacob's ship roared in celebration. Jacob put the ship into idle, ran down the stairs then stood at the side of the vessel. His men followed him. Jacob then pulled down his pants and BA'd the warship. His men followed in suit. Their bare asses hung in the wind, and they were hooting and howling like Marauding warriors.

When the men on the D.M.R. warship saw the display, they knew they'd been bested. The captain and his men just stood there dumbfounded, gawking at the display. Over a loud speaker they heard, "Take that, you bastard sons-of-bitches!" Jacob's comrades continued to mock and laugh at the D.M.R. warship. The best the D.M.R. men could do was make derogatory gestures in Jacob's direction as they cussed and slurred under their breath. Jacob then ran back upstairs and hit the gas. He did a roundabout around the D.M.R. warship, flipped the D.M.R. captain off, and fled the scene like a leopard carrying off its prey.

Chapter 41

▼

Peace, Apostasy, & the Post War Dream

The Tarshish-Magog War started on Dec. 31st, 776 and ended on Feb. 2, 777. Millions lost their lives, and even more were injured. Both Tarshish and the D.M.R.'s armed forces were badly depleted and many more were mourning the loss of their loved ones. In the Land of Nod, the war raged on. The D.M.R. settlers managed to take over most of the major cities to the south in the first year of the war, but the occupation of Native Nodian territory proved costly. Almost everyday a terrorist bomb would go off, and the D.M.R. military would suffer casualties. This dragged on for four more years. The death toll for the two wars now numbered over a billion, and the D.M.R. citizens were growing weary of the conflict. The President's approval rating was at an all time low, and many groups wanted his resignation. Regardless, the President's term was coming to a close the following year, so the people in the D.M.R. held out hope. In 781, Nod's War for Independence was over. The President ordered a withdrawal from Native Nodian territory, and the Natives celebrated in the streets. Finally after hundreds of years of subjugation, Nod was free. The loss of life still weighed heavy on the people in the area, but the Natives were finally free from the oppressive D.M.R. regime.

After the D.M.R. withdrew from Southern Nod, a border was drawn up separating Nod into two countries. There was some dispute over certain regions, but ultimately the two sides came to an agreement and a treaty was signed. The border ran approximately along the same lines of the former U.S. Canadian border before the Kingdom Age, but not exactly. Some of the geography had changed since that period, but it was fairly close. As for the two countries of Nod, the North remained a colony of the D.M.R. and the South became its own country.

In 782, Southern Nod joined the Alliance and became an official member of the Empire Free Trade Pact. They became allies with Tarshish, Sheba, Dan, and De-Dan. Dan helped out tremendously with rebuilding Southern Nod and within a decade, the Natives were prospering again. To the north, the settlers in Nod were aided by Coalition forces, and they were soon back on their feet, but not quite as fast as the Natives to the south.

* * * *

The century following the Nodian War of Independence and the Tarshish-Magog conflict brokered in another era of peace and prosperity for the Outskirts. No wars were being fought and there was cooperation between Alliance and Coalition Forces. During this era, people began to get fat and lazy. The lusts of the flesh prevailed, and many bowed down to foreign gods. Of course, each year, the nations brought forth their tribute to the Lord of Lords, but most did it out of obligation. There was no heartfelt love for the Counselor anymore, and most despised the Kingdom for having to be subjugated to them. In addition, most saw the Kingdom as a backward people. They were living in the stone ages. Progress and technology were the wave of the future, and Gog Incorporated was leading the way. There were many in the Outskirts, however, who missed the simple life in the Kingdom. These New Timers had lived in the Kingdom before Mandate 222 had passed, and they held onto the ancient ways. They were called old fashioned by the young and frowned upon by some, but they were the staples of society. They remembered the Outskirts when it was a wild garden and many despised the fact that it was being replaced by high rises and concrete.

* * * *

"Kasca, over here, you've got to see this," Esmeralda prodded and pointed down at Liberty Square from Gog Inc.'s high-rise building. "That woman is going for the all-time record. She has had sex with more than 900 men in the last twenty hours, and I think she is going to break the record. I didn't think it was possible to beat Dominque Ditz' record of having intercourse with over 1,000 men in a twenty-four hour period, but this woman's on the verge of becoming infamous."

Kasca looked down and asked, "What's her name?"

"Oh, I don't know, but her koochie has to be hurting by now," Esmeralda chuckled. "I went down there an hour ago to get a close-up and her vagina was all enflamed, but she looked determined. I even sent a news crew down there to take pictures and get a holo-image for the viewers at home."

"My oh my," Kasca laughed, "some people will do anything for that fifteen minutes of fame. And look at that line of men waiting to get a piece of her. It must go around the block."

"Yeah, I know. It's kind of scary. Do you think we should do something about it?"

"No, no, let them have their fun," Kasca voiced. "They're not hurting anyone."

"If the Counselor could see us now, He'd be turning over in His grave."

"Well, if He is God, He can see all things," Kasca scoffed, "but the D.M.R. must be out of His range. The Counselor's obviously no king. He's no god. He's a con!"

Esmeralda slapped Kasca across the face at this slur and shouted, "Why must you insult me? You know my sympathies. You know I believe He's the Messiah."

"Ha, ha, ha," Kasca mocked. "After all these years, you still believe in Him. Were you born yesterday? He's like Santa Claus to me. I thought you were wiser than that, Zeze. Can't you see through His bag of tricks?"

"Kasca, you're such a jerk," and she raised her hand to slap him across the face again, but Kasca stopped her in mid-swing and started squeezing her hand real hard.

"Let go, you're hurting me!"

Esmeralda glared into his eyes, but Kasca continued to squeeze harder.

"Let me go!" Esmeralda shouted and Kasca freed her.

"One of these days you're going to have to make a choice, Zeze," Kasca spoke earnestly. "Are you with Him or are you with me? And if you don't want a fight, don't ever bring up His name in my presence again. Understand?"

Kasca gave her a hard look and stormed out of the office building as Esmeralda glanced down at the woman going for the world record one last time, and she began to weep.

* * * *

"'Vanity of vanities, all is vanity' the poet wrote," Matusak preached to his 21st, 22nd, and 39th wife.

All four of them were in bed together, and they had just indulged in an orgy of sex together.

"My dears, do you understand what I am saying?"

None of the wives said a word, but they remained quiet and submissive as Matusak continued his rant.

"King Solomon was the wealthiest King of Israel. He had everything. He had fame. He had fortune. He had power. He had hundreds of wives and all that he desired, but he was still not satisfied. He had no peace, and he was not happy with his lot in life," Matusak stated. "I am like King Solomon. I am not content but displeased with my existence."

"Matusak, please don't fret," his 21st wife comforted. "Let us enjoy the moment. The night is still young. There is a bright future ahead of you."

"Oh hogwash!"

Matusak angrily rose from the bed and started to pace about the room. All three women were watching him carefully.

"There is no future for me. I have been banished from the Kingdom. All that awaits me is judgment and eternal separation from God. Even this so-called paradise brings loathing to my heart. There are no new worlds to conquer. There are no new places to see. What am I suppose to do with the rest of my wretched life? Ah! Better the miscarriage than me. For it goes into obscurity and knows nothing."

Matusak collapsed to his knees and continued to holler out. His wives rushed to his side and tended to him as Matusak wept, "Why Lord, why? Why did you ever make me to walk upon this earth in the first place? This is hell down here. I have no joy. I am bored with all things. Let me out of here!"

As of late, Matusak had been having a lot of these episodes. He had been alive for almost 800 years, and he was tired with life. He even contemplated suicide from time to time, but he couldn't bring himself around to doing it. Instead, he walked around comatose like a zombie. He slept constantly and ignored all his duties. At times he would go on rampages and destroy everything. He would burn buildings to the ground, attack innocent bystanders, and cause turmoil in Alexandria. In general, he was doing a poor job as ruler of the Empire, and there was talk amongst some of the leading Marauders that he should be removed from power. They saw his public displays of emotion as weakness and his rampages as signs that he was losing his mind.

*   *   *   *

In the Year of 890, Alexandria had a surprise guest. They were visited by the King of Kings. He came to the territory secretly, and the first place he visited was Matusak's palace. When Matusak's servants and wives saw the Counselor at their gate, they immediately opened the gates to the palace and welcomed Him as a King. When Matusak's first wife saw Emmanuel, she cried, "My prayers have been answered!" She took Him by the hand and brought him to Matusak's quarters. As they went, she informed the Counselor about Matusak's latest rumblings and all the trouble he was causing. When the Counselor heard her words, He said He would do all He could to aide her husband.

Matusak was found in his bed having a bad dream. He was sweating profusely under the sheets, and he was being chased by a fire-breathing dragon. The situation looked hopeless in his dream, and just when Matusak thought he was going to be burned alive, he awoke to the Counselor sitting at his bedside.

"Am I still dreaming?" Matusak asked himself as he looked at the Counselor, and he started slapping his face to see if he was really awake. Matusak closed his eyes for a moment then reopened them again only to find the Counselor still staring at him.

"You are here!" Matusak said overjoyed. He jumped out of bed, gave the Counselor a huge hug, and spun Him around like a child.

"Yes, my friend, I have returned from the dead," the Counselor joked, "and I have come to help you out."

"Help?" Matusak asked, "Who called for help?"

"Officially no one, but your first wife has been crying out to My Father in heaven for some time now, and I have answered her call."

"Yes, that first wife of mine is always causing trouble," Matusak stated. "She walks around the palace like she owns the place, and I can never get any rest. I suppose that's why I married her."

The Counselor laughed, "Yes, she has done you good all the days of your life. And even though you multiplied your spouses, she did not leave you. She was upset that you married others and at the time jealous, but she has remained by your side. She must truly love you."

Matusak looked away condemned knowing that he wasn't suppose to practice polygamy, so he changed the subject and stated, "So what was her prayer about?"

"She has asked that your reason would return to you and that your life would be spared," The Counselor explained.

"My life in danger?" Matusak questioned. "Who is planning to kill me?"

"Many have risen up against you in the last few years. Even those who have been your most loyal subjects are questioning your rule," the Counselor explained. "For over a decade, you have ruled like a madman. You have become like a King who has drank too much wine and has forgotten the ruling ordinances. At times, you run about your kingdom like a man possessed by a demon."

"Am I possessed, my Lord?"

"No, but I've seen men possessed by a legion of demons function more orderly than you have lately."

"It is true, my Lord," Matusak confessed, and he fell to his lap whimpering like a child. "I ha … a … a … ave been depressed lately, and I ca … a … an't seem to find joy in anything."

"That is because you have over indulged yourself. You have forgotten about sacrifice and pain," the Counselor spoke plainly. "It is time for you to rid yourself of the chains that bind you. You must come with me. We are going to Mt. Sinai. We will both endure a forty day fast to clean our minds and become one with our God. There will be no holoscreen to entertain you. There will be no women to satisfy you. We will reside with the monks at the foot of the mountain, and you will purify your soul. Let's go. We are leaving right now," the Counselor ordered.

"But I have to get prepared," Matusak said. "I have to …"

"You have to do nothing," the Counselor interrupted. "You will go with the shirt on your back. Your first wife will take care of everything while you are gone. Now, let's be on our way."

The Counselor started heading towards the door, and Matusak followed. The Marauder went reluctantly, but he followed like a dog being given orders by his master.

Forty days later, Matusak returned to the Empire a new man. It looked like he lost 100 pounds, but his mind was quick and sharp. To his wives and everyone at the palace, it appeared as if the old Matusak was back. In the months following his retreat to Mt. Sinai, Matusak first put his house in order and the Empire followed in step. Even those who wanted to remove Matusak from his throne were satisfied. There no longer was talk of assassination attempts amongst key leaders, and the Alexandrian Empire was thriving again. As for the Counselor, He returned home to Jerusalem refreshed. The journey to Alexandria and His fast at Mt. Sinai reminded the King of the suffering He had to endure long ago. It brought back a lot of sorrowful memories, but the forty day fast reminded the Counselor why He was willing to step from the throne and sacrifice His life. He did it for Matusak. He did it for man. He bore the cross to bring back those who were lost.

*   *   *   *

During the first century of peace, the Professor had a romantic love affair with a student named Sierra from the University. And although there was a significant age gap between the two lovers, this affair turned into a long term relationship. In fact, they had already been together for over 200 years. This was possible because Patmos and Sierra fit together like chocolate and caramel. The two melded into one when they made love and their minds interlinked. They could talk about anything and there was no fear of rejection or censorship or anything that would bring up their defenses because they fully trusted one another. Nonetheless, the two lovers never married. Patmos had already gone down that path twice before, and he wasn't willing to partake in the public ceremony again. The Professor never liked the idea of marriage in the first place. Instead he preferred a relationship built on mutual trust without all the bondage of a formal commitment. As for Sierra, she understood. She would have married the Professor if he asked, but she was a free spirit, and she saw no use in pushing the issue. In fact, she had all the characteristics of a gypsy, although she did not practice the craft. Sierra was also a happy person and a joy to be around. In any case, the two were intimate lovers, and this bond grew with the passing years. They still had a vibrant sex life despite their many years together. And to keep themselves from getting bored in the relationship, they role-played with one another and occasionally swung with others.

"Sierra, you have the smoothest skin I have ever touched. It feels as if I am running my fingers over velvet," Patmos complimented. "Your scent is divine, and your beauty rivals Aphrodite. I could lie here with you forever and be contented for the rest of my days."

The two stared into each other's eyes and neither one of them looked away shamefully. Sierra smiled gleefully like a child but did not blush or feel ashamed for receiving Patmos' sweet words. The Professor smiled back then Sierra spoke.

"You are too kind, Patmos. You make me want to lock you away and throw away the key, so only I could enjoy the pearls of wisdom rolling from your lips."

"If you did that, my love, I would become embittered, and my affection for you would turn to hate."

"It would not, my dear, because I would make you my love slave," Sierra boasted with an evil grin. "I would have you crawling on your hands and knees for me and you'd willingly do my bidding."

Patmos laughed, "You're so full of yourself. I would not be your love slave. Instead I'd make you submit unto me."

Sierra instantly switched roles at the suggestion and spoke, "O please master, what is it you desire? Would you like me to massage you? Would you like me to pleasure you?"

Sierra crawled on top of the Professor and began to rub him down.

"How does that feel, master," Sierra acted. "Does that please you?"

"Yes slave, carry on. You are doing a wonderful job but press harder."

Sierra's hands gripped firmer, and she continued to work down Patmos' back. When she reached his buttocks, Patmos rolled over, and she began to massage his arms and legs. Then she began to kiss him all over. She kissed his lips. She sucked on his nipples. She worked her way down. When she reached his privates, she began to service him.

* * * *

Patmos was a man who thrived during adversity. During times of peace and prosperity, however, he did not fair so well. Patmos found his way towards trouble during idle times. Simply put, he would get bored when everything was going well. For example, before the Millennial Reign, Patmos lived in Sweden, a prosperous European country. He had everything he wanted. He came from a wealthy and well-respected family. He had a prestigious job working as an executive for a successful company. And he accomplished all of this before the age of thirty. Thus, he started to dabble in evil things. He took ecstasy occasionally, used cocaine from time to time, and he smoked marijuana. In addition, he dabbled with the occult. Being of the rich, elite society, he was exposed to promiscuous behavior that people usually only read about in books. On a monthly basis, a fraternity of men he belonged to called the Crowing Wizards would gather together with a sorority of women, and they would indulge in all sorts of sinful pleasures. Everyone would wear masks like it was a Halloween charade, and people would walk about with their identities unknown. They would sacrifice animals like it was a voodoo ceremony, and some would drink the blood. Usually, people would dance uncontrollably in the blood, smear it all over their bodies, and have orgies of sex in the fluid. Others would indulge in sadomasochistic behavior, and some would buy young children in the Asian slave market, so they could defile them. Sodomy was also considered the norm at these parties. Men slept with men and women lusted after one another.

Patmos was exposed to all of this in his teens, and he never really questioned the behavior. The circles he ran around with were politicians, wealthy businessmen, and people of power. His lineage went way back to Sweden's upper crest. At an early age, he was educated in the most prestigious schools and disciplined firmly for disruptive behavior.

Patmos was one of the few who lived through the Tribulation. During the first 3½ years of Mahdi's rise to power, Patmos witnessed the events first hand. He was not part of Mahdi's inner circle, but he did have connections with people who were part of the outer realm. Therefore, when Mahdi, later known as the Antichrist, began to seize power, the Professor was one of the first to raise the red flag, and eventually Patmos became one of Mahdi's most vocal opponents in Sweden. He would not receive the Mark of the Beast. Patmos believed Sweden should remain a free and independent society. So many of the powerful supporters of the Antichrist tried to silence Patmos, but it only brought him more fame and notoriety. Ultimately, Patmos was blacklisted like the rest of the people who refused to receive the Mark of the Beast, and he was not able to buy or sell. In addition, some people were starting to get arrested for opposing Mahdi, and it was during this time that Patmos learned the truth about God and the Man of Lawlessness.

After Patmos was enlightened, he did his best to oppose Mahdi and his followers, but it was difficult because Mahdi was getting stronger every day. People were starting to praise him as the Messiah, so Patmos was ostracized by many. The Crowing Wizards excommunicated him, and shortly thereafter, he was taken away secretly in the night and thrown into an underground high security prison. Patmos was never seen from again, and he lived out the rest of the Tribulation in confinement.

Chapter 42

▼

The Ancient Myths

"Counselor, tell us about the dragons of yore," a child requested. "Our teacher told us about the Dragon Wars, but can you tell us more about them?"

A group of children were gathered around Emmanuel, and they scooted in closer to hear His story.

"Long ago when man was first created, dragons were one of man's best friends. Both creations were intelligent species that spoke to one another. At times, dragons would even allow men to ride upon their backs. They would travel to distant lands and go on great adventures together. The dragons were also called serpents, fire breathers, or leviathan, but most of the time they liked to be called by their given names. One of these dragons was called Quetzalcoatl. He was a mischievous dragon. He was brave, over-confident, and a tad bit gullible. One day, Quetzalcoatl was resting in the Garden of Eden in the branches of the Tree of Knowledge when he was awakened by an angelic being who had taken the form of a female dragon. When Quetzalcoatl set eyes upon this dragon, he was immediately enamored by her splendor. Quetzalcoatl had never seen such a beautiful dragon, and he couldn't keep his eyes off her. The female dragon then started to excrete a sweet scent, and Quetzalcoatl was mesmerized by it. By and by the dragons became intimate, and the female dragon asked Quetzalcoatl if he wanted to unite and become one. Quetzalcoatl did not understand what the female dragon meant, but he agreed anyway. 'All that you must do,' the female dragon spoke, 'is give me your consent and do as I desire.' Quetzalcoatl was so charmed by the female dragon that he agreed to her wishes and asked, 'What must I do?' 'All that you must do,' the female dragon spoke, 'is close your eyes, listen to my voice, and do as I command.' Quetzalcoatl did as she requested and before he knew it, he was in a trance. The female dragon had hypnotized him."

The children moved in closer. They hung onto the Counselor's words like a kitten clinging to its mother as Emmanuel continued. But just before the Counselor was about to carry on with His story, a child interrupted Him and asked, "What happens next? Did Quetzalcoatl snap out of it?"

"Be patient, my young friend, you shall know the outcome of the story in a matter of moments," the Counselor encouraged.

The child nodded his head impatiently, and the Lord finished his tale.

"Quetzalcoatl did not snap out of the hypnotic trance. Instead, he was fed subliminal thoughts by the female dragon. He was ordered to seduce the woman, known as Eve, and get her to eat from the Tree of Good and Evil."

"Was the female dragon, Lucifer?" a child asked who was familiar with the Biblical stories.

"Yes, Suzie, the female dragon was the Devil, and he was on a quest to bring about the fall of man and the radiant lineage of dragons. As for the rest of the story you already know it. Quetzalcoatl came to Eve when she was in the Garden and fooled her to eat of the Tree of Knowledge. Eve then gave the fruit to Adam, and he willingly rebelled against My orders by eating of the fruit. Hence, they both sinned against Me and were expelled from the Garden. As for the dragon, Quetzalcoatl, he brought a curse upon his species and they were transformed into snakes. Dragons lost their ability to fly and breathe fire, and they were made to crawl upon their bellies."

When the children heard the judgment against man and the dragons, they were saddened by the news and some of the younger ones began to cry. But suddenly out of nowhere, a flock of dragons come out of the sky and landed right next to the Counselor and the children. The children's grief immediately turned to glee and some clapped in expectation. The lead dragon then came forward, bowed unto the King and spoke reverently.

"My King, we have come from the jungles of the North, where the Tribe of Signmonkoala now reside, and they informed us you needed our assistance."

"Yes Quetzalcoatl," the Counselor responded and the children awed when they heard his name, "if you have the time, we would like to go on a pleasure journey across the sky and visit the original destination of the Garden of Eden."

"Your wish is my command," Quetzalcoatl answered, "May I do the honors of carrying my Lord?

The Counselor bowed unto Quetzalcoatl and proceeded to crawl upon his back. The Lord then ordered, "Each of you climb upon the backs of the dragons. Do not be afraid. You are in good hands. The leviathan will take care of you."

One by one the children crawled onto the backs of the dragons and when each child was secure, Quetzalcoatl let out a call and the flock set out in flight.

* * * *

Life in the Kingdom continued as it was from the beginning. There was peace and tranquility. There was no want, nor need. In the Outskirts there were wars, suffering, and plagues, but in the Kingdom, there was no hunger, nor thirst, nor disease. People didn't even get sick. There were no infirmities, no handicaps, nor deformities. At night, one could walk about safely without the fear of being mugged or murdered. There were no locks on people's doors, no bars on anyone's windows, and children could roam about freely without the fear of kidnappings and other abominable deeds. At night, one could fall asleep looking up into the stars without the fear of predators on the prowl. The animals were tame, and there were no crazies on the streets. There were no mosquitoes or spiders feasting on ones flesh, nor flies buzzing around ones face, nor thorns nor thistles. It was a perfect society. The law of the jungle no longer ruled in the Kingdom.

There were a few incidents over the centuries, however, that did raise eyebrows. One time during the 4th Century, a man went on a killing rampage. This man had been reading about some of the famous murderers before the Millennial Reign, and he decided he wanted to experience murder first hand. This savage kidnapped a woman in her twenties. After torturing her for some time, he proceeded to cut off her limbs, then skin her alive. The woman died and most people assumed she had left the Kingdom for the Outskirts. There was a large scale search for the woman, but she was never found. This man went onto kill three other women, and their bodies were found by the Dead Sea stripped of their skin with their limbs missing. When the news went public, people started to panic and an investigation began by the local authorities. They never caught the man, but the King of Kings did. The murderer had captured another woman, and she had already been tortured for several days. It was just a matter of time before the psycho-maniac decided to take her life, but the Lord stepped in before he was able to finish the deed. The woman was rescued, and the murderer was immediately judged and sentenced. The killer's life was taken from him, and his soul was cast into the Lake of Fire where the False Prophet and Antichrist now reside. As for the woman, the Lord erased all memory of the torture she endured, and He resurrected the other victims. They returned to their natural state, and they also had no recollections of the pain they endured.

Other incidents like these occurred from time to time, but the Counselor always stepped in to keep the order. He knew all things like His Father in heaven, and He kept a watchful eye on His flock on earth. Sometimes, the Lord would allow things to play out to give humanity a choice between good and evil, but if someone overstepped their bounds, the Counselor would not allow evil deeds to go on forever. He would set things right and the wicked ones would not go unpunished.

Chapter 43

Autobiography (The Rise to Power)

The following excerpt is taken from *The Autobiography of Queen Sheba*.

* * * *

My rise to power came in 95 K.A., the year my father died. Menelik had ruled for fifty years, but he was dying. He was an Old Timer who bore the Mark of the Beast. Thus, everyone watched as his skin began to wrinkle and his health began to fade. I was forty years old at the time, and no one was sure who would inherit the throne because Menelik had not chosen an heir. The family was asking, "If father dies unexpectedly, will the throne go to the first son as it was in the days of old? Or would the crown go to whoever was the strongest and most ruthless?" I was the first daughter of the second wife, so I knew I was not going to inherit the throne. The first wife had many children. She had thirteen in all, and there were numerous boys. So I knew if I was to win the crown, I would have to do it by force. Luckily for me, I had control over many people because I had collected loads of holo-projections over the years of people partaking in compromised exploits. For the men, I usually had footage of them engaging in homosexual behavior. This was strictly forbidden under Menelik's decrees and anyone engaging in the behavior would be publicly ostracized by society. Of course, behind closed doors at Menelik's Palace, many people were practicing sodomy. For the women, I usually had some piece of gossip that could ruin their reputation, so they usually did my bidding.

One of the most powerful men I had under my thumb was Franklin. He was a wicked boy, a sado-masochist at heart that loved to torture animals and kill things. He had been a puppet of mine for years since childhood, and I knew that I could use his sick and twisted ways to my advantage, if it was required. The second man was Altie, the commander of the Royal Guard. I thought I may be able to manipulate him into helping me take the crown, so I went to him in private and discussed my plans.

"As you know Altie, Menelik is on his last leg. He may die any day now, and he has not picked an heir," I stated.

"Yes, everyone's watching closely. The news of his health has spread far and wide, and there's been some turmoil in the townships," Altie said. "His death may bring about civil war."

"My point exactly," I agreed. "If Mene, the first son, takes over, it's quite possible, the family could lose control to one of our rival tribes. And neither of us wants that. We need a strong ruler who will rule with an iron thumb."

"Do you have anyone in mind?" Altie asked with a hint of derision in his voice.

"Don't give me that B.S. Altie, you know perfectly well who!" I exclaimed. "I am going to take the throne, and you are going to help me!"

"You seem so sure of yourself, Sheba," Altie mocked. "These are changing times. I'd hate to see you get hurt."

"Then let me offer you a little incentive," I bribed. "If I manage to be in a position to take the throne, I plan to make you the lead general of the army. You will answer only to me, and you will have full authority."

"I see, and how do you plan to seize the crown?"

"Don't worry about that. I have a plan," I stated. "Just know that when the time is right, I want the Royal Guard to stand behind me. Do we have a deal?"

For a moment Altie thought, "Sheba's been driven since childhood. She does have the audacity and demeanor to pull this off, but how does she plan to do it. Will she kill Menelik's first son? Hmm ... She does have those holo-projections of me partaking in obscene acts. If I don't support her, she's sure to release them to the public. That would mean I would have to kill her. And if I do kill her, who's to say the projections won't be released anyway to the public? I'm sure she's got a back-up plan ..."

"So what is your answer, Altie?" I pressed. "Do I have your support?"

Altie saluted. "My Queen, I am your loyal subject. I will stand by your side at the appointed time."

"Very good, Altie," I said, *"You will be a man of great power and authority. I think even our history books will remember you as a hero."*

Altie thought, "A hero ... hmm, I like the sound of that," and I went my way.

After I had the support of the Royal Guard, I knew I was one step closer to taking the throne. The next person I needed to manipulate was Franklin, my most trusted companion, so I went down to the science lab and found him working on one of his experiments. But his research wasn't exactly what you would call scientific. Franklin was more like Joseph Mengele of the Nazi regime during WWII. He tortured animals indiscriminately and played with them like a child does with ants. He'd burn them, tear off their wings, and put all sorts of drugs and poisons in their food. In other words, Franklin was sick in the head.

"So Franklin, what do you have there?" I asked.

"Oh, it's just a bat," Franklin responded. *"I'm seeing how far I can stretch the wings before they are pulled out of socket and ripped from its abdomen."*

"I see ... very interesting," I said as I looked away disgusted after seeing the bat struggling and screaming out in misery."

"You know playing with bats is nice and all, but what would you say if I got you a bigger fish to play with?" I asked.

Franklin seemed to be ignoring me.

"How would you like to have your own human being to play with?"

Franklin suddenly looked up from the bat. I knew all about his secret desires to experiment on human subjects.

"Yes, you heard me right, my dear," I enticed. *"As a gift, I plan to give you Ogden, your nemesis, who teased you as a child."*

Ogden was the King's second son of Menelik's first wife, and Franklin despised him.

When Franklin heard this, drool started to form around my mouth as I continued.

"All I need you to do is kill some people for me," I explained.

Franklin's eyes widened a little, and a smile started to form on his face. I then grabbed his crotch and started to rub myself up against him.

"And to top it off ... "

I started to ride myself up and down his leg.

"I plan to let you enter me, something you have always longed for and desired."

Franklin started to breathe hard and heavy as I asked, "Do we have an understanding?"

My half-brother nodded yes as I continued to rub myself up and down his leg, breathed into his ear, and nibbled on his earlobe.

Franklin was hard as steel, then he uttered, "Yes, I will kill them for you."

After I had Franklin in the fold, I made my plans to seize the throne. A week later, Menelik died of poison. I had Franklin sneak into his room at night and give him a dose of something that would be difficult to decipher if an autopsy was to take place. My thinking was, "My father's going to die anyway. I'm just going to speed up the process." That same night, I manipulated Odgen, my half brother, into the underground dungeon. He was easy to seduce. At family gatherings, he always had his eyes on me, so I knew he would be putty in my hands. Once I had him in the chamber, I managed to get him tied up to one of the tables and left him there for Franklin to enjoy later. That same night, I let Franklin loose upon his half brothers and sisters, and he proceeded to murder Menelik's first wife and all of her offspring. Seven of them were together in one of the palace's abodes, so they were easy for Franklin to knock off because they were still children. The rest Franklin had to pick off one by one, and he managed to do the job without getting caught. Even I was surprised that he pulled it off without anyone seeing him.

Early the next morning, the whole palace was in disarray. Everyone was rushing this way and that, trying to figure out what happened, so I took control.

I ordered, "Get the Royal Guard in here at once and find out who's responsible for these wicked acts!"

The servants responded quickly and within fifteen minutes, almost everyone on the palace grounds was gathered in the meeting hall.

I ordered, "No one is to leave this room until the Royal Guard investigates everyone's quarters and discovers who is accounted for and who is missing."

At first, no one seemed to question my authority. Altie jumped into line like I was the reigning queen and before anyone knew what happened, I was running the show.

It was later discovered, according to findings fabricated by the Royal Guard, that our enemies, the Maoris and the Aborigines had plotted together against us, the Meneliks, and killed our king. A day or so later, I ordered an emergency meeting of the Royal Guard, the general of our army, and some of the older siblings. At the meeting, I took control and started barking out orders. One of the older siblings asked, "Who put you in charge?" and everything got quiet for a moment. People looked around, and no one said a word then everyone started to argue with one another. Finally, Altie took one of his guns out and fired it into the ceiling. He yelled, "Fighting amongst each other is not going to help anyone! We need to conduct ourselves in a civilized manner, and in the last few days, only Sheba has had the steady nerve to make order out of chaos!" Everyone looked around at the table and agreed that I was doing a fine job of directing traffic. "So

I say," Altie continued, "until we figure out what's going on, we let Sheba continue with her agenda."

From that point forward, I led the family. In the coming weeks, the Royal Guard together with Menelik's army, marched upon the territories controlled by the Maori and Aborigine tribes, and we rode to victory. The remaining tribes on the continent immediately tried to make peace treaties with us, and we conquered all of Australia and New Zealand within a few months. Unfortunately, the general of our army was killed by sniper fire, which was planned by the Royal Guard, so I put Altie in charge. Within a year, I was pronounced Queen of the land, and my first edict was to rename our empire the Land of Sheba.

Looking back at those days, it's hard to believe that the events really happened. I can't believe I had the impudence to kill so many people for power. I sincerely regret my actions, and I freely admit that I am guilty of the deeds. When I first met the Counselor, I wept for a long time and repented of my sins. He forgave me and even took me as His wife. Do I deserve forgiveness? No, I don't think so. I should be hung by a rope for the crimes I have committed against the people of Sheba and my family. Someday, retribution will probably come my way, but in the meantime, I look to the cross as my source of liberty and justification.

Chapter 44

▼

Turn of the Century

In the late 800's and early 900's, a great plague occurred on the earth. It was the Plague of Old Age. It did not affect citizens in the Kingdom, but it did strike people in the Outskirts. It seemed to hit people hardest in the Outskirts because many of them had not eaten from the Tree of Life for some time. In fact, many of the common folk were lucky if they had eaten a Fruit Pill in their entire life and people started to look older. The rich elite, however, managed to stay young and strong. To be able to eat Fruit Pills at dinner was a status of your wealth and some overindulged themselves while the rest of the Outskirts slowly aged. As for the people in the Kingdom, traces of the Tree of Life were in everything. It was a key ingredient used in fruit juice and most cooks liked to sprinkle it on dishes and other delicacies. The Outskirts, however, were not afforded this luxury. People horded Fruit Pills like diamonds because doctors discovered that a deficiency of the fruit would cause old age. Thus, people became even stingier with the Fruit Pills as mankind's population increased and the supply of Fruit Pills decreased.

During the Millennial Reign, most adults looked like they were in their twenties, but when the 900's rolled around, a lot of people were starting to get a trickle of grey in their hair and many were starting to look like they were in their 30's or 40's by pre-Millennial standards. There were a few cases where people aged exceedingly fast, and some people died of old age. This scared many living in the Outskirts, and they started to envy those living in the Kingdom. There was even talk amongst some circles of invading the Kingdom and taking the Tree of

Life as a spoil of war. This way all of humanity would have access to the fruit and the Plague of Old Age would cease.

*   *   *   *

For 900 years, the people in the Kingdom had been isolated from the rest of the world. They lived a relatively sheltered life, but the perfection of God's creation still remained. The Kingdom still looked like the Garden of Eden unlike parts of the Outskirts that had been drilled, mined, and raped of its resources. Every year though at the Booth's Festival, foreigners would come to Jerusalem and give their tribute to the King. These outsiders would bring in gadgets and nick-knacks from the Outskirts that left Kingdom citizens in awe and wonder. Therefore, many people, especially those born during the Millennial Reign, wanted to know what was going on outside of the Kingdom. The news from the Outskirts would eventually trickle down to the Israeli citizens, but it was slow, incomplete, and many people wondered if the news had been censored. Finally in the year of 902, the citizens of the Kingdom demanded that the holoscreen ban of 262 be lifted. Everyone was curious as to what was really going on in the Outskirts, and if the holoscreen ban was abolished, people in the Kingdom would have access to information outside their borders. They would be exposed to holoscreen stations coming from the D.M.R. and the rest of the world. Their eyes would finally be opened, and it would change life in the Kingdom forever.

The government of the 144 Elders was a long established governing power in the world. When the group was established at the onset of the Kingdom Age, all 144 seats were occupied by Old Timers, but as the centuries passed, many of the original founding fathers resigned, retired, or left their post. These people needed to be replaced, and many of these seats were now occupied by people born during the Millennium. And in the Year of 902, these New Timers finally became the majority when Rhodes Kruger decided to leave his post. People from the Kingdom voted for his replacement, and a New Timer was elected. Now over two-thirds of the 144 Elders were New Timers, and they had the power to change Kingdom Law for better or worse.

The first law to go was the ban on news, information, and holoscreen programs coming from the Outskirts. This radically changed people's perspectives in the Kingdom. Within a few years, the influence of holoprograms from the Outskirts revolutionized fashion, outlooks, and the way people lived their lives. Overnight, the Kingdom was exposed to thousands of holoscreen stations, and it was like the Berlin Wall coming down at the end of the Cold War in the 20th Century. Prior to the lifting of the ban, the Kingdom only had a few holoscreen stations and most citizens didn't pay much attention to them. People were out doing things and living their lives, but holoscreen programs from the Outskirts were pure entertainment. There was also a lot of questionable behavior taking place on these stations, so some of the 144 Elders tried to step in and censor the profane stations, but the attempts proved futile. There were always ways around these clampdowns and after a decade of trying to ban stations that were unacceptable, they just gave up. In fact, it was mostly the Old Timers that were trying to censor them anyway, and they no longer had enough votes to rectify change. As for the Counselor, he let the 144 Elders do as they seemed fit. He found it ironic that they didn't ask His opinion on the issue of lifting the ban, but He was not surprised. The 144 Elders had gone without His counsel for years, and He realized people were starting to forsake Him for new gods, mostly the god of pleasure. Therefore, the Counselor let the ruling stand. Some of the Old Timers were up in arms over the whole debacle and they came to Him, but the Counselor informed them, "It is time to loosen the reigns. The New Timers will be offered fruit from the Tree of Good and Evil. They cannot be forced into belief. The end of the age is coming soon."

The Fog of War that used to protect the Kingdom from outsiders peering into their borders was also affected. For some strange reason, the moment the 144 Elders lifted the ban on holostations coming from the Outskirts, the Fog of War also vanished. Suddenly the D.M.R. could see into the Kingdom. For almost 700 years, Gog Inc. was baffled as to why their satellites could not see beyond a few kilometers into the Kingdom, but now they could see clearly. Some scientists believed the Kingdom had technology that could block out the cameras. They believed that this mechanism also blocked out receiving holostations from the Outskirts, but now that the Israelis were receiving these stations, they were no longer able to use their Fog of War to prevent spying from the Outskirts. The truth, however, was that the Counselor decided that the Fog of War was no longer a necessity now that the Kingdom was being exposed to so much new information. The King decided it just didn't matter anymore, so He made the Fog of War dissipate.

Exposure to Outskirts holoscreen programs was similar to what happened to the world when the internet was introduced to people in the late 20th and early 21st centuries. Kingdom citizens were exposed to improper behavior, and it was just a matter of time before these influences started to pop-up in Kingdom circles. For example, the holoscreen allowed people to interact with the projections and play a character in a script or play. The technology was incredibly complex, and the player felt as if he/she was really in the center of the action. Citizens could be movie stars, porn stars, race-car drivers, and even axe murderers. From the oldest Old Timer to the newest New Timer, almost everyone was using their holoscreen and role-playing in various ways.

* * * *

"Check it out, Billy, I just downloaded this holoprogram from the D.M.R.," the seventeen-year-old boasted. "It's called 'Babes, Breasts, and Blow-whores.' It's about two guys who are on a mission to have sex with every hooker in Amsterdam's Red-Light District. Would you like to come with me on this journey?"

"I don't know. My dad told me to stay away from that stuff," Billy answered. "He told me it's evil."

"C'mon, don't be such a square," his friend mocked. "We'll have the time of our lives, and do you always do what your father says?"

Billy sat silent looking down at the ground then he mumbled, "Mmm ... I don't know if I should."

"Billy, this program is hot," his older friend said convincingly. "It's a best seller in the D.M.R., and my parents won't be back until tomorrow. At least check it out for a while, and if you don't like it, we'll shut it off. Sound like a plan?"

"Oh okay," Billy said, "but you promise to end the program if I say?"

"Sure, of course!" his friend affirmed, "But I doubt you're going to want to turn it off because you're going on a journey where no man has gone before!"

The older teen proceeded to load the program into the holoprojector, and the two were enjoying sexual exploits that they had only dreamed were possible.

Events like these were happening everyday in the Outskirts, and it was just a matter of time before the Kingdom followed suit. The holoscreen had that much effect upon its viewers. It was seductive and sweet like honey on the tongue and more and more immoral programs were becoming available to Kingdom citizens everyday. Many Old Timers saw the holoscreen as the Whore of Babylon, and they hoped that their friends and families would not be led away from the precepts that the Kingdom was founded on. And some found it puzzling that although the Devil and his companions were locked away, mankind still found a way to wallow in the pigsty.

CHAPTER 45

REVIVAL, RELIGION, & SCIENCE

The 900's may have been a degenerate time in the Kingdom, but it was also a time of revival on the planet. Many people in the world were preparing for the end of the age. According to the ancient Scriptures, Lucifer would be released after the thousandth year of the Millennial Reign, and a new era would begin shortly thereafter. The righteous would reign with the Counselor forever and ever, and the wicked would be cast into the Lake of Fire for eternity.

Most people in the world did not believe the ancient tales. In many parts of the Outskirts, the Holy Books weren't even read anymore. In the D.M.R., the stories about Moses, David, and other Biblical characters were viewed as fairy tales. As for the Counselor, he was seen as a man of great power, but hardly anyone believed He was God. Most considered Him a powerful sage but nothing more. They respected Him out of fear, but they did not freely worship Him. As for other places in the Outskirts, it was much the same. Even in countries like Sheba and Tarshish, unbelief was the mainstay. In these lands, a large percentage of people would say they believed the Counselor was the Son of God, but they also believed that all men and women were "Sons of God." They had just not attained the same level yet. Someday they hoped to reach that pinnacle, but in the meantime, most did not seek to find answers to their questions, nor did they read the Holy Books themselves to find out if they were relative.

"Dear brothers and sisters, thank you all for coming here tonight. Some of you have come from distant lands to learn about the Holy Scriptures and you are welcome," the preacher from Tarshish spoke. *"Others have come out of curiosity to find out if these ancient prophecies are true or false. You are also welcome here tonight. So please listen, observe, and study but do not take my word for it. Read the ancient prophecies on your own, and come to your own conclusions. Ask yourself, is the Counselor truly the Son of God or is He a false leader merely fooling us with His bag of tricks? Can we believe in Him? Is it possible that God would become man in hopes of redeeming His creation? Is it true that when the thousand years are over, Lucifer, the great deceiver, will be released from the bottomless pit to wage war against the Kingdom? Is it true that the D.M.R. and its northern coalition will be the instrument that Satan will use to bring about his rebellion? Will one day the heavens and the earth be destroyed? Will a new heaven and a new earth take its place? These are some of the questions we will answer tonight. So be attentive, take notes, and draw your own conclusions, but most of all, when you leave this meeting tonight, I pray and hope that you will take the time to research the Holy Writings yourself. Test to see if they are true. Examine them like the ancient Church of Thessalonica. And I believe you will come to the same conclusion as I, that the Counselor truly is the Son of God ..."*

The preacher continued to expound his message, and the audience listened attentively. The preacher at the gathering went onto answer all of the questions he posed at his introduction, and he gave evidence to support his claims. This meeting was like many others during the century. People were repenting of their sins and turning back to God. They were reading the Holy Books once again, and millions were attending Revivalist meetings all over the globe.

* * * *

There was another group that was taking the nations by storm. They were called the "Sons of God." They believed that the Counselor's great feats of power would one day be available to all. They believed it was the next stop in the evolutionary process. They held the belief that after the thousandth year, the bodies of those who had been enlightened would be transformed into new bodies. These new bodies would enable them to fly and levitate like the Counselor's. These bodies would not die or age and they would not require food and water to survive. Ultimately they would live forever, and after the sun and earth passed away, their consciousness would leave this plane and become part of a new one elsewhere in the universe.

The Sons of God had over a billion believers by the Year of 950, and more and more converts were being added each day because the Sons of God believed if they brought someone to the "Path of Regeneration," they would be given more powers in the coming age. Some of these extrasensory powers included clairvoyance, telepathy, psycho-kinesis, and many more. The Sons of God greatly desired to have these powers. Thus, they worked hard to evangelize others and went to great extremes to find new converts. The truth, however, was that the Sons of God were a cult. Their teachings were based upon a book published in the 3rd Century titled the Lost Book of Gomar. It later became known as the Holy Book of Gomar. No one knows for sure who wrote the book. Some think it was a publicity stunt by the largest publisher in the Outskirts, the Roman Revival Corporation, in order to increase sales and the top executives never leaked the truth. The original manuscript was kept under lock and key, and the myth about the book grew over the centuries. In fact, it was one of the top selling books in the Outskirts because it gave an alternate interpretation of what happened when the Counselor came to earth. In the Kingdom, the book was immediately tagged as a book of heresy and was banned. This only created more interest in the book. Copies of the book were smuggled into the Kingdom during the Booth's Festival and more and more New Timers accepted it as the truth.

※ ※ ※ ※

Most people in the Outskirts did not follow the Sons of God nor believe in the Revivalist's message. They believed in science. They believed in technology. They were atheists or agnostics who had no religious faith. There were others, however, who dabbled in the occult, and witchcraft was a common practice in these circles, but the numbers weren't astronomical. Satanism was also running rampant in the Outskirts. The Satanist awaited Lucifer's return, and they believed they would be rewarded for their dedication to him. As for those who did believe in God, most thought of God as being benevolent to the human race. These people did not believe in the Counselor or any other god. They did not worship Him as the Messiah, nor consider Him worthy of tribute at the Festival of Booths. They simply saw Him as having know-how that was superior to their own. They believed, one day, science would solve the mystery of His miracles, and ultimately remove Him from His throne. And in the year of 975, the people in the north moved one step closer to achieving that goal. Gog Incorporated had learned how to manipulate rain clouds.

"Today is a day of renowned for the Outskirts. On this momentous occasion, we have learned how to control the weather," Kasca announced to the press. *"Gog Incorporated has learned how to recreate rain clouds. We can now cause thunder and lightning to occur naturally in the atmosphere. Our scientists believe within a matter of years, we will be able to control all rain precipitation in the D.M.R. This technology will finally enable us to break free from the Kingdom. We will no longer have to pay homage to the Counselor or any other power monger. We will be free to think and do as we please."* Kasca paused then continued, *"We plan to share this technology with the Coalition, the Alliance, and any other nation that wishes to be free from the bondage of our oppressors to the south ..."*

Kasca finished up his speech, and the whole world marveled at this achievement. More and more people began to seriously question the Counselor's power and by the year 978, the entire D.M.R. and most of the Coalition forces had weather systems in place. In that year, all Coalition nations did not bring forth tribute to the King of Kings. As for the Alliance, they had purchased the technology for a price from the D.M.R., and they too would have weather systems available to them if they desired to build or purchase them. In the meantime, members of the Alliance still brought forth tribute to the Counselor, and the rains fell on their kingdoms. As for the Coalition forces, the rain did not fall on their lands, so they had to rely upon their new weather systems to give them rain. In the beginning these weather systems had flaws and some parts of the D.M.R. did not get rain, but within a decade, the kinks were worked out, and the technology proved successful. Rain fell again on their territories, and almost everyone was pleased with the new discovery.

The weather systems were complex pieces of machinery. They would take regular cumulus clouds and transform them into nimbus clouds, also known as rain clouds. These weather silos would stimulate precipitation from the oceans, and it would bring rain to the land masses nearby. In the D.M.R., there were thirteen of these silos, and it was just enough to provide rain for the entire nation. Therefore, more of these weather machines were being manufactured everyday, and by the year 990, there were enough weather machines mass produced at Gog Inc. to bring water to every nation in the Outskirts.

Chapter 46

▼

Testimony from Nod

I was born in the Land of Nod, a Native by birth, during the 5th Century. I was raised in a fine home, and I was brought up on values that would be considered archaic by today's standards. I had a wonderful childhood, and my parents were honorable people.

As a young man, I decided to head out on the road and travel the world for a spell. I saw magnificent sights and met many strangers on the way. Some were good people and others were not so good. I quickly learned how to survive on my own, but was still conned on many occasions. Luckily, my street smarts got me out of a lot of sticky situations. During my travels, I visited Dan and saw the grand falls of Iguazu. In De-Dan, I trekked across the Valley of Poetry and witnessed spectacles only dreamed of in fairy tales. In Africa, I saw great beasts that walked the earth and a picturesque landscape of rivers, mountains, and lakes. However, in Africa, I witnessed war for the first time in my life. There were areas that were laid to waste with laser fire and bombs, and I saw many people starving and struggling to survive. I then took a ship to Sheba and worked as a sailor to earn my fair. After landing in Perth, I explored the continent by hitchhiking from town to town and picked up odd jobs along the way. I worked as a fruit picker, a ranch hand, a cook, and as a waiter. I got to know the local folk and made some long lasting friendships.

After Sheba, I ventured north and headed to Persia. Being a resident of Nod meant I had D.M.R. citizenship, and I was granted access into the country. Persia was a mysterious place. They spoke a unique dialect, and the people reminded me a lot of the Natives back home. Persia was not as developed as other places in the world, and I enjoyed the simplicity of the realm. After Persia, I headed further north and visited the largest city in the world, the City of Liberty. Some Old Timers call it the New York of the Kingdom Age.

I spent a few years in the City of Liberty working on the metro and rented out an apartment. During those years, I had a romantic love affair with a woman who ultimately broke my heart, so I left town and headed west through Beth-Togar-Mah and Gomar. After spending about a year in Europe hopping from one place to the next, I took a ship over to Tarshish and landed in Canaan. I worked for about a decade on a transport that brought goods from Tarshish to Greenland. It was a good job. I had many great adventures, but after twenty-five years on the road, I was longing for home. So I took the next available transport and returned to Nod.

After traveling the world, I felt well-rounded as a human being. I had experiences that can never be taught in a geography class, and I learned far more from travel than I ever learned in school. Still, there was an emptiness inside. In Nod, I tried to fill that void. I engaged in gluttonous behavior. I drank a lot and daily took Bliss. I was a wreck, and it did not make me feel whole inside. After a decade or so of living this way, I kicked Bliss cold turkey and didn't drink alcohol for over a century. Shortly thereafter, I met my soul mate, my wife Cindy. She gave me many children, and it was the happiest time of my life.

During this period, there was a lot of animosity towards the Settlers and the D.M.R. in the Land of Nod. A majority of Natives on the continent felt like their rights were being violated. There was civil unrest, and a lot of protests started taking place in the cities. The main reason the Natives were upset was because they felt like they had no representation in the Senate. For example, in the Year of 556, the Nodians voted in favor of joining the Empire Free Trade Alliance, but they were vetoed by the President of the D.M.R. long ago. For over two centuries, the Native Nodians felt like they had no voice in the political process. Many were tired of being used as a doormat, so in the Year of 775, the Natives rose up against their oppressors. Revolution was in the air, and in 776, the Native Nodians declared their independence. The Settlers to the north, however, did not sign the declaration, and the division between the two clans was engraved in stone. War was declared on us by the D.M.R. almost immediately, so I did what any patriot would do, I joined the resistance.

During the war, I saw atrocities that should never be spoken of or written down on paper. The brutality of man never ceases to amaze me. Even I found myself as being nothing more than a savage. I did anything to survive because food was as scarce as Fruit Pills during the war. And one time, I was so hungry that I stole food from a mother nursing her baby. When the war finally came to a close, I had lost three sons and my right arm. I was one of the lucky ones because over a billion people died in the war.

After the Natives won the war, we rebuilt our society with the help from the Alliance. The continent was divided into two, and we finally gained our freedom. As for me, I was never the same man. My bionic arm made me feel incomplete even though the arm worked perfectly. I would get the shakes from time to time, and I still have nightmares on a regular basis. Even after more than a century, I can't get the images from the war out of my head.

Immediately following the war, I was a wreck. To wash away the pain of losing so many friends and family members, I started drinking again, and if I had enough credits, I would buy the Purple Fruit to ease the pain. I was useless to my wife, but she took care of me. I fell into the worst depression I've ever known, and I couldn't lift myself out of the doldrums. I thought about suicide all the time and found no purpose in waking in the morning. After a few years of this behavior, my wife finally got me to see a psychiatrist for post-war veterans. I figured I had nothing else to lose, so I went to her sessions. A group of about a dozen army veterans gathered together, and we shared our stories. This outlet was the one thing that saved my sanity, and I made a full-recovery. But even going to hell and back, I still felt like there was something missing in my life. Spiritually I was vacant, so I went on a quest to find myself.

On my spiritual journey, the first place I stopped was at the Church of the Sons of God. I listened to their teaching and wholeheartedly gave myself over to their beliefs. I went through the Path of Regeneration. I went out earnestly and tried to convert others to the cause, so that I would receive more powers in the coming age. Ultimately, I was still unsatisfied, so I left the group, much to the delight of my family. I also did research on the Sons of God, and discovered that a lot of their teaching was based on untruths.

After a decade of being with the Sons of God, I considered religion to be foolhardy, and put my energy into my family. I had more kids with my wife, became the coach at all their sporting events, and things were good for a spell. My children took up all my time. In the end, about three decades later, I found myself hanging from another rope. The emptiness was still inside, and I figured there had to be something more. Therefore, I ventured out and decided to start my own business. I bought an old theater and turned it into a holo-house. In other words, people would watch the latest movie projections on an open space in the middle of the room. Business went very well, so I opened up a chain of them and became a successful businessman. This kept my mind occupied because I was so busy trying to keep everything up and going. In some ways, the work was good for me because it prevented me from moping about, but I think I was running around from place to place because I didn't want to think about the greater picture.

My business aspirations were going well, but in the Year of 910, a new holo-projection was released. It was the *Autobiography of Queen Sheba*. Her story greatly touched me. She had killed innocent people to gain control. I had killed people in the war. She had lived through many trials and tribulations. I had suffered in vain. And comparing our lives, there were many commonalities between us. But the one area that moved me the most was when she repented of our sins and bowed unto the Counselor and became a changed woman.

I experienced a similar experience. After watching her story in one of my holo-houses, I went into the back office and kneeled down upon my knees. I prayed, "God, if you're out there, please hear me. If the Counselor truly is the Son of God, please reveal yourself to me. Although I am not worthy of your grace, I beseech you to hear my prayer. I am a sinner. I'm a murderer, a drunkard, and an evil man. Please Lord, forgive me of my sin." I began to weep for some time then suddenly something happened. I felt a tinkling sensation up my spine. It was like the wind was running through my body, and I felt the presence of the Lord. His Spirit was upon me, and I was reborn. Now I know it sounds insane that I say God was with me in the room, but He was. He didn't speak to me in words, but He was still conveying a message unto me. He was telling me that He is with me and that everything will be alright. At that moment I felt like a caterpillar in a cocoon that had turned into a butterfly. I was free, and I had become a true believer.

Since my conversion, my life has changed in many ways. I sold my chain of holo-houses and have given a large percentage of my profits to help spread the Revivalist's message. I've shared my faith with many people and done my best to present the facts about the Messiah in an intelligent way. As for Southern Nod, the whole country is booming. All our cities have been rebuilt, and some are calling it a renaissance in the territory.

Chapter 47

Business, Break-ups, & Speculation

After the Counselor's visit to Alexandria in the late 800's, Matusak was a new man. His forty day fast at Mt. Sinai revived his soul, and Matusak went south to Ethiopia on a mission. His goal was to unite the tribes of Ethiopia and form a trade pact with them. At first, the tribes did not believe Matusak. The Marauder had always been viewed as a conqueror, not a man of peace; thus, they looked upon his motives suspiciously. Eventually, the southern tribes came around to Matusak's way of thinking. It was better to have him as an ally than an enemy. This way, Ethiopia was able to focus on their economy and infrastructure instead of preparing for war and spending money on weapons.

By the time 900 came around, Alexandria and Ethiopia were intricately connected economically. During the same period, Matusak was able to bridge the gap that had divided Libya and Alexandria after the 13 Year War. In fact, Madmenah II and Matusak ended up becoming close friends after years of enmity between the two men. Africa then became a thriving financial market. It was a place where Coalition and Alliance businessmen could trade freely without the burden of going through the proper channels. In Africa, business was business whether you came from the north or the south. The motto was, "No one cares where you got it, but how much do you want for it?"

As for Matusak, he put all his soul into buying and selling, and he became a successful businessman. By the mid-900's, Africa rivaled the Alliance and the Coalition, and Matusak was the one who put them on the map. Matusak found that his business adventures were as challenging as the wars he fought in the past. He used his aggressive techniques on the battlefield and applied them to the workplace. These pursuits kept the Marauder's mind occupied, and he was able to lift himself out of the doldrums. He was once again the linebacker that put fear into his opponents on the football field. He was a champion in business, and his racketeering satisfied his ever-growing ego.

* * * *

During the mid-900's, Patmos continued in his relationship with Sierra. The love affair with his former student was open and free. Patmos loved Sierra for many reasons. She was intelligent, full of life, and artistic. Patmos also loved her hazel eyes and the cinnamon tone of her skin. To Patmos, Sierra moved like a panther in full-stride, and the sex between the two was passionate and sensual. Nevertheless, Patmos still thought about Esmeralda. She was the love of his life, and there was nothing he could do to rid her from his system. The love Patmos had for Sierra just differed with the love he had for Esmeralda. His love for Esmeralda was true and unadulterated. Patmos' love for Esmeralda went to the marrow of his bones. She completed him. With Esmeralda, Patmos felt as if he was one with the universe, but with Sierra, he felt he was witnessing the beauty of the universe. With Sierra, God's creation was magnificent, and he saw it through children's eyes once again.

In 970, Sierra went through the "Path of Regeneration," and she became a member of the "Sons of God." Sierra became a fanatical member of the cult, and this strained the relationship between Sierra and Patmos. Sierra went to great ends to convert Patmos, but he wanted to have nothing to do with it.

"See, Patmos, it says right here in the holy book," Sierra explained. "At the dawn of the new millennium, an evolutionary change will take place. Those who have been purified will experience extra-sensory abilities and will transform into a higher being."

Patmos laughed, "You have to be kidding me. Do you actually believe this hogwash? Think about it Sierra. Who wrote this book? Who came up with these grand ideas?"

"Gomar, the Great, said it long ago," Sierra answered.

"Who is this Gomar, and where did he come from? Where has he gone?"

"They say he was the brother of the Counselor. That he transfigured and went up into the heavens but left behind the Holy Book of Gomar."

Patmos chuckled even louder at this comment.

"Sierra, don't you realize I was there when the Counselor returned to the earth? There was no Gomar. It's all a myth. It never happened. There's no historical or archeological evidence to prove any of Gomar's claims. And this book wasn't even published until 369 K.A. It's all a lie. It's just another story. In fact, when this book first came out, it was considered a work of religious fiction. Only later did people turn it into a religion."

"Patmos, you're always so negative. I've gone through the Path of Regeneration, and it changed my life, and one day I'm going to transform into a higher being too."

"Best of luck with that," the Professor sarcastically remarked.

"You're such a jerk sometimes," Sierra said, and she stormed out of the room.

In general, the Professor thought the Sons of God were fools, and he wasn't buying any of their propaganda. Patmos tried to convince Sierra otherwise, but a veil covered her eyes. She was lost in the elaborate pantomimes created by the Sons of God. For nine months, Patmos tried to keep their relationship together, but eventually he couldn't take it anymore. Sierra spent all her time at the fellowship of the Sons of God, and she wasn't the same person. Therefore, the Professor left her, and the two went their separate ways.

* * * *

Kasca paraded around his estate like Nero, the mad emperor of Rome. He was screaming wildly and making a scene at his home.

"Kasca counselor, Kasca sings, Kasca conqueror, Kasca king! Kasca counselor, Kasca sings, Kasca conqueror, Kasca king!"

When Esmeralda and the other servants saw him behaving like a madman, Esmeralda stood in his path and prevented him from heading down the hall.

"Move fast, young woman!" Kasca stated. "Make way for the king. He is heading for Jerusalem. He is coming for the Tree."

"But where is Kasca going?" Esmeralda asked playing along with his delusion.

"I said make way, young woman!" Kasca ordered. "Kasca's coming for the Tree."

"King Kasca," Esmeralda said, "would you bless me before you head on your way?"

Esmeralda fell to her knees and bowed at his feet. When Kasca saw this, it slightly snapped him back to his senses, and he stopped ranting for a moment. He then starting rubbing his hands through Esmeralda's hair and looked off into the distance. Esmeralda rose to her feet and looked at Kasca's mindless stare. She then took him by the hand and escorted him to his room. She laid him down upon the bed, and Kasca returned to sleep.

In the morning, Kasca awoke with no recollection of what happened the night before. Esmeralda made sure he was okay and did not prevent him from going into work the next day. She was still worried about him though. As of late, Kasca had been having a lot of these crazed, sleep-walking episodes. Esmeralda pondered, "Is Kasca losing his mind? Is he planning to invade the Kingdom?" Esmeralda did not know the answers to these questions, but she was afraid. Kasca was running for President again in the upcoming election of 992, and he was a guaranteed victor. After all, Kasca was the most famous man in the D.M.R. He was the hero of the Libertines, and he was now about to seize power at a pivotal moment on the time line. Esmeralda thought, "Kasca already has a firm grip on the D.M.R.'s power base. He is the top executive of the largest company in the world, and if he also takes over the presidency, he could become a ruthless dictator, especially if he's going mad." So Esmeralda worried, and she tried to keep focused on her tasks at the estate. Meanwhile, she had recently been attending secret Revivalist meetings in the outskirts of town. She was utterly befuddled by the message coming from the pulpit, and it appeared to her that all the ancient prophecies about Gog and Magog in the Book of Ezekiel were falling into place. She hoped the prophecies about the D.M.R. were not true, but she could not deny the coincidences. There were too many of them. It made her fret about the future and she wondered about her eternal resting place.

In the D.M.R. and the rest of the Coalition, the Revivalists were seen as conspirators. They were pointing the finger at the D.M.R., Gog Inc., and the Coalition as being the forces of evil. Therefore, the Libertines and those loyal to the D.M.R. viewed the Revivalists as enemies of the state. Some people wanted the "traitors" locked away, and Esmeralda knew that if she was caught attending these meetings, she could be putting her life in danger.

Unaware to Esmeralda's knowledge, the D.M.R.'s secret service had been keeping tabs on the Revivalist meetings. People's names were being written down, holo-pictures were being taken, and Esmeralda's name was on the top of the list as one of the co-conspirators. Her name had already been brought to Kasca, but the Libertine told the secret service to take no action. He informed them to keep the file classified and that he would deal with the problem himself.

Kasca did not take action against Esmeralda because he loved her. With anyone else, he would have immediately removed them from his home or had them locked away, but with Zeze it was different. She was someone close to his heart. She was one of the few people who treated him like a human being and not a star. She didn't put up with his pretence, but made him accountable for his actions. To Kasca, Zeze was one of the most important people in his life, and she took care of him like a mother. And although Kasca could not remember his neurotic episodes, deep down in his soul, Kasca knew that Esmeralda tendered him like a child.

* * * *

In the 900s, Tarshish had been doing well. For over 700 years the colony of the Kingdom had been a beckon of light in the Outskirts. Chieftain James ruled justly, and the success of the Alliance he formed years ago proved to be beyond his wildest dreams. James had no idea that this small sect of colonists would come to rival Kasca and the Libertines. In the beginning, Tarshish numbered in the hundreds while the Libertines numbered in the millions. James believed their success must have been the blessing of God. Tarshish had been a thorn in the D.M.R's flesh for many years, and if Tarshish did not exist, the D.M.R. most likely would have gone on to conquer the world. The Alliance would have never existed, and most believed the Outskirts would have been a darker place. Nevertheless, the D.M.R's dominion still managed to corrupt the world. Even James had been touched by their influence. Overall, he had been a just ruler, but his character was not unblemished. James had been head Chieftain over Tarshish for centuries, and some saw him as a dictator. Most people believed, outside of the Coalition, that James did all these glorious deeds to save the world from the corruption of the D.M.R., but James also did it for selfish reasons. James enjoyed the status of being a world leader. He liked the prestige that came with the position. It made him feel important. It gave him a sense of pride. Some said if Tarshish never existed, the Outskirts would have been a safer place. In the 700 years that Tarshish had been a country, they had been involved in more wars than any other nation. Only the Marauders had been in more conflicts. Tarshish also had been one of the most prolific arms dealers and Purple Fruit distributors. In addition, James was the one who gave the orders to use the superweapon against the D.M.R. This explosion killed close to a million people. So in reality, James was no saint. There was blood on his hands.

Jacob O'Donohue wasn't unclean either. He was the one who carried out a lot of James' orders. And after the death of his wife in the Tarshish-Magog War, Jacob became hateful. His soul was blackened by Hannah's death, and he could think of nothing else but revenge. He blamed Kasca and the D.M.R. for the war, and the brother of James wanted them to pay for their indiscretions. In the meantime, Jacob made plans for another war while the rest of the world was at peace. He thought about it all day long, and even his dreams were filled with murder and ill will. Sometimes Hannah would come to Jacob in his dreams, and it was the only time he felt at ease. The rest of the time, he squirmed about in bed and got very little sleep.

"*He, he, he, he,*" *Hannah laughed and dashed through the bushes as she headed towards the shoreline.*

"*Where are you going, Hannah?*" *Jacob shouted as he ran after her.*

"*You can't get me, Jacob!*" *Hannah yelled. "I'm too fast for you. You'll never catch me!*"

"*We'll see about that!*" *Jacob hollered back.*

Jacob charged after her and ran her down. When he caught up to her, he tackled her on the shoreline of Africa.

"*I told you I'd catch you,*" *Jacob breathed as Hannah struggled half-heartedly trying to get away. Jacob then sat on top of her, and Hannah went limp as she stared into his eyes. There was a moment of stillness as the tide went in and out on the beach. Jacob then bent down and kissed her.*

Jacob was remembering a kiss he and Hannah shared long ago on the shores of Egypt in his dream. The moment of bliss did not last long though because the dream quickly took a detour and transformed into distress. Suddenly from out of nowhere, a giant wave came out of the sea and swept the two lovers apart. Jacob was cast upon the shoreline, and Hannah was taken out to sea. She screamed, "Jacob, save me!" and at that instant he awoke from his night vision.

Chapter 48

Return of the Prophets

"Gather around, my friends," the Counselor spoke. "I am about to send you out on another important mission to the Outskirts. You are going to prophecy unto the nations and forewarn them about the impending doom. Inform them that the Kingdom Age is coming to a close, and the final judgment is at hand. Warn them that if they decide to attack the Kingdom, they will lose their eternal souls to the Lake of Fire. Firmly exhort them to not follow the D.M.R.'s lead. Plead with them, beseech them, and do not stop preaching until your lives are taken from you."

When the prophets heard the last line, some trembled in fright.

"But do not fear," the Lord comforted. "My Spirit is with you always, and at the end of the age you will be with Me by My side."

In June of 996 the prophets went out and arrived in the Outskirts. Patmos was sent to the D.M.R. Kruger was sent to Africa, and Micah was sent to Tarshish. Queen Sheba returned to the land of Sheba, and other prophets went forth to the corresponding nations.

The first week did not go well for the prophets sent to the Coalition nations. In Persia, the prophet was immediately captured and executed. In Meschech and Tubal, the prophets were imprisoned. In Gomar, the prophet was beaten to death by a mob of anti-Revivalists, and in Beth-Togar-Mah, they wouldn't allow the prophet to enter the country. This prophet's ship was later lost at sea and never heard from again.

The two prophetesses sent to Dan, De-Dan and Nod were treated with mixed signals. Some saw them as heroes while others viewed them as charlatans. Wherever the two women spoke, confrontations arose. Those who believed the prophetesses' message joined together, and those who opposed them gathered on the other side. On many occasions, the two sides would start taunting one another, then a fight would break out, and riot police would have to be brought in to restore order. This happened in almost every city the women traveled to. There was civil unrest, riots, and the prophetesses' were causing an uproar. In Southern Nod, it was much the same; however, more Native Nodians backed the prophet's message than those who opposed them. Therefore, there were fewer confrontations in Southern Nodian cities. In Nod, most of the time, the people just stood around and watched, and after six months of proclaiming the Counselor's message, the people started to lose interest and only a handful would come to their speaking engagements.

* * * *

When the Queen returned to the Land of Sheba, she was catered to in every way. After all, she was the leader of their empire for hundreds of years. Many were surprised that she willingly gave up the throne to be with the Counselor. Then again, others were not shocked at all. The Counselor was the most powerful man in the world, and who could resist a marriage proposal from the Son of God? Even so, the Queen was welcomed by her family, and they gave her airtime on the holoscreen to proclaim her message. Two of her sons were opposed to the idea, but eventually they conceded being outnumbered by the other siblings. Her message was broadcast everywhere in the world. Even the Coalition press covered the story on their news-stations. The Queen was a well-known world leader. Her autobiography had been read by billions, and she was one of the most respected women in the world.

"For centuries, I have lived in the Kingdom with the Counselor," the Queen addressed, *"and I have been blessed beyond measure. Emmanuel and I have raised children together. We've walked hand in hand with one another, and we've shared our intimate thoughts. I probably know the Counselor better than anyone on the planet. And I have come here today to inform you that the Counselor is a good and righteous Man. The rumors that you have heard over the centuries are lies. He is not power hungry. He does not desire your worship or obedience. He could have had your veneration if that's what He wished for. The Counselor merely wanted to have fellowship with the human race. He is not an evil ruler as many of you have been led to*

believe. He is the Son of God. He is the Lord of Lords, but He is also the suffering Servant that many of you have come to know. Now I do understand the difficulty in accepting the fact that the Creator of the universe would come down and become a man, but it is the truth. I, like you, had my doubts at first, but I have seen His power. I have heard the Father speak from heaven, and I have been filled with His Spirit. But most of all, I have seen the Counselor's deeds first hand. He is gentle. He is honest. He is just, but I promise you that if anyone comes against Him and His people, the Counselor will bring retribution. It is the end of the age as spoken of by the Word of the prophets, and I have come as His representative to exhort, comfort, and edify the Land of Sheba and the entire world today ..."

* * * *

The O'Donohue brothers greeted Micah with banners and flags. It was a grand celebration that honored the return of the General who helped put Tarshish on the map. If Micah had never come back in 255, it is likely that they would have lost the Tarshish-Gomar War and would have been overrun by their enemies. Micah was the one who supplied Tarshish with an abundance of Fruit Pills and laser technology that enabled the colony to defend themselves. On the contrary though, Micah also was the one who started the arms race. If he had not supplied Tarshish with laser technology, the D.M.R. would have never been able to steal the idea. Gog Inc. probably would have figured out how to make lasers eventually, but it may have taken them decades or possibly centuries to figure it out, and that would have saved many lives. Micah, nevertheless, was celebrated as a hero in Tarshish. He was in all the history books, and children learned about him in their early education. A holiday was also celebrated in his honor on February 2nd of every year. It was called "General's Day."

Before Micah left for Tarshish, he informed James that he was coming. He told the Chieftain that he had an urgent message from the Counselor and to prepare for his arrival. Micah flew by dragon. He scared a lot of people upon his arrival because leviathan had not been seen for centuries in the Outskirts. They had all been killed for game, and it was dangerous for dragons to fly outside the Kingdom. Micah and the dragon both knew this, but the General wanted to enter Tarshish in an ingenious way. As for the dragon, Quetzalcoatl, he owed Micah a favor, so he agreed to take the flight.

As soon as Micah landed, the great dragon breathed fire for all the people to see then sped off into the heavens. The dragon knew that he was not safe in the Outskirts, so he made haste and headed back towards the Kingdom. As for

Micah, the people gathered around him. They patted him on the back. They were cheering for him, and some were asking for autographs. After all, it wasn't everyday that a great hero came back from the past, so the people were flabbergasted.

After the ceremony, Micah was taken to James' estate. He was greeted by James, Jacob, Simon, and some of the other chieftains, and the men talked business. After the Queen's speech yesterday, most guessed why he was there, and they were right. But Micah always thought like a man of war, and he was able to surprise them at the meeting. Before the Millennium, he spent almost his entire life in the service, and it was difficult for him to rid himself of thinking like an enlisted man. Even during the Kingdom years, Micah wanted walls built to defend the Kingdom and all sorts of other military barricades, but the Counselor would reject every plan passed by the 144 Elders. The Counselor would tell Micah and the others who supported the General's plans that "This is the Kingdom. It's the golden era. We don't need weapons or fortifications." But in Tarshish, Micah had a new plan, and he pronounced it to the chieftains at the meeting.

"The prophecies predict that a northern confederacy will come against the Kingdom and try to destroy it. This confederacy will be destroyed, but the prophecies don't exactly say how this will come to pass. All it states is that 'fire will come down from heaven and devour them.' I suggest that Tarshish create a weapon with that kind of magnitude and destroy the invaders."

Simon spoke, "Are you suggesting that we are the Counselor's instrument for judgment against the Coalition? Did the King approve of this?"

"No, not exactly," Micah explained, "but He didn't disapprove either. And who knows, maybe we are written about in prophecy?"

"Did you tell Him about your plan?" Simon asked.

"No, but you know the Counselor can read our minds," Micah went onto explain. "And He did nothing to dissuade me."

When the chieftains heard this, there was an upheaval. James got up and started pacing around the room while Jacob and Simon started arguing with one another. Micah kept trying to explain his case to the other chieftains, and this went on for about ten minutes. Eventually James spoke, and the other chieftains quieted.

"Do we have the technology? Could a weapon like this be created?"

Micah reached into his pocket. He took out a computer chip, and he smiled. The rest of the men stood back in fear, and Micah spoke.

"Lane Hofmann created a weapon of this magnitude years ago, and before I left, he handed the technology over to me. It's a weapon that could change the landscape of the world. It just needs to be built."

*   *   *   *

Rhodes Kruger rode into Alexandria on horseback. In the Kingdom it was a common form of transportation, but if you had to go far, you took the subway. Hardly anyone owned hovercars in the Kingdom. The train system was superb, and most of the trains traveled over 300 kilometers per hour, so it was easy to get from place to place in the Kingdom.

As Kruger crossed the border, he was greeted by Marauding guards. He told them him name, and that he wanted to be escorted to Matusak's palace and ranch. When the guards saw him, they instantly recognized the Zulu Warrior, and they made way. After all, Kruger was as much of a hero in Africa as he was in the Kingdom. The legendary fight between Matusak and Kruger became a museum in the City of Alexandria. A statue of the Marauder fighting the Philistine with drawn swords was one of the major sites in the city, and the true story was told. Everyone knew about Matusak's fall from grace, his imprisonment in the Kingdom, and his return to glory. It was what legends were made of. And when the border police saw Kruger with a sword on his belt riding on horseback, they felt a sense of pride. Kruger symbolized everything that the Marauders once stood for. He fought hard. He fought to the death. He fought with pride.

Kruger rode on and arrived at Matusak's gate near sundown. He was welcomed onto the grounds, and he rode forward towards the palace. When he got outside the palace, he hollered with all his might.

"Hear yea, Alexandria! The hour of judgment is upon you! All men who oppose the Crown will be crushed by the wrath of God!"

Kruger then rode back and forth across the estate shouting the message over and over again until everyone came out of the palace and living quarters. Hundreds of servants stood gawking in awe. Matusak's wives came out of the harem, and many of his children stood from the balconies and the doorways. Finally, Matusak came out from his office and joined the others. He looked like a D.M.R. businessman dressed in the finest clothes. When Kruger saw Matusak, he laughed, then shouted, "Look at what we have here, how far you have fallen? Have you sold your soul to the Devil? Have you compromised with the D.M.R.? Once upon a time you were a warrior of renowned. You were like King Arthur, but look at what you've become! You're a hypocrite, Matusak. You're no Marauder. You look like a Libertine to me!"

When Matusak heard Kruger's taunt, he felt like charging the Philistine and making him pay for his insult, but instead Matusak stood there like the others. Kruger had obviously been training for his mission to the Outskirts. Ever since he left the 144 Elders, he had studied the martial arts, and he had become a black-belt. He also became an expert swordsman under the tutelage of a Marauder who returned to the Kingdom in 262. The Philistine's body was cut up like a body builder as compared to Matusak who had grown fat and lazy. Kruger wanted revenge for the humiliation he suffered long ago. He wanted a fair fight, and this time he was ready.

"That's right, Matusak!" Kruger hollered, "I am challenging you to a fight today. After the thousandth year, I am going to meet you in the City of Alexandria, and we are going to have a rematch. We will play by the old rules. There will be no modern weaponry or laser fire. We will fight again with clubs and fists, and I will cut off your head with my sword!"

Kruger then raised his sword in the air and pointed it at Matusak.

"I will then take the crown upon your head and place it on my own. I will rule over Alexandria in your place. And when the Time of Tribute comes around in the fall, I will throw the crown at the Counselor's feet and pay homage to the King of Kings."

Kruger was making reference to the fact that since Alexandria bought weather systems from the D.M.R., they had not brought forth tribute to the Counselor. Matusak decided he no longer needed to pledge his allegiance unto Him. He wanted to rule on his own accord.

"I challenge you by the Marauder's ancient Code of Ascendancy!"

Kruger ripped his shirt, cut his hand with his sword and used the torn piece of cloth to suck up the blood. Kruger then tossed the bloody shirt at Matusak and spit on the ground.

When Matusak saw Kruger perform the Code of Ascendancy, he stood dumbfounded. The Marauder hadn't seen a bloody shirt thrown at the ground in centuries. Only a few still remembered it. One of the Marauders in the Kingdom must have taught the Philistine the old ways, and his heart sank in his chest. Matusak then watched Kruger ride away unchallenged. He knew he didn't have the strength to fight him on the spot, and he also felt remorse for forsaking the Counselor by using weather machines.

The next morning Matusak awoke in rage. He opened his newspaper, and Kruger's challenge to Matusak was the headline story. Someone who was present leaked the story to the press and managed to get a holoprojection of the scene. The holoprojection was being run over and over again in the Outskirts, and pretty soon everyone knew about Kruger's challenge to Matusak's authority.

As the weeks passed, Matusak's remorse over forsaking the Counselor slowly slipped away. Instead, his guilt was replaced with hatred, and Matusak wanted nothing more than revenge against Kruger and the King of Kings. After all, Matusak reasoned, the Counselor sent Kruger to Alexandria in the first place, so He must have made this decree. Therefore, Matusak despised both of them. He wanted Kruger's head upon a stick, and if he had the chance, he wanted to declare war against the Kingdom.

* * * *

Patmos returned to the straight and narrow path after the break-up with Sierra. In some ways the ending of the relationship was a positive thing for the Professor. He was able to focus on the important concerns in his life. With Sierra, Patmos was constantly distracted, and he couldn't think of anything else when she was around. She had a way of possessing one's soul, and the Professor was enraptured by her. But after Sierra joined the Sons of God, he was able to see clearly again. It was like his mind had been in a fog for centuries, and the haze had finally gone from his thoughts.

After Patmos and Sierra went their separate ways, the Professor paid a visit to the Counselor and the two men spoke. Patmos divulged his soul to the Prince of Peace, and the Counselor listened. It was good therapy for the Professor. His relationship with the King had been somewhat breached after his return from the D.M.R. back in 262. It took centuries for the bitterness to heal, and looking back he couldn't figure out why he was so angry with the Lord. It wasn't the Counselor's fault that he fell in love with a woman that was not his wife and that he was tempted by her. The Professor did all of this on his own, and in some ways he wanted to bring about his undoing. Falling into sin made his life exciting again. In fact, Patmos never really liked the consecrated life. It was too much of a bore for him. The Professor liked living on the edge. He enjoyed running with the Devil. Despite Patmos' desire for sin, he did love God. He just didn't like worshipping Him in the traditional ways. It seemed liked too much of a farce, and that's probably why he was so turned off by Sierra's involvement with the Sons of God.

Before Patmos left for the North, the Counselor had long sessions with Patmos speaking to him about the D.M.R. and the importance of his undertaking.

The King made it clear that he would have the most difficult time of all the prophets, so He counseled him before he went on his mission.

"You will be tempted beyond measure in the North. You will endure animosity, beatings, and imprisonment. It will be worse off than it was before. The people in the D.M.R. have become haughty and proud. They have grown to hate Me, and they will also hate you. But I want you to speak My words whether they listen or not. You are my representative out there, and if they deny you, they will be denying Me. Do not take offense. Stand strong with a firm upper lip, and hopefully a remnant will return unto Me."

Patmos arrived in the City of Liberty a few days later. He went to the bank to see if his account was still active, and it was. He accrued so much interest in the time that he was gone that he was a very wealthy man in the Outskirts. Not only did he have a lot of credits, Patmos owned stock in Gog Incorporated, and he was a large shareholder. Luckily, he kept all the paperwork from long ago. If not, he would have had nothing. Patmos then found a furnished home on the outskirts of town and paid for the house with some of his shares. He then got himself settled and spoke at Liberty Square the next day.

Patmos made his way to the staging area at Liberty Square. In his backpack, he had a robe made of sackcloth, and he put it on. His head was shaved. He wore sandals, and the people eating lunch in the square stared at him like he was a freak. Patmos then spoke to the scattered crowd.

"I have come from the Kingdom to bring forth a message from the King of Kings and the Lord of Lords! A great judgment is about to be cast down upon the D.M.R. unless the people of the North repent of their sins. Eternal outcomes weigh in the balance, and your immortal souls are on the line …"

When the people in the square heard Patmos speak, they thought he was just another Revivalist breathing fire and brimstone, and the people were immediately turned off by his message. A man yelled from the crowd, "Go home, you scum-bag! I don't want to hear this crap while I'm eating my lunch!" "Get out of here, you jerk," another man voiced his opinion. "What are you supposed to be anyway? Do you think you're Elijah? Why don't you go back to the quack-farm you came from?" But Patmos did not quit exhorting the crowd. He went on for another fifteen minutes, and people started to move away from him. A young child wandered over towards the Professor and his mother quickly swept the child off his feet. As she went, she shunned Patmos and said, "You should be ashamed of yourself," and scuttled off into the distance. A gang of adolescents riding holoboards came up to Patmos and laughed at him. They then started spitting at him, but the Professor chased them away and went back to his public address. Another man came forward and took several holo-pictures of Patmos. He started writing something in a book, but Patmos tried to ignore him. Finally, Patmos' speech came to a close when a man pulled down his pants, whipped out his penis, and started pissing on the Professor. Patmos had urine all over him, and after that he walked away discouraged. People started to clap as he left the square and someone shouted, "Nice speech crack-wipe!"

When Patmos got home, he was disheartened. He didn't expect the D.M.R. to be this callous and cold. Back in the old days, the people in the North were open minded and receptive to new ideas. Liberty Square was a place where one could speak freely without this sort of discord. Patmos thought, "How far has the D.M.R. fallen?" He stripped off his clothes, took a shower, and napped shortly thereafter. When he awoke, he thought about visiting Esmeralda, but he wasn't ready yet. Instead, he sank into the couch and watched the Holo-TV.

The next day, Patmos was back at Liberty Square speaking to the people meandering about. He spoke for about an hour, and the day went better than his previous outing. Some kids were trying to hit him with a Frisbee as he spoke, but once they hit the Professor, they left him alone because instead of getting mad, the Professor simply tossed the Frisbee back to them. As for the rest of the people, most ignored him as they passed by. Some stopped for a few minutes and listened, but the rest could care less. Some gawked, some laughed, but most just stared at the freak in the long robe. On the third day, a man kept screaming at him. Every time Patmos tried to speak, he would yell real loud and start jumping up and down. So the Professor would move to a new location, but the man kept following him around. Eventually, Patmos just gave up and went home. On the fourth day, the minute he started speaking, a man came up to him and socked him in the jaw. Patmos bit his tongue and wasn't able to continue, so he packed up his things and went home for the day. The fifth and sixth days, Patmos stayed home and let his tongue heal. He was planning on visiting Esmeralda on the sixth day, but his wounded tongue kept him away. On the seventh day, the Professor was back at Liberty Square, but he wasn't permitted to speak. At one of the restrooms, Patmos was attacked by three men and knocked unconscious. The men carried him out to a hovercar, and he was later imprisoned.

Chapter 49

The Countdown

Patmos had been locked in a prison cell for six months before he received his first visitor. It was Kasca, the current President of the D.M.R. When the Professor saw Kasca, he felt mixed emotions. He hadn't seen his friend in centuries, and he felt ecstatic, but on the other hand, their last meeting didn't go so well. Patmos punched Kasca in the face after he found out that he and Esmeralda had lied to him. So Patmos did not know what to expect. He eyed his old friend suspiciously and did not speak. Kasca came forward and spoke first instead.

"How are they treating you in here," Kasca asked.

"Compared to imprisonment during the Tribulation, this is a cake-walk," Patmos answered. "There are no torture chambers, no medical experiments, and I get a meal three times a day, but I do miss seeing the moon and stars at night."

Kasca looked at Patmos inquiringly, but he seemed distant. His eyes had dark shadows under them, and he appeared to be under a lot of stress.

"So are you here to get me out?" Patmos asked.

Kasca did not answer. Instead he paced around in front of the jail cell looking at the ground.

"I assumed you're here to give me a 'Get out of jail free card.' That is why you're here, isn't it?"

"Not exactly," Kasca answered, "It all depends on a few things. If you're willing to stop speaking out against the D.M.R. and head back to the Kingdom, you'll be free to go, but if you're set on causing mayhem, I can't help you. The D.M.R. is arresting all Revivalists and enemies of the State."

Patmos laughed, "You've got to be kidding me. So much for freedom of speech."

Kasca's voice rose, "These are changing times, my friend. We are doing this for the safety and security of our people."

"Safety and security," Patmos mocked. "Don't play me for a fool. You're starting to sound more like Mahdi everyday."

Patmos was referring to the Antichrist's rise to power during the Tribulation. Mahdi was able to play on people's fears after the early nukes went off during the war, and the people were so afraid of being next on the hit list that they embraced him as the Prince of Peace. Western democracies became part of his fascist regime and all authority was given unto him.

"Don't be so dramatic, Professor!" Kasca belched. "We're just removing a few rabble-rousers. We can't have them upsetting the natural order of things. After all, it's the end of the Millennium and a new era is about to begin."

Patmos shook his head in revulsion and said, "History does have a way of repeating itself."

"Yes it does!" Kasca said in anger. "And I'm not going to permit another exodus from the Libertine Republic!"

"So this is the new world order," Patmos stated. "Who's going to be on the throne? Let me see, I'll take a wild guess. Could it be Kasca, the new lord and king?"

"Professor, I'm sick of listening to your nonsense," Kasca explained emphatically. "You and the Kingdom have been in isolation for far too long. How can the Outskirts permit a backward and oppressive regime rule over us? It's illogical. The Counselor's reign is coming to an end."

"In some ways you're right," Patmos countered, "but it's not His reign, it's yours. I know you've read the ancient prophecies. How can you possibly think of invading the Kingdom after knowing what the outcome will be?"

"First, I don't believe in the Counselor, and second of all, the prophecies were created to keep us in line and make us slaves," Kasca explained. "And after we eliminate the Counselor once and for all, we'll take back the Tree of Life and usher in a new era of peace."

"My friend, I truly feel sorry for you," Patmos said sympathetically. "If I didn't know the Devil was locked away, I'd say he was pulling your strings. Instead you've outwitted yourself, and it will be your undoing. Kasca, please listen to reason. Do not invade the Kingdom. I'm your friend and not your enemy.

I'm sorry if I hurt you long ago. I should have forgiven you. At any rate, I have put all that behind me. If you'll have me, I'd like to be your friend again."

Previously Kasca was brooding, but after the President heard Patmos' kind words, it seemed to soften his heart a little. There was silence for a moment as the two men collected their thoughts. Finally, Patmos spoke again and he asked, "How's Zeze? Is she still alive? Is she here in the D.M.R?"

"She's fine," Kasca answered.

"I was planning to hunt her down on my free time and make reconciliation, but I was thrown in here before I had the chance."

"Well, she's doing well," Kasca explained. "She and I have remained close friends, and …"

Kasca was about to explain how intimate they had become, but he stopped in mid-sentence. He didn't want to make matters worse by informing his friend that he was romantically involved with her. Instead, he changed the subject and asked, "So are you willing to stop speaking like a Revivalist and head home? And if you want, I could find you a job at Gog Inc. We could use a top executive like yourself."

"Kasca …"

Patmos' tone grew quiet.

"Thanks for the offer, old buddy, but I can't take the position. As for public speaking, I can't stop. I'm on a mission from the Lord. I've been ordered to keep warning the masses until I'm six feet under."

Kasca looked at Patmos and took a deep breath. The President knew he would not be able to change the Professor's mind, but he asked anyway.

"Patmos, would you please take the offer? I can't have you out there spreading the Counselor's propaganda, and I don't want you locked up in here, but if you refuse, I'll have to keep you behind bars like the rest of the fanatics."

Kasca opened up the jail cell and stated, "You're free to go. It's up to you."

Patmos sat on the bed in the cell and stared at the bars dreaming of sunny days and blue skies. He wanted so badly to be free again, but he couldn't leave.

"I'm sorry, Kasca, you're going to have to keep me here."

Kasca tried to stare down the Professor, but Patmos wouldn't budge, so he grabbed the cell door and slammed it shut. He walked away waving his hands in disgust and shouted, "Suit yourself, you stubborn fool! But if you change your mind, you know who to call for!"

Kasca left the cell-block as Patmos rolled over on his side and began to weep.

*   *   *   *

"Is that all you got!" Matusak taunted. "C'mon, challenge me. I haven't even broken a sweat."

Matusak's sparring partner was breathing hard and straining with all his might to keep the blunted blade from his neck. Finally, Matusak grew tired of the affair, pulled his sword back, and knocked his sparring partner out with the handle of the weapon. The man fell to the floor and Matusak hollered, "Next!"

The trainer approached Matusak and said, "Let's take a break," but Matusak protested.

"I'm not finished yet!"

"Well they are," the trainer answered as he pointed to the five men nursing their wounds. One had a broken arm, another a black eye, two had concussions, and the fifth was being carted off on a gurney.

"How can I possibly train if there are no men to spar with?" Matusak asked. "Hire more fighters. This time, I only want heavyweights. Double the offer on credits, and if there are still no men willing to fight me in all of Alexandria, head down to Ethiopia and get me some real warriors."

The trainer looked at a man in the corner, snapped his fingers, and the man left hurriedly from the gymnasium to carry out the orders.

It had been three years since Kruger offered his challenge. In six more months, Kruger would return from his mission to Ethiopia and Libya, and the fight for the throne of Alexandria would take place. Who would win? No one knew for sure. The bookies had Matusak favored 55 to 45, but it was really a toss up. Kruger looked like a comic book superhero. He was cut-up and noble. He had the martial arts skills of Bruce Lee, and he was one of the toughest linemen to ever play in the Kingdom Football League. Matusak, on the other hand, had the strength of Hercules and was known as a barbarian with dexterity and wit. Matusak had also won the first fight long ago.

The outcome of the fight would determine many factors politically. If Matusak won, it was highly likely that Alexandria and the rest of Africa would join the D.M.R. in their invasion of the Kingdom. If Kruger was victorious, Alexandria would be ruled by a man loyal to the Counselor, and he would not endorse an offensive against the Kingdom. A man like Kruger might even fight to defend the Kingdom. Therefore, there was a lot on the line, and the people in the Outskirts waited expectantly for the "Fight of the Century."

* * * *

For three years, Tarshish had been making the mechanism created by Lane Hofmann. If the apparatus worked, it could change the outcome of the war against the Kingdom. Officially no declaration of war had been proclaimed, but all the signs were pointing to it. Coalition propaganda against the Kingdom, the Counselor, and the 144 Elders was so vicious that even people who lived in the Kingdom and knew the Counselor were starting to have doubts about Him. The King of Kings was viewed as a tyrant and political cartoons had no mercy upon Him. For instance, one cartoon had the Counselor sitting on His throne with his feet up during the time of tribute. He was lazing around with the 144 Elders. These men were all fat, and they looked like tycoons. Men from the Outskirts were bringing forth their tribute at the Booth's Festival and two of the previous tributaries were massaging the Counselor's feet. The King was joking with the 144 Elders and saying, "Do you think we should have them clean the toilets or fix us a meal to eat?"

In general, there was a lot of animosity towards the Kingdom, and people in the Outskirts were not afraid of the Counselor anymore or the Kingdom. After the holoscreen ban was lifted in 902, people from the Kingdom were able to see what was going on in the Outskirts, but it also allowed people from the Outskirts to see into the Kingdom. Most of the people in the Outskirts saw the Kingdom as a place of savages. The Kingdom was technologically behind the nations in the Outskirts, and most people in the Outskirts viewed them similarly to how the colonial nations viewed the natives of North and South America during the 15th and 16th centuries. Not only did the Coalition and the Alliance view the Kingdom as being behind the times, they also noticed there were no walls or barriers to prevent an invasion. This made the Kingdom very seductive to entrepreneurs and businessmen. Its resources were practically untouched, and Jerusalem was the place where the Tree of Life resided. The Tree promised everlasting life, and it was a prize worthy of warfare.

* * * *

"So Simon when do you think the weapon will be ready to launch?" James asked.

"It's actually ready right now," Simon answered, "but our scientists said they want to first do a few more tests before they give the okay."

"Have you seen any of these trial experiments?"

"Yes, as a matter of fact, there's one scheduled for today," Simon said. "If you'd like to come along with me to the lab, you might witness something that's beyond belief."

"How could I deny an offer like that?"

"Well, let's go. I have a hovercar waiting downstairs. We could be there in a jiffy."

The two men arrived at the lab right before the simulation began. A model city lay on a large table in an adjacent room. It looked like the City of Jerusalem. One of the scientists walked over to the city and put the secret weapon in the center of the model. He then walked away, hit a button on his remote control, and a bubble formed over the model. It was translucent, but one could still see an outline of the bubble if one looked closely. The scientist left the room and a man in goggles, armed with a laser weapon entered the room. He stood behind a large steel plate and fired the weapon through a small crack in the plating. The armed man fired it at the model. The laser fire was absorbed by the bubble, but the model was undamaged. The armed man then took a small explosive and threw it at the model. It exploded, but most of it was absorbed by the bubble. The rest of the debris fell to the ground nearby outside the perimeter. He then took another explosive, tied it to a long stick and held it within inches of the bubble. It exploded, but the bubble and the model were unscathed once again.

After the experiment was complete, the scientists started patting themselves on the backs, and they seemed pleased. As for James and Simon, they were ecstatic.

"Did you see that?" Simon boasted. We've created a force field. It cannot be penetrated by weapons or explosives."

"My oh my!" James exclaimed, "I thought a force field was only possible on Sci-Fi holoprograms, but now I've witnessed it with my own eyes. So how strong is the force-field?"

"Thus far we have found nothing that can penetrate its defenses," Simon boasted. "Even a small superweapon was unable to break the shielding."

James stood looking at the model with a glow on his face. He thought, "There is now a way to protect the Kingdom and the Alliance from invaders. If the Coalition dares attack us, we will have a way of protecting ourselves. This technology will bring about a new era. It baffles the mind to think that these days were prophesied thousands of years in advance. How could it be? The Scriptures must be true, and the Revivalists were right all along."

* * * *

Lucifer's release was imminent. In less than a month, Lucifer would be loosed upon the earth and the people began to panic. Some dug shelters in the earth. Others fled to the caves and mountains. Some stockpiled food and water, but most went about their lives unconcerned about Lucifer's return. In the Kingdom, people were the most unsettled. This would be the first time the Israeli citizens would face an unpredictable future. No one was sure how long Lucifer would be free. The ancient Scriptures were not clear. They only said he'd be set loose for a "short time." Did that mean a year or a thousand years? Even the Counselor did not reveal the hidden secret. He knew the answer to the mystery, but he wouldn't reveal it even to those closest to him. He'd say, "I am like Hamlet, and you are like Guildenstern. If I told you the answer to your question, it would pluck out the mystery of the future, and it would ruin the final act."

Lucifer, meanwhile, sat impatiently in confinement. In a matter of weeks, he would be free again. He contemplated being a faithful angel and doing all that God required of him, but these thoughts quickly slipped away. Instead, he thought about the beautiful Eves and a harem of them at his feet. He saw myriads of slaves bowing down unto him, and he held the keys to their release. These thoughts gave him a warm and fuzzy feeling inside and a slight grin showed on his face.

Lucifer contemplated many things. He wondered if the heavens and the earth had changed. Would he find the Counselor as a suffering servant or a conquering king? He did not know, and in some ways, he did not care. In the back of his mind he still hoped for forgiveness, and he thought, "Maybe the Lake of Fire won't be that bad after all." He did not believe it would be like heaven, but at least he would be able to do as he pleased. Then again, forever was for infinity. He had lived a long time, but could he endure an eternity of gnashing and bitterness of teeth?

Chapter 50

The New Age

"10, 9, 8, 7, 6, 5, 4, 3, 2, 1 ... Happy new year!" the Kingdom citizens chanted. Hugs and kisses were given. People were celebrating everywhere. The streets of Jerusalem were in an uproar. Some were singing, others were drinking, and many were eating of the Purple Fruit. It was a glorious day. The thousandth year had finally come. But for many the end of the Millennium did not bring pleasure. It brought about uncertain times. And these people were not celebrating. They knew about the giant army to the north, and they were afraid for their lives. They hoped the Counselor would protect them, but many of the New Timers born during the Kingdom Age were unsure of His power.

One New Timer asked, "Do you really think the Counselor can protect us from Kasca and the Coalition? Do you think we have a chance?"

"I don't know for sure," another New Timer responded, "but if I was a betting man, I bet against it. Look at the Coalition's strength. They have superweapons, tanks, an air force, a navy, laser fire, and a billion-man-army," he said convincingly. "What do we have? We have one man who can turn water into wine, a few flocks of dragons to protect us, and the rest of the leviathan. We don't stand a chance. If the Coalition decides to attack, we'll be overrun. The Counselor will not save us."

"I do hope you're wrong, buddy. And what about the Alliance or the Marauders, do you think they'll come to our aide?"

"I hope so. If not, we're dead meat. But I don't really trust the Alliance or Matusak. They'll probably make a big stink about the war, but when push comes to shove, our Kingdom will be on its own."

"Tarshish won't forsake us," the first New Timer protested. "They've always stood by us."

"Maybe so, but you and I both know Tarshish will not be able to hold off the D.M.R. for long. They're no longer the superpower they used to be."

Overall, these were the thoughts of many Kingdom citizens. They were afraid, and the future was in doubt.

In other parts of the world, the end of the Millennium crushed some people's hopes. For example, the Sons of God had gathered at their holy temple in Gomar. Half a billion gathered from all over the globe at the site in expectation of the transformation. According to the cult's teaching, at the end of the thousand years, the believers would transform into gods themselves. They would become like the Counselor with certain powers and abilities, but at midnight, the Sons of God dreams were shattered. There was no transformation. They did not become like gods. The believers were exactly as they were before the clock struck twelve. They remained mere men and women without superpowers like they were led to believe.

The next day, one of the priests of the Sons of God came forward and explained to the believers what happened. "I'm sorry to inform you, but we have misinterpreted prophecy. The priests thought there would be an instant transformation after the thousandth year, but we have now learned from one of the holy seers that it will be a gradual transformation …" The priest went on to offer a further explanation and some of the followers believed him. Most, however, felt betrayed and left the group. Within the first month after the thousandth year passed, the Sons of God's numbers quickly diminished from a billion to a few million, and they could not recover from the debacle. Sierra, Patmos' former lover, was one of the ones who left the cult.

The Satanists weren't sure how to react after the dawn of the New Age turned out to be a dud. Some thought the Devil and his demons would bring forth evil and destruction upon the earth at the stroke of midnight, but it did not come to pass. Instead, it was just like any other new year. Therefore, some of the Satanists went out and started fires themselves to prove their worth. Some went about causing chaos and others caused trouble in the streets.

Most people in the world weren't surprised when the thousandth year passed calmly like any other day. Some made fun of the whole thing, and it confirmed their doubts about God and the Devil. It reaffirmed their lack of belief and proved once again that science and reason was the answer, not faith and hope. The end of the Millennium was similar to what it was like during the 20th and 21st centuries. To believe in God was seen as contrary to logic. Even the teaching of a Greater Power in the public schools was frowned upon, especially in the Outskirts. In the Land of Tarshish and Sheba, the idea that the Counselor was the Son of God was still taught to the children, but the belief in Him was highly criticized. Even in the Kingdom where the Counselor walked amongst the populace, the people had doubts. As for the D.M.R. and the rest of the Outskirts, a person who believed in Him suffered persecution from the unbelievers. It was similar to what the Jews experienced throughout the ages. They were spit upon, hated, and racially discriminated against especially in the North. Derogatory jokes against the Revivalists, Old Timers, the 144 Elders, and the Counselor Himself were common place. Most people, nevertheless, remained civilized. They wouldn't bother someone who believed in the Counselor. It was usually the uneducated who bought into all the propaganda against these groups, but overall, to be a believer during this period was frowned upon and difficult.

As for most of the Old Timers and Revivalists, they were not fazed by the negativity or the passing of the Millennium. Some of them were hoping that the thousandth year would mark the end of the age and that the Counselor would create a new heaven and earth, but it did not happen that way. Most believed the change would come soon, but they realized they might have to wait a little longer. Some of the pessimists surmised that they might have to wait another thousand years for the change to come about. Many on the Old Timers had begun to loathe their existence, and they were ready for a new day. They had lived for over a thousand years, and for many, it was too many years to walk the earth. Of course, many felt blessed to have been able to live in a paradise with their Lord and King, but they still wanted to start anew. They were ready to be reborn. They wanted to see things with fresh eyes again. They desired to dream new dreams. They wanted the Lord of Lords to remold the earth as the potter does with the clay.

The Counselor was able to relate to those who were tired of living because after all, He was a man. He was also the Son of God, and He knew all things, but He could still relate to His creation. He may have been the potter, but He understood their pain and anguish. He knew His creation was weak. So silently, the Counselor prayed unto the Father for mankind's strength as He was tending the Temple garden. He then started to converse with the Father in His mind. He thought, "I truly have enjoyed my fellowship on earth with man and woman, but it is time for a change. This generation has walked with Me, talked with Me, but most do not believe in Me. This has brought tears to My eyes. I have tried for a thousand years to relate to this generation, but they are a stubborn and obstinate people. They bring me much sorrow and grief. They have become as evil as Noah's generation. They even plan to proclaim war against Me. All this I have already known would take place, but to experience it first hand as man is distressing. There are so many souls that will be lost to the Lake of Fire for their unbelief. But I cannot force man to put His trust in Me. If so, my relationships with men and women would not be real. Man must choose His own fate. Although I already know the outcome, it still makes me weep to see so many turning away from Me. Still, a new age is coming. I will recreate all things. Those who have been faithful and true will join Me. I will wash away the sorrow and usher in a new reign. Those who choose to live out their lives apart from Me will continue on their path. They will live in darkness forever not knowing what they have lost. I will not intercede. They will not get to partake in the adventures I had planned for them. It is a shame. As for the rest, they will join Us on our quests together. It will be glorious. It will be new. Man will see things they have never seen before!"

Chapter 51

Fight of the Century

Immediately after Michael, the archangel, released Lucifer from his chains, the Devil flapped his wings and flew out of the bottomless pit. Once Lucifer reached the atmosphere he transformed into a bird of flight, and he felt the wind across his face. He was finally free from his imprisonment, and he was baptized by the earth and sky.

The first place Lucifer visited was the City of Jerusalem. He perched himself upon the Tree of Life and looked down upon the Kingdom. It was magnificent, and it sort of reminded him of the Throne of God. There were many similarities. The Kingdom was like the Garden of Eden. Last time he saw the planet's surface, it was torched and almost everything was dead, but now it was beautiful again. Lucifer then flew to the Temple of God and witnessed a vibrant and tranquil city surrounding it. He then saw the Counselor. He was working in the garden, and He took no notice of the Devil. Some time passed, and finally the Counselor called out, "So are you going to pay Me a visit or are you going to stay perched on that wall all day long?" Lucifer immediately flew from the Temple, after he heard the Lord's invitation, and landed at the Counselor's feet.

"How does it feel to be free again?" the Lord asked. "Are you enjoying yourself?"

"After being bound for a thousand years, I think You know the answer to that question," Lucifer answered.

"Now that you have served your time, what do you plan to do next? Are you going to Disneyland?" the Counselor joked.

"I haven't decided yet, but I thought I might go to and fro and see what is happening on the earth."

The Counselor nodded his head in understanding as He continued to pick fruit from a tree.

"What do you think I should do with the time allotted me?" Lucifer asked.

"That's up to you. You are free to do as you wish. But remember this is My domain, and if you decide to act wickedly, there will be consequences for your actions."

"Understood."

"Why don't you try starting a new leaf?" the Counselor suggested. "Instead of accusing people and leading them astray, you could help them out and be an administering spirit."

"That's not a bad idea, but what purpose will it serve?" Lucifer asked. "According to prophecy, I'm already doomed."

"Your point is well-taken, but it might be a rewarding experience for you."

"Did you say rewarding or revolting?" Lucifer snickered.

"See, comments like that is what got you into trouble in the first place."

"True, but at least I'm entertaining."

"Actually, your comment was somewhat funny, Lucifer, but that's not your problem," the Counselor stated. "Your dilemma runs deeper. And I think you already know the root of your predicament, so I won't go into it."

Lucifer did not respond. He knew the Counselor was right. Instead he stood humbled in His presence. Also, his time of imprisonment was still fresh in his mind, and he did not want to return to the bottomless pit. Instead, Lucifer was agreeable and subservient to the Lord. Soon enough, the Devil would be out conquering and deceiving, but in the meantime, he was observing the Counselor's movements and the Kingdom itself. Lucifer was looking for a weakness. He was trying to find a way to change his fate. He thought, "If there is a way to overcome the Son of Man, I will not have to spend eternity in the Lake of Fire. I will reign in His place. I will exalt my throne above the stars and usher in a new heaven and a new earth. I will be the Most High, the anointed cherub, the wise and beautiful king. All I must do is find a crack in His armor, a way to change my destiny. But I must be vigilant. My time is short. The end is drawing near."

* * * *

Lucifer went west after leaving the Kingdom, and he arrived in Alexandria. He quickly discovered who was in power and found himself at Matusak's palace. He learned about the "Fight of the Century" and the animosity that Matusak had for the Counselor. Lucifer knew that he could use this bitterness to his advantage, and he quickly went to work building the deception. As for Kruger, Matusak's challenger, Lucifer put a fork in the road at every turn. First, Kruger's well-trained horse got spooked by something, and the Philistine fell to the ground and injured his shoulder. Second, he was attacked by a group of possessed bandits as he was making his way out of Ethiopia. Kruger successfully fought off the men, but he dislocated a finger in the process, and he slightly sprained an ankle. Kruger hoped his injuries would be fully healed by the time of the fight which was in a week, and he took several Fruit Pills to buffet the healing process. Lucifer, in the meantime, visited Libya and Ethiopia and quickly went to work to build more hatred against the Counselor and the Kingdom.

After 3 ½ years of waiting, the "Fight of the Century" had finally come in January of 1000. The outcome could possibly determine the fate of the Kingdom, and everyone knew what was on the line. Bets were being made, and bookies were being kept busy. This fight guaranteed to bring in more credits than any other world event in Millennial history. It was bigger than the Olympics. It was grander than the Kingdom Bowl, and it put the Millennial Cup to shame. Who would win? No one knew for sure, but everyone was watching. The actual fight took place in Alexandria, but due to the holoscreen, it felt as if the fight was happening right in everyone's living rooms.

Kruger entered the arena first. He was wearing the outfit of a Zulu warrior. One side of his face was painted white in contrast to his naturally blackened skin. His ears were pierced. He bore a Mohawk on his head, and he had a stolid look on his face. When the crowd saw him, they roared mightily. The boos outweighed the cheers, but it didn't matter. Win or lose Kruger was making his stand for the King.

Matusak followed moments after Kruger entered the ring. He was dressed in vintage Marauder fashion from a vanished time when the Marauders first crossed the Nile. He wore no shirt, and he bore a Samoan lava-lava around his waist. It was silver and black like the Alexandrian flag, but it looked more like a Scottish kilt. As for Matusak, he had a new tattoo that covered his back. It was a drawing of a man getting his throat cut.

The crowd cheered madly when Matusak entered the ring and one young man was so excited that in the hysteria, he fell from the upper balcony and crushed his skull on the floor. He was carted off by security, and the crowd roared even louder at the blood and gore. Matusak then taunted Kruger by raising his fist at him. Matusak also made it look like he was going to charge him, but it was a bluff. He knew his manager and trainer would hold him back. Eventually, after several taunts and a continuous strut around the ring, Matusak was sent to his corner as the ring announcer called out.

"Welcome ladies and gentlemen. Are you ready to RUUUUMBLE?"

The crowd cheered madly and the announcer continued.

"Tonight we have the Fight of the Century! I must remind you that this is a fight to the death. The winner will rule all … of … AL-EX-AN-DRI-A!!!!"

The crowd roared again.

"If the challenger wins, the crown will be his and a new era will begin."

There was a slight pause then the announcer continued.

"And to my left, we have the challenger, also known as the Philistine lineman, the Zulu warrior, the Counselor's spokesman, Rhodes Kruger!!!"

There were boos and cheers from the audience. Some were spitting in disgust and others were clapping frantically.

"And to my right, we have the Marauding madman, the relentless raider, the Emperor of Alexandria, Matusak!!!"

The crowd went mad. People started jumping up and down. Some were screaming like psycho-maniacs as the audience grunted out the Marauders' chant, "WHO-MA-TAL-A, WHO-MA-TAL-A, WHO-MA-TAL-A, HA! WHO-MA-TAL-A, WHO-MA-TAL-A, WHO-MA-TAL-A, HA! …"

This chant went on for sometime, and Matusak kept waving his arms in the air to keep the chant going. Finally, the crowd died down. The fighters met in the center of the ring, and the rules were laid out. Matusak kept taunting Kruger while the Philistine stared coldly into the distance. When the rules were fully explained, Kruger grabbed the mike and shouted, "For the Kingdom!" and headed to his corner. The crowd booed him, and the fight started shortly thereafter.

In the first round, the two warriors were scheduled to fight in hand to hand combat without any weapons. In the second round, the men were to be given a shield and a club. The club would be traded for a sword in the third round, and the fight would not come to an end until one of the men lay dead.

The opening round favored Kruger. He was a black belt at Karate, an excellent kick-boxer, and a superb technician at hand to hand fighting. Matusak was more skilled with weaponry and he used his superior strength to get him out of tough situations.

The bell rang and Matusak instantly charged Kruger trying to catch him off guard, but the Philistine was ready for him, and he deflected Matusak off into the ropes. The Marauder stumbled, but he did not fall. Instead he hulked his way towards Kruger again as the crowd ooohd and aaahd at the prowess.

The two men were about equal in height, but Matusak outweighed Kruger by about fifty pounds. Nevertheless, Kruger was built like a young stallion, and he appeared to have superior fighting skills.

Matusak continued to make his attacks, but every time he moved in, Kruger would hit the Marauder across the jaw or kick him in the ribs, and Matusak would go flailing. After about ten minutes of failure, Matusak managed to get Kruger in a head lock and bring him to the floor. This was the Emperor's plan all along. He knew he had an advantage over Kruger in a wrestling match, and he did his best to keep him down. The Philistine, however, was too fast for Matusak and he slipped out of his grasp.

The first round came to a close shortly thereafter. For fifteen minutes, Matusak struggled to make his move, but Kruger had the upper hand. When the bell rang, everyone in the audience knew who won the first round. The Zulu warrior took it by a landslide.

The two men rested and prepared themselves for the second round. Each man was given a club and a shield and when the bell rang, Kruger was the one who came out swinging. Matusak blocked each hit with his shield and the Marauder hoped Kruger's attacks would wear him out. This went on for about five minutes, and Matusak still had not swung his club at Kruger. He was in a defensive stance, and the crowd started to boo him. It was like watching Muhammad Ali, the boxer, in his latter years. Finally Matusak raised his club and struck the Philistine in the thigh. It was a solid hit, but it didn't seem to faze Kruger. In fact, the hit appeared to anger Kruger, and he went on a flurry by swinging his club madly at the emperor. Matusak just laughed at Kruger and started to taunt him again. This brought back the favor of the crowd as the battle continued.

After Kruger went on his rampage, Matusak went on a rampage of his own. He struck high several times, using his weight to push back his opponent. It was an effective attack, and for the first time in the round, Kruger was on the defensive. Matusak struck high. He struck low, but Kruger was able to block every stroke. Kruger then started to strike back, and the warriors exchanged blows. Back and forth they went across the ring. Occasionally, a body part would be hit in the crossfire, but the blows were not serious hits.

The second round came to an end with the ringing of the bell, but the fighters continued swinging their clubs at one another and didn't stop. The referee tried to break it up but was unable to. Finally, he was able to divide the two men, but he paid a price for interfering. The referee was hit several times, but he did manage to bring about order. As the two men were being separated, they yelled obscenities at one another across the ring, but eventually they went to their respected corners.

The two warriors breathed heavily after the second round as their trainers prepared them for the final event. This round had no time limit, and it would not come to an end until one man lay dead on the floor.

When the third round began, the two men circled one another slowly and methodically in the ring. Each man had a shield in one arm and a sword in the other. This was the moment of truth. The final hour had come upon them. Matusak no longer taunted his opponent. Instead, he moved slouched over like the hunchback of Notre Dame and grunted with each step he'd take. Kruger's eyes were bulging out of his head. He looked like he had been up all night on a cocaine binge, and he moved like a robot across the ring.

Matusak swung his sword first, and Kruger blocked it with his shield, but the power of the blow knocked him backward. Matusak moved in closer and swung again. The same result occurred, but this time Kruger slipped on some sweat on the ground and fell to the floor. The crowd cheered thinking they were about to witness the final blow, but Kruger scurried out of the way before Matusak was able to finish him off.

The two men continued to pace around the ring. The Marauder was making advances and Kruger was reacting accordingly. Matusak was sensing victory, and he swung his sword several times in expectation, but in his haste, Kruger managed to counter his attack and sliced Matusak across the shoulder. It was a flesh wound. Blood gushed out on the floor, but it did not deter Matusak. The hit seemed to infuriate the Emperor, and he charged Kruger with a barrage of swings. Kruger deflected most of these attacks, but one got through and struck him on the arm. It was a serious injury. It made his arm practically immobile and a hush settled on the crowd as Kruger mopped about. But Kruger was not done. He was acting more hurt than he really was, and he managed to catch Matusak off guard. The Philistine leg kicked Matusak at the feet, and the Marauder fell to the floor. Kruger lifted up his sword to finish him off, but before Kruger was able to strike, Matusak raised his sword and struck Kruger in the heart.

As Kruger breathed his last breath, he reached out for Matusak, but he caught only air. Kruger then fell back on the canvas and died. The crowd fell silent after

Kruger expired. Matusak slowly rose to his feet and stood over his dead opponent. A slow chant started to build that kept getting louder and louder. "Who-Ma-Tal-A, Who-Ma-Tal-A, Who-Ma-Tal-A, WHO-MA-TAL-A ..." Matusak then took his sword, raised it in the air and cut off Kruger's head. He raised the Philistines head in the air and held it out for all to see. He paced back and forth across the ring as the horde continued to chant. The sound reverberated throughout the arena as Matusak basked in the glory of victory.

Chapter 52

Memoirs from a D.M.R. Jail

July

I've been in a D.M.R. jail for about three years. It's been miserable to say the least, even though I've been well-fed and taken care of. I'm given recreational time and allowed to interact with the other prisoners, but the one thing I miss the most is the earth and sky. Everything is enclosed, so we're not permitted to breathe fresh air, but in comparison to when I was imprisoned during the tyrannical reign of Mahdi where I was starved, tortured, and used as a human test subject, prison in the D.M.R. is a cakewalk. So I'm taking my time behind bars in stride and making the best of my solitary moments. Thus far I've learned how to play the trumpet. I've taken up painting, and I'm trying to write a book. But none of these activities have kept my mind occupied, especially in the last few months. All I can think about is getting out of here, and I'm considering lying to Kasca about not spreading the Revivalist's message, so I can have a few more days on the outside. The hourglass of the Millennial Age is coming to a close. I have nothing to lose either way. Even if I am killed by the Libertines, at least others will say that Patmos Svenson made a stand for the Lord.

August

Lately, I've been hearing a lot of disturbing news from my fellow prisoners. Many people have gone missing. According to the stories, two armed guards come for you in the middle of the night, and you are never heard from again. Are these people being released or just exterminated? Is this Kasca's final solution to rid the world of Revivalists and anyone who opposes his rule? I hope not. I truly pray Kasca has not gone to these extremes. I always knew he had a few demons running loose in that head of his, but we're talking genocide here. Is the Prince of Rosh capable of such atrocities? I don't know. I just don't know.

September

I've been doing a lot of reading lately, but the selection of books in here is limited. What I would give to be walking through the University of Jerusalem's Library again or even having access to my home library and research books. I suppose I'll have to kiss them all goodbye. It probably doesn't matter anyway. A few of my friends have gone missing, and the guards are getting more sadistic everyday. They used to treat me like Kasca's special guest, but I've become just another number. A new age is about to begin, and everything we once held as true will become a figment of our imagination. If I live or die, I'm ready for a change. Living for over a thousand years has been a blessing, but at times the journey has been too much to bear. Just dealing with the loss of Esmeralda took me almost a century to recover from.

I wonder how Esmeralda is these days. I'm sure she's changed in many ways, but at heart she's probably the same old girl she used to be. Oh, I would give any thing to look into those brown eyes and hold her close again. And Zeze, if you're reading this, someday when I'm dead and gone, remember that I love you. I've always loved you. Although we were together for only a short time, you were the first love of my life. May we have an eternity to spend together! As for Sierra, I miss you too. You were also a soul-mate of mine. It's a shame that religion got between the two of us. I hope one day you will see the light, so we can share the beauty of the universe together.

As for my family and friends, I doubt you will ever get to read any of my writings, but I've learned over the centuries to not be so cynical about the future. So in case you're out there, just know I love and miss all of you. The times we shared together and the intimate moments are something I will never forget. The adventures that we traveled and the experiments and dreams will be with me forever. There were so many blessed times we had. I wouldn't change a thing. You are the ones who stood by my side when I was down and out. You lifted me from the abyss and picked me up. You are the ones who made my life meaningful.

October

If I was on my deathbed, and I had one final speech, what words of wisdom would I want to pass onto the next generation? King Solomon said, "Fear God and keep His commandments." In a sense I agree with Solomon but after walking with the Lord for so many centuries, I don't know if I would be so dogmatic when it comes to God. Instead I might say, "Know the Lord, and He will guide you." In other words, get to know God personally, and He will show you the way. All you need to do is look at God as a friend instead of a supernatural being. If you do this, you will be one step closer to understanding Him. One must remember that God did not create man to control us and put us in chains. He made us so we could have a relationship with Him. He is a God of love, not a God of hate. He is a God of forgiveness, not a God of wrath. Don't get me wrong, He will discipline us from time to time like a father does with a child, but it's because He wants to mold us into better human beings. God wants intimacy. Our love is His desire.

Now that I have the platform, I find it rather funny that I have very little to say. My mind has drawn a blank. You'd think after living a thousand years, I'd have something more profound to declare, but that's not the case. Maybe that's the knowledge I'm imparting??? When it's all said and done, does any of it really matter? Over the centuries, I've amassed great knowledge and have learned many things, but I still know very little. I've only explored a microbe of all the wonders in the universe. Still, I'm tired. These old eyes have seen too much. I'm ready to move onto the next realm and experience another dimension. I want to go through a metamorphosis and transform into something else. I suppose my dreams are based on promises spoken of in the Holy Scriptures. The new heavens await me and for all the faithful on earth.

November

Prison life is wearing me down. I'm tired. My neighbor next door was taken away, and I was beaten up by one of the guards. I'm sure my days are numbered. I even made a request last month to summon Kasca to let me out, but I haven't heard back from the warden. Have I been forgotten? Has my friend betrayed me? Maybe Kasca has had a change of heart. Maybe he never intended to let me go in the first place. All I know is I can't take another day in here. I'm losing heart. Oh God, please show mercy upon your prodigal son, and let me out of here! The remaining prisoners are on edge and our recreational time has been limited. Even the portions are getting scarce. It was only a few months ago that we were getting full course meals, but now it's bread, goulash, and some juice. And even though I believe I'll live forever, I'm still scared. I don't know if I could go through the torture I once endured during the Tribulation. Instead, I pray they shoot me in the head and get it over with quick.

December

Another month has passed, and I still have not heard a word from Kasca. Either the message has not reached him, or he's leaving me in here to rot. For a while there, I thought I was going to take my life, but instead the Spirit has filled my soul. Now I smile at the guards when they're beating me and shrug it off when they curse my name. I know my reward awaits me in heaven. It's still hard to believe that these abuses are taking place in the Kingdom Age. I think a lot of us were under the illusion that everything would be perfect, and that we would never have to suffer through the age. But to be honest, in some ways it's been harder to live through the Millennium than it was living through the days when everything was discombobulated. But that's my commentary on the period. I'm sure there are many who would beg to differ. As for my present situation, I'm in hell. Things have gotten worse, and I'm waiting for the day when they take me away.

Chapter 53

Temptation

Lucifer left Alexandria pleased with the outcome of the "Fight of the Century." He now believed that all of Africa would join him in his fight against the Kingdom. Therefore, he left Africa and visited the southern provinces of Sheba, Dan, and De-Dan. In the Land of Sheba, Lucifer met the Lord's children, and he attempted to seduce the Queen of Sheba. Satan was the most beautiful of all the angels, and he believed his beauty and charm would sway Sheba away from the Counselor. When Sheba first met Lucifer, it was at a cocktail party. It was a formal affair that had many of her family members and political leaders there. Lucifer posed as the correspondent from Perth, and no one seemed to notice. In actuality, the real correspondent came down with a plague of boils on the plane, and he had to return home due to his health. This small plane crashed in the South Pacific and no one realized until much later. As for Lucifer, he deceived everyone including the Queen of Sheba. He posed as Garrett Faust while the real correspondent lay dead at the bottom of the sea.

The Queen was immediately swept off her feet by Faust. He was refined, intelligent, and immaculate looking. In fact, all the women at the party were drooling over him, but Faust was only weaving his web to catch one woman, and that woman was the Queen of Sheba. Lucifer hoped to lead the Queen away from the Lord for many reasons. First, it was a matter of pride. He saw the Counselor's wife as a trophy to be taken. If Lucifer could tempt her into adultery with him, he would once again bruise the Son of Man's heart. To Lucifer, it was like deceiving

Judas into betraying the Lord. It brought him satisfaction to mislead one of Emmanuel's closest disciples and to watch him self-destruct in the end. Second, it was a matter of importance. The Queen was one of the Counselor's strongest spokespersons, and she had great influence upon the Alliance and the Outskirts. She was a thorn that needed to be removed, and Lucifer did all he could to bring about her ruin.

"Mr. Faust, this is the Queen of Sheba," the correspondent from Adelaide introduced.

"Pleased to meet you, my Queen," Faust stated as he took her hand and kissed it dearly. "Please call me Garrett."

The Queen blushed being captivated by his splendor and gentleman's touch.

"Usually these meetings are such a bore," Faust said. "Everyone's so formal at these occasions, but I see you are wearing a Kingdom necklace bore from an Ent tree."

"How did you know this wood is from an Ent?"

"I've been around for a long time, and I consider Ent wood to be more valuable than diamonds and jewels."

Faust pulled out a piece of Entwood from his pocket. The wood piece was attached to his keychain, and the Queen marveled at the coincidence. Faust held the wood up to the light and attempted to compare the relic to her necklace from a distance.

"With your permission, may I compare the two closer?"

The Queen nodded yes and Faust touched the necklace on her neck. He also managed to touch a sensitive spot on her neck, and the Queen felt a moment of desire. After all, she had been away from the Counselor for over three years, and she had been longing for sexual contact for some time. The Queen was also seduced by Faust's scent. His body seemed to give off a seductive aroma, and when Faust looked deep into her Polynesian eyes, she felt he was peering into her soul. She only felt that way with the Counselor, and now this man from Perth was having the same effect upon her.

"Yes, I must say they are similar. Even the texture is alike. Would you like to compare the two?"

The Queen reached out her hand and touched the two pieces of wood. Faust also managed to caress her hand a little, and the Queen was filled with hope and desire. The two stood very close to one another for a moment, and there seemed to be a connection between the two, but there were too many people around, so they could not pursue it.

The two broke apart from one another as soft music started to play in the background. Many people were heading out on the dance floor, so Faust asked if the Queen would care to dance, and she agreed. Faust moved like a skilled dancer across the floor, and the Queen was swept up in the moment.

Later on in the evening, the two shared drinks, started to get tipsy, and spent time talking personally to one another on the balcony. When the night came to a close, Faust asked if she would like a ride home to the palace in his hoverlimo, and she agreed. The two held hands all the way home in the back seat. When they arrived at the palace, Faust gave the Queen a long intimate hug, and she reciprocated. Her heart was beating fast, and she greatly wanted to kiss him and invite him in, but the Queen resisted the temptation. Instead she kissed him on the cheek and fled from the limousine like Joseph did when he was being pursued by his master's wife.

The next week, Lucifer tried on several occasions to set up another encounter with the Queen, but he was unable to persuade her. The Queen felt guilty over the whole incident, and she would not see Faust. Thus, Lucifer left the Land of Sheba angry and flew west to Dan and De-Dan. When he arrived, he immediately took out his wrath on the two prophetesses speaking in the region. Lucifer incited a riot at one of their speaking engagements. He possessed one of the police officers, who was a devil worshipper, and singed the two prophetesses with laser fire. The gun was set on the highest setting, and there was nothing left of them but burning embers.

* * * *

Lucifer flew north after killing the two prophetesses in Dan. He visited Nod and came to understand the division between the Natives and the Settlers. He hoped one day to build on the hatred between the two factions and start another war, but in the meantime, he flew across the sea and found himself in the City of Liberty. This is where he wanted to be all along, but he kept getting distracted by other events in the Outskirts. There was so much going in the world, and he couldn't resist planting seeds of descent in man. In fact, before Lucifer was imprisoned, destroying people's souls became a pastime for him. He would keep a running record of all the people he had damned to hell, and his fellow demons would do most of the dirty work. As for those who were doing God's work, he would keep a close eye on them and did all he could to bring about their fall. This wasn't too difficult. Lucifer had many associates. Usually he would keep the chosen ones distracted with all sorts of gods and other nick-knacks. For example, before the Millennial Reign, he had everyone so mesmerized by television that even God's elect couldn't find their way through the fog. There were sports and movies and video games and computers and a barrage of other entertainment devices that seemed to occupy everyone's time. These were the modern gods that mankind bowed down to. And if God's people couldn't be distracted by these devices, he attempted to destroy them by their own fleshly desires. For instance, he used the god of sex to destroy many believers. The internet provided easy access to pornography, and suddenly people who had never lusted or thought about these wicked desires were being ensnared by deviant practices. After awhile, these cravings became needs, and soon enough, many men and women were living out their fantasies in real life.

As Lucifer cruised through the City of Liberty in the D.M.R., he had to chuckle to himself. He had been gone a thousand years and mankind still found a way to engage in wicked deeds without his help or persuasion. The holoscreen seemed to be man's greatest downfall, but there were others activities in the D.M.R. that took the Devil by surprise. Still, he couldn't figure out why the people in the D.M.R. hated the Counselor so much. He had to do research on the subject and eventually came to understand why. He learned about Kasca and the Libertines. He read up on the Coalition and the Alliance. He found out about the strife between Tarshish and the D.M.R. and became educated on many areas of concern before he made his acquaintance with the President of the Magog Republic.

Lucifer dwelt in Kasca's estate for many days, and he observed the movements of the Libertine. Kasca was like many other men he had known in the past. He was a power monger. He was a conqueror like himself, and the Devil knew he could use this to his advantage. Kasca had the same dream as Hitler. He was like Napoleon. He was similar to Alexander, and of course, he was like Mahdi, the Antichrist who ruled the world during the Tribulation.

Lucifer knew on every occasion that he tried to defeat God, he had failed. In heaven he waged war against Him, and he was cast out. On earth he tried to eliminate the Israelites, but he was unsuccessful. He tried to destroy the Messiah when He was a child, but it proved futile. He tried to tempt Emmanuel in the wilderness, but it did not work. He even tried to kill Him on the cross, but Jesus came back to life. The Devil tried to eliminate the Jews during the Holocaust and tried to destroy them during the Tribulation, but once again he failed. Lucifer thought, "Why should I believe I'll be successful this time? Is not this quest in vain? Maybe the Counselor is right. Maybe I should try working for Him instead of going against Him all the time? But did I not serve Him loyally for many millennia before the fall? Servitude only brought me despair and misery. I will not return to bondage! There must be a way to overthrow His Kingdom. I will find a way, even if it brings about my ruin. But be sure of this, if I go down, I'm bringing mankind with me!"

Lucifer first visited Kasca in his dreams. Some were pleasurable and others were nightmares. The Devil used the dreams as experiments to find weaknesses, strengths, and others desires. With Kasca, the Devil used a recurring dream to buffet the President's aspirations for fame and glory. The vision started with a large army heading towards the Kingdom. Kasca was leading the army. Their number was like the sand on the seashore, and they were preparing to invade the Kingdom. In the dream, the army overran the Kingdom, and the Counselor was slain at the temple like a human sacrifice. Kasca was the one who raised the blade and took His life. Kasca then saw himself sitting on the throne. The leaders of the nations were bowing down unto him, and they were throwing their crowns at his feet.

Kasca usually woke up at this moment in the dream. Sometimes, however, Lucifer would not be able to control the dreams. The mind of man was a complex mechanism, and the brain had a way of creating its own pathways. These dreams usually turned into nightmares, and Kasca would wake up screaming. Sometimes a giant earthquake would occur, and it would shake his throne. The earth would crack open, and he would fall into an abyss that had no bottom. Other times he would see himself sacrificed at the temple instead of the Counselor. And other nights Kasca would envision his army being destroyed by fire coming down from heaven, and he would be left to blame. In general, the dreams changed with each night vision, but most of the time Lucifer would be successful in tweaking the dreams, and Kasca would be the conquering king.

Chapter 54

A Reunion of Sorts

By the fall of 1000, Esmeralda had become a hard-core believer in the Revivalist's message. There were too many coincidences falling into place, and she could no longer believe the deception. The Holy Scriptures were clear, and she meditated on them daily. She now believed the age was coming to a close and that the D.M.R. was going to be destroyed after leading a rebellion against the Kingdom, so she was terrified and expectant in the same breath. A year ago she repented of her sins and stopped committing acts of fornication. Also, she became part of the underground movement, and she did all she could to help the Revivalists who were in trouble. Of course, Kasca knew all about her misdeeds against the State, but he did nothing about it. Zeze was the one person who comforted him during these trying times, and he wasn't about to imprison her. Kasca was being tormented by his dreams at night. He was losing all sense of reality, but Esmeralda seemed to ease his mind. Zeze would sing to him like David used to soothe King Saul long ago. She would massage and bathe him, and she acted like his caregiver. Esmeralda was Kasca's peace. She was the light of his life.

During the day, Kasca seemed to function normally. Even with his mind playing tricks on him from time to time, he was still a mastermind. In fact, when he was young, he was diagnosed as a genius. Kasca always downplayed his abilities, but deep down inside, he had a superiority complex due to his sharpened intellect. Kasca only considered a few men on equal ground with him. Patmos was one of these men. The Counselor was another, and he used to play chess with

Lane Hofmann, the great inventor, when he still resided in the Kingdom. He also kept his mind occupied by working with the scientists at Gog Incorporated. These were the only people he was able to have an intelligent conversation with and Kasca found himself spending most of his time with them. The rest of his waking hours, he spent on lewd and lascivious behavior, but lately he had been occupied. He was the President of the D.M.R., and it required many menial tasks that he loathed and despised. Also, Kasca had been working on a strategy for invading the Kingdom. He was calculating the costs, forming war pacts, and wondering how Tarshish and the rest of the Alliance would react if the D.M.R. declared war on the Kingdom.

Esmeralda, meanwhile, was doing research of her own. She wondered why no prophet was sent to the D.M.R. Almost every other nation had a prophet come to their lands, but in Magog no prophet made his appearance. She believed that he was either arrested or killed. She also wondered if Patmos was the one sent, and if so, it brought up suppressed feelings in her heart. She had tried for many years to forget about Patmos, and in some ways she had, but deep down she knew her heart. She still loved him, and if he was here, she would do all she could to save him, but Esmeralda was not sure if she was willing to die for him.

Esmeralda first asked an old friend of hers, a private investigator, to see if Patmos had returned to the D.M.R. He found very little information, but he did discover a few strange coincidences. He tried to access the files on Patmos: his bank account, his stock, and other personal data, but it had all been deleted over three years ago. He wondered why the government waited so long to delete him from the system. He asked Esmeralda, "Shouldn't the government have deleted his files long ago when he led the exodus back to the Kingdom? And not only that, I found eye-witnesses who say there was a man who spoke in Liberty Square a few years back. He had a shaved head. He dressed in sackcloth and spoke a Revivalist's message. Apparently, he was quite bold and daring, and a few of the local transients remembered him. But as soon as he came, he was gone. No one knows what happened to him."

"Hmm, that's odd," Esmeralda mumbled. "Patmos dressed the exact same way when he led the people back centuries ago. There must be a connection."

"That's it for me though, Zeze," the investigator announced. "I know we're old friends and all, but this case is starting to get touchy. Since I accessed Patmos' account on the holocomputer, I've had people following me, and all sorts of other problems. That's why I met with you in secret today. I didn't want to lead them to you."

"Thanks, old friend, I hope I didn't cause you any trouble," Esmeralda stated. "That was never my intention, and I'd hate to see you suffer because of me."

"Don't worry about me, Zeze. I'm a survivor. I'm always one step ahead of Big Brother. Even the secret service can't keep up with me."

The two departed from one another and when Esmeralda returned to the estate, she used the holocomputer in her room to research the files and realized she was locked out like her friend, the private investigator. She wondered why this was so. She had top security clearance, so she went into Kasca's office and used his holocomputer to see if he was also locked out, but when she put in the commands, the file opened and she found out all she needed to know about the Professor. Esmeralda knew she wasn't supposed to be using Kasca's machine, but this was too important to her. If Kasca found out, she would fess up, but in the meantime she found out about Patmos' arrest, his imprisonment, and visited the detention cell some time later.

Esmeralda arrived at the prison an hour later. She found Patmos in his cell sitting on the floor. The Professor was reading a book, and he did not notice her standing outside his cell. At first Esmeralda said nothing. She stood there admiring Patmos. He looked thinner than he once had. He had a thick beard, and it was graying on the edges. His time away from the Tree of Life was already starting to take its effect on him. To Pre-Millennial standards, Patmos looked like a man in his early thirties, and Esmeralda thought he looked quite distinguished. Finally, the Professor looked up, and he saw the woman that he loved dearly. At first, he couldn't believe his eyes, but he zoomed in with his vision and realized that Zeze was really standing outside his cell. As for Esmeralda, she did not know what to expect. "Had Patmos forgiven her?" she thought. "Or was the deception still fresh in his mind?" Esmeralda did not know. All she knew was that when she laid eyes on him, old feelings that had been dormant for so long came to the surface and were revived.

When Patmos saw her, he immediately put down his book. He rushed towards her, reached through the bars, and hugged Zeze the best he could. He said, "I'm sorry," and tears began to build in his eyes. When Esmeralda saw the tears start to fall, she could not hold back her demeanor. She also started to cry then she ordered, "Open up the cell!" and the two were reunited.

The two lovers wept for some time in each other's arms. They kissed and held each other tight. Patmos kept asking, "Are you really here?" and she answered, "Yes I am, my love," as Patmos continued to weep. Patmos could not believe that it was truly her. It was like a dream becoming reality. To Patmos, she was as beautiful as a fairy princess. Her skin smelled like baby's-breath, and her lips were as soft as rose petals.

The two lovers touched base and caught up on each other's lives, but Esmeralda seemed more concerned with getting him released than talking about her jaded past. Finally, she said, "Let's go. I'm getting you out of here." But Patmos wouldn't move. She asked, "Is there something you're not telling me?"

The Professor went on to inform her about his dealings with Kasca. He told her about his mission in the D.M.R. and why he could not leave. But Esmeralda seemed unconcerned. She said, "I don't care. I'm taking you home with me today. If Kasca has a problem with that, we'll deal with him together. Now get your things. We're getting out of here."

Patmos stood comatose thinking about what he was going to do. He then turned around, grabbed his personal items, and left the prison cell.

* * * *

Kasca came home from work fuming. He had learned about Esmeralda's illegal access of his holocomputer and about the release of Patmos, so when he saw Esmeralda sitting quietly on the couch reading a book like nothing had happened, he was livid. Kasca walked up to Zeze, grabbed her roughly by the arm, and picked her up. He was squeezing her arm real hard, and he started yelling. Veins were sticking out of the side of his head, and he looked like a madman.

Esmeralda looked back at him with anger and screeched, "Let go of my arm!"

Kasca did not release it. Instead he squeezed harder.

"I said let go of my arm, you jerk!" and she stared coldly into Kasca's eyes.

Finally Kasca released her, and he threw her back down on the couch with force. Kasca then paced back and forth in front of her and was about to yell again, but Esmeralda put a finger up to her mouth informing him to remain quiet, and she pointed at her bedroom door. "He's in the other room. Now be quiet and control yourself," Zeze ordered like a mother scolding a child.

Kasca then started whispering to her angrily.

"You had no right to release him. He's a Revivalist and all of them deserve to be behind bars. And you had the nerve to go behind my back, using my access codes on my computer. Where's the trust?"

"Where's the trust?" Esmeralda mocked. "Well, if you had not locked me out of the files, I wouldn't have had to use your holocomputer."

"I'm the President of the D.M.R. There are some things you don't need to know about."

"And Patmos is one of those?" Esmeralda questioned.

"He had a choice," Kasca explained. "If he wanted to walk free, he could have been here with us long ago.

"Yes, that might have been true, but why didn't you inform me he was here?"

"Because ... because I ..."

Kasca tried to explain, but he could not defend his position.

"I'll tell you why," Esmeralda answered her own question. "It's because you didn't trust me. You thought I'd try to get him released, and you were right, I would have. What harm could he have done?"

"What harm?" the President derided her. "I'll tell you what harm. Last time he was here, he led an exodus of people back to the Kingdom, and he upset the whole Republic. He also betrayed me, and he left you at the crossroads. It took you decades to recover from that relationship, and I nursed you back to health like a wounded animal."

Esmeralda did not have a rebuttal to Kasca's claims. Instead she looked at the ground and did not speak. His words were hurtful, and it brought up a lot of bad memories. Tears started to build in her eyes, and she started to walk away, but Kasca grabbed her by the hand and pulled her close. He said, "I'm sorry," and comforted her with a hug.

A moment later, Patmos entered the room. He asked, "Am I interrupting anything?"

When Esmeralda saw Patmos, she immediately let go of Kasca, and her face brightened. Her sorrow turned to joy, and it became apparent to Kasca that she was still in love with the Professor. This did not sit well with Kasca. He was jealous of Patmos, and it brought up his greatest fears. A little voice inside his head said, "Patmos is going to take your Zeze away from you." It was the Devil speaking. "She is going to forsake you and leave you all alone. Your precious, Zeze, will be gone. You will have no one to take care of you. You will go crazy, and your aspirations will be lost. You must destroy Patmos before he destroys you."

Chapter 55

Dealings & Death

Micah returned to the Kingdom by means of conventional methods. He flew back to the Kingdom on James' private jet instead of flying on the back of a dragon. He landed at the Island of Crete, the Kingdom's airport for Outsiders and from there took a ship to the Kingdom like most of the others during the Booth's Festival. The ship was privately owned, and they were able to move the shield mechanism secretly into the Kingdom. Micah was still one of the 144 Elders, and when he arrived at Jaffa Port near Tel Aviv, he was permitted entrance into the Kingdom. Immediately after Micah's arrival, his cargo was moved to Jerusalem by a hover-truck, and it arrived in the Kingdom's capital shortly thereafter.

Few people in the Kingdom knew about the shield technology. Lane Hofmann, the scientist, was one of these men, and a few others close to the General, like Peter, his nephew, helped Micah achieve his task of bringing the technology to the Kingdom. Once the mechanism was delivered to Lane Hofmann's lab, the great scientist inspected it and proceeded to run tests on it to make sure it would work. Hofmann was impressed with the devise which was based on his schematics, and he prepared the shield technology to be hooked up to one of Jerusalem's solar power plants. It would take a whole power plant to generate enough energy to create a bubble big enough to protect the entire Kingdom, so Micah and the others moved fast to get the device ready in case of a sneak attack from the north.

* * * *

"Now I know that we have been at odds with one another for some time," Kasca addressed Matusak, "but I have a business proposition for you. Madmenah, my old friend, has informed me that you and the Counselor had a falling out. Am I correct?"

Matusak did not speak, but he nodded in agreement.

"Well, the Coalition and its allies ..." Kasca pointed to Madmenah II of Libya and the leaders of Ethiopia. "have decided to invade the Kingdom. We plan to take the Tree of Life and divide its fruit amongst us equally. As for the Kingdom itself, we plan to divide the territory between us. Each nation will be allocated a certain section of the Kingdom, as you can see by the projection in front of you. Alexandria would get a large portion of land east of the Nile River. Alexandria would also seize control of the Red Sea. Your country would be given a generous amount of territory because of the role you would play in the battle. We would like the forces of Africa to gather at the Nile River and launch a simultaneous invasion from there as the Coalition crosses into the Kingdom from the North. As for the people of the Kingdom, they can either join us or be relocated. And if they resist, we will have no other alternative than to eliminate them."

"What about the Counselor?" Matusak asked. "Do you think He's going to stand by idly as we storm into His country?"

"No, I doubt it, but He is only one man," Kasca reassured. "And Gog Incorporated has invented ear protectors to guard us against the Counselor's voice. If He decides to use His sonic voice against us, we will be ready. Also, we outnumber the Kingdom 1000 to 1. They have no walls, no defenses, and no weapons. This should be an easy victory. We should roll right over them. Our generals project that it will only take a few hours to overrun the cities in the Kingdom. First, we'll knock out their communications, take Jerusalem, and invade by land, air, and sea. The leviathan will resist us, but they are no match for our modern warfare."

Matusak looked at the plans, and it seemed too simple. The odds were against the Kingdom, but in the back of Matusak's mind, he kept worrying about the Counselor. He thought to himself, "What if He really is the Son of God? They say that one of His angels can kill a thousand men with a single stroke. Then again, this offer is generous. I'd be a fool not to take it ..."

"So what do you say?" Kasca asked. "Is Alexandria going to be part of the greatest battle ever conceived?"

Matusak did not answer immediately. Hushed voices filled the room. One could hear a pin drop from across the room. Then Matusak answered by raising his fist in the air. He voiced, "We shall be one! We will destroy the menacing Counselor and the 144 Elders! We shall loot the Kingdom of all its riches and have women from the Kingdom as spoils!"

When the men in the room heard this, they cheered mightily like they were at a Marauder bonfire. They drank as one, hugged one another like old friends, and ate heartily.

* * * *

"I hate to break the news to you, Jacob, but we've heard through our spy network that Alexandria has now joined the Coalition and the rest of Africa for the coming invasion of the Kingdom," James announced.

"That backstabbing son of a bitch!" Jacob protested. "After all we've been through together? Matusak has turned his back on us. We've fought side to side together in many wars, and now he's joined forces with his enemy, Kasca and the Libertines??? I don't get it. You sure he doesn't have some trick up his sleeve?"

"I hope so," James answered. "If not, we are greatly outnumbered. Alexandria was always our ace in the hole, and now he has abandoned us for wealth and greed."

"I wouldn't count him out yet, brother. It's just not the Marauding way to turn your back on your friends. Even though the Counselor and Matusak had a falling out, it would be hard for me to imagine Matusak taking up arms against the King of Kings."

"I hope you're right, bro, but as a precaution, we have to proceed without Alexandria on our side. Simon has already projected the losses, and it doesn't look good. Sheba, Dan, and De-Dan don't seem to want to get their hands dirty, so we might have to go this battle alone. It might just be us and the Kingdom against the rest of the world."

* * * *

"Gathering the forces of men against the Kingdom has been too simple," Lucifer mused, "but men are always easily deceived. Everything is falling into place like the prophecies said. How could Ezekiel have known so far in advance? I've never liked the seers. They've always been a thorn in my side. And that Patmos is such a loyal subject of the King. He must be exterminated. I don't see a hedge around him. As for the Queen, I have plans of my own for her. When the Counselor is overcome, I plan to make her my sex slave. I'm going to impregnate her like the Watchers did long ago and build my own little army of demons. He he he … Then again maybe I'll just torture her for eternity. After all, she's the one who rejected me. What? Is she a prude? I'm the most beautiful species in the universe, and she's fallen for that do-gooder, Jesus …"

Lucifer paced around Kasca's estate, and he seemed to be deep in thought. He contemplated. "And what if I'm wrong? Maybe God plans to have mercy upon the fallen angels in the long run. Maybe this is all just a ruse to see how we'll react. If so, I'm in serious trouble. But without me, there would not be a reason for the cross. Without my insurrection, there would be no testing ground for man. Have I been a pawn all along? Have I been played for a fool? Maybe that's why the Son of Man suggested I start a new leaf. Is it possible that He was giving me a second chance? I don't know. I'm torn in two. I'm at a fork in the road. There's still time for me to change my mind and manipulate Kasca to stop the attack. Then again, He says His word is unchanging from beginning until end, and I've already been sentenced. This might be my last chance to break out of prison! I must go through with it! The Kingdom will be destroyed!"

* * * *

The Queen of Sheba had just finished a broadcast on Sheba's largest radio station. She was exhorting the nation to not join the invasion against the Kingdom. She was telling the people about the love that she and the Counselor shared. She spoke about the intimacy between the two, and the miracles she had witnessed over the years. Her radio broadcast was very similar to the one she gave on the holoprogram years ago.

When the Queen left the station, she was escorted to a holo-limo and taken home. In the car, she was reminiscing about the Counselor and the good times they had together. She was feeling elated as the holo-limo sailed over the countryside. Then from out of nowhere, a missile struck the car. Neither the driver nor the Queen saw it coming until the last second, and it blew the car into a thousand fragments. As for the Queen and the driver, they were incinerated. Their bodies were blown apart, and their flesh slowly burned on the ground.

The death of the Queen was a sad day for the Land of Sheba and the entire planet. She was well-liked and renowned. When the Queen spoke, people stood mesmerized by her words, and one could tell that she was being honest and upfront. Her personality was alluring, and she was loved by many. Thus, when people heard the news, it was a day of mourning. It was similar to what happened in the 20th Century when John F. Kennedy and Martin Luther King, Jr. were assassinated. People were saddened, and the death hit home.

Due to the fact that the Queen's body was so badly obliterated, there was no way of reviving her with Fruit Pills. Some hoped the Counselor would come to her aide and bring her back to life like he did with Rhodes Kruger hundreds of years ago, but the Counselor did not come. He didn't even show up at the funeral in Sheba, which took place later that week. Many frowned upon the Counselor's absence, and it didn't help His public image. Some thought He didn't care. Others thought He was afraid to step outside the Kingdom. The truth, however, was that the Counselor was distraught by her death, but He foresaw the event long ago. He even sent her to the Outskirts to die like the rest of the prophets. The Lord knew that one day they would be reunited, so He did not weep. The Counselor knew her death would serve a greater purpose. The Queen would become a martyr for His cause.

The Sheba investigators never figured out who fired the missile. Many people thought the D.M.R. did the deed, but there was no evidence to verify these claims. The rocket was fired from an SS-37 bazooka that could be bought on the black market. These models were outdated and were hardly used by any modern armies. After the invention of the laser, no one used this technology anymore except in places like Ethiopia and the remote Islands of Sheba. As a result, no one was convicted of the crime.

The true culprit was a vigilante by the name of Mercado Romero. He was a Northerner from Gomar who had a few screws loose in his head. He was one of the Queen's biggest fans. In fact, he was infatuated with her and had a shrine back home of her in one of his rooms. When Mercado found out that the Queen had left the Kingdom and was now residing in Sheba, he immediately booked a flight to the South and planned to meet her. After one of her radio presentations, Mercado did manage to shake her hand, but he wouldn't let go of it. The security, therefore, made him let go. They knocked him to the floor and kicked him in the ribs. After his humiliation, Mercado realized he would never get to have the Queen, so he reasoned, "If I can't have her, no one will." Mercado then bought a bazooka on the Black Market and proceeded to execute his neurotic plan.

Sheba's death passed. The people moved on, and a great museum was planned to be built in her honor.

Chapter 56

Request Denied

"Kasca, wake up!" Esmeralda screamed. "What are you doing? It's me, Zeze. Put down the gun."

Kasca was sleep walking again, but this time he was holding a laser gun at Esmeralda and Patmos. The two were in bed together, and Kasca looked like he was going to shoot them for their indiscretions.

"Honey, please it's me, Zeze, and your best friend, Patmos."

"If he was my best friend he wouldn't be sleeping with my girl," Kasca objected. "Now get your hands off her, you traitor. I know all about your plans. You want to lead another exodus back to the Kingdom and steal all my people. We will have none of that. Instead, I'm going to singe you with laser fire and watch your body burn."

Kasca raised the gun and was about to pull the trigger but stopped midway when he heard Esmeralda's voice.

"Please Kasca, you don't know what you're doing," Esmeralda begged. "We are your friends, not your enemies. Now put the gun down before you do something rash."

"Then why is he here? I'll tell you why. He's trying to stop me from taking my rightful place on the throne. But I'm too smart for him. I'm going to take the Kingdom and put the Counselor's head in a noose. And the Tree of Life will be mine, mine, mine!!!"

Kasca raised the gun again, but while he was having his tangent, Esmeralda had snuck out of bed and managed to grab his arm before he exterminated Patmos. As she grabbed him, the gun went off. She distracted the shot just enough and the laser fire missed Patmos and burned a hole in the wall instead.

At the sound of the laser gun, Kasca snapped out of his trance and said, "What … what's going on here? Why am I standing here naked, and who burned a hole in my wall."

Kasca then looked down at his arm and noticed a laser in his hand.

"Zeze, what's happening to me?"

"It's okay, darling," Esmeralda comforted. "Let me take that from you. Let's go back to bed."

Esmeralda put her arm around Kasca and escorted him to the other room like a child having a bad dream as Patmos stood frozen on the bed with sweat dripping down his forehead.

When Esmeralda returned, Patmos asked, "What's wrong with him? Is he losing his mind?"

"It's a long story, honey, but he's been having these episodes for some time now, but lately they've increased tenfold. It's like he's possessed or something."

"You're telling me. He almost killed me."

"You wouldn't be the first. Before you returned, he went on a rampage and killed three of the servants and seriously injured four others. Since then, we've removed all the guns from the house. We must have missed this one, or maybe he brought it in recently."

"Maybe security should do a more thorough job of searching the house!" Patmos exclaimed.

"It was an accident, honey. It won't happen again."

"And what about the three servants who are dead already?"

"Let's just say that's classified information. No one knows about it and no one ever will."

"My God, we've got a psycho-maniac in power, and now he's planning on invading the Kingdom. We've got to do something before it's too late. The D.M.R. must be warned. If the people join him in this attack, it's quite possible all of Magog will be destroyed and suffer eternal consequences. We must warn the people. It's our duty!"

"What do you want me to do?" Esmeralda objected. "I can't just go into the Liberty Broadcasting Station and make an announcement. They won't let me through the gate."

"Possibly so, but if you had Kasca's authorization, I bet you could get off an announcement. I saw you signing his name earlier, and you have access to his personal codes on his holocomputer. I know we could pull it off if we tried."

"No, I don't think so. It's too dangerous."

"But we have to, Zeze. If we don't warn the people in the North, their blood will be on our hands!"

"Keep your voice down. He's just in the other room."

Patmos started to whisper. "It's the end of the age, Zeze. There's no time left to hesitate. You've read the ancient prophecies about the invasion from the North. We already know the outcome. The Counselor is going to destroy the invaders. Their end will be like Sodom, and they will pay for their insurrection."

"But what about Kasca?"

"I know darling. You can try to change his mind, but I don't know if it will help."

Esmeralda started to weep. "Patmos, I love him like a brother. I don't want to lose him. Why don't we ask him first to see if we can make an announcement? This way we won't be betraying him. And if he says no, then I'll go along with your plan."

"It is agreed. We will ask him tomorrow."

The next day rolled around and Patmos proceeded into Kasca's office at home to see if he could have some air time on the Liberty Broadcasting Station.

"So, my old friend, apparently I almost singed you into a million molecules last night," Kasca joked. "Are you alright?"

"I'll survive, but you scared the living hell out of me. I was almost a goner."

"You are correct. When I have my sleep walking episodes anything is possible. I must have forgotten to take my medicine. I'm sorry. I'm also sorry about letting you rot in that cell. Zeze tells me you tried to contact me about getting out. I never received a message."

"It's okay. No worries. I survived, and thank God Zeze was there last night. If she didn't hit your arm, I wouldn't be speaking to you right now."

"Once again, I'm sorry, old buddy. I just didn't know what I was doing at the time."

"Don't worry about it. I know you didn't do it on purpose."

Deep down Kasca wished he would have killed Patmos, but he played it off like he was earnestly sorry and lied to the Professor.

"So Zeze tells me you have a favor to ask," Kasca stated. "What can I do for you?"

Esmeralda slipped into the room and stood behind Patmos as the Professor made his request.

"I would like to get some air time on the holoscreen. Do you think you can arrange that?" Patmos asked.

"Well, it all depends on what you want it for," Kasca answered. "For what purpose will you be using it?"

"I plan to warn the people about the danger of siding against the Counselor and invading the Kingdom."

"In other words, you want to spread the Revivalists' message," Kasca stated sarcastically.

"In a matter of speaking, yes, but there's more to it than that."

"Patmos, we've already been over this. I granted you your freedom, but there is no way in hell I'm going to allow you to address the D.M.R. public. People are being imprisoned for preaching the Revivalist's message out here. If I let you go on the air, it's going to go against the Republic's policy."

"But isn't this a free country?" Patmos countered. "By allowing me to speak, you will be showing the Republic that freedom of speech still exists. Isn't that what you've been fighting for all along? By silencing the Revivalists, you are silencing the voice of freedom."

"Yes, that might be so, but the Revivalists are a threat to our security. They are preaching a message that is putting the whole D.M.R. at risk."

"I don't see how a little freedom of speech is going to hurt anyone. Show me the evidence. The Revivalists don't carry arms. It's not like they are trying to overthrow the government."

"I don't have to prove it to you!" Kasca objected. "They've caused civil unrest. They've upset many proceedings, and they've spread lies about the D.M.R. And not only that, some are suggesting that I'm the Antichrist. One of them even tried to assassinate me over a decade ago. The Revivalists only speak lies! I won't put up with them! They must be exterminated!"

When Patmos heard the last words, he knew that Kasca had gone over the edge. Kasca had officially become everything he once despised. Kasca had now become the ruthless dictator who squashed human rights to propagate his own lust for gain and power.

"So be it, my old friend," the Professor stated indifferently. "I will find another way to proclaim my message."

"And if you do, I will have you arrested. I don't care if our friendship goes back hundreds of years. If you overstep your bounds, I'm going to have you imprisoned. And I'm quite sure you know what happens to the Revivalists in prison," Kasca said dogmatically. "And this time, Zeze's not going to be able to save you."

Kasca glared over at Esmeralda and she looked away being frightened by his stare. There was something evil in his gaze. She had not seen it before. She was blinded by love like the type of blind admiration a mother has for her own child. They cannot see beyond their affection. But now she saw a glimpse of what Kasca had become-an evil genius who had plans for world domination.

"Then we are done here," Patmos said frankly.

"Yes we are, and I'm not bluffing Professor. Don't test me. If you decide to preach the Revivalists' message, you will be going to jail for a long time."

Patmos looked at Kasca one last time then he exited the room. Esmeralda did the same, but as she left, she gave Kasca a disapproving glare and went her way.

Chapter 57

The Gathering Storm

"Run to the hills. Run to the hills, I say!" a man hollered from the streets of Jerusalem. "The D.M.R. is coming! The Coalition's on its way! Matusak's coming for revenge! Flee the cities was Kasca's decree!"

People were running this way and that in the Kingdom. The President had just announced to the world that they had declared war on the Kingdom, and everyone was in a state of panic. People were fleeing to the mountains. Others had taken all their belongings and were heading to the Outskirts like refugees. A great army was gathering to the North and Israeli citizens were afraid for their lives.

A newscaster from Tarshish repeated the holo announcement for the third time today as people were gathered around their holoprojectors waiting to hear the next word on the war.

"At 5:00 P.M. today, the D.M.R., together with the Coalition forces and all of Africa, have declared war on the Kingdom. Coalition forces have made a blockade of the borders, and they appear to be moving into position for an assault on the Kingdom."

Holoprojections of refugees fleeing to the Outskirts were being projected in the background as the newscaster continued his breaking news story.

"As you can see from our satellite images, billions of troops have started moving into position in the North, and they are settling in Meschech and Tubal. There is also a large constituency of troops gathered from the tribes of Ethiopia, Libya, and Alexan-

dria at the Nile River, but no official invasion has begun. Encampments are being built. The troops are settling in, but no shots have been fired yet. We will now replay the official declaration of war made by the President of the D.M.R. earlier today."

Kasca appeared in everyone's living rooms. He was wearing a black suit and tie, and standing behind a podium with a speech in his hand.

"It is with deep regret that I must give this proclamation today, but the D.M.R., the Coalition, and the forces of Africa have exhausted every other means of engagement. We have tried diplomacy with the Kingdom, but it has failed. We have attempted to use sanctions, but it has not been successful. We have tried to reason with the Counselor and the 144 Elders, but they will not speak with our representatives. Therefore, the allies of the D.M.R. have decided to declare war on the Kingdom."

There was a pause, then Kasca continued making his speech.

"Now I know these are difficult words to hear, but there are many reasons to justify our actions. First of all, the Plague of Age increases in the Outskirts. More and more people are growing older and Fruit Pills are getting scarcer by the day. The Kingdom, however, has been hording the pills for over a thousand years, and it is time for the Israelis to share the Tree of Life with the rest of humanity. Our coalition plans to retake the Tree and share it with all peoples of the earth. In addition, the Counselor and the 144 Elders have been ruthless dictators over the years. They have forced us to bring tribute year after year, and if we do not bring forth their praises, they have withheld the rains from falling upon our regions. Is this just? Is this fair? I think not. But thank Gog Incorporated for making the technological advancements in creating weather machines to free us from this bondage. And not only that, these tyrants have shot down innocent victims over the years. I hope you all remember Aero-plane 22764, and the countless other victims that have been shot down over the centuries. The blood of these blameless men and women has been crying out to us for years, and today we will make retribution for these crimes."

Kasca took a breath and resolutely looked into the eyes of the holoprojection audience. He then continued.

"The D.M.R., with its allies, plans to launch an invasion into the Kingdom in the coming days. We will bring freedom and liberty to the Israeli people. Our coalition wants to make it clear that our fight is not against you. It's against the Counselor, the 144 Elders, and all those who have supported them throughout the years. Therefore, we are granting amnesty to any Kingdom citizen that wishes to be liberated. You may cross the borders freely into the Outskirts, and you will be cared for and received. But those who remain behind will have to suffer the consequences of your actions. We hope to spare as many lives as possible, but we cannot guarantee your safety. For this reason, we entreat you to come to your senses and join us in our quest to eliminate this dicta-

torship from the world. Fight with us. Join our cause, and we will have peace in our time."

*   *   *   *

"Can you believe that bull rolling from Kasca's lips?" Jacob objected. "Does he really think anyone's buying his propaganda?"

"Well, he's obviously convinced two-thirds of the Outskirts and a whole lot of people in the Kingdom," James answered. "Our sources say there are millions of refugees fleeing the Kingdom and trying to escape the coming war."

"So what are we going to do about it, James?" Jacob asked. "Don't tell me you're just going to stand by idly and watch this atrocity unfold."

"Of course not, Simon is already down at one of the holostations preparing to make a formal protest against the invasion. I've already called the leaders of Dan and De-Dan, but they don't want to get involved. They said they're willing to publicly denounce the invasion, but they are not willing to go to war over it. As for Southern Nod and Sheba, I haven't spoken with them yet. If they are also unwilling to go to war, we won't have a chance. We need the Alliance to be united against this war. If not, we won't have a leg to stand on."

"Arghhh!" Jacob grunted as he pulled at his curly, red hair. "Don't they realize, the time is now to make a stand! The Counselor needs our support! We must rise to the occasion and fight for what is right!"

"Yes, I know brother, but we must temper our passions and remain calm. Tarshish needs our reason, not our rage."

"Forget reason!" Jacob yelled. "Eternal souls are on the line here. This is not a game. All those who oppose the King of Kings are going to be destroyed and cast into the Lake of Fire for eternity. Have you forgotten your reason?"

James did not have a rebuttal. He knew his brother well, and he knew it was better to let Jacob's temper die down before he pursued the issue. So James went over to the wet bar, pulled out a glass, poured himself a shot, then drank it down.

"Would you like one?"

Jacob didn't answer. Instead, he looked out the high rise window as James proceeded to pour himself another drink and also one for his brother. James walked over to Jacob and handed him a glass. The two toasted each other, and they drank down the shot together. Then Jacob spoke solemnly.

"So what do you want to do?"

James' eyes rolled back into his head. His mind was working. He then spoke like a man who had nothing left to lose.

"I say we gather all the leaders of the Alliance together and make a big stink about the war. Let's inform the whole world that there are those who are standing by the Counselor and the Kingdom. Then I say we let the force field do its job. Micah's over there already, and he says the bubble's ready to go. We just have to hope it works. We've never tried the shields on this grand of a scale. Lane Hofmann said it would take a whole solar plant to protect the entire Kingdom. They have the network set-up, but if there are any technical difficulties, the Kingdom's going to be in trouble.

So if the force-field fails, we have to be ready. I suggest we send our navy to the Arctic Ocean, scatter our ships across the sea, and destroy the D.M.R. with laser fire and superweapons if their invasion is successful."

"But what if the D.M.R. fires back?" Jacob asked. "We didn't have enough time to construct force fields for us and the rest of the Alliance. We'll be destroyed as well."

"So be it! It's the end of the age anyway. We might as well go out with a bang rather than a whimper."

Jacob laughed and a huge smile formed on his freckled face. He gave his brother a firm hug and James smiled insanely. "To the death!" the O'Donohue brothers said in unison, and they both screamed madly, "Ahhhhhh!!!"

※　　※　　※　　※

Some of the leading members of the 144 Elders came to the Counselor secretly.

"What are we going to do?" the lead speaker asked. "Some of the Elders have already fled to the Outskirts. We need your help. They're coming for us. What counsel do you give?"

"That's funny," the Counselor answered. "For over a hundred years, the 144 Elders have not sought My advice. Now you come to Me in your time of need. Why should I help you? Why don't you flee like the rest of the cowards?"

"Where would we go, Lord?" the lead speaker asked. "They will come for us. There is no where to hide from the satellites of the D.M.R."

"Yes, that is true. You were the ones who voted to lift the ban on holoprograms coming from the Outskirts. You were the ones who took the Fog of War away. Before that, the Kingdom was shrouded from the rest of the world, but now they can see that there are no walls or fortresses to defend us. What would you do if you were in My shoes? Most of the 144 Elders forsook Me a long time ago. Why should I come to your aide?"

"You are right, my Lord. We have been rebellious servants for some time, but now we come to You humbly asking for forgiveness. Will you receive us unto You?"

"Do you take Me for a fool?" the Counselor asked. "If you believed in Me, you would know that I can read your innermost thoughts. You are only here to save yourselves, and you are not truly sorry. Therefore, I'm going to do nothing. I'm going to let you fend for yourselves. You have been doing that for a long time now. Let's see if you survive this conflict. Maybe if you bow down to Kasca, he will have mercy upon you."

"Counselor, it's not true. I swear," the lead speaker lied.

"Depart from Me and take the rest of the worms with you. I don't want to hear your falsehood anymore," the Counselor ordered. "Only if you genuinely repent will I receive you back unto Me. Now depart from Me and go your way."

The elders withdrew like rats when they're exposed to electric light, and they quickly scurried out of the Temple.

Not all the 144 Elders were corrupted by the times, but most of them had fallen into sin like the rest of the Kingdom. They had been exposed to life in the Outskirts for too long and many of them could no longer walk the straight and narrow path. Even some of the Old Timers were having a difficult time refraining from sin, but most still had faith in the Lord. As for the Counselor, He knew man's shortcomings. He was the one who created man and woman in the first place, so he expected most to fall by the wayside. And even though there were millions who were fleeing for the Outskirts in fear, there were billions in the Kingdom who stayed behind. They knew they were outnumbered. Most were scared for their lives. They knew that if the Counselor did not save them, they would be destroyed. They knew their chances were bleak, but they had faith that the Counselor would come through in the bottom of the ninth.

✳   ✳   ✳   ✳

"Matusak, I had a horrible dream last night," Matusak's first wife stated in a panicked voice. "We were in a dark and dreary place. It was a place of torment. There was no peace there. There was a river of fire. It was a great blaze that burned with intensity. There was no water there, nor birds, nor any living thing. It was a wasteland, a place of chaos, and we were bound in chains. We could not escape. We were locked away forever."

"Oh please, my husband, do not invade the Kingdom. This is a warning from God. If you make war with the Counselor, I believe we are going to suffer eternally for our actions. Make peace with the Counselor and withdraw your troops. Emmanuel has been a friend to you, not your enemy. He has disciplined you from time to time, but He has stood by your side. Don't you remember when you were depressed and downtrodden? The Counselor was the one who came to your aide and rescued you. He answered my cry and restored you to your old self before your enemies came to destroy you."

"Matusak, don't listen to her," the Emperor's thirteenth wife responded from the other side of the bed. The three of them were lying in bed together, and both women had their arms wrapped around Matusak. The Emperor was in the center, and he was listening to the two women quarrel.

"Sasha has always been a crazy fool, and here she goes with those visions again. You're the ruler of Alexandria, not her. Are you going to let your decisions be made by a mad woman?"

When Matusak's first wife heard these words, she immediately sat up in bed and gave the Emperor's thirteenth wife an evil glare. The two women never saw eye to eye, and they had both fought for control of the palace for years.

"Now be nice," Matusak said. "I don't feel like breaking up a cat fight right on top of me."

Sasha lay down again on his shoulder and pleaded, "Please, my husband, don't follow the Coalition into war. I think our eternal souls are at risk here."

The thirteenth wife started to laugh, and she mocked Matusak's first.

"Eternal outcomes, don't be ridiculous! If you don't join the battle, you will be seen as a coward. And if you don't fight along side the Coalition, you are going to miss out on all the spoils. All of Alexandria will suffer for your inept leadership, and it will bring about your fall."

Matusak looked over at his thirteenth wife and said, "Hmm ... maybe I shouldn't have married you, but made you an advisor instead."

"Don't listen to her, my husband," Sasha argued, "she's just trying to sideswipe you."

"Sideswipe him!" Matusak's thirteenth wife warned as she sat up and stared down Sasha. "I'm trying to give him reasonable advice, and you're trying to confuse him with your crazy dream."

"If you call me crazy again, I'm going to make you pay!"

"Crazy, crazy, crazy ... Crazy, crazy, crazy ..."

Sasha immediately leapt over Matusak's body and started strangling the Emperor's thirteenth wife. The thirteenth wife tried to fight back, but she was losing consciousness, so Matusak had to step in and separate the two women. He grabbed his first wife and tore her from the other woman then threw her to the other side of the room. The thirteenth wife started gasping for air, but when she recovered, she started yelling, "You crazy bitch! I'm going to kill you one day! You just wait and see!"

"I'll be waiting for you!" his first wife hollered back. "You come for me, and I'll cut your throat!"

As Matusak's first wife was yelling out her threats, Matusak was pulling his thirteenth by the arm and dragging her across the floor. Then he threw her out of the room and locked her out. In the background, one could hear threats being made from the other room. Eventually they faded and stopped altogether.

When Matusak turned around, he saw his first wife looking in the mirror. She was tending to a scratch that she received in the conflict. The emperor started walking towards his first wife, but she threatened him.

"Don't you dare do that to me or I swear I'll cut you!"

She raised a knife in the air to show she was serious, and Matusak stopped in mid-step.

"Ugh!" Matusak grunted. He threw his arms down in protest then walked away into the bathroom and started running himself some bath water.

Twenty minutes later, Matusak was lying passed out in the tub. His first wife was naked, and she had just sneaked into the room. She was holding a knife behind her back, and she slowly stepped into the tub with him. Sasha then leaned over the Emperor like she was going to cut his throat, but just when she was close enough to make her move. Matusak reached out with one hand and crushed her wrist until she dropped the knife. His first wife tried to fight back, but it was useless. Instead she kissed him hard on the mouth, bit his lip, and the two made passionate love.

Chapter 58

Behind the Scenes

"Patmos, over here," Esmeralda whispered. "If we are going to make our move, tomorrow is the day. I walked in on Kasca earlier in the middle of a telo-prompter call and overheard that there will be an important meeting at Gog Incorporated with the leaders of the nations gathered against the Kingdom. That will be our chance to get into his office. He's almost barricaded in there lately with the pressures of the war. This might be our only chance to access his computer."

"What time's the meeting at?"

"9:00 A.M. I'm sure he'll be out of here earlier than that, so we'll just have to wait and listen. So tomorrow morning, be ready to go. And look your best. If everything goes well, you are going to be on the holoscreen."

The next day rolled around and Kasca was out of the house by 7:00 A.M. This allowed Esmeralda and Patmos to infiltrate Kasca's home holo-computer."

"What are you doing?" the Professor asked.

"First of all, I have to put in the access codes," Esmeralda answered. "Hopefully he hasn't changed them. He does that from time to time, but last time he forgot his passwords, and we had to have a government technician out here to fix the problem."

"But don't you need a thumb print to get out of the batter's box on the holo-computer?"

"Don't worry, I have that taken care of."

Zeze pulled out a thin piece of plastic that looked like a thumb. It was amazingly detailed, and Esmeralda slipped it over her left thumb then proceeded to the scanner.

"Look closely Patmos, the Republic's been making these for years. It's allowed Gog Inc. to access computers all over the world. All the secret service needs is a solid thumb print left behind, and they can go anywhere. Glasses are the best, but you'd be amazed at what computers can do these days. This technology has allowed the Republic to stay one step ahead of the other nations in the Outskirts. Only the D.M.R. has access to the technology, not even the other Coalition nations like Persia know about it."

Esmeralda put her left thumb up to the scanner and proceeded to first base on Kasca's holo-computer. A pad appeared out of thin air in front of her. It was an access panel and a password needed to be entered.

"Well, here it goes," Zeze said as she punched a series of numbers on the holo-panel.

There was a slight delay as a holo-computer appeared in front of her. It spoke in a woman's voice. "Welcome Mr. President, what can I do for you today?"

"I would like you to get a hold of the Liberty Broadcasting Station and inform them that we are going to have a special guest today on Kennedy King's morning talk show. Send the information over to King's secretary, and let her know that Patmos will be the one being interviewed by the talk show host today. The questions King will be asking the Professor are attached and background information on Patmos' previous interview with King long ago is also to be sent over."

"Thank you, Mr. President, would you like me to record the request right now or would you prefer a holo-image."

"A holo-projection will be fine. I don't look my best this morning."

"Is there anything else I can do for you, Mr. President?"

"Yes, I would like you to generate two V.I.P. access passes to Liberty Broadcasting Corporation for Patmos Svenson and Esmeralda Sanchez."

"Thank you, computer, Kasca signing out."

"Goodbye, Mr. President, your passes will be generated in five seconds."

"Alright, let's go!" Esmeralda ordered. "We don't have a moment to spare. We're on at 9:15, and we still have to fight the morning rush hour."

"But Zeze, let me go put on a tie," Patmos objected. "I didn't realize I was going to be on Kennedy King's show."

"No, you look fine," Esmeralda comforted. "You look professional, but you have a casual feel to you. It will appeal to the masses."

"Are you sure?"

"Yes, now let's go."

"One last thing …"

"What now?" Esmeralda shrugged.

Patmos did not speak. Instead he grabbed Zeze, spun her around, and kissed her firmly on the lips.

"Okay, now I'm ready."

Esmeralda smiled, and the two swiftly exited Kasca's office and the estate.

* * * *

When Patmos and Esmeralda arrived at Liberty Broadcasting Studio, they were late. It was 8:45 A.M. already, and King's show went on a 9:00 A.M. They were rushed through the door, and the two were brought to the make-up room. Patmos was tended to by several make-up artists, and they quickly went to work on the Professor. When 9:15 A.M. rolled around, Patmos only had a few minutes to collect his thoughts. The next thing he knew he was being escorted to the stage and sitting next to the most famous talk-show host in the world, Kennedy King.

"When I got the news, you were going to be on the show today, I was absolutely flabbergasted," King exulted. "After all, it's been centuries since you led the exodus back to the Kingdom in 262. Do we have any footage from that period? There have been a lot of New Timers born since then, and they don't even remember that era."

Instantly in the background footage was being run of Patmos leading millions of people back to the Kingdom and making a speech at Liberty Square.

"And if I remember correctly, weren't you and the President good friends?"

Once again footage was being run in the background. It was Patmos and Kasca being interviewed centuries ago on King's show.

"Yes, that's how I made it on the show today," Patmos answered. "Kasca and I are strongly opposed to one another on the invasion of the Kingdom, but he's still my buddy."

"My o my," King shook his head, "we are on the brink of a new era. Our country has already declared war on the Kingdom, yet our president has allowed a spokesman for the Kingdom to come on the air today. This proves that Kasca truly is a Libertine. Freedom of the press still reigns supreme in the D.M.R!"

When the audience heard this, they clapped madly as the talk show host shook his head. King knew the truth though. For over a century, the Libertines had been dictating to him what will be allowed and what will be censored on his program. The reality was that King hated the Libertines and the President. King was an educated African, an Old Timer from the United States of America, and he despised what the D.M.R. had become. He saw through their lies, and he experienced their deception day in and day out, so to have Patmos on the air was a breath of fresh air to the talk show host.

"Well, Professor, we are on the brink of war here. What message do you have for the D.M.R. and the rest of the Outskirts? The floor is yours."

"It's simple," Patmos spoke earnestly. "Don't partake in the battle. Resist this government. Kasca is about to make a fatal mistake. If the D.M.R. and its allies invade the Kingdom, the armies will be destroyed. And all those in support of the attack might lose their eternal souls to the Lake of Fire. The Coalition is waging a war against the Son of God. This battle cannot be won. I strongly urge the people in the Outskirts to make a stand against the invasion. The D.M.R. is about to start a conflict that will be the war to end all wars. We must not comply. The voice of the people must be heard before it's too late."

There was a moment of silence. Kennedy King sat shell-shocked after hearing the Professor's words then finally he regained his composure.

"My God, you sound like a Revivalist," King stated.

"If that's what you want to call me, that's fine with me. And the reason you haven't heard from the Revivalists lately is because they are all in prison and many have been murdered in jail. In fact, I came to the D.M.R. years ago to forewarn the North, but I was locked away like the rest of them, but I luckily got out. Please do not join this rebellion against the Kingdom and the Counselor. All that you've heard about Him are lies. It's all propaganda. I know the Counselor personally. He is a kind and just King. And not only that, He is God. This is a test my friends. This is a battle for your eternal souls. The thousand years are up. Think about it. Read the Holy Scriptures. Go and find yourself an old Bible and look up Ezekiel, chapter thirty-eight and Revelation twenty. It's evidence to support my claims. Don't take my word for it. This has all been prophesied thousands of years ago. Look it up, please! This might be your last chance!"

At that moment D.M.R. security forces appeared on the set, and the interview was cut short. A holo-image of Kennedy King appeared on everyone's projectors. The holo-image said, "And we'll be right back folks. Here's a message from our sponsors."

The truth was that Patmos and King were arrested. Esmeralda was also taken captive. As for the viewers, they had no idea what was going on. When the program came back on the air after the commercial break, Patmos was not there. Kennedy King was sitting by himself on the couch, and he was announcing his next guest. It was an old interview of an actor from a century ago, and the show continued without interruption. Most viewers did not have a clue that they had just been hoodwinked, but it did not matter. Patmos' managed to get his message out before it was too late, and he reached many people in the world viewing the program that day.

* * * *

Patmos and Esmeralda were escorted to one government hovercar, and King was ushered to another, but right before they were thrown into the cars, Zeze pulled out a laser hidden between her breasts and managed to stun the agents. King hollered, "Run for it! I'll try to keep them occupied!" The two lovers made a break for it as King fought off the agents. One of the government agents was not pleased though, and he fired in anger at the talk show host. His laser was set at the highest setting, and King was burned alive.

"Oh my God, did you see that!" Esmeralda hollered. "They killed King!"

"Let's go! It's too late for him!" Patmos ordered. "Don't make his sacrifice be in vain!"

The two continued to flee. They got lost in the city crowd. And when they were far enough away, they started to walk briskly and made their way towards the subway.

After hopping on one of the trains, the two looked out the window to see if anyone was following them. No agents appeared as the train pulled away, and they were safe for the moment. The two lovers were wrapped in each other's arms, and Esmeralda was shaking.

"It's going to be okay," the Professor comforted as he held onto her and rubbed his hand up and down her back. "King will be rewarded like the rest of the martyrs at the end of the age. We will see him soon. God be our witness."

Five minutes passed as they continued to ride the train then they exited at the next stop and switched lines. They knew the agents would be onto them soon enough, so they tried to get as far away as possible and not follow a predictable pattern.

Patmos was just about to pick a line to take, but Esmeralda spoke up. She finally seemed to snap out of it. "No, let's take the green line. I know a place at Ukraine Junction that the Revivalists used to meet at before it was overrun by agents. It's abandoned now. I think we'll be safe there for the time being."

Patmos acted quickly. He took her hand, and the two made their way to the place of refuge.

* * * *

When Patmos arrived at the Revivalists building, it was all boarded up. It looked like no one had been there for sometime, so the two found a comfortable place in the corner and slept on the floor. They cuddled up to one another to keep each other warm, and they fell asleep in each other's arms.

Two hours later the couple was awakened by the sound of the door being kicked in. They had been found, and there was no where to hide. Minutes later, two agents appeared with lasers in their hand, and they had them aimed at Patmos and Esmeralda. Zeze wanted to use the little laser gun she had in defense, but the Professor took it from her and laid it on the floor. Kasca then appeared in the shadows. He was weeping.

"You have both betrayed me!" Kasca said hysterically. "My closest friends have turned their backs on me and forsaken me."

"Kasca, please …" Patmos tried to explain, but he was cut off in mid sentence.

"You shut up!" and he aimed his laser at the Professor. "I've had enough of you!"

Patmos fell back into Esmeralda's arms, and the two cringed together.

"You have betrayed me. You are Benedict Arnolds. Now I have no one. Patmos, you were my closest friend, and Zeze, I loved you more than all the others. But none of that matters now. You have left me no choice. I must sacrifice you for a better tomorrow …"

"Kasca, please, listen to reason …" Esmeralda tried to interrupt.

"And don't you start on me!" the President voiced, but Esmeralda did not stop speaking.

"Arrest us, put us in jail, but don't murder us. If you take our lives, you won't be able to live with that. I know you better than anyone else. We still love you, Kasca …"

"Stop! Don't talk about love!" Kasca protested. "If you loved me, you would not have stabbed me in the back. You would not have accessed my computer against my will again nor allowed this traitor to speak words of blasphemy against me. So don't insult my intelligence!"

"Kasca, listen to her," Patmos joined in. The Professor rose from the floor and started walking towards the President. "Don't put our blood on your hands. It will live with you forever …"

"Don't take a step closer! If you do I'm going to kill you."

Kasca pushed a button a few times on the laser and set it to its highest setting.

"If you move one step closer, I'm going to execute you!"

Patmos stopped in his tracks then he spoke again, "I'm sorry, old friend. I had to do what I thought was right. Please forgive me."

The Professor took another step forward, and Kasca pushed the fire button on the laser. Patmos was killed instantly. When Esmeralda saw this, she charged towards Patmos trying to save him, but he was already incinerated. She then looked at Kasca incredulously, and she reached for her laser on the ground. The President's two security officers fired at Esmeralda. Kasca yelled, "Nooooo!!!" but it was too late. She was also burned alive. When Kasca witnessed this, he put the laser to his head and was just about to pull the trigger, but luckily for him, one of the security guards tackled him before the laser went off, and Kasca was knocked unconscious. At that moment, Lucifer entered Kasca's body and possessed him, and from that point forward, the President's life would never be the same.

Chapter 59

Blood Brothers

Jacob arrived at the Emperor's palace in Alexandria and was greeted by Matusak and his harem. Matusak reached out to shake Jacob's hand, but instead of shaking the Emperor's hand, he punched him in the face.

"You betrayed us!" Jacob hollered. "We took a blood oath long ago, and now you've turned your back on us!"

Matusak felt his lip and noticed blood dripping from his finger. He was angry at the chieftain from Tarshish, but he was also impressed. And instead of striking Jacob, he ordered his servants and concubines out of the room.

"Leave us! The chieftain and I have business to discuss!"

The two men waited for everyone to leave the room. Each man was eyeing the other. Jacob had his hand on his hip pocket which contained a knife, and he was preparing for a battle. Matusak, on the other hand, held his hands in the air, as a sign of peace, and the two men sat down at a table. Jacob then began.

"You are a traitor, Matusak. Our blood oath goes back to the 13 Year War. We supplied the Marauders with weapons, supplies, and Fruit Pills. Without Tarshish, the Marauders would be no more. And now you have formed an alliance with our greatest enemy, the Prince of Rosh. How could you do this to us? We were counting on you to protect our back."

Matusak looked at Jacob, and he felt a sense of pride. Although the chieftain was from Tarshish, Jacob had fought side to side with Matusak many times, and the Emperor was as close to him as any Marauder.

Matusak then spoke, "Come with me. There are too many peering eyes in this palace."

Jacob followed Matusak to his bedroom and locked the door behind him. He then proceeded to open a secret passage in the floor. They entered an elevator, and the two men went down many levels until they found themselves in a bunker beneath the earth.

"This bunker was made centuries ago after the 13 Year War," Matusak spoke earnestly. "Only a few know about its existence. After the death of so many members of my family during the war, I decided to never let that happen again, so I built this shelter under the earth. It's built to hold 500 people, and there are enough supplies to last ten years."

"So why have you brought me here?" Jacob asked.

"First of all, I know my secret is safe with you. It's also the only place I know that's free from spies. I don't even know whom I can trust anymore. I've lost faith in many of my companions and several of my wives would stab me in the back if they had the chance. And I can't go outside because the D.M.R.'s watching me 24 hours a day. They're making sure I won't betray them, so we must outfox them with your visit."

"Why are you telling me all this?"

"Because I have not forsaken the Counselor as many have been led to believe. Initially I was upset with Him, but after speaking with my first wife, I realized I had misjudged the Counselor. He has been a true friend to me over the years. At times His rulings have upset me, but if the Lord did not care for me, He would not have chastened me. As for the alliance against the Kingdom, I have only joined them to get the upper edge in the battle. When the war is about to begin, I plan to turn my troops around and destroy the armies gathered in Africa then I plan to attack the D.M.R. I guarantee you the Nile will not be crossed. As for my family, I plan to send them here and wait for the outcome of the battle. I know it's quite possible Alexandria will be destroyed, so I have prepared for the worst. As for the blood oath between the O'Donohue brothers and I, it's as strong as ever. You are family to me. We will either die in battle fighting for the Kingdom or we will be destroyed. Either way, I'm hoping the Counselor will forgive me for my indiscretions, and I will enter into glory with the rest of the martyrs and saints."

Jacob gave Matusak a firm hug, and the bond of friendship was as it was before.

"I'm sorry for ever doubting you, Matusak," Jacob said.

"I forgive you, but I'm going to make you pay for your unbelief. You and I are going to get into a fight when we return to the surface, and I'm going to kick the living crap out of you. It's the only way they'll believe us. We must put on a good show. We must prove to them that our negotiations have failed. This way the Coalition will not become suspicious of us."

"Please don't break anything."

"I'll try my best, but I have to make it look real."

"Oh yeah, I almost forgot. Strap this to the inside of your leg. It's a secret communication device created by Gog Inc. With this instrument, you'll be able to monitor everything I hear. It might give you an edge in battle.

"Okay, are you ready?

Jacob shook his head yes.

"This might be the last chance I get to speak with you, so when we get to the surface, I want you to call me a traitor and a whole bunch of other vile things. An argument will ensue then I'm going to make you pay for your indiscretions. And here's a few Fruit Pills. Put these in your pocket. You're going to need these later."

Jacob swallowed harshly, and sweat started to form on his forehead, but Matusak comforted him, "It'll be fun. When's the last time you were in a fight?"

Jacob shook his head in disbelief as the elevator doors opened.

They both exited the elevator, took a few steps then Jacob yelled, "You bastard, traitor, son of a bitch! I hope you burn in hell!" And the chieftain proceeded to slap Matusak solidly across the face as an insult.

"Oh, you're going to pay for that!" And Matusak punched Jacob in the jaw as a reply to the offense.

At that moment, one of Matusak's wives unlocked the door, and the servants tried to rush in and break up the brawl.

"Stand back, I say!"

Matusak threw one of the servants against the wall.

"This is between me and him! Now stand aside!"

A large crowd started to grow in Matusak's quarters, so the Emperor grabbed Jacob and threw him out the door. He must have traveled fifteen meters as he slid across the floor. Matusak and the others followed him out of the room. Jacob then pulled his knife from his hip, and Matusak yelled, "Bring it on! Let's see what you have!"

Jacob moved in closer and started to make quick swings at Matusak, but missed every time. Matusak managed to grab Jacob's arm and wrestle the knife out of his hand. It fell to the floor, and Matusak kicked it aside. Matusak then threw Jacob in the air and he landed on top of a table. Jacob grunted in pain and rolled off the table onto the floor, but he managed to rise to his feet. Matusak walked over to Jacob, picked him up again and threw him across the room, closer to one of the exits. Jacob slammed into the door and was barely moving. Matusak strutted over to Jacob, picked him up two feet off the ground and held him in the air. He said, "This is what you get for disrespecting me and my family. Consider our alliance over."

But Jacob wasn't done. He spit in Matusak's face and said, "That's what I think of our alliance.

When Matusak heard these words, "He kicked down the door and threw Jacob out of the palace. He boasted, "Take that Tarshish!" and Matusak started to beat his chest like King Kong.

Jacob crawled away in the dirt. His body was all bloody and battered. As he went, he hollered one last taunt. "You'll pay for this someday, Matusak, you and all your household!"

Matusak acted like he was about to finish him off, but his first wife held him back. "He's had enough, old man. You've already taken his pride from him."

Matusak looked at his first wife and the rest of the crowd gathered around him. He spit on the ground in Jacob's direction then turned around and entered back into the palace.

*   *   *   *

"So Mr. President, did you hear about the fight between Matusak and Jacob of Tarshish?" one of his advisors asked.

"Yes, how could I miss it?" Kasca answered. "It's been on almost every channel since this morning."

"I guess now all your fears of Alexandria switching sides can be put to rest."

"I suppose so, but this battle almost seems staged. I mean how is it possible that someone just happens to have a holo-camera handy at that very moment?"

"Mr. President, I don't mean any disrespect, but everyone has them now. Even my kids carry them around with them. These tri-corders can do everything now. You can listen to music, talk on the phone, record holo-images, scan for life signs, and everything else in between."

"Yes, you might be right, but it just doesn't sit well with me," Kasca objected. "I want you to continue monitoring Matusak and his actions. There's something fishy in the water, and I don't want to be caught off guard."

"Yes sir!" the advisor cadenced and left the room.

Kasca then rose from his chair and paced around the room. He poured himself a drink and looked in the mirror. There was something behind his eyes that he could not pin down, and he felt different inside. The sensation made him feel strong and powerful. As of late, he truly did feel like a god. With Patmos and Esmeralda out of the way, all his doubts and indecisions slipped away. Kasca thought he'd feel guilty about their deaths, but he did not. The President could not believe he almost took his life at the very moment he was about to reach his glorious destiny, but by killing his closest companions, Kasca proved to himself that he could do anything. He was now willing to kill billions of people to achieve his goals. In a matter of days, he would be the ruler of the world. The D.M.R. was at red alert. His air force was already in the air 24 hours a day, and if Tarshish decided to move against the D.M.R. and interfere, they would be exterminated. His laser silos were geared up to defend against any superweapons attacks, and his missiles were ready to be launched at the push of a button. This time, Kasca would not hesitate. He no longer felt fear or regret or sorrow. His mind was focused on the prize awaiting him. He would be proclaimed as the sovereign ruler of the earth. The Counselor would be defeated, and the Tree of Life would be taken as a spoil of war.

Chapter 60

The Final Battle

The drums of war were playing in soldiers' minds. The orders were given by their commanders earlier that night, and they were informed the invasion would begin at 5:00 A.M. Kingdom time. The soldiers were nervous and edgy. The tanks were ready to rumble, and the Battle of Gog was about to begin. It was December of 1000. The outcome of this battle would decide the fate of the world for ages to come. The victors would reap the bounty, and a new age would dawn.

Shortly after the announcement was made to the troops, Kasca received a private call from James, the ruler of Tarshish. James asked, "What's the true purpose of the invasion? Is it for spoil and the taking of the Tree of Life?"

"Yes, that is one reason, but it's also to pave the path to freedom and to rid the world of the Counselor's dictatorship," the President answered.

"That's the generic response you've been giving the press, but why Kasca? You know the Counselor's power. He's going to repel your invasion and bring you to judgment for your crimes."

"As far as I can see, there are no walls to stop our tanks, and there's no military to defend them. The Counselor may have some power, but He cannot stop us all. We will overrun the Kingdom, and the Counselor will fall."

"But what if you're wrong, Kasca? What is it you want? Do you require more Fruit Pills? Maybe we could strike a bargain with the King and end this war before it begins. There's still time for diplomacy."

"Forget diplomacy! The time is now for war!" Kasca reacted. "You're trying to make one last feeble attempt to save yourselves. For a thousand years, Tarshish has had the upper hand on Fruit Pills, but that's all going to change. The D.M.R. and the Coalition will now rule the world, and Tarshish will be subservient to us."

"Kasca, if I didn't know you better, I'd say you've gone crazy. Are you starting to believe your own propaganda," James expounded. "I personally saw the King of Kings return in glory and set up His Kingdom on earth. With a word from His mouth, the Counselor returned the earth to its natural glory, and all of mankind has been blessed. Think about what you're doing. You're waging a war against the Creator of the universe. You cannot win."

"Yes, that's the lies you've been telling us for a thousand years, and I'm not buying it. All of you Old Timers say the same thing, but it's time for a new reign. The old will be replaced by the new, and we will usher in an era of peace and freedom."

"Of course with you at the top!" James protested.

"James, I'm tired of this conversation. I have a war to wage, and I can't be bothered with this frivolous dialogue. But be aware, if Tarshish or any other nation decides to interfere, they will be destroyed. I'm not bluffing. Tarshish is either going to go down with the Kingdom or you will salute the new head of state. Understand?"

"Yes, I understand, Kasca. You've made yourself perfectly clear. You truly have gone mad. James out."

James hung up his telo-communicator and his holo-image evaporated from Kasca's office. After the call, Kasca took his stapler and threw it at the wall. He thought, "I'm going to make Tarshish pay for their insolence."

* * * *

After Matusak was informed about the attack, he proceeded to gather his commanders together, and told them his plans for conquest.

"Gentlemen, the attack against the Kingdom will begin at 5:00 A.M. We will partake in this invasion; however, I have different plans for Alexandria. The forces of Africa are gathered in one place to the southwest of us. I see easy pickings. Instead of turning our firepower against the Kingdom, we will be using it against Libya and the tribes of Ethiopia. And after we destroy their militaries, we will march into their capitals and take all of Africa as plunder. We will then send a regiment across the Nile to fulfill our duty unto the D.M.R., and we will capture the Tree of Life."

Matusak had no intention of sending forces across the Nile, but he had to make his commanders believe he would. Instead, he planned to fire upon the D.M.R. and help Tarshish against the Coalition. Matusak also knew that it was quite possible his forces would be destroyed after breaking the agreement with Libya and Ethiopia, but he did not voice these concerns.

"We will be," Matusak continued, "the rulers of all of Africa and each of you will have a piece of the pie! Each of you will rule a region, and the Kingdom will also be divided! We will be one of the strongest nations in the world, and the Marauders will put fear in our enemy's hearts! So who is with me?"

The commanders all looked at one another, not knowing how to respond, but their indecision was soon replaced by chants of victory, and they all hollered into the night. "Who-ma-tal-a … Who-ma-tal-a … Who-ma-tal-a …"

* * * *

The ships of Tarshish moved into position across the Arctic Ocean. They were spread out equally across the sea to make it difficult for the D.M.R. Air Force and Navy to destroy them. Kasca knew Tarshish's Defense Forces would not sit idly by when the attack against the Kingdom began, so he planned to destroy the Tarshish military with superweapons. Kasca also planned to fire them at Southern Greenland and Tarshish's cities. The D.M.R. had been stockpiling superweapons for years, and he knew Tarshish would not be able to defend against the barrage of superweapons coming at them. As for Jacob, the commander of the Tarshish navy, he waited impatiently for the war to begin. He was ordered by James to not fire a single shot until the D.M.R. started the conflict against the Kingdom.

At 4:45, the war began. It was supposed to begin at 5:00 A.M., but Kasca did not want Tarshish to have the first strike capability. All along the President had been planning to annihilate Tarshish. He knew they would get involved in the war, and even if they didn't, James would be a thorn in his side. Therefore, his pilots took off for Tarshish, as his silos shot superweapons at the Arctic Ocean and the cities of Tarshish.

"Incoming! The war has begun!" James shouted into the loud speaker. "The D.M.R. is attacking us! Shoot down anything in the sky! Our future depends on it!"

Jacob quickly relayed the message to his navy, and they fired upon the missiles coming in their direction. There must have been over 50,000 missiles fired in the first wave, but the TDF Navy defended their ships well. Only a few superweapons got through, but that was enough to do serious harm to the left flank in the Arctic. Also one of the cities in Greenland was destroyed. The D.M.R. then fired the second wave at Tarshish just as their Air Force arrived. This time, they had to fight off over 100,000 missiles and laser fire from the planes, and it was too much for them to overcome. Southern Greenland was wiped off the map, and most of the TDF navy was destroyed, along with the Arctic Ocean.

"Come in! Right flank are you there?" Jacob asked, but there was no response.

"North flank, come in! Please respond."

Once again there was no answer.

"South flank! Left flank. Is anybody out there?"

"We're here, commander. The South flank is still standing. What are your orders?"

"Fire upon the D.M.R. with everything you have! Destroy the port cities and knock out those silos!"

The remaining ships fired upon the D.M.R. but one by one the ships were picked off by the D.M.R. Air Force. The southern flank was hit by a superweapon, and Jacob's vessel was also hit and sinking quickly. Everyone in the command vessel was dead. Only Jacob was still alive, but he was badly injured and dying fast.

Jacob crawled over to the communications counsel. He spoke with half his breath. "Brother, are you there? Can you hear me?"

"Yes Jacob, I hear you," James answered.

"Our navy's been destroyed, and my ship is going down. I'm the last one alive. I love you, brother. I'll see you in the ... next ... life. I'm going ... home ... to ... Hannah."

Jacob spoke his last words, and his body sunk to the floor. The rest of the ship slipped under the tide as another superweapon hit the Arctic Ocean destroying everything in its path.

"Jacob ... Jacob! Are you there?" James screamed into the microphone. "Please respond!"

But the Chieftain knew the truth. His brother was gone. As for mainland Tarshish, it was overrun with superweapons and shots fired from the D.M.R. Air Force. Tarshish did manage to get some of their planes up in the air, but they were heavily outnumbered, and they were shot down. The TDF silos did manage to shoot down most of the weapons being fired at them, but by the third wave of superweapons, Tarshish was helpless. The entire country was annihilated, including the Twin Islands and every other territory belonging to the colony. Only those who were burrowed in the ground survived. James and his commanders were still alive in the Dublin command center under the earth, but it did not matter. Tarshish was defeated in less than 15 minutes, and the Kingdom was now all alone.

* * * *

As soon as Micah heard Tarshish was being attacked by the D.M.R., he erected the force-field. A giant bubble of defense formed over the Kingdom, and the Coalition generals wondered at the phenomena.

"What is that?" the Persian general asked.

"Our satellites show it as a giant translucent bubble covering the entire Kingdom," the D.M.R general answered.

"What does it do? What's it for?" the Persian general asked again.

"We're sending the pictures over to our scientists at Gog Inc. We're having them look at it."

A few minutes passed then a holo-image appeared in the bunker. "We believe the bubble is some sort of force-field, but we're not for sure," the scientist said. "We suggest you shoot a missile into it and see what happens."

A holo-image of Kasca was also standing in the bunker. He was not there, but he was partaking in the conversation. His real body was in an underground base in the D.M.R. He said, "It's settled then. Ready a missile and see what happens."

The Coalition fired a missile at the force-field, but when it hit the bubble it exploded and burned up. Some of the debris fell on the troops of men gathered near the explosion, and many died or were seriously injured.

When the generals of the coalition saw the effect, they immediately started to worry.

"Try the lasers," Kasca ordered. "Let's see if they have any effect."

The Persian general ordered one of his tanks to fire upon force field, but it was absorbed into the bubble and no damage was done.

"Interesting," the Persian general said above the others, but Kasca shouted above him. "Interesting! This is a disaster! Send forth a brigade of tanks! Have them focus on one spot of the bubble and see if they can penetrate the shield."

A brigade of tanks moved forward. They fired at one spot in the shield as they went, but it had no effect. The laser fire was absorbed into the bubble like the previous shots. When the tanks reached the force-field, they stopped, but they were ordered to keep moving forward. The tanks that rushed into the bubble were immediately incinerated. The ones that moved in slowly first started to shake then they were blown backwards. Other tanks just exploded. Some of the men even tried to run through the bubble, but their bodies immediately turned to ash like when one was hit with laser fire.

The brigade was completely destroyed. Some of the tanks near the rear refused to go forward, so the generals called off the attack.

"Now what do we do?" the general from Meschech asked.

"I think we made a mistake attacking the Kingdom," the general from Tubal answered. "We should call off the attack. There's still time to turn back."

But Kasca stepped in and calmed them, "The battle has just begun. The shield may be able to hold off a few tanks and missiles, but how about a whole arsenal of superweapons. We just need to weaken the shield then we'll be able to enter the borders."

The generals in the bunker all agreed by shaking their heads and the attack continued.

Kasca ordered, "Bring the superweapons back online. Fire at will, but do not target Jerusalem. We want to leave Jerusalem and the Tree of Life intact."

Each general ordered their troops to fire upon the force-field, but the bubble remained impenetrable. The force-field even held up against a barrage of superweapons. Most of the impact was absorbed by the force-field, but some of it reflected off the shield and killed over a hundred thousand men closest to where the bombs impacted. Not one of them was able to penetrate the shield. Thus, they called off the attack. Everyone looked disheartened and many started to panic. Suddenly, something strange started happening to the shield. It started to flicker on and off. Something was wrong with the bubble. The force-field was starting to falter.

* * * *

"What's wrong, Lane?" Micah asked. "The shield seems to be weakening. Can you rectify the problem?"

"I don't know, General. It looks like we're having an overload," the great scientist answered. "We might have to shut the power plant down. If not, I think it's going to blow."

"We can't shut it down!" Micah exclaimed. "If we do, the Kingdom will be left defenseless!"

"Yes, I know that," Hofmann responded, "but if we don't shut it down, the power plant will explode and the force-field will go down anyway."

"How long do you think it will take to get the power plant back online after shutting her down?"

"I'd say at least thirty minutes. If we don't give her time to cool off, the pressure will build up and we'll have to start over again."

Micah shouted, "Thirty minutes is too much time. If we shut her down, the Coalition will overrun us. We can't risk it. We have to keep her online and hope for the best. Do you agree?"

"Either way, we're doomed," the scientist answered. "I died long ago during the Second World War. I suppose it won't hurt to die again. Long live the King!"

"Yea, long live the King!" Micah hollered back.

* * * *

As soon as Matusak saw the force-field flickering on and off, he ordered his commanders to follow his earlier orders. The Alexandrian tanks slowly turned around, and before Libya and the Ethiopian tribes knew what was happening, they were being fired upon by Matusak's forces. Alexandria's Air Force also took out the armory of their enemies and a full-scale battle had begun. As a result, Madmenah II ordered his men to fire upon Alexandria, and the Ethiopian tribes started to shoot at one another. It was complete chaos. All of Africa was in disarray, and millions of soldiers were falling by the wayside.

When Kasca saw what was happening to his allies in Africa, he knew he'd been betrayed by Matusak. He was angry, so he ordered, "Re-configure the missile silos. I want you to nuke the whole territory with superweapons. Leave no city untouched. We'll make Alexandria pay for their treachery."

Matusak went down like the rest of his soldiers. He died with a gun in his hand fighting for the Kingdom. He knew his cause was lost, but he fought to the death like the ancient warriors of long ago. His life ended like most of the troops gathered in Africa, he was incinerated in a matter of seconds by one of the superweapons that the D.M.R. fired upon them. The war in Africa was over quickly. Matusak went out with a bang, but he kept his honor and pride by fighting for the Counselor and the Kingdom.

* * * *

The force-field continued to flicker on and off a few more minutes after Matusak's death, but ultimately the pressure at the power plant continued to build and it exploded. Micah and Lane Hofmann were both blown to bits in the blast then the shield went down.

When the Coalition troops saw the bubble disappear, they started to cheer. Billions of soldiers started to celebrate including the generals at the bunker. Victory over the Kingdom now seemed secure, and when the rejoicing died down, the generals ordered their men to cross the border.

"Forward!" the general from Gomar ordered. "The Kingdom is ours for the taking!"

Beth-Togar-Mah's general followed in step, and ordered his soldiers to attack. Persia's troops were on the left flank. The D.M.R. was in the center, and Gomar was to the right. Beth-Togar-Mah was right behind Gomar because they had the smallest amount of troops deployed in the area. The number of troops attacking the Kingdom was like the sand on the seashore. It was estimated that over a billion troops were involved in the assault, but no one knew for sure.

As soon as the Coalition crossed into the Kingdom, they were attacked by dragons. "Ahh!" screamed one of the D.M.R. troops as Quetzalcoatl swept down and bit off his head. The great dragon proceeded to scorch a whole regiment, but as he veered left, hundreds of lasers bore into his flesh from the troops to his right, and Quetzalcoatl was shot from the sky. The other dragons and beasts defending the Kingdom fell much the same way. They fought to the death and killed many men, but they were greatly outnumbered. They soon were killed like the rest of those defending the Kingdom, and the Coalition troops advanced.

The people who remained behind in the Kingdom were worried. The force-field was down. The leviathan had been destroyed, and now they were defenseless. The situation looked hopeless. An army without number was advancing upon them, and they were without arms. Some held knives and pitchforks in their hands and swore they'd fight to the death, but they knew that a knife against a laser gun was suicide. Therefore, they waited for death and held out hope that the Counselor would rescue them.

"Victory is in our hands," Kasca snickered to himself. "We are on the verge of conquest. In a matter of hours I will be the ruler of the earth. The Counselor will be putty in my hands. I will set my throne above all others. I will bring freedom and justice to the earth. The Kingdom will be liberated, and I will set the captives free! It will be mine … mine … mine!"

A huge grin started to form on Kasca's face. He looked like the manifestation of a villain in a comic book story. He was blinded by his own quest for power and glory. And just when everything seemed to be going so well, the battle turned upside down. First, the earth began to shake violently. It was the largest earthquake ever felt in Millennial history, and many soldiers began to stumble and fall. The Coalition soldiers looked up into the sky and saw flames of fire coming towards them. They only had a second or two to admire the display because in the next instance, they were being scorched by fire and brimstone.

"Retreat! Retreat!" the general from Persia ordered, but it was too late. The bombs from heaven seemed to be tripling by the second. It was like Sodom and Gomorrah all over again. The Coalition Air Force was immediately destroyed. Men were screaming with their bodies on fire, and some were incinerated by the impact of the blasts.

"No, this can't be happening!" Kasca's holo-image said to the other generals in the bunker. Order a ..."

But there were no orders left to give because in the next moment, the bunker with the generals was hit by a barrage of burning meteorites. Kasca's image disappeared, and he found himself back at headquarters in the underground base.

"We have failed!" Kasca admitted. "But if we're going to die, we're going to take the Kingdom with us. Launch whatever superweapons we have left and destroy Jerusalem!"

The President's generals in the underground bunker tried to carry out Kasca's orders, but there was no time. The D.M.R. and all of the north were now being hit by the fire and brimstone from space, and there was no time to launch the missiles. The silos that carried the superweapons were destroyed. The Coalition air force and navy were also exterminated, and the D.M.R. was no more.

"I thought you said this underground base was impenetrable!" Kasca screamed at one of the scientist who helped build the base.

The scientist at Gog Inc. did not answer. He was too busy trying to stay on his feet. The D.M.R.'s headquarters was rocking back and forth from the great earthquake and the situation looked hopeless. There was no where to run. There was no where to hide. The roof on the D.M.R.'s headquarters was starting to buckle, and it was just a matter of time before the whole thing collapsed.

"Why? Why?" Kasca screamed with his fist in the air. He then looked at one of the steel beams holding up the infrastructure and saw his reflection in the light. Kasca saw the Devil in his eyes. He screamed, "No ... no ... it can't be!" At that moment, the large steel frame started to buckle and the whole ceiling came down. One steel beam hit Kasca on the head, and it squashed the President's skull. Kasca's brains were guacamole on the ground, and he had fallen like the rest of the Coalition.

The invasion against the Kingdom had failed. The Day of Judgment had come.

Chapter 61

New Beginning

Picking up the pieces after a war is always the hardest part of any confrontation. Both sides suffer loss and pain. In fact, it took seven months to bury the remains of the dead and salvage anything worth recovering. Those who survived used the fuel from the weapons to stay warm and keep themselves alive because there was no sunlight on the earth. There was too much smoke in the atmosphere from the burning cities and the brimstone from heaven. As for the Kingdom citizens, they went beyond their borders. They brought with them food and Fruit Pills and helped anyone in need. It was greatly required because almost all of Asia and Europe were destroyed by the fires. Only a sixth of the people survived. Tarshish was completely wiped off the map, and only the people in James' underground base lived through the war, along with a few other shelters in various parts of the country. Africa was also decimated. Alexandria was the worst off, and only Matusak's family survived the conflict. When the war began, they ran for cover under the earth. Some of the family did not take refuge under the earth like Matusak's thirteenth wife and a few others. They died in the attack, but the rest were as healthy as ever. When Matusak's family crawled out of the belly of the earth, everything was scorched. There was nothing left. The lands of Libya and Ethiopia were also ravaged by superweapons. Kasca wasn't sure who was on his side during the battle, so he decided to bomb everyone. The President also fired over a thousand missiles at the rest of the Alliance, but these missiles were destroyed before they hit the mainlands. Only Southern Nod was hit hard by the blasts. Sheba, Dan, and Dedan remained untouched. Their defenses were sound like Tarshish, but they were able to fend off the attack by the Coalition because not that many superweapons were fired at them. These countries resided so far to the south that most of the Coalition bombs could not travel that far.

After the Magog War was over, the Counselor disbanded the 144 Elders. The borders of the Kingdom were also lifted. The Counselor went out like the others and helped those in need. When the seven months were completed, and everyone was accounted for, the Counselor made an announcement to the people of the earth.

"Long ago, the Father, the Spirit, and I embarked on a journey together. From the dust of the earth, We created man in our image. But those days are over. A new dawn has begun. As prophesied long ago, We are going to make a new heaven and a new earth. It will be like nothing you have ever known before. It is unspeakable. It cannot be put into words, but just know there will be joy and happiness there. Every tear shall be wiped away from your eyes, and there will no longer be any death. There will be no mourning, nor crying, nor pain. The first things will have passed away. There will no longer be any sun in the sky nor moon at night for We shall be your illumination, and the righteous will reign forever and ever with Us."

The Counselor paused for a moment and smiled. The people who survived the war in the Outskirts could finally see the Counselor for who He was, the Lord of Lords. The haze of propaganda was lifted, and the people's eyes were opened and their ears unplugged. For many, it was like being a blind man who had just regained his sight. The scales had fallen from their eyes.

"But for the unbelieving and all those who have rejected Me throughout the ages, they will suffer eternal consequences. They will be cast in the Lake of Fire. Eternally they will be separated from Us. This is the second death," the Counselor explained. "But for those who have been faithful and true, you will join Me. You will not remember those who have fallen by the wayside. You were chosen long ago, so do not sorrow nor weep. Have faith. You will soon understand everything-all your questions-all your doubts-all your objections. The knowledge of today will transform into a simple equation. This passing age will be like two plus two equals four. It will be as if you had a dream. You will wake up and realize that nothing is as it seems. So, my friends, be strong. We will all be One in the blink of an eye."

The Counselor then snapped his fingers together, and suddenly everyone on earth could see the other realms. Heaven and hell were exposed to man-holy angels flying in the heavens-demons burning in the embers. It was a sight that knocked everyone off their feet. The Counselor exposed Himself in all His glory, and no one could move for a long time. The people of the earth became like Daniel, the prophet, when he was lifted up into the heavens. Daniel saw a vision of the Lord, but when the prophet's eyes looked upon Him, Daniel lost his strength, and he fell into a deep sleep. But redemption for all the righteous was just around the corner. Angels beyond number started lifting men and women from the ground, and their old bodies were transformed into glorious new ones. James was lifted up. Jacob and Hannah were reunited. The Queen of Sheba was clothed in glory. Esmeralda and Patmos were celebrating. Matusak was present, and Kruger was nearby. Micah was standing by his family. And there were many others that had been overcomers. It was a reunion like no others. The righteous were filled with joy and great songs were being sung to the King of Kings.

The elevated mood did not last long, however, because shortly after the righteous were resurrected into glory, the Great White Throne judgment began against the wicked. All those who were bound in hell were cast into the Lake of Fire. It was a terrible sight to see because many of the righteous saw their own families and friends being thrown into the Fire. Therefore, many began to weep because they knew this judgment would last forever. Some were pleased knowing that justice would be served, but most had loved ones that were being sent to the Lake of Fire, and they were in distress. One by one the unrighteous struggled to break free, but there was no means of escape. The holy angels had them firmly in their grasp, and even if they did break free, there was no where to flee to.

Lucifer was being held by Michael and a couple of other angels. He was not going down quietly, but even Lucifer could not escape. He screamed, "I'll have my revenge someday, but it was really a powerless threat. He was greatly outnumbered and compared to the Son of God, he looked as small and frail as a mouse does to a lion. Kasca was also thrown into the Lake. He looked perturbed as he was being escorted away. He joined the False Prophet, the Antichrist, and the rest of the fallen angels. The Lord did relent on casting some of the fallen angels into the fire. These Watchers were spared because some of the men on earth had prayed for their redemption. It went against the Lord's previous ruling, but it did not surprise many. He had relented from casting judgment upon the people of Nineveh when they repented and had done so on many other occasions throughout history, but this was the first time known to man where the angels were granted the same grace. In addition, most recognized that the Counselor was a God of mercy, and if He decided to change His mind on a few rogue angels, they figured it was the Lord's prerogative. No one objected.

As far as those men and women who were being cast into the fire, they far outweighed those who were being lifted up and called righteous; however, the heavens were filled with many glorious species other than men. There were angels, men, dragons, signmonkoalas, and numerous other beings that men had never laid eyes on before. They must have come from somewhere else in the universe, and most of these species did not have anyone being sent to the Lake of Fire.

As the judgment proceeded, many were weeping. They thought heaven would be a place of joy, but witnessing this event put a damper on the celebration. Many felt ashamed because they knew they were no better off than those who were being cast into the fire. The only difference is that they had believed in the Lord and the others had not. It just didn't seem fair to many. For example, Patmos and Esmeralda could not bear to watch Kasca being sent away. They knew that he had done wrong and that he deserved his fate, but they still loved him. He was their friend, and they were never going to see him again. Only gnashing and bitterness of teeth awaited Kasca, and they felt sorry for him. How could they be happy in heaven knowing that someone they loved was damned for all time. Suddenly people started to cry. The wailing resonated throughout the heavens. One of the righteous mothers wept, "Please Lord, have mercy upon my son. Don't send him to the Lake of Fire." Many others were pleading for their loved ones too, and this went on for sometime as each of the unrighteous was cast in the burning flames. When the judgment was completed, the Counselor recognized that many were grieved, so he comforted the righteous. He said, "Remember what I spoke earlier? I said that in the blink of an eye you would understand everything. Do you recall My words? Well, that moment has come ..."

The Counselor snapped His fingers again. All the righteous through the ages were gathered at the Counselor's feet like a first grade classroom during story time. The Counselor was the teacher, and He was reading the final words to a story. He read, "... the forces of evil had been destroyed. The righteous had been saved. Everyone lived happily ever after, and there was no recollection of the former things."

The Counselor showed the final picture. A bunch of children were holding hands and dancing around the Tree of Life. They all had smiles on their faces.

"The End."

For a moment the children stirred in their seats with awe and wonder as the Counselor closed the book. They were pondering what it all meant. To some it felt like they were experiencing deja-vu, but suddenly the bell rang for recess and distracted their thinking. The children charged out of the room screaming with joy and laughter. They had already forgotten about the wicked being cast into the Lake of Burning Fire.

TERMS, COUNTRIES, CHARACTERS & PRECEPTS

7 Principles of Truth: 1. You shall love the Lord your God with all your heart, mind, and soul. You shall have no other gods before thee. You shall not worship them or serve them. You shall worship the Father, the Son, and the Holy Spirit. 2. Love your neighbor as yourself. 3. Treat the earth and all that dwell thereon with respect and dignity. 4. You shall not murder, commit adultery, or steal. 5. You shall not bear false witness against your neighbor, nor covet your neighbor's house, your neighbor's wife, or anything belonging to your neighbor. 6. Honor your father, your mother, your elders, and your God. 7. You shall live righteously, avoid wickedness, and take full responsibility for your actions.

20 Precepts: 1. Love and help one another. 2. Forgive one another. 3. Be truthful and honest. 4. Be patient and long suffering. 5. Do good and avoid evil. 6. Give and share. 7. Be just and fair. 8. Be supportive and caring. 9. Be kind and generous. 10. Be humble, not proud. 11. Work together and stand united. 12. Look after the well being of your body and mind. 13. Clean up after yourself and return what you borrow. 14. Obey the rules, but follow your conscience. 15. Avoid jealousy and outbursts of anger. 16. Avoid gossip and greed. 17. Avoid envy and covetousness. 18. Don't lie, steal, or cheat. 19. Right your wrongs and amend your ways. 20. Treat others like you want to be treated.

144 Elders: Ruling authorities in the Kingdom

Age of Accountability: Age of adulthood in the Kingdom & Tarshish; Age 21

Alaskan-Kamchatka Passageway: Land bridge connecting Asia to North America

Alexandria: Territory ruled by Matusak and the Marauders; Part of Egypt

Algiers: Country in Ethiopia; Later conquered by Matusak & Alexandria

Alliance: Empire Free Trade Pact between Tarshish, Sheba, Dan, De-Dan & later Southern Nod

Altie: Commander of the Royal Guard that helped Queen Sheba rise to power

Angolans: Country in Africa; Formerly the territory of Madagascar

Athalia: Evil Queen of the Algiers; Conquered by Alexandria

Azazel: City that was destroyed in the Tarshish-Gomar War

Azrial: Leads Town of Paradise to safety during Tarshish-Gomar War

Battle of Gog: War between the D.M.R. allies versus the Kingdom and her allies
Behemoth: Leviathan; Large dinosaurs; Godzillas
Beth: Daughter of Jacob & Hannah
Beth-Togar-Mah: Territories in Eastern Europe; Trading partners with the D.M.R.
Bluebeard: Made slaves of mermaids; Killed in a revolt
Bliss: From the Purple Fruit trees on Signmonkoala Island; Euphoric & aphrodisiac effect upon its users
Book of Gomar: The Sons of God based their religion on this fictional book
Booth's Festival: Festival of Booth's; 8 Day Carnival celebrated in the Kingdom each year; Time of Tribute
Captain 1: Landed on Signmonkoala Island & his men burned down the island
Captain 2: Led expedition back to the Kingdom from the D.M.R.
Cherubim: Angels of God
Cindy: Wife of a war veteran from Nod
City of Liberty: Capital of the D.M.R.
City of Canaan: Capital of Tarshish
Coalition: Northern Coalition of Free Trade between the D.M.R., Persia, Meschech, Tubal, Beth-Togar-Mah, Gomar, & Nod
Code of Ascendancy: Bloody shirt thrown at the ground as a way of challenging authority amongst the Marauders
Corinne: Princess/Queen of De-Dan
Counselor: King of Kings; Lord of Lords; Messiah; Jesus; Ruler in the Kingdom Age
Credits: Money; Called Shekels in the Kingdom; Cashless society that scanned the left thumb as a way of determining how much you're worth monetarily
Crowing Wizards: Patmos was a member of this Swedish group before the Kingdom Age; The group would engage in questionable behavior
Dan: King/General in the Land of Dan; Conquered the land & became the 1st king; Territory of South America
De-Dan: Originally a colony of Dan; Became independent after the death of King Dan; Ruled by Queen Corinne; The Continent of Antarctica
Democratic Magog Republic (D.M.R.): Nation north of the Kingdom; A republic based on democratic principles; Kasca & the Libertines rule the land
Dispersal Gun: Gun that fires thousands of lasers at the same time and protects Tarshish ships from incoming fire
Dominique Ditz: Holds a world record in the area of fornication
Dragons: Leviathan; Fire-breathers; Serpents

Dragon Wars: Wars between rival dragon kin; The wars later turned into a sporting event
Dragon Rider: Men & Signmonkoala who ride dragons during the Dragon Wars
Emperor of Persia: Reigns over an empire in Asia
Entwood: Type of tree found in the Kingdom; very rare and unique
Esmeralda: ZeZe; Lover of Patmos & Kasca; Former model & business woman; Latina; Dark brown hair; Brown eyes
False Prophet: Helped Mahdi rise to power during the Tribulation
Fight of the Century: Fight to the death between Matusak and Kruger
Fog of War: A shroud that covers the Kingdom and prevents satellites from peering into the territory
Franklin: Half brother of Queen Sheba that does her bidding
Fruit Pills: Fruit from the Tree of Life with healing powers
Gabriel: Angel cursed with old age: Protects Kingdom borders
Garrett Faust: Correspondent from Perth; Lucifer poses as him
Gog Incorporated: Largest & most successful company in the Outskirts; Kasca is the President of the company
Gomar: Country in Western Europe with economic ties to the D.M.R.
Gomar the Great: The Sons of Gods' religion is based upon the teaching of this fictional character
Great White Throne Judgment: Final judgment at the end of the age
Greenland: Territory divided into two; The North is D.M.R. territory & the South belongs to Tarshish
Greenland Pact: Accord between Tarshish & the D.M.R. over land rites in Greenland
Hades: Hell
Hannah: Wife of Jacob; Commander in the Tarshish Navy; Long, auburn hair
Harrick Kim I: 2nd President in the D.M.R. after Kasca leaves office
Harrick Kim III: President of the D.M.R. during the 7 Year Drought
Holo-camera: Camera that takes holo-image pictures
Holo-computer: Computer that projects images but the images do not have any substance or frame
Holo-house: A theatre that would project the latest movies on a large open space in the center of a room
Holo-image: Life-like image that can be projected into a room or space
Holo-pictures: Picture of someone taken by a holo-camera

Holo-projection: A series of holo-images that can be projected into a room or space

Holo-recorder: Records live footage and transforms it into holo-projection/image

Holoscreen: Like a television but projects images in three dimensions in the center of a room or space

Holostation: Studio or station that runs holoscreen programs throughout the day; these images can be projected anywhere in the world

Holo-TV: Similar to television except the programs and scenes are in holo-projections

Hosea: Prophet and Old Testament book

Hover-car/limo/truck: Automobiles that do not touch the earth, but hover above the ground like a helicopter

Hover-craft: A ship that skims across the ocean like a hover-car

Isaiah: Prophet and Old Testament book

James O'Donohue: Chieftain of Tarshish; Leader of the Alliance; Irish/English; Large man with a deep voice

Jacob O'Donohue: Lead Commander of the Tarshish Navy; Married to Hannah; Irish/English; Curly, red hair; Freckled face

Jerusalem: Center of the world; The Counselor, the Temple, and the Tree of Life reside there

Jerusalem Square: City center in New Jerusalem

Jonas: Commander of the Marauders during Matusak's absence

Kasca: Prince of Rosh; Libertine; Leader of the D.M.R; President of Gog Inc; Dark and handsome; 6' 3"; Genius; Black hair

Kennedy King: Talk show host from the D.M.R.

Kingdom: The region between the Euphrates and Nile Rivers; The territory is ruled by the Counselor & the 144 Elders; Also called Israel

Kingdom Age: 1000 year reign of Christ; also called the Millennial Reign

Kruger, Rhodes: Fought Matusak in the Fight of the Century; Prophet sent to Africa; Zulu tribe; Dark, black skin

Lake of Fire: Lake where the unrighteous are sent to after the final judgment; Eternal separation from God for both men and fallen angels

Lane Hofmann: Great inventor; Created laser guns, the Force-Field, and other technology

Leviathan: Dinosaurs; Dragons; Serpents; Behemoths

Leviathan Hunter: Tracker who helps people hunt great beasts

Libertines: Disciples of Kasca; Founders of Freedom in the D.M.R.

Libya: Country in Africa; Ruled by Xavier Laxamana I & II; Part of Egypt
Liberty Broadcasting Station: Holoscreen station in the D.M.R.
Liberty Square: Open forum in the center of the City of Liberty
Lucifer: Devil; Locked away in the abyss for 1000 years
Madmenah I, Xavier: Anointed Emperor of Egypt after Matusak's fall from grace
Madmenah II, Xavier: Emperor of Egypt/Libya & fought against the Marauders during the 13 Year War
Magog: The far North in Asia; The D.M.R.
Magog War: War between the D.M.R. and its allies against the Kingdom & their associates
Mahdi: Antichrist; Man of Lawlessness; Reigned during the Tribulation period
Manasseh: Evil King of the Algiers; Conquered by Alexandria
Mandate 1: Banning of firearms/weapons in the Kingdom
Mandate 2: Each year during the Festival of Booths it is required that a representative from each nation or tribe brings forth tribute to the King of Kings. If a nation of tribe fails to bring forth tribute, rain shall not fall upon that territory for one year.
Mandate 222: Any person who has reached the Age of Accountability and is unwilling to follow the dictates outlined by the Lord of Lords and the 144 Elders shall be banished to the Outskirts. They will lose their citizenship and may never return to Israel. If an individual chooses to leave Israel on their own free will he/she may do so on their own accord. They and their descendents will be banished until the end of the age.
Marauders: Clan of men that follow after Matusak; Territory in Africa
Mark of the Beast: Number given to those who followed Mahdi during the Tribulation
Martin: A boy who fell from a cliff's edge during Kasca's childhood
Massacre of Nod: Riot where D.M.R. soldiers killed many Native Nodians
Matusak: Marauder; Emperor of Alexandria; Strongest man in the world; Stringy, black hair; Thick beard
Menelik: 1st ruler in Australia; Father of Sheba
Meneliks: Tribe in Australia; Clan originated with Rastafarian beliefs
Mercado Romero: Assassin of Queen Sheba
Mermaids: Species of women/fish visited by Jacob & his crew
Meschech: Territory north of the Kingdom; Close economic ties with the D.M.R.

Micah McCalister: General; Husband of Sarah; Father of Simon & Hannah; Irish-American; Originally from the South (Georgia); Crew-cut
Michael: Arch-angel of God; Speaks with Lucifer while he's imprisoned
Millennium: 1000 year Reign of Christ; Period following the Tribulation
Modelo Espana: Successful modeling agency in Europe before the Tribulation; Owned by Esmeralda
Nathan: Son of Patmos
Natives: Nodians who were born in the Land of Nod whose ancestors were originally from North America.
New Timers: Anyone born after the Millennial Reign began
Nigerians: Territory in Ethiopia
Nod: North America; Divided between the Natives & the D.M.R. Settlers
Nodian Testimony: A testimonial from a war veteran in Nod
Nodians: People from North America (Natives from the South; Settlers from the D.M.R.)
Ogden: 2nd son of Menelik that teased Franklin as a child
Old Timers: Anyone born before the Millennial Reign began
Outskirts: The land and territories of the world outside the Kingdom borders
Patmos: The Professor; Prophet sent to the D.M.R; Esmeralda's & Sierra's lover; Blond hair; Turquoise-blue eyes
Path of Regeneration: The Sons of God would partake in this ritual
Persia: Empire in Asia with strong economic ties to the D.M.R.
Peter: Son of Jacob & Hannah; Returns to the Kingdom with Micah
Plague of Old Age: Caused by a deficiency of fruit from the Tree of Life
Private Investigator: Helps Esmeralda track down Patmos
Private Wilhelm: Soldier from the D.M.R. that befriended the Signmonkoalas
Prophetesses: Prophets sent to Dan, De-Dan, and Nod
Purple Fruit: Also called Bliss; From the trees on Signmonkoala Island; Euphoric & aphrodisiac effect upon its users
Queen Sheba: Leader of the Land of Sheba; Married to the Counselor; Polynesian; Straight, black hair
Quetzalcoatl: Dragon/Serpent in the Garden that tempted Eve
Raphael: Angel of God; Protects Kingdom borders
Raguel: Angel of God
Rameel: City that was destroyed in the Tarshish-Gomar War
Revelation: Last book in the New Testament that speaks about Armageddon, the Tribulation, and the Kingdom Age
Sabbath: A day of rest in the Kingdom

Sarah: Wife of Micah
Sasha: Matusak's 1st wife
Semjaza: City that was destroyed in the Tarshish-Gomar War
Settlers: Nodians who are from the D.M.R. and they colonized the Land of Nod
Sheba: Land ruled by Queen Sheba, her children & the Meneliks; Continent of Australia & islands of the South Pacific
Sierra: Love of Patmos; Former student of Patmos; Member of the Sons of God; Braided hair; Cinnamon skin
Signmonkoala Island: Native homeland of the Signmonkoala; Origin of the Purple Fruit
Signmonkoalas: Intelligent species that uses sign language to communicate with one another; They look like a Koala bear and/or monkey with sharp claws; Friendly species
Simon: A Chieftain in Tarshish; Hannah's brother; Son of Micah
Silver Kin: Race of Dragons; Patmos & Kasca were dragon riders of this kin
Silverstreak: Dragon Patmos rode during the Dragon Wars
Sons of God: Cult that believed in the Book of Gomar; Believed that one day its members would evolve and inherit supernatural abilities
Superweapon: A bomb of mass destruction that can destroy an entire city
Sydney: 3rd daughter of the Counselor & Queen Sheba
Tanzanians: Territory in Ethiopia
Tarshish Defense Force (TDF): Military forces in Tarshish
Telo-prompter: Similar to a phone
Telo-communicator: A means of communicating in the Outskirts
Thirteenth wife: One of Matusak's wives
Timothy: Son of Jacob & Hannah
Town of Paradise: Town invaded by Gomar in the Tarshish-Gomar War
Tree of Life: Biggest tree in the Kingdom; Fruit has healing powers; Resides in Jerusalem; Fruit resembles dates of a palm
Tree of Knowledge (Good & Evil): Adam & Evil ate from the fruit of this tree, and they were cast out of the Garden of Eden
Tribulation: 7 Year period during the Reign of Mahdi that had terrible wars, plagues, & judgments
Tribute: A tribute given to the Counselor each year during the Booth's Festival. If a tribe or nation fails to bring forth their tribute, rain will not fall upon that territory for one year
Tubal: Country north of the Kingdom with close economic ties to the D.M.R.

University of Jerusalem: Prestigious college in the Kingdom; Patmos & Kasca both taught there
Uriel: Angel of God; Lost a wing in a fight with Lucifer
Valley of Poetry: Mystical valley in De-Dan
Watchers: Angels who slept with women; Written about in the Book of Enoch
Water-hole whales: A new type of whale found during the Kingdom Age
Whore of Babylon: Religious & commercial Babylon that rides the Beast during the Tribulation period
Zadok: Chief Priest at the Temple
Zechariah: Prophet and Old Testament book
Zulus: Country in South Africa; Part of Ethiopia
Zzyzx: Prince/King in Dan after his father's death; Leper

978-0-595-52467-9
0-595-52467-2

Printed in the United States
121352LV00003B/1-48/P